Clive Cussler is the author or co-author of a great number of bestselling novels, including the famous Dirk Pitt® adventures, such as *Arctic Drift*; the NUMA® Files series, which include *Medusa*; the *Oregon* Files books, such as *Corsair*; and two historical adventures, *The Chase* and *The Wrecker*. He lives in Arizona.

Dirk Cussler, an MBA from Berkeley, worked for many years in the financial arena, and now devotes himself full-time to writing. He is the co-author, with Clive Cussler, of *Black Wind*, *Treasure of Khan* and *Arctic Drift*. In recent years he has been an active participant and partner in his father's real-life NUMA® expeditions and served as president of the NUMA® advisory board of trustees. He lives in Arizona.

Praise for Clive Cussler:

'Impossible to put down . . . a compelling sense of adventure that can rival any cinematic blockbuster' *Big Issue*

'No holds barred adventure . . . a souped-up treat' *Daily Mirror*

'Frightening and full of suspense . . . unquestionably entertaining' *Daily Express*

'Clive Cussler is hard to beat' *Daily Mail*

'The guy I read' Tom Clancy

Black Wind

CLIVE CUSSLER
and DIRK CUSSLER

PENGUIN BOOKS

PENGUIN BOOKS

Published by the Penguin Group
Penguin Books Ltd, 80 Strand, London WC2R ORL, England
Penguin Group (USA) Inc., 375 Hudson Street, New York, New York 10014, USA
Penguin Group (Canada), 90 Eglinton Avenue East, Suite 700, Toronto, Ontario, Canada M4P 2Y3
(a division of Pearson Penguin Canada Inc.)
Penguin Ireland, 25 St Stephen's Green, Dublin 2, Ireland (a division of Penguin Books Ltd)
Penguin Group (Australia), 250 Camberwell Road, Camberwell, Victoria 3124, Australia
(a division of Pearson Australia Group Pty Ltd)
Penguin Books India Pvt Ltd, 11 Community Centre, Panchsheel Park, New Delhi – 110 017, India
Penguin Group (NZ), 67 Apollo Drive, Rosedale, North Shore 0632, New Zealand
(a division of Pearson New Zealand Ltd)
Penguin Books (South Africa) (Pty) Ltd, 24 Sturdee Avenue,
Rosebank, Johannesburg 2196, South Africa

Penguin Books Ltd, Registered Offices: 80 Strand, London WC2R ORL, England

www.penguin.com

First published in the United States of America by G. P. Putnam's Sons 2004
First published in Great Britain by Michael Joseph 2004
Published in Penguin Books 2005
Reissued in this edition 2009

1

Typeset by Rowland Phototypesetting Ltd, Bury St Edmunds, Suffolk
Printed in England by Clays Ltd, St Ives plc

ISBN 978-0-7181-5956-6

www.greenpenguin.co.uk

Penguin Books is committed to a sustainable
future for our business, our readers and our
planet. This book is made from paper certified
by the Forest Stewardship Council.

In memory of my mother, Barbara, whose love, compassion, kindness, and encouragement are deeply missed by all who knew her.

D. E. C.

Acknowledgments

With appreciation and gratitude to Scott Danneker, Mike Fitzpatrick, Mike Hance, and George Spyrou of Airship Management Services, for sharing the wondrous world of airship flight.

Thanks also to Sheldon Harris, whose book *Factories of Death* has helped open the door to the horrors of biological and chemical warfare practiced during World War II and its thousands of forgotten victims.

Makaze

Japanese Imperial submarine *I-403* and Seiran floatplane

Lieutenant Commander Takeo Ogawa glanced at his wristwatch and shook his head in irritation.

'Half past midnight already,' he muttered anxiously. 'Three hours late and still we wait.'

A young ensign staring through the glazed eyes of a sleep-deprived insomniac nodded slightly at his superior's grieving but said nothing. Waiting atop the conning tower of the Japanese Imperial Navy submarine *I-403*, the two men gazed across the naval yard searching for signs of a pending arrival. Beyond the expansive naval base, a haphazard twinkling of nighttime lights glistened about the scenic Japanese city of Kure. A light drizzle fell, lending an eerie tranquility to the late hour, which was broken by the distant sounds of hammers, cranes, and welding torches. Repairs to enemy-damaged ships and new vessel construction persisted around the clock in other parts of the shipyard, in a futile rush to aid the increasingly bleak war effort.

The distant whine of a diesel truck soon echoed across the water, the sound rising in intensity as the vehicle approached the submarine docks. Rounding the corner of a brick warehouse, a slate-colored Isuzu cargo truck rumbled into view and turned along the wharf. The driver inched his way cautiously toward the submarine's pen as he struggled to make out the edges of the darkened pier, barely visible under the truck's wartime-blackened headlights. Pulling alongside a large gangplank, the truck ground to a halt as its worn brakes squealed loudly in protest.

A moment of silence ensued, then six heavily armed soldiers sprang from the truck bed and enveloped the vehicle in a perimeter guard. As Ogawa made his way down from the conning tower to the dock, he sensed one of the guards pointing a weapon in his direction. The soldiers were no Imperial Army regulars, he noted, but elite members of the feared Kempei Tai military police.

Two uniformed men exited the cab of the truck and approached Ogawa. Recognizing a superior officer, Ogawa stood at attention and saluted smartly.

'I've awaited your arrival, Captain,' Ogawa stated with a tinge of annoyance.

Captain Miyoshi Horinouchi ignored the innuendo. As staff operations officer for the Sixth Fleet, his mind was occupied with graver matters. The Japanese submarine fleet was slowly being decimated in the Pacific and the Imperial Navy had no answer for the antisubmarine warfare technologies being deployed by the American forces. Desperate battles by the fleet's submarines against overwhelming odds inevitably resulted in the loss of crew and vessels, which weighed heavily on Horinouchi. His short-cropped hair had turned prematurely white, and stress lines creased his face like dry riverbeds.

'Commander, this is Dr. Hisaichi Tanaka of the Army Medical College. He will be accompanying you on your mission.'

'Sir, I am not accustomed to carrying passengers while on patrol,' Ogawa replied, ignoring the small bespectacled man at Horinouchi's side.

'Your patrol orders to the Philippines have been rescinded,' Horinouchi replied, handing Ogawa a brown folder. 'You have new orders. You are to take Dr. Tanaka and his cargo aboard and proceed immediately per fleet directives to strike at the enemy's doorstep.'

Glancing at one of the guards holding a German Bergman MP34 submachine gun pointed in his direction, Ogawa asserted, 'This is most unusual, Captain.'

Horinouchi tilted his head to the side, then took a few steps to his right. Ogawa followed, leaving Tanaka out of earshot. Speaking softly, Horinouchi continued.

'Ogawa, our surface fleet was annihilated at Leyte Gulf. We counted on a decisive battle to stop the Americans, but it was our own forces that were defeated instead. It is just a matter of time before all of our remaining resources will be assigned in defense of the homeland.'

'We will make the Americans pay heavily in blood,' Ogawa said harshly.

'True, but there is no question that they have the

will to conquer, regardless of the losses. The slaughter of our own people will be appalling.' Horinouchi contemplated the sacrifice of his own family and fell silent for a moment.

'The Army has approached us for assistance in a valiant operation,' he continued. 'Dr. Tanaka is affiliated with Unit 731. You will take him and his cargo across the Pacific and launch an attack on the American mainland. You are to avoid detection and protect your boat at all costs en route. Succeed, Ogawa, and the Americans will bow to a truce and our homeland will be preserved.'

Ogawa was stunned by the words. His fellow submarine commanders were waging a mostly defensive battle to protect the remnants of the surface fleet, yet he was to cross the Pacific single-handedly and launch an attack that would end the war. He might have ridiculed the idea, had it not been a fleet staff officer dictating the order to him out of desperation in the middle of the night.

'I am most honored by your confidence, Captain Horinouchi. Rest assured my crew and officers will uphold the honor of the emperor. If I may ask, sir, what exactly is Dr. Tanaka's cargo?' Ogawa inquired.

Horinouchi gazed forlornly across the bay for several seconds. *'Makaze,'* he finally muttered quietly. 'An evil wind.'

Under the watchful eye of Dr. Tanaka, a half-dozen oblong wooden crates were carefully loaded by

6

the Kempei Tai guards into the forward torpedo room of the *I-403* and tightly secured. Ogawa ordered the submarine's four diesel engines turned over and the deck lines released. At half past two in the morning, the iron sub nosed slowly into the inky harbor and inched its way past several other fleet I-boats docked in the yard. Ogawa noted with curiosity that Horinouchi sat silently in the darkened truck on the pier, refusing to leave until after the *I-403* was well out of sight.

Creeping past the docks and warehouses of the sprawling navy yard, the sub soon approached a massive shadow looming against the darkness ahead. Lying quietly in a repair dock, the massive battleship *Yamato* towered above the submarine like a behemoth. With its massive eighteen-inch guns and sixteen-inch-thick armor plating, the *Yamato* was the most feared vessel afloat. Ogawa admired the lines and armament of the world's largest battleship as he sailed past, then felt a touch of pity toward her. Like her sister ship, the *Musashi*, recently sunk in the Philippines, the *Yamato*, he feared, was destined to find her way to the bottom of the sea before the war was over.

Gradually the lights of Kure fell away as the submarine snaked around several large islands, then entered the Seto Inland Sea. Ogawa ordered increased speed as the mountainous island outcroppings fell away and the first gray patches of predawn light tinted the eastern sky. As he marked their route in the conning tower with the *I-403*'s navigator, Ogawa was approached by the executive officer climbing up from below.

'Hot tea, sir,' Lieutenant Yoshi Motoshita said, thrusting a small cup toward the commander. A thin man with a warm demeanor, Motoshita mustered a grin even at five in the morning.

'Yes, thanks,' Ogawa replied crisply before gulping at the tea. The hot liquid was a welcome tonic against the chill December air and Ogawa quickly drained the cup.

'The sea is unusually calm this morning,' Motoshita noted.

'Fine conditions for fishing,' Ogawa said reflectively. The son of a fisherman, Ogawa had grown up in a small village on the southern island of Kyushu. Accustomed to a hard life on the water, Ogawa had overcome a modest background by passing the formidable entrance exams to Etajima, the Japanese naval academy. After gaining his commission, he was drawn to the growing prewar submarine force and served on two boats before attaining command of the *I-403* in late 1943. Under his leadership, the *I-403* had sunk a half-dozen merchant ships, along with an Australian destroyer in the Philippines. Ogawa was considered one of the top submarine captains remaining in the rapidly shrinking underwater fleet.

'Yoshi, we'll initiate a zigzag running pattern when we reach the strait, then submerge before we leave the mainland. We can take no chances with enemy submarines patrolling off our coast.'

'I will alert the crew, sir.'

'And Dr. Tanaka. See that he is situated comfortably.'

'I have offered him my cabin,' Motoshita said with a pained look. 'Judging by the stack of books he brought with him, I think he will keep himself occupied and out of our way.'

'Very well,' Ogawa replied, wondering silently about his unwanted passenger.

As a crimson sun crept up over the eastern horizon, the *I-403* veered south from the Inland Sea into the Bungo Strait, a pathway above Japan's southern island of Kyushu that poured into the Pacific Ocean. A gray destroyer limped past the sub on its way back to port, listing heavily to one side and showing a rash of gaping holes in its bridge and decks, the result of a nasty encounter with a pair of U.S. Navy Hellcats. On the submarine, several petty officers crowded the conning tower to take a final glimpse of their green island nation, uncertain as all seamen departing for battle whether they would return home again.

When the approach to the Pacific became visible to the lookout, Ogawa issued the command to dive. A loud bell clanged throughout the submarine and sailors scurried to secure the deck and hatches.

'Submerge to fifteen meters,' Ogawa ordered from the bridge.

Large ballast tanks were flooded with seawater and the diving planes tipped forward. With a rush of collapsing water, the *I-403*'s nose dipped downward and the entire submarine was quickly gobbled up by the murky green sea.

In the Pacific waters off the Bungo Strait, aggressive American submarines lurked in the depths hunting merchant supply ships or armed vessels en route from the Kure Navy Base. Submarine-against-submarine attacks were not unheard of and Ogawa was not about to make himself easy fodder. Entering the Pacific waters, he quickly aimed the *I-403* northeast and away from the bulk of the wartime traffic traveling south toward the Philippines.

As were most subs of its era, the *I-403* was powered by diesel and electric motors. In daylight hours, the *I-403* would operate submerged, powered by battery-operated electric motors that pushed the sub along at a sluggish 6 knots per hour. Under cover of darkness, the *I-403* would surface and crank up the diesel engines, which propelled the boat to better than 18 knots, while recharging the batteries. But the *I-403* was no ordinary submarine. Stretching over 390 feet long, the *I-403* was one of a handful of Sen toku-class submarines, which were the largest built in their day. The massive iron vessel displaced over 5,200 tons and was pushed through the water by four 7,700-horsepower diesel engines. The *I-403*'s truly unique feature, however, was the vessel's armament of aircraft. The *I-403* could carry three Seiran floatplanes, which were small converted dive-bombers that could be launched from a catapult on the center bow. While traveling at sea, the planes were disassembled and stored in a 110-foot-long watertight hangar that stretched along the sub's deck. A shortage of aircraft had forced Ogawa to give up one of his seaplanes for coastal reconnaissance, however, and his vessel now carried just two of the Seiran aircraft.

Once the *I-403* had safely entered the Pacific, Ogawa retired to his cabin and reread the brief mission orders Horinouchi had given him. The succinct commands called for him to sail a northerly route across the Pacific, with a refueling stop in the Aleutians. He was to proceed to the northwest coast of the United States, where his two aircraft were to launch air attacks on the cities of Tacoma, Seattle, Victoria, and Vancouver.

On the face of it, it appeared a futile gesture, thought Ogawa. Japan needed her submarines for homeland waters defense rather than instigating minuscule attacks with a pair of small aircraft. But there was the question of Dr. Tanaka and his unidentified cargo.

Summoned to Ogawa's cabin, Tanaka bowed gracefully before entering the cramped quarters and seating himself at a small wooden table. The slightly built scientist bore a shrewish and unsmiling face. A pair of vacant black eyes that were magnified by thick glasses augmented his sinister appearance.

Dispensing with formalities, Ogawa pressed immediately for the nature of the doctor's presence.

'Dr. Tanaka, my written orders are to sail this

vessel to the west coast of North America and launch an airborne attack on four cities. There is no mention of your duties or the nature of your cargo. I must ask what your role in the mission is.'

'Commander Ogawa, rest assured that my assignment here has been authorized at the highest levels,' Tanaka replied in a quiet monotone voice. 'I will be providing technical assistance for the attack operation,' he continued.

'This is a warship. I fail to understand how a medical officer will assist in a naval strike,' Ogawa countered.

'Commander, I am with the Army Medical School's Epidemic Disease Prevention Study Group. We have received materials from a research facility in China that have enabled us to develop an effective new weapon against the enemy. Your submarine has been chosen as the means to launch the weapon for the first time against American forces. I am responsible for the security and deployment of the weapon on this mission.'

'These "materials." They will be dropped from my aircraft?'

'Yes, in special canisters that can be accommodated by your bombers. I have already made the necessary arrangements with your aviation ordnance crew.'

'And the men on my vessel. Are they in any danger with this weapon aboard?'

'None whatsoever.' Tanaka's face was inscrutable as he lied.

Ogawa didn't believe him, but figured the risk of the American Navy's antisubmarine warfare forces were a greater risk to his sub than anything carried on board. Ogawa tried to procure what little information he could from Tanaka, but the Army doctor volunteered few additional facts. Whatever mystery was associated with the weapon, he kept close to the vest. There was something ominous about the man, Ogawa decided, and it made him uncomfortable. After sharing a quick cup of tea, he dismissed the eerie scientist. Sitting silently in his cabin, Ogawa cursed the Fleet Command for selecting his vessel for the assignment. It was a mission that he didn't want.

The sporadic ocean traffic of merchant ships and fishing boats soon dissipated as the Japanese mainland fell behind the sub's wake and the vessel crawled farther north in latitude. For the next twelve days and nights, the crew embraced a normal operating schedule as the sub nosed northeast, surfacing at night to run at higher speed. The prospect of being detected by an Allied plane or ship was more remote in the north Pacific, but Ogawa took no chances and ran submerged during all daylight hours. Operating under the waves, the bottled-up sub became like an oven to the men who drove her. Interior temperatures would climb into the nineties from the machinery, while the confined air would grow foul to the breath over the hours. Evening darkness was eagerly anticipated by each crewman, knowing the sub would finally surface, open its hatches, and vent cold, fresh sea air into the dank interior.

Naval authority on submarines was notably relaxed, even in the Japanese Navy, and operations on the *I-403* were no different. Officers and enlisted crew mixed easily, sharing the same meals and suffering the same miseries aboard the cramped vessel. The *I-403* had survived depth charge attacks on three different occasions and the near-death experiences had bonded the crew tightly together. They were survivors in a deadly game of cat and mouse and felt the *I-403* was a lucky ship that could defy the enemy.

On the fourteenth night, the *I-403* surfaced near the Aleutian island of Amchitka and quickly found the supply ship *Morioka* anchored in a small cove. Ogawa gently brought his vessel alongside the surface ship and mooring lines were tossed across. As diesel fuel was pumped into the submarine's reservoir tanks, crewmen on each vessel bantered back and forth in the freezing cold.

'Aren't you a little cramped in that anchovy tin?' asked a bundled yeoman at the ship's rail.

'No, we've got plenty of room for our canned fruit, chestnuts, and sake!' yelled back a submariner, boastful of the superior food the undersea services were provided.

The refueling operation was completed in less than three hours. One of the submarine's crewmen, diagnosed as suffering an acute bout of appendicitis, was transferred to the ship for medical attention. After rewarding the supply ship crew with a box of hard candies, the *I-403* cast off on an eastward tack toward North America. The skies gradually turned black and the gray-green ocean waters frothed with spray as the *I-403* found herself sailing into the teeth of an early winter storm. The sub was tossed violently for three nights as waves flooded across the low deck and crashed into the conning tower as the sub attempted to recharge its batteries. A lookout was nearly washed overboard into the icy seas on one occasion, and many of the experienced crew succumbed to bouts of seasickness. Strong westerly winds aided the voyage, however, pushing the sub briskly through the swells and quickening its trek east.

Gradually, the winds began to ease and the seas flattened. Ogawa was pleased to find his vessel had survived Mother Nature's buffeting with no damage. The battered crew regained their sea legs and their fighting morale as the seas stabilized and the submarine neared the enemy's homeland.

'Captain, I have a final plot to the coast,' Seiji Kakishita remarked as he unrolled a chart of the northeast Pacific Ocean in front of Ogawa. The *I-403*'s navigator had ceased shaving, like many crewmen upon leaving port, and sported a straggly tuft of hair from his chin that created a cartoonish look about him.

'What is our present position?' Ogawa inquired as he studied the map.

'Right here,' Kakishita replied as he pointed to a spot on the map with a pair of dividers. 'Approximately two hundred kilometers west of Vancouver Island. We have two more hours of darkness for surface running, which will bring us to within 150 kilometers of land by daybreak on our current heading.'

Ogawa studied the chart intently for a few moments before speaking. 'We are too far north. I wish to launch the attack from a point central to the four targets in order to minimize flight time. Bring us south and we'll approach the coastline here,' he said, stubbing his finger at the map. Beneath his fingertip lay the northwest tip of Washington State, an angular peak of land that jutted into the Pacific Ocean like the snout of a hungry dog. Just to the north lay the Strait of Juan de Fuca, which created a natural border channel with British Columbia and was the main thoroughfare for maritime traffic from Vancouver and Seattle into the Pacific Ocean.

Kakishita hurriedly plotted a new route on the map and recalculated the distances. 'Sir, I compute that we can arrive at a position fifteen kilometers offshore from the point marked "Cape Alava" in twenty-two hours.'

'Excellent, Kakishita,' Ogawa replied smugly as he eyed a nearby chronograph. 'That will allow us plenty of time to commence the attack before dawn.' The timing was right. Ogawa wished to spend as little time as possible in high-traffic areas where they might be spotted before launching the strike. Things seemed to be falling into place, he thought. With a little luck, they might just be on their way home from a successful mission in just over twenty-four hours.

A buzz of activity overtook the *I-403* after it surfaced again that evening as preparations were made to launch the aerial strike. Mechanics pulled out the fuselage, wings, and pontoons of the aircraft and began piecing the parts together like some giant toy model. Seamen rigged the hydraulic catapult and carefully tested the device by which the planes would be launched. The pilots attentively studied topographic maps of the region, plotting their course to the drop zones and back. And the ordnance men, under the cautious direction of Dr. Tanaka, configured the bomb racks of the Seiran bombers to hold the twelve silver canisters still stored in the forward torpedo room.

By three in the morning, the *I-403* had crept quietly to its staging point off the Washington coast. A light drizzle was falling and the six lookouts Ogawa had stationed on deck strained to peer through the murky darkness for signs of other vessels. Ogawa himself paced the open bridge nervously in anxious wait to see the aircraft off, so that he could hide his submarine under the protection of the rolling seas.

Another hour had ticked by when a hurried squat man in a grease-stained jumpsuit approached Ogawa tentatively.

'Sir, sorry to report we are having troubles with the aircraft.'

'What is the problem at this late hour?' Ogawa countered, clearly annoyed.

'Aircraft number one has been found to have a faulty magneto. We must replace it with a spare for the motor to operate. Aircraft number two has a damaged elevator, apparently due to shifting that occurred during the storm. This we can repair also.'

'And how long will it require to complete both repairs?'

The mechanic looked skyward for a moment, contemplating his response. 'Approximately one hour for the repairs, sir, plus another twenty minutes to load the ordnance from belowdecks.'

Ogawa nodded grimly. 'Proceed with all haste.'

One hour turned into two and still the planes were not ready. Ogawa's impatience grew as he noticed gray streaks in the eastern sky, signaling the approaching dawn. The drizzling rain had stopped and was replaced by a light fog that enveloped the sub, cutting visibility to less than a third of a mile. Sitting ducks, perhaps, but at least ducks in a blind, Ogawa thought.

Then the stillness of the morning air was shattered as a cry from the sound-detection operator belowdecks pierced the air.

'Captain, I have an echo!'

'I've got you this time, Big Brother!' Steve Schauer yelled into the radio transmitter with a grin, then pushed a pair of throttles to their stops. Alongside him in the fishing trawler's cramped cabin, two teen-age crewmen, exhausted and reeking of dead fish, looked at each other and rolled their eyes. Schauer ignored their looks as he lightly fingered the wooden wheel of the plodding fishing boat and began whistling an old drinking tune.

A pair of fortyish siblings with youth in their veins, Steve and Doug Schauer had spent their lives fishing the waters in and around Puget Sound. With skill and hard work, they had thrown all their earnings into ever-larger fishing boats until they traded up for a matched pair of fifty-foot wooden hull trawlers. Working as a team, they successfully fished the Washington and Vancouver shorelines with an uncanny ability to sniff out large schools of halibut. After a three-day excursion, with their holds full of fish and their coolers empty of beer, the brothers would race each other back to port like a pair of kids on roller skates.

'It ain't over till the paint scratches the dock,' Doug's voice crackled over the radio. After a particularly good haul during the 1941 season, the brothers had splurged on two-way radios for their boats. Though intended to help each other coordinate the catches, the brothers spent most of their time on the airwaves goading each other instead.

As Schauer's boat chugged along at its top speed of 12 knots, the skies lightened from black to gray and a spotlight beam shining on the water ahead of the bow gradually lost its illuminating effect. Ahead, in the mist, Schauer saw the faint outline of a large black object lying low in the water. A second later, a small orange flash emanated from the object's center for a brief instant.

'Is that a whale off the starboard bow?' The words had barely escaped his lips when a shrieking whistle creased past the cabin, followed by a volcanic explosion that erupted in the water off the port beam, showering the trawler in a downpour of seawater.

Schauer stood stunned for a moment, his mind unable to comprehend what his eyes and ears had just absorbed. It took the sight of a second orange flash to jolt him into action.

'Get down!' he shouted at the two men in the cabin as he spun the ship's wheel hard to port. The laden trawler was slow to respond, but it was enough to avoid the second shell from the *I-403*'s 5.5-inch deck gun, which screamed into the water just astern of the boat. This time, the force of the explosion lifted the entire trawler out of the water and slammed it back down again hard, shearing the rudder off in the upheaval.

Wiping blood out of his eyes from a gash to the temple, Schauer groped for the radio microphone.

'Doug, there's a Jap sub. It's blasting the hell out of us. No joke. Keep to the north, and get help.'

He was still talking when the third shell found its mark, piercing the forward hold of the fishing boat before detonating. A furious explosion of splinters, glass, and mangled halibut blasted into the cabin, throwing the three men viciously to the back wall. Struggling to his feet, Schauer peered out a gaping hole in the front of the cabin and saw the entire bow of the trawler disintegrate into the sea before him. Instinctively grabbing the wheel for support, he looked on in disbelief as the remains of the boat began to sink rapidly beneath his feet.

Peering through binoculars, Ogawa watched with grim satisfaction as the trawler slipped beneath the waves amid a scattering of flotsam. Rescuing survivors was out of the question, so he wasted no time in looking for bodies in the water.

'Motoshita, have there been any additional sound recordings?' he asked his exec.

'Negative, sir. The sound operator reported a possible secondary target before we initiated firing but the reading faded. It was either background noise, or a small vessel at best.'

'Have him keep sweeping. With this visibility, we will hear a vessel well before seeing her. And have the chief aircraft mechanic report to me. We've got to get those planes launched.'

As Motoshita scurried off, Ogawa stared toward the hidden coastline of Washington. Perhaps we'll get lucky, he thought. The trawler was likely a lone fishing boat and wouldn't have a radio. The guns could have been heard ashore, but, at this distance, would sound like an innocuous muffle. The charts showed few inhabitants residing along that stretch of coast as well. Perhaps – just perhaps – they could still pull off the mission undetected.

The hairs on the back of Radioman First Class Gene Hampton's neck stood up like a grove of ponderosa pine. The voice ringing through his earphones had an air of urgency and authenticity that could not help but be believed. After confirming the message twice, Hampton popped out of his chair like a jack-in-the-box and bounded to the center of the bridge.

'Captain, I just picked up a civilian Mayday message,' he blurted excitedly. 'A fisherman says there's a Jap sub offshore shelling his brother's boat.'

'Did he sound coherent?' replied the ship's bearded, heavyset commander in a skeptical tone.

'Yes, sir. Said he didn't see the sub because of the fog but got a radio call from his brother on another fishing boat. He heard a couple of shots fired from a big gun, then lost contact with his brother. I received a call from another boat confirming the sound of gunfire.'

'Did they provide a fix on the location?'

'Yes, sir. Nine miles southwest of Cape Flattery.'

'Very well. Contact the *Madison* and tell her we are headed out of the strait to investigate a reported enemy contact, then provide a location fix to Navigation. Mr. Baker,' he continued, turning to a tall lieutenant standing at his side, 'let's go to General Quarters.'

As an alarm bell rang throughout the ship, the

crew of the USS *Theodore Knight* scrambled to their battle stations, adorning helmets and kapoks as they ran. It wasn't the first time the Farragut-class destroyer had seen action. Launched in 1931 at the Bath Iron Works shipyard in Maine, the *Theodore Knight* had an active service duty garnering North Atlantic convoy duty in the early stages of the war. After dodging several U-boat attacks while escorting the merchant fleets, the 341-foot-long destroyer was sent back for patrol and escort duty off the West Coast, sailing the waters from San Diego to Alaska.

Trailing three miles behind, in the Strait of Juan de Fuca, was the Liberty Ship *Madison*, bound for San Francisco with a cargo of lumber and tinned salmon. Leaving the assigned cargo ship in its wake, the *Theodore Knight* broached the mouth of the Pacific as its captain, Lieutenant Commander Roy Baxter, ordered flank speed. The ship's twin diesel turbines churned the sleek gray ship through the water like a hound chasing a rabbit. The crew, accustomed to quiet, routine patrols, was at an unusually heightened sense of readiness at the prospect of facing the enemy.

Even Baxter felt his heart beat a little faster. A twenty-year Navy man, he had seen action in the Atlantic but had grown bored with his recent assignment on the home shores. He relished the thought of tasting battle again, though remained skeptical about the radio report. Japanese subs had not been seen off the coast for over a year, he knew, and the Imperial Navy was now clearly on the defensive.

'Radar?' he demanded loudly.

'Sir, I have three small vessels approaching the channel, two from the north and one from the west,' replied the radarman without taking his eyes off his monitor. 'I have another indefinite target that appears to be stationary lying to the southwest.'

'Take us to the southern mark,' Baxter barked. 'And have the forward batteries stand by for action.' The commander had to suppress a grin of excitement as he issued the orders. Maybe we'll earn our pay today, he thought while strapping on his helmet.

Unlike their American counterparts, most Japanese submarines in World War II were not equipped with radar. The early-warning technology was only first deployed on Imperial submarines in mid-1944, and then installed only on selected vessels. Most Japanese submarines instead relied upon sound-detection equipment to reveal a distant enemy. Although more limited in range than radar, sound detection could be utilized underwater, and aided many a sub in avoiding a fatal rendezvous with depth charges.

Absent a radar unit, it was the *I-403*'s sound operator who first became aware of the destroyer bearing down on them.

'Vessel approaching ahead ... sound intensity one,' he reported at the first registering on his equipment.

On deck, both of the aircraft had been moved out of their hangars, where the wings and pontoons were affixed, while repairs continued. It was the situation

Ogawa feared most. With both planes assembled but neither ready for flight, they would have to be sacrificed should the submarine have to make an emergency dive.

'Deck gun at the ready,' he ordered, hoping the unwelcome intruder was yet another fishing boat.

'Sound intensity two and increasing,' the sound operator relayed calmly. 'It's a ship,' he added, to no one's surprise.

'Secure all aircraft and clear the aviation deck,' Ogawa ordered an ensign, who sprinted down the large deck shouting at the mechanics and pilots as he ran. Tying down the two airplanes, the aviation crew quickly grabbed their work tools and scurried to the hangar. The watertight doors of the hangar were closed and sealed; then the men dropped down another hatch into the secure body of the submarine.

'Sound intensity three, off our bow. May be a destroyer,' the operator reported, correctly identifying the churning sound of the tin can's twin propellers.

As if on cue, the gray ship materialized out of the fog a half mile away, the apparition of a steel wraith charging across the moor. White foam burst off the bow in angry torrents while wisps of dark smoke billowed from the funnel. The lean ship drove straight at the sub, an attacking lancer not to be denied.

In an instant, the *I-403*'s deck gun boomed as the submarine's experienced gun crew attempted to halt the oncoming dervish. The slim, head-on profile of the destroyer made for a difficult target, however, and the shell passed harmlessly to one side. Hurriedly, the gun crew took aim and fired again.

Once identifying the ship as a destroyer, Ogawa recognized the futility of a surface duel with a superior vessel and immediately ordered a crash dive. The mission would have to be sacrificed for the safety of the ship and crew, he reasoned, if it wasn't already too late.

As the dive alarm sounded, the gun crew fired off a last desperate shot before scrambling belowdecks to safety. The gunner's accuracy was nearly dead-on, but he overcompensated the approaching speed of the destroyer. The shell splashed into the water fifty feet directly ahead of the American ship's bow, blasting a spray of water onto its deck but causing no damage.

The two forward batteries of the *Theodore Knight* at last came to life, lobbing five-inch shells in succession toward the Japanese sub. The inexperienced and adrenaline-fortified gun crew fired high, however, placing the destroyer's shells harmlessly beyond the now-accelerating submarine.

On the exterior bridge of the *I-403*, Ogawa hesitated momentarily before dropping down the hatch, taking a final glance at his approaching stalker. Movement caught his eye on the forward deck, where he was surprised to see a crewman striding toward one of the airplanes. It was a pilot, ignoring the dive command and climbing into his plane. In the spirit of the kamikaze, the pilot could not bear the thought of losing his aircraft and was willing to die with it instead. Ogawa cursed his foolish bravery, then ducked down into the bridge below.

The ballast tanks were opened and a rush of seawater began flooding in to weigh the submarine down. The huge hull of the *I-403* was a liability in this situation, requiring a notoriously long time to submerge. As Ogawa waited for the sub to make its agonizingly slow descent, he played one more card.

'Prepare to fire torpedoes!' he commanded.

It was a gamble, but a calculated one at that. With the destroyer directly ahead, Ogawa could let go a shot in the face of the ship and make the hunter fall prey to the victim.

'Tubes loaded,' the torpedo officer reported.

'Stand by tubes number one and number two,' Ogawa ordered.

The destroyer was barely two hundred yards away and still belching fire from its five-inch guns. Amazingly, the destroyer's guns continued to miss their mark. The point-blank target of the sub slowly began to diminish as the nose of the undersea craft dipped beneath the waves and a wash of seawater gradually flooded over the forward deck.

'Fire one!' Ogawa shouted. Counting off three seconds silently, he paused, then ordered, 'Fire two!'

With a blast of compressed air, the two torpedoes burst out of the forward tubes on a deadly streak toward the advancing destroyer. Each packing an

890-pound lethal warhead, the twenty-three-foot-long, oxygen-powered torpedoes accelerated quickly, racing toward the *Theodore Knight* at better than 45 knots.

An ensign standing on the bridge wing of the destroyer noticed a seam of white trails under the water's surface burrowing toward the ship.

'Torpedoes off the port and starboard bow!' he shouted, though his body remained frozen in rapt fascination as he watched the speeding explosives approach.

In an instant, the torpedoes were on them. But either by miscalculation, divine intervention, or just plain luck, the two deadly fish somehow missed their target. The immobile ensign watched in amazement as the two torpedoes skimmed past both sides of the destroyer's bow, then raced down the length of the ship no more than ten feet from either side of the hull before disappearing beyond the stern.

'She's diving, sir,' noted the destroyer's helmsman as he watched the waves slosh over the bow of the sub.

'Steer for the conning tower,' Baxter commanded. 'Let's go right down her throat.'

Firing from the forward batteries had ceased, as the guns could no longer be trained on a target so low to the ship's bow. The battle became a race, the destroyer boring in like a charging ram in an attempt to batter the *I-403*. But the submarine was gaining depth and, for a moment, appeared like it would successfully slip beneath the stalking ship. The *Theodore Knight* had crossed over the bowline of the sub, its keel missing the top deck of the descending sub by a matter of feet. But the destroyer drove forward, intent on crushing the submersing vessel.

The aircraft were the first to feel the sharp wedge of the destroyer's prow. Partially submerged on the receding deck, the tandemly aligned airplanes just caught the surging bow of the ship at midheight and were instantly dissected into large sections of mangled metal, fabric, and debris. The defiant pilot, who had climbed into the cockpit of the first airplane, received little time for impudence before realizing his wish to die with his plane in a crushing blow.

The *I-403* itself was now half submerged and had so far avoided damage from the assault. But the sub's conning tower was too great a protrusion and could not escape the charging wrath of the ship. With a crunching shear, the bow of the destroyer tore into the vessel's console, slicing through it like a scythe. Ogawa and his operations officers were killed instantly as the ship crushed into and through the control center of the sub. The entire structure was ripped away from the body of the submarine as the destroyer continued its onslaught, carving a mutilating gash along the rear spine of the *I-403*. Inside, the doomed crew heard the screeching grind of metal on metal before the torrents of seawater burst in and flooded the compartments. Death came quickly but painfully to the drowning men as the sub lurched, then dropped rapidly to the seafloor. A smattering of air bubbles and oil boiled to the surface to mark the gravesite, then all was silent.

Aboard the *Theodore Knight*, the crew and officers cheered their destruction of the Japanese submarine as they watched the telltale slick of black oil and fuel pool on the surface like a death cloud above the sunken boat. How lucky they were to have found and destroyed an enemy vessel right on their own home shores, with not so much as a casualty on their own ship. Though the enemy had fought with valor, the victory had come easily. The crew would return to port as heroes, with a great tale to tell their grandchildren. What none of the men on the destroyer could have suspected or imagined, however, was the unspeakable horror that would have befallen their countrymen had the *I-403* succeeded in its mission. Nor could they know that the horror still awaited, silently beckoning from the depths of the shattered wreckage.

PART ONE
Air of Death

Mystery trawler and NUMA helicopter

I

May 22, 2007
The Aleutian Islands, Alaska

The winds swirled lightly about the faded yellow tin hut perched on a small bluff overlooking the sea. A few light snowflakes danced about the eaves of the structure before falling to the ground and melting amid the grass and tundra. Despite the nearby hum of a diesel generator, a wooly Siberian husky lay on a sun-exposed patch of loose gravel enjoying a deep sleep. A white-feathered arctic tern swooped by for a look, then stopped momentarily on the small building's roof. After curiously examining the odd assortment of antennae, beacons, and satellite dishes adorning the rooftop, the small bird seized a gust of wind and flew away in search of more edible offerings.

The Coast Guard weather station on Yunaska Island was as tranquil as it was remote. Situated midway along the Aleutian chain of islands, Yunaska was one of dozens of volcanic uprisings that curved off the Alaskan mainland like an arched tentacle. Barely seventeen miles across, the island was distinguished by two dormant volcano peaks at either end, which were separated by rolling grass hills. Absent a single tree or high shrub, the green island rose like an emerald from the surrounding frigid ocean waters in the late spring.

Lying central to the North Pacific currents, Yunaska was an ideal location for tracking sea and atmospheric conditions that would brew into full-fledged weather fronts as they moved eastward toward North America. In addition to collecting weather data, the Coast Guard station also served as a warning and rescue relay station for troubled fishermen working the surrounding marine-rich waters.

The site could hardly be considered a paradise for the two men assigned to man the station. The nearest village was ninety miles away across open water, while their home base in Anchorage was more than a thousand miles distant. The isolated inhabitants were on their own for a three-week stint until the next pair of volunteers was airlifted in. Five months out of the year, brutal winter weather conditions forced closure of the station except for minimal remote operations. But from May to November, the two-man crew was on call around the clock.

Despite the seclusion, meteorologist Ed Stimson and technician Mike Barnes considered it a plum assignment. Stimson enjoyed being in the field to practice his science while Barnes relished the time off he would accrue after working a station shift, which he would spend prospecting in the Alaskan backcountry.

'I'm telling you, Ed, you're going to have to find a

new partner after our next R&R. I found a fissure of quartz in the Chugach Mountains that would knock your socks off. I know there's got to be a thick, juicy gold vein lying right beneath it.'

'Sure, just like that strike you made wild claims about on the McKinley River,' Stimson chided. Barnes had a naive sense of optimism that always amused the elder meteorologist.

'Just wait till you see me driving around Anchorage in my new Hummer, then you'll believe,' replied Barnes somewhat indignantly.

'Fair enough,' Stimson replied. 'In the meantime, can you check the anemometer mounting? The wind readings have stopped recording again.'

'Just don't file a claim on my goldfield while I'm up on the roof,' Barnes grinned while pulling on a heavy coat.

'Not to worry, my friend. Not to worry.'

Two miles to the east, Sarah Matson cursed leaving her gloves back in the tent. Although the temperature was almost fifty, an offshore breeze made it feel much cooler. Her hands were wet from crawling over some sea-washed boulders and the sensitivity was evaporating from her fingertips. Climbing across a gully, she tried to forget about her icy hands and concentrate on moving closer to her quarry. Stepping quietly along a boulder-strewn path, she eased herself slowly to a prime vantage point beside a shallow rock outcropping.

Barely thirty feet away lay a noisy colony of Steller's sea lions basking at the water's edge. A dozen or so of the fat-whiskered mammals sat huddled together like tourists jammed on the beach at Rio while another four or five could be seen swimming in the surf. Two young males barked loudly back and forth at each other, vying for the attention of a nearby female, who showed not the slightest sign of interest in either mammal. Several pups slept blissfully oblivious to the rancor, cuddled up close to their mother's belly.

Pulling a small notepad from her jacket pocket, Sarah began jotting down particulars about each animal, estimating their age, sex, and apparent health condition. As accurately as she could, she carefully observed each sea lion for signs of muscle spasms, eye or nasal secretions, or excessive sneezing. After nearly an hour of observation, she replaced the notepad in her pocket, hoping that she would later be able to read the scribbled handwriting created by her frozen fingers.

Slowly retracing her steps, Sarah edged away from the colony and made her way back across the gully. She found that her original footsteps had left indentations in the short grass and she easily followed her imprints leading inland and over a gradual rise. The cool sea breeze felt refreshing to her lungs as she hiked while the sparse beauty of the island made her feel energized and full of life. Belying her slender frame and delicate features, the flaxen-haired woman of thirty actually relished working outdoors. Growing up in rural Wyoming, Sarah had spent all her summer days hiking and horseback riding in the Teton Mountains with a pair of rambunctious brothers. A love of outdoor wildlife led her to study veterinary medicine at neighboring Colorado State University. After a number of research positions on the East Coast, she followed a favorite professor to the federal Centers for Disease Control with the promise that she wouldn't be stuck in a lab every day. In the role of field epidemiologist for the CDC, she was able to combine her passion for wildlife and the outdoors by helping track the spread of communicable diseases among animals that posed a health threat to humans.

Finding herself in the Aleutian Islands was just the sort of outdoor adventure she craved, although the reason behind it tugged at her animal-loving heart. A mysterious number of sea lion deaths had been reported along the western Alaska Peninsula, although no known environmental catastrophe or human-induced culprit was suspected. Sarah and two associates had been sent from Seattle to diagnose the extent of the die-off and determine its range of dispersement. Starting with the outward Aleutian island of Attu, the team had begun island-hopping eastward, searching for signs of the outbreak while working their way toward the Alaskan mainland. Every three days, a small seaplane would pick the team up, then ferry them to the next designated island with a fresh drop of supplies. The second day on

Yunaska had failed to reveal indications of the ailment in the local sea lion population, which added a small sense of relief to Sarah.

Blessed with high cheekbones and soft hazel eyes, the pretty scientist quickly ambled the two miles back to camp, easily spotting the trio of bright red tents some distance away. A squat, bearded man wearing a flannel shirt and a worn Seattle Mariners baseball cap was rummaging through a large cooler when Sarah approached the campsite.

'Sarah, there you are. Sandy and I were just making plans for lunch,' Irv Fowler said with a smile. An easygoing man on the thin side of fifty, Fowler looked and acted like a man ten years his junior.

A petite redheaded woman crawled out of one of the nearby tents clutching a pot and ladle. 'Irv's always making plans for lunch,' Sandy Johnson responded with a grin while rolling her eyes.

'How did you two make out this morning?' Sarah inquired as she grabbed an empty campstool and sat down.

'Sandy's got the stats. We checked a large colony of Steller's on the eastern beach and they all looked fat and healthy. I found one cadaver, but by all appearances the fellow looked like he expired from old age. I took a tissue sample for lab analysis just to be sure.' While he spoke, Fowler pumped the primer on a propane gas camp stove, then lit the hissing gas escaping beneath the burner, the blue flame igniting with a poof.

'That's consistent with what I observed as well. It appears that the affliction has not spread to the sea lions of charming Yunaska,' Sarah replied, her eyes sweeping the green landscape around them.

'We can check the colony on the west coast of the island this afternoon, since our pilot won't be back to pick us up until morning.'

'That will be a bit of a hike. But we can stop for a chat at the Coast Guard station, which I recall our pilot saying was manned this time of year.'

'In the meantime,' Fowler announced, placing the large pot on the portable stove, 'it's time for the specialty of the house.'

'Not that fire-belching –' Sandy tried to declare before being cut off.

'Yes, indeed. Cajun chili du jour,' Fowler grinned, while scraping the lumpy brown contents of a large tin can into the heated pot.

'As they say in N'Awlins,' Sarah said with a laugh, *'Laissez le bon temps rouler.'*

Ed Stimson peered intently at a weather radar monitor watching a slight buildup of white electronic clouds fuzz up the upper portion of the green screen. It was a moderate storm front, some two hundred miles to the southwest, that Stimson accurately predicted would douse their island with several days of soggy weather. His concentration was interrupted by a rapping sound overhead. Barnes was still up on the tin roof fooling with the anemometer.

Static-filled chatter suddenly blared through the hut from a radio set mounted on a corner wall. Nearby fishing boats, their captains yakking about the weather, constituted most of the garbled radio traffic received on the island. Stimson did his best to tune out the meaningless chatter and, at first, failed to detect the odd whooshing sound. It was a low resonance emanating from outside. Then the radio fell silent for a moment and he could clearly hear a rushing sound in the distance, something similar to a jet aircraft. For several long seconds, the odd noise continued, seeming to diminish slightly in intensity before ending altogether in a loud crack.

Thinking it might be thunder, Stimson adjusted the scale view on his weather radar to a twenty-mile range. The monitor showed only a light scattering of clouds in the immediate vicinity, with nothing resembling thunderheads. Must be the Air Force up to some tricks, he figured, recalling the heavy air traffic in the Alaskan skies during the days of the Cold War.

His thoughts were broken by a crying wail outside the door from the pet husky named Max.

'What is it, Max?' Stimson called out while opening the door to the hut.

The Siberian husky let out a death-shrieking howl as it turned, shaking, toward his master in the doorway. Stimson was shocked to see the dog's eyes glazed in a vacant stare while thick white foam oozed from his mouth. The dog stood teetering back and forth for a moment, then keeled over on its side, hitting the ground with a thud.

'Jesus! Mike, get down here quick,' Stimson yelled to his partner.

Barnes was already climbing down the ladder from the roof but was having a hard time catching the rungs with his feet. Nearing the ground, he missed the last rung with his left foot altogether and lurched to the ground, staying semierect only by a hearty handgrasp on the ladder's rung.

'Mike, the dog just . . . are you okay?' Stimson asked, realizing something was not right. Running to his partner's side, he found Barnes in a state of labored breathing, and his eyes were nearly as glassy as Max's. Throwing his arm around the younger man's shoulder, Stimson half carried, half dragged Barnes into the shack and set him down in a chair.

Barnes bent over and retched violently, then sat upright, clinging to Stimson's arm for support. Gasping in a hoarse voice, he whispered, 'There's something in the air.'

No sooner had the words left his mouth when his eyes rolled up into the back of his head and he fell over stone dead.

Stimson stood up in a state of shock, then found that the room was spinning like a top before his eyes. A throbbing pain racked his head while the grip of an iron vise suddenly began squeezing the air out of his lungs. Staggering to the radio, he tried to let out a brief cry for help but was unsure whether his lips could move because of numbness to his face. A burst of heat flared internally, like an invisible fire was consuming his organs. Choking for air and losing all sense of vision, he staggered and fell hard to the floor, dead before he hit the ground.

Four miles east of the Coast Guard station, the three CDC scientists were just finishing their lunch when the invisible wave of death struck. Sarah was the first to detect something wrong when a pair of birds flying overhead suddenly stopped in midflight as if they had struck an invisible wall and then fell to the ground wriggling. Sandy fell victim first, clutching her stomach and doubling over in agony.

'Come now, my chili wasn't that bad,' Fowler joked before he, too, became light-headed and nauseous.

Sarah stood and took a few steps toward the cooler to retrieve some bottled water when fire shot through her legs and her thigh muscles began to spasm.

'What's happening?' Fowler gasped as he tried to comfort Sandy before staggering to the ground in distress.

For Sarah, time seemed to slow as her senses became dulled. Sluggishly, she dropped to the ground as her muscles weakened and refused to obey the commands sent by her brain. Her lungs seemed to constrict upon themselves, making each breath a painful stab of agony. A thumping noise began to ring through her ears as she fell prone on her back and stared blurry-eyed at the gray sky above. She felt the blades of grass dance and rustle against her body, but she was frozen, unable to move.

Gradually, a fog enveloped her mind and a field of blackness began to encroach the edges of her vision. But a sudden intrusion jarred her senses momentarily. Into the sea of gray popped an apparition, a strange ghost with a tuft of black hair over a rubbery face that seemed to melt away like plastic. She felt the alien gaze upon her with frightening giant, three-inch-wide crystal eyes. But there appeared to be another set of eyes beyond the crystal lenses, gazing intently at her with a sense of grace and warmth. A pair of deep, opaline green eyes. Then everything turned to black.

2

Sarah opened her eyes to a gray canopy above her, only this one was flat and without clouds. Shaking off the blurriness, her eyes slowly regained focus and she could see that it was not the sky above her but a ceiling. A softness beneath her revealed that she was lying in a bed with a thick pillow under her head. An oxygen mask was covering her face, which she removed, but she left alone the intravenous needle that was stuck in her arm. Carefully taking in the surroundings, her eyes gazed upon a small, simply decorated room featuring a small writing desk in one corner with an impressive painting of an old ocean liner above it, while off to the side was a small bath. The bed she lay in was mounted to the wall and the open door to a hallway had a stepover threshold. The whole room seemed to be rolling, and she was uncertain if it was her head creating the motion as a result of the deep throbbing sensation that pounded at her temples.

A movement caught her eye and she turned back to the doorway to find a figure standing there, looking at her with a slight grin. He was a tall man, broad-shouldered, but on a fit and somewhat wiry frame. He was young, perhaps in his late twenties, she guessed, but moved with the confidence of a more mature man. His skin showed the deep tan of someone who spent a good deal of time outdoors. Wavy black hair set off a rugged face that was more intriguing than classically handsome. But it was the eyes that radiated an aura about the man. They were a deep shade of iridescent green and revealed a sense of intelligence, adventure, and integrity all rolled into one. They were the eyes of a man who could be trusted. And they were the same green eyes, Sarah recalled, that she had seen before blacking out at the camp.

'Well, hello, Sleeping Beauty.' The words came from a warm, deep voice.

'You ... you're the man at the camp,' Sarah stammered.

'Yes. My apologies for not properly introducing myself on the island, Sarah. My name is Dirk Pitt.' He neglected to add 'Junior,' although he shared the same name as his father.

'You know who I am?' she asked, still confused.

'Well, not intimately,' Dirk smiled nonthreateningly, 'but a brainy scientist named Irv told me a little about you and your project on Yunaska. Irv seemed to think he poisoned everyone with his chili.'

'Irv and Sandy! Are they all right?'

'Yes. They took a little nap, like you, but are fine now. They're resting just down the hall,' Dirk said, motioning with his thumb toward the corridor. He could see the look of bewilderment in Sarah's eyes and touched her shoulder with his hand in a reassuring squeeze.

'Don't worry, you're in good hands. You're aboard the National Underwater and Marine Agency research ship *Deep Endeavor*. We were returning from an underwater survey of the Aleutian Basin when we picked up a distress call from the Coast Guard weather station on Yunaska. I flew to the station in a helicopter we have on board and happened to see your camp while flying back to the ship. I gave you and your friends an all-expense-paid aerial tour of Yunaska, but you slept through the whole thing,' Dirk added with mock disappointment.

'I'm sorry,' Sarah murmured, feeling somewhat bashful. 'I guess I owe you a big thanks, Mr. Pitt.'

'Please, call me "Dirk." '

'Okay, Dirk,' Sarah replied with a smile, feeling an odd flutter as she spoke his name. 'How are the Coast Guard people?'

Dirk's face went dark and a look of sorrow crossed his brow. 'I'm afraid we didn't make it in time. We found two men and a dog at the station. They were all dead.'

A shiver went up Sarah's spine. Two men dead, and she and her companions nearly as well. None of it made any sense.

'What on earth happened?' Sarah asked in shock.

'We don't know for sure. Our ship's doctor is running some tests, but, as you can imagine, his

46

resources are somewhat limited. It appears to have been some sort of airborne fume or toxin. All we know for sure is that the Coast Guard station thought there was something in the air. We flew in with gas masks and were not impacted. We even took some white mice from our shipboard lab with us. They all survived fine, without any apparent symptoms. Whatever it was, it must have dissipated by the time we landed at the Coast Guard station. You and your team were apparently far enough away from the source to be impacted less severely. You probably didn't receive a full dose of whatever it was.'

Sarah's eyes dropped and she fell quiet. The horror and pain of the whole ordeal came back to her with a showering of fatigue. She wanted to sleep it all off and hope it was just a bad dream.

'Sarah, I'll have the doctor check on you, then let you sleep some more. Perhaps later I can buy you a plate of king crab legs for dinner?' Dirk asked with a smile.

Sarah smiled briefly in return. 'I'd like that,' she murmured, then fell fast asleep.

Kermit Burch stood at the helm reading a fax communiqué when Dirk stepped into the bridge from the starboard wing door. The seasoned captain of the *Deep Endeavor* shook his head slightly as he read the document, then turned to Dirk with a slightly annoyed look on his face.

'We've notified the Coast Guard and the Department of Homeland Security, but nobody intends to do anything until the local authorities have filed their report. The village public safety officer from Atka is the area law enforcement official and he can't get to the island until morning,' Burch snorted. 'Two men dead and they treat it as an accident.'

'We don't have much to go on,' Dirk replied. 'I spoke with Carl Nash, our saltwater environmental analyst, who is well versed on terrestrial pollutants. According to Nash, there are naturally occurring environmental emissions, such as sulfuric volcanic releases, which could have killed the men. High concentrations of industrial pollutants are another potential culprit, although I'm not aware of any neighborhood chemical plants in the Aleutians.'

'The public safety officer told me it sounds to him like a classic case of carbon monoxide poisoning from the station house generator. Of course, that doesn't explain our friends from the CDC succumbing to similar effects four miles away.'

'Nor does it explain the dog I found dead outside of the station house,' Dirk added.

'Well, perhaps the CDC crew can shed some light on the matter. How are our three guests doing, by the way?'

'A little groggy still. They don't remember much, other than that it struck pretty rapidly.'

'The sooner we get them to a proper medical facility, the sooner I'll rest easier. The nearest airfield is Unalaska, which we can make in under fourteen hours. I'll radio ahead for a medical flight to transfer them to Anchorage.'

'Captain, I'd like to take the helicopter back out and reconnoiter the island. We didn't have much of a chance to look around on the last flight. Maybe there's something we missed. Any objections?'

'No . . . just so long as you take that Texas joker with you,' Burch replied with a pained grin.

As Dirk ran through a preflight checklist from the pilot seat of the NUMA Sikorsky S-76C+ offshore helicopter, a sandy-haired man with a bushy mustache ambled across the flight platform. With scuffed cowboy boots, chiseled arms, and a ubiquitous scowl that hid a mordant sense of humor, Jack Dahlgren looked like a bull rider who got lost on the way to the rodeo. A notorious practical joker, Dahlgren had already worked his way under Burch's skin by spiking the galley's coffee urn with a cheap bottle of rum on their first night at sea. An engineering whiz who grew up in west Texas, Dahlgren knew his way around horses and guns, as well as every type of mechanical equipment that operated above or below the sea.

'Is this the scenic island tour my travel agent recommended?' he asked Dirk, sticking his head through a sliding cockpit window.

'Step right up, sonny boy, you won't be disappointed. All the water, rocks, and sea lions your eyes can absorb.'

'Sounds swell. I'll give you an extra quarter if you can find me a bar with a short-skirted waitress.'

'I'll see what I can do,' Dirk grinned as Dahlgren climbed into the copilot's seat.

The two men had become fast friends years before, while studying ocean engineering at Florida Atlantic University. Avid divers, they regularly cut classes together in order to spearfish the coral reefs lying off Boca Raton, using their fresh-caught fish to woo local sorority girls with barbecues on the beach. After graduating, Jack completed his college ROTC commitment in the Navy while Dirk obtained a master's degree from the New York Maritime College and trained at a commercial dive school. The two men were reunited when Dirk joined his father at NUMA as a special projects director and convinced his old friend to accompany him at the prestigious research agency.

After years of diving together, there was almost an unspoken bond between the two men. They knew they could depend on each other and performed at their best when the chips were down. Dahlgren had seen the look of determination in Dirk's eyes before and knew the dogged persistence that came with it. The mysterious events on Yunaska were weighing on his friend, Dahlgren noticed, and he wasn't likely to let it go.

The main rotor blade of the Sikorsky wound to a high pitch as Dirk gently eased the helicopter up and off a small landing platform mounted amidships of the *Deep Endeavor*. Climbing to one hundred feet,

Dirk held the helicopter stationary for a moment, admiring the bird's-eye view of the NUMA research ship. The wide-beamed, turquoise-colored survey ship had a stubby look to her 270-foot length. But the lack of a svelte streamline made for a stable work platform, ideal for operating the myriad cranes and hoists strategically positioned about the large, open stern deck. In the middle of the deck, a bright yellow submersible sparkled like a jewel in the late afternoon sunlight as it rested on a large wooden cradle, while several technicians tinkered with its thrusters and electronics. One of the technicians stood and waved his cap toward the suspended helicopter. Dirk threw the man a quick wave, then banked the chopper and headed northeast toward the island of Yunaska, less than ten miles away.

'Back to Yunaska?' asked Dahlgren.

'The Coast Guard station we scouted this morning.'

'Great,' Dahlgren moaned. 'We acting as a flying hearse?'

'No, just checking out the source of whatever killed the men and dog.'

'And are we looking for animal, vegetable, or mineral?' Dahlgren asked through his headset, his teeth mashing a large wad of gum.

'All three,' Dirk replied. 'Carl Nash told me that a toxic cloud could be created by anything from an active volcano to an algae bloom, not to mention your garden-variety industrial pollutant.'

'Just stop at the next walrus and I'll ask for directions to the closest pesticide factory.'

'That reminds me, where's Basil?' Dirk asked, his eyes glancing about the cockpit.

'Right here, safe and sound,' Dahlgren replied, grabbing a small cage from beneath his seat and holding it up in front of his face. Inside, a small white mouse peered back at Dahlgren, his tiny whiskers twitching back and forth.

'Breathe deep, little friend, and don't go to sleep on us,' Dahlgren requested of the furry rodent. He then strung the cage from an overhead lanyard, like a canary in a coal mine, so they could easily see if the mouse succumbed to any toxins in the air.

The grassy island of Yunaska crested out of the slate green water ahead of them, a sprinkling of light cirrus clouds dancing about the larger of the island's two extinct volcanic peaks. Dirk gradually increased the helicopter's altitude as they approached the craggy shoreline, then banked left along the water's edge. Flying counterclockwise around the island's perimeter, it took only a few minutes before they spotted the yellow building of the Coast Guard station. Bringing the helicopter to a hover, Dirk and Dahlgren carefully examined the ground surrounding the station for any unusual signs. Dirk eyed the body of Max the husky still lying outside the hut's door and it brought back to mind the look of pain and horror on the dead men's faces inside when he and Dahlgren first landed at the station earlier in the day.

He carefully shelved his emotions and shifted his mental motor to discovering the source of the deadly toxic breeze.

Dirk nodded past the windscreen to the right. 'The prevailing winds come from the west, so the source would likely have come from farther up the coast. Or possibly from offshore.'

'Makes sense. The CDC team was camped to the east of here and they obviously caught a less lethal dose of the mystery gas,' Dahlgren replied while peering at the ground through low-power binoculars.

Dirk applied a gentle force to the cyclic control lever and the helicopter edged forward and away from the yellow structure. For the next hour, the two men strained eyeballs searching the grassy island for signs of a natural or man-made origin to the toxin. Dirk traced wide semicircular arcs north and south across the island, expanding their way west until they reached the western coast and returned to the vicinity of the Coast Guard station.

'Nothing but grass and rocks,' Dahlgren grumbled. 'The seals can keep it, as far as I'm concerned.'

'Speaking of which, take a look down there,' Dirk replied, pointing to a small gravel beach ahead of them.

A half-dozen brown sea lions lay stretched out on the ground, seemingly enjoying the rays of the late afternoon sun. Dahlgren looked closer, his forehead suddenly wrinkling in puzzlement.

'Jeez, they're not moving. They've all bought it, too.'

'The toxin must not have come from Yunaska but from the sea, or the next island over.'

'Amukta is the next rock pile to the west,' Dahlgren replied, running his finger across a chart of the region.

Dirk could clearly see the dirty gray outline of the island on the horizon. 'Looks to be about twenty miles from here.'

Eyeing the helicopter's fuel gauge, he continued, 'I think we've got time for a quick gander before our fuel runs low. Okay if you miss your pedicure treatment in the ship's salon?'

'Sure, I'll just reschedule it with my body wrap tomorrow,' Dahlgren replied.

'I'll let Burch know where we're headed,' Dirk said, dialing up the ship's radio frequency.

'Tell him to hold supper in the galley,' Dahlgren added while rubbing his stomach. 'I'm working up an appetite taking in all this scenery.'

As Dirk radioed the survey ship, he guided the Sikorsky toward the island of Amukta, skimming low over the open water. The powerful helicopter, designed for offshore oil transport, flew straight as a rail under Dirk's firm hand. After cruising steadily for ten minutes, Dahlgren quietly lifted an arm and pointed out the cockpit window to an object on the horizon. It was a white speck, growing larger by the second, until it slowly revealed itself as a large boat complete with trailing wake. Without a word, Dirk applied gentle pressure to his left pedal control until the helicopter eased about on the same line as the boat. Approaching rapidly, they could see it was a steel-hulled fishing trawler, running to the southwest at full bore.

'Now, there's a tub calling out for a little spit and polish,' Pitt remarked as he eased off the throttle to match speeds with the boat.

Though not appearing particularly old, the fishing vessel had obvious signs of hard use over the years. Scrapes, dents, and grease marks abounded both on the hull and throughout the open deck. Its original coating of white paint was worn thin in the spots where rust had not yet declared victory. By outward appearance, she looked as tired as the frayed bald tires hanging over her sides like a string of donuts. Yet like many disheveled-appearing workboats, her twin diesel engines were newly rebuilt and pushed the hulk hard through the waves with a barely a wisp of black smoke from the funnel.

Dirk studied the boat carefully, noting with interest that no flags flew from the mast, which might identify nationality. Both the bow sides and the stern were absent a ship name or home port. As he perused the stern deck, two Asian men in blue jumpsuits stepped into view and peered at the helicopter with looks of angst.

'Don't look overly friendly now, do they?' Dahlgren remarked before waving and grinning toward the boat. The two jumpsuits simply scowled in return.

'You wouldn't be, either, if you worked on that mangy derelict,' Dirk said as he steadied the Sikorsky in a hover just aft of the churning boat. 'Anything strike you as odd about that fishing boat?' he asked, eyeing the stern deck.

'You mean the fact that no fishing equipment is anywhere to be seen?'

'Precisely,' Dirk replied, inching the helicopter closer to the boat. He noted an odd trestle mounted in the center of the deck, built up approximately fifteen feet high. No streaks of rust could be seen on the metal framing, indicating it was a recent addition to the boat. In a star-shaped pattern at the base of the trestle was a gray powdery marking that appeared singed into the surface of the deck.

As the helicopter crept closer, the two men on deck suddenly began jabbering animately with each other, then ducked down a stairwell. At the head of the stairwell, five sea lion carcasses were stretched out on the deck side by side like sardines in a tin. To the left of the corpses was a small steel pen, which contained three live sea lions.

'Since when has the demand for seal blubber surpassed the market for crab legs?' Dahlgren said idly.

'Not sure, but I don't think Nanook of the North would be too happy about these guys stealing his dinner.'

Then came the flash of fire. Dirk detected it out of the corner of his eye and instinctively pressed hard on the left foot pedal, throwing the Sikorsky into a quick half spin. The move saved their lives. As the helicopter began to turn, a spray of bullets found their mark and burst into the machine. But rather than smashing into the forward section of the cockpit, the hail of fire entered in front of the pilots and ripped into the instrument panel. The console, gauges, and radio shattered into bits, but the pilots and critical mechanical components went unharmed.

'Guess they didn't like the Nanook comment,' Dahlgren deadpanned as he watched the two men in jumpsuits reappear and fire into the helicopter with automatic rifles.

Dirk said nothing as he throttled up the Sikorsky to its maximum thrust and attempted to swing clear of the gunmen. On the port half deck of the trawler, the two men were continuing to fire their Russian-made AK-74s at the helicopter. Without contemplating their target, they foolishly aimed their fire at the cabin rather than the more susceptible rotors. Inside the helicopter, the rackety sound of the machine-gun fire was lost to the whine of the engine and rotors. Dirk and Dahlgren could hear only a slight tapping behind them on the fuselage.

Dirk wheeled the helicopter around in a wide arc to the starboard side of the trawler, putting the ship's bridge between him and the gunmen, shielding themselves from the gunfire. Temporarily free from attack, he muscled the helicopter level, then aimed it toward the island of Amukta looming in the distance.

But the damage had been done. The cockpit began filling with smoke as Dirk fought the fiercely bucking controls. The rain of lead had smashed into the electronics, pierced hydraulic lines, and riddled the control gauges. Dahlgren detected a warm trickle on his ankle and felt down to find a neat hole shot through his calf. Several rounds had also found the turbine, but still the rotor chugged on, coughing and cajoling itself in gasps.

'I'll try for the island, but be prepared to ditch,' Dirk shouted over the racket of the disintegrating engine. A foul blue smoke filled the cockpit, accompanied by the acrid odor of burning wiring. Through the haze, Dirk could barely make out the island ahead, and what looked like a small beach.

In his hands, the control stick shook like a jackhammer. Dirk used all his strength to hold the craft steady and willed it forward as it began to shake itself apart. Agonizingly close, he could see the shoreline beckoning as the aircraft lurched ahead low to the sea, smoke belching, its wheels skimming just above the surf. But just short of the shoreline, the shot-up turbine could take no more. Digesting a handful of its own parts, the turbine wailed before grinding to a halt with a loud pop.

As the turbine died, Dirk pulled on the collective control lever with all his might to keep the nose up as power to the rotors was lost. The tail rotor sliced down into the water, acting as an anchor to slow the forward progress of the entire craft. The Sikorsky hung suspended for a moment in the air before gravity caught up and the cabin dropped to the water, slapping the surface with a smack. The main rotor spun into the surf, attempting to whip through the sea, but the sudden impact with the water cracked the main spindle and the entire rotor cartwheeled off to the side fifty feet before sinking in a spray of foam.

The cabin of the Sikorsky remarkably held together during the crash and bobbed on the surface for a second before being sucked under the waves. Through the smashed windshield, Dirk caught a glimpse of a wave breaking over a sandy beach before the icy water filled the cockpit and stung his body. Dahlgren was trying to kick out a side-panel door as the green water enveloped them rapidly, rising to the cockpit ceiling. In unison, each man raised his head and took a last gasp of air before the murky cold water rose over them. Then the turquoise helicopter disappeared completely from the surface in a swirl of bubbles, sinking swiftly to the rocky seafloor.

3

Captain Burch immediately launched a search-and-rescue mission after he lost radio contact with Dirk and Dahlgren. He brought the *Deep Endeavor* to Dirk's last reported position, then began a visual search for the two men, sailing west in a zigzag pattern from Yunaska to Amukta. Every available crewman was called to the deck to scan the horizon for signs of the men or helicopter, while in the ship's radio shack the radioman continued a tireless call for the missing aircraft.

After three hours of searching, no trace was found of the helicopter and an apprehensive dread fell over the ship's crew. The *Deep Endeavor* had worked its way close to Amukta Island, which was little more than a steep volcanic cone popping out of the sea. Dusk was approaching and the sky turned a purplish red on the western horizon as the day's light slowly diminished. Executive Officer Leo Delgado was studying the steep shape of the mountainous island when a faint blur caught his eye.

'Captain, there's smoke on the shoreline,' he reported, pointing a finger toward the hazy spot on the island.

Burch held a pair of binoculars to his eyes and

looked intently at the spot for several moments.

'Burning debris, sir?' Delgado asked, fearful of the answer.

'Perhaps. Or it could be a signal fire. Can't tell from here. Delgado, take two men in the Zodiac and see what you can find on shore. I'll bring the ship in behind you as close as I can get.'

'Yes, sir,' Delgado responded, already crossing the bridge before the captain had finished speaking.

A gusty breeze had kicked up, making the evening seas choppy by the time the Zodiac was lowered into the water. Delgado and the two crewmen got doused with cold sea spray repeatedly as the rubber boat bounced over the swells in their anxious drive to the shore. The skies were nearly dark and the helmsmen had a difficult time tracking the wisps of smoke against the black backdrop of the peaked island. The island appeared to be surrounded by a steep and rocky shoreline and Delgado wondered whether they would even be able to get ashore. Finally, he spotted a quick glimpse of the fire's flame and directed the Zodiac toward it. A small channel through the rocks opened up, leading to a pebble-strewn patch of beach. Gunning the motor to ride the crest of a wave in, the twelve-foot rubber boat bounded through the channel and ground to the shore with a crunch as the hull plate scraped some small rocks before sliding to a stop.

Delgado jumped out of the inflatable boat and ran apprehensively toward the smoky fire. Two shadowy figures could be seen hunched over the smoldering driftwood fire trying to keep warm, their backs turned to Delgado.

'Pitt? Dahlgren? Are you guys okay?' Delgado shouted out hesitantly before approaching too close.

The two soggy-looking derelicts slowly turned toward Delgado as if rudely interrupted from an important meeting. Dahlgren was holding a half-eaten crab claw in one hand, while the head of a white mouse peeked out of his chest pocket sniffing the night air. Dirk stood holding a sharp stick, the end of which pierced the shell of a huge Alaskan king crab whose spiny legs Dirk dangled over the open flame.

'Well,' Dirk said, tearing a steaming leg off the big crustacean, 'we could use some lemon and butter.'

After briefing Burch on their encounter with the fishing trawler, Dirk and Dahlgren limped to the ship's medical station for treatment of their wounds and to slip into some dry clothes. Dahlgren's bullet wound had pierced the meaty section of his left calf but, fortunately, had missed damaging any tendons. As the ship's doctor inserted sutures to close up the wound, Dahlgren nonchalantly lit up a cigar while lying on the examination table. When the smoke hit the physician's nostrils, he nearly ripped out the sutures by hand before forcing Dahlgren to douse the smelly tobacco. With a grin, the doctor handed

Dahlgren a pair of crutches and told him to stay off his leg for three days.

Dirk had his bloodied cheek and forehead cleaned and bandaged after catching a face full of shattered glass when the helicopter hit the surf. Remarkably, the two men incurred no other injuries from the crash and sinking of the Sikorsky. Dirk had saved them from drowning when he noticed a fuselage door had popped off during the crash landing. After the helicopter filled with water, Dirk grabbed Dahlgren and swam out the opening and made for the surface. With the aid of Dahlgren's trusty Zippo lighter, they were able to ignite some dry driftwood on the beach and stave off hypothermia until Delgado arrived in the rubber boat.

Captain Burch, meanwhile, reported the loss of the helicopter to NUMA headquarters, as well as reporting the incident to the Coast Guard and the Atka village public safety officer. The nearest Coast Guard patrol vessel was hundreds of miles away at Attu Island. Information about the fishing trawler was reported in detail but the odds for an interdiction were slim at best.

After donning a black turtleneck sweater and jeans, Dirk made his way to the wheelhouse. Burch was leaning over the chart table plotting a course through the Aleutian Islands.

'Aren't we heading back to Yunaska to retrieve the bodies of the Coast Guardsmen?' Dirk asked.

Burch shook his head. 'Not our job. Better to leave

them be and allow the proper authorities to handle the investigation. I'm laying a course for the fishing port at Unalaska to disembark the CDC scientists.'

'I'd rather make for that trawler,' Dirk said.

'We've lost our helicopter and they have an eight-hour lead on us. We'd be lucky to find them, assuming we could even outrun them. The Navy, Coast Guard, and local authorities have all been alerted to your description. They have a better chance of finding that trawler than we do.'

'Perhaps, but their resources are all thin in this part of the world. Those chances are slim at best.'

'There's little more we can do. Our survey work is finished and we need to get those injured scientists appropriate medical care. There's no sense in hanging around any longer.'

Dirk nodded. 'You're right, of course.' Wishing there was a way to find the trawler, he headed down the ladder to the ship's galley for a cup of coffee. Dinner had long since been served and a cleanup crew was working over the kitchen before shutting down. Dirk filled a mug of coffee from a large silver urn, then turned and spotted Sarah sitting in a wheel-chair at the end of the dining hall. The golden-haired woman sat alone at a table, peering out a large port-hole at the moonlit water outside. She was dressed in the dull medical ward attire of cotton pajamas, slippers, and a blue robe but still gave off a vibrant glow. As Dirk approached, she looked up and her eyes twinkled.

'Too late for dinner?' he asked apologetically.

'Afraid so. You missed the chef's special Halibut Oscar, which was truly excellent.'

'Just my luck,' Dirk replied, drawing a chair and sitting down directly across from her.

'What happened to you?' Sarah asked with concern in her voice as she eyed the bandages on Dirk's face.

'Just a little accident with the helicopter. I don't think my boss is going to like the news,' he said with a grimace, thinking about the expensive helicopter sitting at the bottom of the sea. Dirk proceeded to describe the events of the flight, all the while gazing intently into Sarah's hazel-colored eyes.

'Do you think the fishing boat had something to do with the death of the Coast Guardsmen and us getting sick?' she asked.

'It only goes to figure. They obviously weren't too keen on us seeing them poaching sea lions, or whatever else they were up to.'

'The sea lions,' Sarah murmured. 'Did you see any sea lions on the west end of the island when you flew over?'

'Yes, Jack spotted several just past the Coast Guard station on the western shore. They all appeared to be dead.'

'Do you think the *Deep Endeavor* could obtain one of the cadavers to study? I could arrange to have the specimen sent to the state lab in Washington we are working out of.'

'Captain Burch isn't eager to stick around the area,

but I'm sure I can convince him to retrieve one for scientific purposes,' Dirk said before taking a long draw from his coffee. 'We are actually headed back to port in Seattle, so could deliver it there in a few more days.'

'We could perform an autopsy of the animal and determine the source of death relatively quickly. I'm sure the Alaska state authorities will take some time to release the cause of death of the two Coast Guardsmen, and they might not want the CDC looking over their shoulder.'

'Do you think there might be a link with the dead sea lions that were found on the other Aleutian islands?'

'I don't know. We believe the cadavers found near the mainland were infected by a canine distemper virus.'

'Distemper? From dogs?'

'Yes. A viral outbreak likely occurred through contact between an infected domestic dog and one or more sea lions. Distemper is very contagious and could spread rapidly through a concentrated sea lion population.'

'Wasn't there a similar outbreak in Russia a few years ago?' Dirk tried to recall.

'Kazakhstan, actually. Thousands of Caspian seals died in 2000 due to an outbreak of distemper near the Ural River along the Caspian Sea.'

'Irv told me you found healthy, uninfected sea lions on Yunaska.'

'Yes, the distemper did not appear to have reached this far west. Which will make an examination of the dead sea lions you saw from the helicopter that much more intriguing.'

A quiet pause fell over the couple and Sarah could see a faraway look in Dirk's eyes as the wheels churned inside his head. After a moment, she broke the silence.

'The men on the boat. Who do you think they were? What were they doing?'

Dirk stared out the porthole for a long minute. 'I don't know,' he replied quietly, 'but I intend to find out.'

4

The twelfth hole of the Kasumigaseki Golf Club stretched 290 yards down a tight fairway before it doglegged left to an elevated green tightly guarded by a deep bunker in front. The U.S. ambassador to Japan, Edward Hamilton, waggled the head of his oversized driver several times before swinging hard into the golf ball, sending it soaring some 275 yards off the tee box and straight down the fairway.

'Fine shot, Ed,' offered David Monaco, the British ambassador to Japan and Hamilton's weekly golf partner for nearly three years. The lanky Brit teed up his ball, then punched a long arcing shot that rolled twenty yards past Hamilton's ball before bounding into a patch of tall grass on the left fringe of the fairway.

'Nice power, Dave, but I think you found the rough,' Hamilton said as he spotted his playing partner's ball. The two men proceeded to walk down the fairway while a pair of female caddies, in the unique tradition of Japan's oldest country clubs, manhandled their golf bags a respectable distance behind them. Lurking nearby, four not-so-inconspicuous government bodyguards maintained a rough perimeter around the duo as they made their way around the course.

The weekly outing at the golf course located south of Tokyo was an informal way of sharing information about the goings-on in and around their host country. The two allied ambassadors actually found it one of their most productive uses of time.

'I hear you are making good progress on establishing the economic partnership agreement with Tokyo,' Monaco remarked as they hiked up the fairway.

'It just makes sense for everyone involved to ease trade restrictions. Our own steel tariffs may still get in the way of an agreement. The trade attitudes here are certainly changing, however. I think South Korea will even forge a partnership agreement with the Japanese shortly.'

'Speaking of Korea, I understand that some chaps in Seoul are going to issue another appeal for the removal of U.S. armed forces in the Korean National Assembly next week,' Monaco said in a soft but accented voice.

'Yes, we've heard that as well. The South Koreans' Democratic Labor Party is using the issue as a divisive wedge to gain more political power. Fortunately, they still only represent a small minority within the National Assembly.'

'It's a damn mystery how they can think that way, given the past aggressiveness of the North.'

'True, but it does play on a sensitive cultural issue. The DLP tries to compare us to the historical foreign occupations of Korea by the Chinese and the Japanese and it strikes a chord with the average man on the street.'

'Yes, but I would be surprised if the leaders of the party are operating on a simply altruistic motive,' Monaco said as the two approached Hamilton's ball.

'My counterpart in Seoul tells me we have no definitive proof, but we are pretty sure that at least some party officials are receiving support from the North,' Hamilton replied. Taking a 3-iron from his caddy, Hamilton lined up the pin, then knocked another straight shot that cut the corner of the dogleg and landed on the far side of the green, avoiding the large bunker.

'I understand that support for the measure extends well beyond the DLP, I'm afraid,' Monaco continued. 'The economic gains from reunification are catching a lot of blokes' attention. I heard the president of South Korea's Hyko Tractor Industries remark at a trade seminar in Osaka how he could reduce labor costs and compete internationally if he had access to the North's labor force.'

Monaco strode through the rough grass for a minute before locating his ball, then lofted a 5-iron shot that bounced up onto the green, rolling shy of the pin by thirty feet.

'That's assuming a reunification would maintain free markets,' Hamilton replied. 'It's still clear that the North would have the most to gain from a re-unification of both countries, and even more so if American forces are not in play.'

'I'll see if my people can find any connections,' Monaco offered as they approached the green. 'But, for now, I'm just glad we're working this side of the Sea of Japan.'

Hamilton nodded in appreciation as he attempted a chip shot to the hole. His club scuffed the ground before striking the ball, which caused it to plop short of the pin by fifteen feet. He waited as Monaco putted out in two strokes for par, then bent over the ball with a putter for his own attempt at par. But as he swung through the ball, a sudden thump emanated from his head, followed by a loud crack in the distance. Hamilton's eyes rolled back and a shower of blood and tissue sprayed out from his left temple and onto the pants and shoes of Monaco. As the British diplomat looked on in horror, Hamilton fell to his knees in a pool of blood, his hands still tightly clutching the putter. He tried to speak but only a gurgle rolled from his lips before he toppled stiffly onto the manicured grass surface. A fraction of a second later, the dead man's bloodstained golf ball found the rim of the hole and dropped into the cup with a clink.

Six hundred yards away, a short, stout Asian man dressed in blue stood up in the bunker of the eighteenth hole. The sun glared off his bald head and brightened a lifeless pair of coal black eyes that were made more menacing by a long, thin Fu Manchu mustache. His squat, powerful build was more aptly suited to wrestling than golf, but his fluid movements revealed a flexibility to his strength. With the bored demeanor of a child putting away his toys, the man carefully disassembled an M-40 sniper rifle and placed the gun parts in a concealed compartment inside his golf bag. Pulling out a sand wedge, he forcefully lofted an overpowered shot out of the bunker in a spray of sand. He then calmly three-putted to finish his round, then strolled slowly to his car and stowed his clubs in the trunk. Exiting the parking lot, he patiently gave way as a flood of police cars and ambulances came streaking up to the clubhouse with sirens blaring, then he eased his car into the adjacent road where he quickly became lost in the local traffic.

5

A pair of technicians wearing protective gear steered the *Deep Endeavor*'s Zodiac to the western shore of Yunaska, where they selected a young male sea lion from the assortment of dead mammals strewn about the beach. The animal was carefully wrapped in a synthetic sheet, then placed into a heavy body bag for transport back to the ship. The NUMA research vessel stood off nearby with spotlights beaming on the water, guiding the rubber boat back in short order. A section of the galley was cleared away and the sealed cadaver was stored in a cold freezer for the remainder of the voyage, just next to a crate of frozen sherbet.

Once all was secured, Captain Burch pushed the research vessel hard toward the island of Unalaska, with its port city of the same name, situated more than two hundred miles away. Running at top speed all through the night, Burch was able to bring the *Deep Endeavor* into the commercial fishing port just before ten the next morning. A weathered ambulance waited at the dock to transfer Sarah, Irv, and Sandy to the town's small airfield, where a chartered plane was waiting to whisk them to Anchorage. Dirk insisted on pushing Sarah to the ambulance in her wheelchair and gave her a long kiss on the cheek as she was loaded in.

'We've got a date in Seattle, right? I still owe you a crab dinner,' Dirk said with an engaging smile.

'I wouldn't miss it,' Sarah replied sheepishly. 'Sandy and I will be down just as soon we're okay to leave Anchorage.'

After seeing the CDC team off, Dirk and Burch met with the village public safety officer and gave him a full report of the incident. Dirk provided a detailed description of the mystery fishing trawler and convinced the VPSO to furnish him with a listing of registered fishing vessels from the state licensing authority. The VPSO also agreed to check with the local commercial fishing entities for information but didn't hold out much hope. Japanese and even Russian fishing boats were known to ply the territorial waters illegally on occasion in search of fertile fishing grounds and had the habit of disappearing whenever the authorities tried to pursue them.

Burch wasted little time in the port city before turning the *Deep Endeavor* south and sailing toward Seattle. Like everyone else, the crew of the ship had plenty of questions about the events of the preceding day but few answers.

Sarah, Irv, and Sandy endured a noisy and bumpy flight to Anchorage on one of the local twin-engine island-hoppers, arriving at the city's international airport late in the evening. Two exuberant college interns from the regional CDC office met them at the airport and transferred them to Alaska Regional Hospital, where they underwent a battery of toxicology tests and examinations. By this time, the threesome had regained their strength and were showing no outward signs of illness. Oddly, the medical staff was unable to diagnose any abnormal toxicity levels or other ailment with any of the three. After an overnight stay for observation, Sarah, Irv, and Sandy were released from the hospital with a clean bill of health as if nothing at all had happened to them.

Six days later, the *Deep Endeavor* cruised quietly into Puget Sound, turning east into the Shilshole Bay just north of Seattle. The research vessel tied up momentarily at the Ballard Locks, where controlled floodgates raised the ship and released it into the fresh water of the ship canal. The *Deep Endeavor* continued on into Lake Union before slowing along the north shore. Burch inched the vessel up to a private dock jutting from a small modern-looking glass building that housed the NUMA northwest field office. A gathering of the crew's wives and children lined the dock, waving enthusiastically as the ship approached.

'Looks like you've got your own welcoming committee, Dirk,' Burch remarked, pointing to two figures waving at the end of the pier. Dirk looked out the bridge window and recognized Sarah and

Sandy among the happy throng greeting the turquoise ship. Sarah looked radiant in a pair of blue capri pants and a maize satin blouse, which complemented her trim figure.

'You two look like the model of health,' Dirk said as he warmly greeted the pair.

'No small part in thanks to you,' Sandy gushed. 'Just one night in Alaska Regional Hospital and we were on our way good as new.'

'How's Irv?'

'He's fine,' Sarah replied. 'He's staying in Anchorage for a few more weeks to coordinate the completion of our sea lion study with the Alaska Department of Fish and Game. They agreed to provide field support to help finish our research investigation.'

'I'm so glad everybody is well. So what was the medical diagnosis in Anchorage?' Dirk asked.

Sandy and Sarah glanced at each other briefly with a searching look, then shrugged and shook their heads in unison.

'They didn't find anything,' Sarah finally said. 'It's something of a mystery. We all showed signs of an inflamed respiratory track, but that was about it. Blood and urine samples came back clean. If we did inhale a toxin, it was purged from our systems by the time we reached Anchorage.'

'That's why we're here to pick up the sea lion. Hopefully, there will be some indicators still evident in the animal's tissue,' Sandy said.

'So, you're not here to see me?' Dirk intoned sadly with an exaggerated frown on his face.

'Sorry, Dirk,' Sarah laughed. 'Why don't you come meet us at the lab later this afternoon after we do our analysis? We can go grab a late lunch.'

'I would like to know the results,' he agreed, then led the two on board to retrieve the frozen sea lion.

Once the mammal was hauled away, Dirk and Dahlgren helped secure the ship, transferring ashore the sensitive high-tech survey gear that was stored in an adjacent warehouse. With their docking shores complete, the crew of the *Deep Endeavor* gradually dispersed to enjoy a few days of R&R before the next project set sail.

Dahlgren approached Dirk with a rucksack tossed over one shoulder and the pair of crutches under one arm. Only a slight limp was noticeable from his calf wound when he walked.

'Dirk, I'm off to rustle up a date with a sexy teller I met at the bank before we shipped out. Should I see if she has a cute friend?'

'No, thanks. Think I'll get cleaned up and go see what Sarah and Sandy discovered from our sea lion Popsicle.'

'You always did have a thing for the brainy types,' Dahlgren chuckled.

'What's with the crutches? You've been off those things for three days now.'

'Never underestimate a woman's sense of sympathy,'

Dahlgren grinned, placing one crutch under an arm and pretending to limp in agony.

'If I were you, I wouldn't underestimate a woman's ability to detect bad acting,' Dirk replied with a laugh. 'Happy hunting.'

Dirk borrowed the keys to a turquoise NUMA jeep Cherokee and drove a short distance to his rented town house overlooking Lake Washington. Although he called Washington, D.C., his home, he enjoyed the temporary assignment in the Northwest. The lush wooded surroundings, the cold, clear waters, and the youthful and vibrant residents who thrived in the sometimes bleak and damp weather made for a refreshing environment.

Dirk showered and threw on a pair of dark slacks and a thin pullover sweater, then downed a peanut butter sandwich and an Olympia beer while listening to a litany of messages on his answering machine. Satisfied that the earth had not come to a stop in his absence, he hopped into the Jeep and headed north on I-5. Exiting east past the lush Jackson Park Golf Course, Dirk turned north and soon entered the parklike grounds of Fircrest Campus. Fircrest was an old military complex that had been turned over to the state of Washington and now housed offices and operations for a variety of state government agencies. Dirk spotted a complex of square white buildings surrounded by mature trees and parked in an adjacent lot fronted by a large sign, stating: WASHINGTON STATE PUBLIC HEALTH LABORATORIES.

A perky receptionist phoned up to the small CDC office shared by the state lab and a few moments later Sarah and Sandy appeared in the lobby. A portion of the cheeriness they showed earlier in the day had clearly left their faces.

'Dirk, it's good of you to come. There's a quiet Italian restaurant down the street where we can talk. The Pasta Alfredo is great, too,' Sarah suggested.

'Sure thing. Ladies first,' Dirk replied as he held the front door open for the two scientists.

After the threesome shoehorned into a red vinyl booth at the nearby neighborhood restaurant, Sarah explained their findings.

'An examination of the sea lion revealed the classic signs of respiratory seizure as the cause of death. An initial blood test failed to reveal any concentrated levels of toxicity, however.'

'Similar to the test results for you three in Anchorage,' Dirk added between bites of bread.

'Exactly. Our vitals showed fine, though we still experienced weakness, headaches, and signs of respiratory irritation by the time we reached Anchorage,' Sandy added.

'So we went back and carefully reexamined the animal's blood and tissue and finally detected trace elements of the toxin,' Sarah continued. 'Though not one hundred percent certain, we are fairly confident the sea lion was killed by hydrogen cyanide poisoning.'

'Cyanide?' Dirk asked with an arched eyebrow.

'Yes,' Sandy replied. 'It makes sense. Cyanide is actually expelled rapidly from the human body. In the case of Sarah, Irv, and me, our bodies had naturally purged most, if not all, of the cyanide toxins before we stepped in the door of the Anchorage hospital. Hence, no trace remained when our blood samples were taken.'

'I've contacted the Alaska State Coroner's Office and informed them of our findings. They have not completed the autopsy report on the two Coast Guardsmen yet, but they will know what to look for. I am convinced that is what killed them,' Sarah said with a tinge of sadness.

'I always thought cyanide had to be ingested in order to be lethal,' Dirk remarked.

'That's what's commonly known, but it's not the only deadly form of the poison. Everyone knows of cyanide tablets carried by wartime spies, the deadly Jim Jones cyanide-laced Kool-Aid that killed hundreds in Jonestown, Guyana, and the Tylenol poisonings, which used cyanide. But cyanide gas has also been used as a killing agent. The French tried variations of cyanide gas against the Germans in the trenches during World War One. And though the Germans never used it on the battlefield, they did use a form of cyanide in the concentration camp gas chambers during the Second World War.'

'The infamous Zyklon B,' Dirk recalled.

'Yes, a beefed-up fumigant originally developed to kill rodents,' Sarah continued. 'And, more recently,

Saddam Hussein was suspected of using a form of cyanide gas in attacks on Kurdish villages in his own country, although it was never verified.'

'Since we packed in our own food and water supplies,' Sandy piped in, 'the airborne poisoning makes sense. It would also explain the deaths of the sea lions.'

'Is it possible for the cyanide to have originated from a natural source?' Dirk inquired.

'Cyanide is found in a variety of plants and edibles, from lima beans to chokecherries. But it's as an industrial solvent where it is most prevalent,' Sarah explained. 'Tons of the stuff are manufactured each year for electroplating, gold and silver extraction, and fumigants. Most people probably come in contact with some form of cyanide every day. But to answer your question, it's unlikely to exist in a gaseous state from a natural source sufficient to reach any sort of lethality. Sandy, what did you find in the historical profile of cyanide deaths in the U.S.?'

'There's been a slew of them, but most are individual accidents or suspected homicides or suicides resulting from ingestion of solid cyanides.' Sandy reached down and picked up a manila folder she had brought along and skimmed through one of the pages inside.

'The only significant mass death was related to the Tylenol poisonings, which killed seven people, again by ingestion. I found only two references for multiple deaths from suspected cyanide gas. A family of four died in the Oregon town of Warrenton back in 1942, and in 1964 three men were killed in Butte, Montana. The Montana case was listed as a mining accident due to extraction solvents. The Oregon case was listed as undetermined. And I found next to nothing for prior incidences in and around Alaska.'

'Then a natural-occurring release doesn't sound very likely,' Dirk remarked.

'So if it was a man-made airborne release, who did it and why?' Sandy asked while jabbing her fork into a bowl of angel-hair pasta.

'I think the "who" was our friends on the fishing boat,' he said drily.

'They weren't picked up by the authorities?' Sarah asked.

Dirk shook his head in disgust. 'No, the trawler disappeared. By the time the local authorities arrived in the area, they were long gone. The official assessment is that they were presumed to be foreign poachers.'

'I suppose it's possible. It sounds a little dangerous to me, but I guess they could release the gas from their boat upwind of a sea lion colony,' Sarah replied, shaking her head.

'A fast way to do a lot of killing,' Dirk added. 'Though poachers armed with AK-47s does seem a little extreme. And I'm still wondering about the retail market for sea lions.'

'It is perplexing. I haven't heard of anything like it before.'

'I hope that you two don't suffer any ill effects from the exposure,' Dirk said, looking at Sarah with concern.

'Thanks,' Sarah replied. 'It was a shock to our system, but we'll be fine. The long-term effect for minimal exposure has not been proven to be dangerous.'

Dirk pushed away a cleaned plate of Pasta Alfredo and rubbed his taut stomach with satisfaction.

'Excellent dining choice.'

'We eat here all the time,' Sarah said as she reached over and outgrabbed Dirk for the bill.

'I insist on returning the favor,' Dirk said, looking at Sarah with a serious smile.

'Sandy and I have to travel to the CDC research lab in Spokane for a few days, but I'd love to take you up when we return,' she replied, intentionally leaving Sandy out of the equation.

Dirk smiled in acknowledgment. 'I can't wait.'

6

The landing wheels of the Gulfstream V jet dropped slowly from the fuselage as the sleek aircraft aligned its nose at the runway. Its wings cut through the moist, hazy air like a scalpel, as the nineteen-passenger luxury business jet dropped gracefully out of the sky until its rubber tires touched the tarmac with a screech and a wisp of blue smoke. The pilot guided the plane to the corporate jet terminal of Tokyo's modern Narita International Airport before shutting down the high-pitched turbines. As a ground crew chocked the wheels of the jet, a gleaming black Lincoln limousine glided up, stopping precisely at the base of the plane's passenger stairwell.

Chris Gavin squinted in the bright sun as he stepped down from the jet and climbed into the waiting limo, followed by a legion of assistants and assorted vice presidents. As chief executive officer of SemCon Industries, Gavin commanded the largest semiconductor manufacturing company in the world. The flamboyant and free-spending corporate chief, who inherited the company from a visionary father, had alienated many of his countrymen in the United States by closing profitable factories and brusquely laying off thousands of workers at home in order to move production to newer and cheaper facilities offshore. Profits would be higher, he promised his shareholders, while taking personal delight in broadening his elaborate lifestyle to a worldwide setting.

Exiting the airport grounds located some sixty-six kilometers northeast of Tokyo, the limo driver entered the Higashi Kanto Expressway and headed toward Japan's capital city with his cargo of high-salaried executives. Twenty minutes later, the driver turned south, exiting the highway some twenty kilometers short of Tokyo. The limo soon entered the industrial section of Chiba, a large port city on the eastern edge of Tokyo Bay. The driver wound past a number of large drab manufacturing buildings before pulling up in front of a sleek glass building overlooking the bay. The modern structure looked more like an executive office building than the industrial fabrication plant it contained, with its shimmering face of gold reflective windows rising four stories high. Mounted on the roof in huge block letters was a blue SEMCON neon sign, which could be seen for miles away. A large crowd of factory workers, all clad in pale blue lab coats, waited anxiously on the grounds for the arrival of their CEO to officially open the new facility.

The crowd cheered and cameras flashed as Gavin exited the limo and waved to the assembled employees and media, baring a wide, capped-tooth grin. After a pair of long-winded welcome speeches by the mayor of Chiba and the new plant manager, Gavin offered a few polished words of thanks and inspiration to the employees, then hoisted a comically oversized pair of scissors and cut a thick ribbon stretched tight across the entrance to the new building. As the crowd applauded politely, a muffled boom echoed from somewhere in the depths of the building, which some mistook for a firing of celebratory fireworks. But then a succession of louder explosions rocked the building and the assembly of employees suddenly gasped in confusion.

In the heart of the building's silicon chip fabrication center, a small timed charge had detonated on a tank of silane gas, a highly flammable substance used in the growth of silicon crystals. Exploding like a torpedo, the tank had flung metallic fragments at high velocity into a half-dozen additional silane and oxygen tanks stored nearby, causing them to burst in a series of concussions that culminated in a massive fireball inside the building. Soaring temperatures soon caused the exterior windows to blast out in a burst of hot air, showering the stunned crowd with a hail of glass and debris.

As the building shook and flames roared from the roof, the panicked employees began to scramble in all directions. Gavin stood holding the pair of giant scissors, a look of stunned confusion on his face. A sharp pain suddenly pierced his neck, jolting his senses. Instinctively rubbing the ache with his fingers, he was shocked to feel a small barbed steel ball the size of a BB lodged in his skin. As he extracted the tiny pellet with a trickle of blood, a nearby woman screamed and ran by him, a large sliver of fallen window glass protruding from her shoulder. A couple of terrified assistants quickly grabbed Gavin and led him toward the limo, shielding him from a nosy photographer eager to snap an embarrassing shot of the corporate mogul in front of his burning building.

As he was whisked to the limo, Gavin's legs suddenly turned to rubber. He turned toward one of his assistants to speak but no words came from his lips. As the car door was opened, he sprawled forward into the car, falling chest first onto the carpeted floor. A confused aide rolled him over and was horrified to find that the CEO was not breathing. A panicked attempt at CPR was performed as the limo screeched off to a nearby hospital, but it was to no avail. The mercurial self-centered leader of the global company was dead.

Few people had paid any attention to the bald man with dark eyes and droopy mustache who had crowded up close to the speaker's platform. Wearing a blue lab coat and plastic identification badge, he looked like any other SemCon employee. Fewer still noticed that he carried a plastic drinking cup with an odd bamboo straw sticking out the top. And in the confusion of the explosions, not a single person had noticed as he pulled out the straw, placed it to his lips, and fired a poisoned bead at the head of the giant corporation.

Casually losing himself in the crowd, the bald

assassin made his way to the edge of the property's grounds, where he tossed his cup and lab coat into a streetside trash can. Hopping onto a bicycle, he paused briefly as a clanging fire truck roared down the street toward the engulfed building. Then, without looking back, he casually pedaled away.

A dinging bell echoed in Dahlgren's mind like some distant train at a railroad crossing. The feverish hope that the sound was part of a dream fell away as his consciousness took hold and told him it was a ringing telephone. Groping for the receiver on his nightstand, he yawned a weary 'Hullo.'

'Jack, you still sawing logs?' Dirk's voice laughed over the line.

'Yeah, thanks for the wake-up call,' he replied groggily.

'I thought bankers didn't like to stay up late.'

'This one does. And likes to drink vodka, too. I think a dinosaur crapped in my mouth during the night,' Dahlgren said with a belch.

'Sorry to hear. Say, I'm thinking of taking a drive to Portland to stretch out my sea legs and take in a car show. Care to ride shotgun?'

'No thanks. I'm supposed to take the teller kayaking today. That is, if I can still stand up.'

'Okay. I'll send over a Bombay martini to get you started.'

'Roger that,' Dahlgren replied with a grimace.

*

Dirk headed south from Seattle on Interstate 5 in the NUMA jeep, enjoying the sights of the lush forested region of western Washington. He found cross-country drives relaxing, as they allowed his mind to roam freely with the open countryside. Finding himself making good time, he decided to detour west along the coast, taking a side road to Willapa Bay before continuing south along the Pacific waters of the large bay. Soon he reached the wide blue mouth of the Columbia River, and cruised the same shores upon which Lewis and Clark had triumphantly set foot back in 1805.

Crossing the mighty river over the four-mile-long Astoria-Megler Bridge, Dirk exited at the historic fishing port of Astoria. As he stopped at a red light on the bridge off ramp, a road sign caught his eye. In white letters on a green field, WARRENTON 8 MI. was preceded by an arrow pointing west. Prodded by curiosity, he followed the sign right, away from Portland, and quickly traversed the few miles to Warrenton.

The small town at Oregon's northwest tip, originally built on a tidal marsh as a fishing and sport boat passage to the Pacific, supported some four thousand residents. It took Dirk only a few minutes of driving about the town before he found what he was looking for on Main Street. Parking his jeep next to a white Clatsop County official vehicle, he strolled up a concrete walkway to the front door of the Warrenton Community Library.

It was a small library but looked like it had been in existence for six or seven decades. A musty smell of old books and older dust wafted lightly in the air. Dirk walked straight to a large metal desk, from which a fiftyish woman with contemporary eyeglasses and short blond hair looked up suspiciously. A plastic green badge pinned to her blouse revealed her name: MARGARET.

'Good morning, Margaret. My name is Dirk,' he said with a smile. 'I wonder if you might have copies of the local newspaper from the nineteen forties?'

The librarian warmed slightly. 'The *Warrenton News*, which went out of print in 1964. We do have original copies from the nineteen thirties through the sixties. Right this way,' she said.

Margaret walked to a cramped corner of the library, where she pulled out several drawers of a filing cabinet before discovering the location of the 1940s editions.

'What exactly is it that you are looking for?' she asked, more out of nosiness than of a desire to help.

'I'm interested in the story of a local family that died suddenly from poisoning back in 1942.'

'Oh, that would be Leigh Hunt,' Margaret exclaimed with a knowing smugness. 'He was a friend of my father. Apparently, that was quite a shock around here. Let's see, I think that happened during the summer,' she said while flipping through the cabinet. 'Did you know the family?' she asked Dirk without looking up.

'No, just a history buff interested in the mystery of their deaths.'

'Here we go,' the librarian said, pulling out an edition of the daily newspaper dated Sunday, June 21, 1942. It was a small journal, mostly containing weather, tide, and salmon-fishing statistics combined with a few local stories and advertisements. Margaret flattened out the paper on top of the filing cabinet so Dirk could read the headline story.

Four Dead on DeLaura Beach

Local resident Leigh Hunt, his two sons Tad (age 13) and Tom (age 11), and a nephew known only as Skip, were found dead Saturday, June 20th, on DeLaura Beach. The four went out clamming in the afternoon, according to Hunt's wife Marie, and failed to return home for dinner. County Sheriff Kit Edwards discovered the bodies, which showed no signs of a struggle or physical injury. 'Not finding any physical marks, we immediately suspected smoke inhalation or poisoning. Leigh had a large supply of a cyanide treatment in his workshop that he used for tanning leather,' Edwards remarked. 'He and the boys must have been exposed to a strong dose before they went to the beach, and the poison caught up with them there,' he stated. Funeral arrangements are pending examination of the bodies by the county coroner.

'Is there a follow-up news report on the coroner's findings?' he asked.

Margaret rifled through another dozen editions of the *News* before finding a small article related to the deaths. Reading out loud, she cited that the coroner's office confirmed accidental cyanide inhalation as the suspected cause of death.

'My father never did believe it was an accident,' Margaret added, to Dirk's surprise.

'It doesn't make sense that they would have died later at the beach after inhaling the fumes in Hunt's workshed,' Dirk mused.

'Papa said the same thing,' Margaret replied, letting down her guard slightly. 'And he said the authorities never did consider the birds.'

'Birds?'

'Yes. About a hundred seagulls were found dead on the beach around the area that Hunt and the boys were found. Fort Stevens, the Army base, was right near that beach. Papa always suspected it was some sort of Army experiment that accidentally killed them. Guess nobody will ever know for sure.'

'Wartime secrets can be difficult to unlock sometimes,' Dirk replied. 'Thank you for your help, Margaret.'

Dirk returned to the jeep and drove through the town to the coastal highway and turned south. A short stretch of pavement later, he approached a small side road marked DELAURA BEACH ROAD. The road led though an open pair of gates marked FORT

STEVENS STATE PARK before narrowing through thick underbrush. Dirk jammed the jeep into low gear and surged over a jagged ridge before descending to a large abandoned gun emplacement overlooking the ocean. Battery Russell had been one of several coastal defense sites guarding the entrance to the Columbia River which sprang up during the Civil War, then were later updated with huge long-range guns during World War II. From the emplacement, Dirk had a clear view of the shimmering blue waters at the mouth of the Columbia River, as well as the DeLaura Beach below, which was dotted with afternoon picnickers. Dirk soaked in a few deep breaths of the fresh sea air, then drove back out the small road, pulling off nearly into the brush at one point to let an oncoming black Cadillac pass by. Driving a quarter mile farther, he stopped the car at a large historical marker along the roadside that caught his eye. Carved on a massive gray slab of granite was a highly detailed engraving of a submarine, beneath which was inscribed:

On June 21, 1942, a 5.5" shell exploded here. One of 17 fired at Columbia River Harbor Defense Installations by the Japanese Submarine 25. The only hostile shelling of a military base on the U.S. mainland during World War II and the first since the War of 1812.

As he read the inscription, he instinctively moved away from the road as the Cadillac returned and passed by slowly, to avoid kicking up dust. Dirk studied the submarine carving for a long moment and started to walk away. But something caught his eye and he looked again. It was the date. June 21, just a day after Hunt and the boys were found dead on the beach.

Dirk reached into the jeep's glove compartment and pulled out a cellular phone, leaning against the car's hood as he dialed the number. After four rings, a deep and jolly voice boomed through the handset.

'Perlmutter here.'

'Julien, it's Dirk. How's my favorite nautical historian?'

'Dirk, my boy, so good to hear from you! I was just enjoying some pickled green mangoes your father sent me from the Philippines. Pray tell, how are you enjoying the Great White North?'

'We just finished our survey in the Aleutians, so I am back in the Pacific Northwest. The islands were quite beautiful, though, but it was a little cold for my blood.'

'Heavens, I can imagine,' Perlmutter's voice bellowed. 'So, what's on your mind, Dirk?'

'World War Two-era Japanese submarines, to be exact. I'm curious about their record of attacks on the U.S. mainland and any unusual weaponry in their arsenals.'

'Imperial submarines, eh? I recall they made some fairly harmless attacks on the West Coast, but I have not delved into my Japanese wartime files in some time. I'll have to do some nosing about for you.'

'Thanks, Julien. And one more thing. Let me know if you run across any references to the use of cyanide as an armament.'

'Cyanide. Now, that would be nasty, wouldn't it?' Perlmutter asked rhetorically before hanging up.

Contemplating the enormous collection of rare maritime history books and manuscripts jammed into his Georgetown carriage house, St. Julien Perlmutter needed only a few seconds of pondering to pinpoint the material he was looking for. Perlmutter resembled an overgrown Santa Claus, with sparkling blue eyes, a huge gray beard, and an enormous belly that helped him tip the scales at nearly four hundred pounds. Besides a penchant for gourmet foods, Perlmutter was known as one of the world's foremost maritime historians, in large part due to his peerless collection of sea-related ephemeris.

Clad in silk pajamas and a paisley robe, Perlmutter padded across a thick Persian carpet to a mahogany bookcase, where he examined several titles before pulling down a book and two large binders with his meaty hands. Satisfied it was the material he was looking for, the immense man returned to an overstuffed red leather chair, where a plate of truffles and a hot pot of tea beckoned him.

*

Dirk continued on his drive to Portland, where he found the antique auto auction he was looking for at a large, grassy fairgrounds at the city's edge. Scores of people milled about the gleaming autos, most from the forties, fifties, and sixties, which were neatly lined up on the wide grass field. Dirk sauntered by the cars, admiring the paint jobs and mechanical restorations, before heading to a large white-canopied tent where the auctioning was taking place.

Inside, loudspeakers blared out the auctioneer's grating staccato voice as he spat out price bids like a rapid-fire machine gun. Grabbing a side seat away from the blare, Dirk watched in amusement as the team of auctioneers, wearing a ridiculous combination of seventies-style tuxedos and cheap cowboy hats, pranced around in a futile attempt to hype the excitement, and price, of each car. After several Corvettes and an early Thunderbird were passed through, Dirk sat up as a 1958 Chrysler 300-D drove up onto the stage. The huge car was painted an original Aztec turquoise, enhanced by miles of gleaming chrome and a pair of rear tail fins that jutted into the air like the dorsal fin of a shark. In a reaction only a true car fanatic could understand, Dirk felt his heartbeat quicken simply at the sight of the artistic mass of steel and glass.

'Perfectly restored to concourse condition by Pastime Restorations of Golden, Colorado,' the auctioneer pitched. He resumed his vocal convulsions, but bidding on the car surprisingly stalled early. Dirk raised his hand in the air and was soon dueling for the car with an overweight man wearing yellow suspenders. Dirk quickly countered his opponent's bids in rapid succession, showing his intent was serious. The tactic worked. Yellow Suspenders shook his head after the third bid and headed toward the bar.

'Sold to the man in the NUMA hat!' the auctioneer barked as the surrounding crowd applauded politely. Though it cost him several months' salary, Dirk recognized it was a good buy, knowing that less than two hundred Chrysler 300-D convertibles were manufactured in 1958.

As he arranged to have the car shipped up to Seattle, his cell phone started to ring.

'Dirk, it's Julien. I have some information for you.'

'That was fast service.'

'Well, I wanted to get back to you before supper,' Perlmutter replied, contemplating his next meal.

'What can you tell me, Julien?'

'After Pearl Harbor, the Japanese placed nine or ten submarines on station along the West Coast, but they were gradually pulled off as the battle action moved to the South Pacific. The Japanese submarines were primarily on reconnaissance missions, observing the major bays and harbors while trying to track major ship movements. They did manage to sink a handful of merchant ships early in the war and create a dose of psychological fear in the general public along the way. As for actual land attacks, the first occurred in early 1942, when the *I-17* lobbed a few shells near Santa Barbara, damaging a pier and an oil derrick. In June of '42, the *I-25* fired upon Fort Stevens, near Astoria, Oregon, while the *I-26* bombarded a radio station on Vancouver Island in Canada. No fatalities were recorded in either of the attacks. In August of 1942, the *I-25* returned near Cape Blanco, Oregon, and launched a seaplane armed with incendiary bombs in an attempt set fire to the nearby forests. The attack was a failure, as only one small fire was ignited in the region.'

'Sounds like they were primarily nuisance attacks,' Dirk commented.

'Yes, there was nothing overly strategic about their actions. Things slowed down after the incendiary attack, as the submarines were moved north to support the Aleutian campaign. Imperial submarines were heavily involved in supporting the capture and later evacuation of Attu and Kiska islands during fighting in 1943. The Japanese lost five subs during the Aleutian battles as our sonar technology really began to pick them out of the seas. After the fall of Kiska, just a few Imperial submarines continued to operate in the north and western Pacific. The *I-180* was attacked and sunk near Kodiak, Alaska, in April of 1944, then things were pretty quiet on the home front until the *I-403* was sunk off Cape Flattery, Washington, in January 1945.'

'Odd that one would get tagged off the West Coast at a point in the war when their navy was on its last legs.'

'It's even more queer when you consider that the *I-403* was one of their big boats. Apparently, it was planning an air attack when it was surprised by an American destroyer.'

'Hard to believe they constructed submarines back then capable of carrying an airplane,' Dirk marveled.

'Their big boats could carry not just one but actually three airplanes. They were massive beasts.'

'Did you find any indication that the naval forces used cyanide weapons?'

'None that was recorded in battle, but they did exist. It was the Imperial Army, I believe, and its biological warfare unit in China, that experimented with biological and chemical weapons. They did fool around with cyanide artillery shells, among other things, so it is possible the Navy tried experimenting with them, but there is no official record of their use.'

'I guess there is no way to prove it, but I suspect the *I-25* launched a cyanide shell that killed four people the day before it attacked Fort Stevens.'

'Quite possible. May be hard to prove, as the *I-25* was later lost in the South Pacific, presumably sunk near Espiritu Santo Island in 1943. But with one possible exception, all accounts I have seen indicate that the Japanese vessels were armed only with conventional weapons.'

'And the exception?'

'The *I-403* again. I found a reference in a postwar Army journal stating that a shipment of *Makaze* ordnance was transferred to the Navy and delivered to the submarine in Kure prior to her last sailing. I've never seen a reference to *Makaze* before, however, and could find no other references in my ordnance and munitions files.'

'Any idea what the term means?'

'The best translation I can make of it is "Black Wind."'

Dirk made a short phone call to Leo Delgado, then reached Dahlgren, who was drinking a beer in a lounge overlooking Lake Washington following his morning kayak with the bank teller.

'Jack, you up for a dive tomorrow?' Dirk asked.

'Sure. Spearfishing in the Sound?'

'I've got something a little bigger in mind.'

'King salmon are game for me.'

'The fish I'm interested in,' Dirk continued, 'hasn't swum in over sixty years.'

7

Irv Fowler woke up with a raging headache. Too many beers the night before, the scientist mused as he dragged himself out of bed. Chugging down a cup of coffee and a donut, he convinced himself he felt better. But as the day wore on, the pain seemed to swell, with little relief offered despite his multiple hits on a bottle of aspirin. Eventually, his back joined in the game, sending out waves of pain with every movement he made. By midafternoon, he felt weak and tired, and left early from his temporary office at Alaska State Health and Social Services to drive back to his apartment and rest.

After he downed a bowl of chicken soup, his abdomen started firing off streaks of shooting pain. So much for home remedies, he thought. After several fitful naps, he staggered into the bathroom for another dose of aspirin to help kill the pain. Looking into the glassy-eyed worn and weary face that stared back at him from the mirror, he noticed a bright red rash emerging on his cheeks.

'Damndest flu I've ever had,' he muttered aloud, then fell back into bed in a heap.

*

Security was tight at the Tokyo Hilton Hotel and guests for the private banquet were required to pass through three separate checkpoints before gaining entry to the lavish dining hall. The Japan Export Association's annual dinner was an extravagant affair featuring the best local chefs and entertainers performing for the country's top business leaders and dignitaries. Executives from Japan's major exporting companies helped sponsor the dinner on behalf of their major trading partners. In addition to key customers, in-country diplomats from all the Western and Asian countries that constituted Japan's primary trading partners were treated as special guests.

The recent assassination of U.S. Ambassador Hamilton and the bedlam at the SemCon factory opening had created a buzz in the crowd and heads turned when the American embassy's deputy chief of mission Robert Bridges entered the room, accompanied by two undercover security men.

Though a career diplomat, Bridges was more at home working policy strategies or conducting business security briefings rather than socializing in mass crowds. Hamilton had been by far the better glad-hander, Bridges thought as he made small talk with a Japanese trade representative. A dinner host soon arrived and escorted him to a small banquet table, where he was seated with a number of European diplomats.

As traditional dishes of sashimi and soba noodles were brought to the tables, a troupe of geisha dancers glided elegantly about a raised stage, dressed in brightly colored kimonos and twirling bamboo fans as they pirouetted. Bridges downed a shot of warm sake to help deaden the pain of listening to the French ambassador drone on about the poor quality of Asian wines while he watched the dancers spin.

As the first course was finished, a litany of corporate executives took to the stage to promote their self-importance with blustery speeches. Bridges took the opportunity to visit the restroom and, with a large bodyguard leading the way, walked down a side corridor and into the men's room.

The bodyguard scanned the tiled restroom, finding only a waiter washing his hands in a sink at the far end. Letting Bridges pass to the urinal, the bodyguard closed the door and stood facing the interior.

The bald waiter slowly finished washing his hands, then turned his back to the bodyguard as he dried his hands from a paper towel rack. When he spun back toward the door, the bodyguard was shocked to see a .25 automatic in the waiter's hand. A silencer was affixed to the muzzle of the small handgun, with the business end pointed directly at the bodyguard's face. Instinctively grabbing for his own weapon, the bodyguard had barely moved his hand when the .25 emitted a muffled cough. A neat red hole appeared just above the bodyguard's left eyebrow and the large man raised up and back momentarily before collapsing to the floor with a thud, a river of red blood running from his head.

Bridges failed to detect the muffled gunshot but heard the bodyguard collapse. Turning to see the waiter pointing the gun at him, Bridges could only mutter, 'What the hell?'

The bald man in the waiter suit stared back at him with deathly cold black eyes, then broke into a sadistic grin that revealed a row of crooked yellow teeth. Without saying a word, he squeezed the trigger two times and watched as Bridges grasped his chest and fell to the ground. The assassin pulled a typewritten note out of his pocket and rolled it up tight into the shape of a tube. He then bent over and wedged it into the dead diplomat's mouth like a flagpole. Carefully disassembling his silencer and placing it in his pocket, he gingerly stepped over the two bodies and out the door, disappearing down a hall toward the kitchen.

8

The fiberglass bow of the twenty-five-foot Parker workboat plunged through the deep, wide swells, cutting a white foamy path as it rolled through the trough before cresting on the peak of the next wave. Though tiny in comparison to most vessels in the NUMA fleet, the durable little boat, identified on the stern as the *Grunion*, was ideal for surveying inland and coastal waterways, as well as supporting shallow-water dive operations.

Leo Delgado rolled the helm's wheel to the right and the *Grunion* quickly nosed to starboard and out of the path of a large red freighter bearing down on them near the entrance of the Strait of Juan de Fuca.

'How far from the strait?' he asked, spinning the wheel hard to port a moment later in order to take the passing freighter's wake bow on.

Standing alongside in the cramped cabin, Dirk and Dahlgren were hunched over a small table studying a nautical chart of their present position near the entrance to the Pacific Ocean, some 125 miles west of Seattle.

'Approximately twelve miles southwest of Cape Flattery,' Dirk said over his shoulder, then dictated latitude and longitude coordinates to Delgado. The

Deep Endeavor's first officer reached over to a keyboard and tapped the position into the small boat's computerized navigation system. A few seconds later, a tiny white square appeared in the upper corner of a flat-screen monitor that hung from the ceiling. At the lower edge of the monitor, a small white triangle flashed on and off, representing the *Grunion* as it motored into the Pacific. With the aid of a satellite Global Positioning System interface, Delgado was able to steer a path directly toward the marked position.

'Now, you guys are sure Captain Burch isn't going to find out we borrowed his support boat and are burning his fuel just for a pleasure dive?' Delgado asked somewhat sheepishly.

'You mean this is Burch's private boat?' Dirk replied with mock horror.

'If he comes snooping, we'll just tell him that Bill Gates stopped by and offered us a few million stock options if he could take the *Grunion* out for a spin,' Dahlgren offered.

'Thanks. I knew I could trust you guys,' Delgado muttered, shaking his head. 'By the way, how good is your fix on the submarine's location?'

'Came right out of the official Navy report on the sinking that Perlmutter faxed me,' Dirk replied, grabbing the cabin door sill for balance as the boat rolled over a large swell. 'We'll start with the position that was recorded by the destroyer after she sank the *I-403*.'

'Too bad the Navy didn't have GPS back in 1945,' Delgado lamented.

'Yes, the wartime action reports weren't always entirely accurate, especially where locations are concerned. But the destroyer had not traveled very far from shore when it engaged the sub, so their reported position ought to put us in the ballpark.'

When the *Grunion* reached the marked position, Delgado eased the throttle into neutral and began keying a search grid into the navigation computer. On the back deck, Dirk and Dahlgren unpacked a Klein Model 3000 side-scan sonar system from a reinforced plastic crate. As Dirk hooked up the cables to the operating system, Dahlgren reeled a yellow cylindrical sonar towfish out over the stern gunwale and into the water.

'The fish is out,' Dahlgren yelled from the back deck, whereupon Delgado applied a light throttle and the boat edged forward. In a matter of minutes, Dirk had the equipment calibrated, resulting in a continuous stream of contrasting shadowy images sliding across a color monitor. The images were reflections of sound waves emitted from the towfish, which bounced off the seafloor and were recaptured and processed into visual recordings of protrusions or cavities on the sea bottom.

'I have a one-mile-square grid plotted around the *Theodore Knight*'s reported position at the time she rammed the sub,' Delgado said.

'That sounds like a good starting range,' Dirk

replied. 'We can expand the grid if we need to.'

Delgado proceeded to steer the boat down a white line on the monitor until the end of the grid was reached, then he spun the wheel around and brought the boat down the next line in the opposite direction. Back and forth the *Grunion* sailed, in narrow two-hundred-meter paths, slowly chewing up the grid while Dirk kept a sharp eye for a long, dark shadow on the sonar monitor that would represent the I-boat lying on the bottom.

An hour went by and the only recognizable image that appeared on the sonar screen was a pair of fifty-five-gallon drums. After two hours, Dahlgren broke out tuna sandwiches from an ice chest and tried to relieve the tedium by telling an assortment of weakly humorous redneck jokes. Finally, after three hours of searching, Dirk's voice suddenly cut through the damp air.

'Target! Mark position.'

Gradually, the fuzzy image of an elongated object rolled across the screen, joined by two smaller protrusions near one end and a large object lying next to it amidships.

'Lord have mercy!' Dahlgren shouted, studying the image. 'Looks like a submarine to me.'

Dirk glanced at a scale measurement at the bottom of the screen. 'She's about 350 feet long, just as Perlmutter's records indicate. Leo, let's take another pass to verify the position, then see if you can park us right on top of her.'

'Can do,' Delgado replied with a grin while swinging the *Grunion* around for another run over the target. The second-pass image showed that the submarine was clearly intact and appeared to be sitting upright on the bottom. As Delgado punched the precise location into the GPS system, Dirk and Dahlgren hauled in the sonar towfish, then unpacked a pair of large dive bags.

'What's our depth here, Leo?' Dahlgren called out as he poked his feet through the leggings of a black neoprene wet suit.

'About 170 feet,' Delgado replied, eyeing a humming fathometer.

'That will only give us twenty minutes of bottom time, with a twenty-five-minute decompression stop on the way up,' Dirk said, recalling the recommended dive duration from the Navy Dive Tables.

'Not a lot of time to cover that big fish,' Dahlgren considered.

'The aircraft armament is what I am most interested in,' Dirk replied. 'According to the Navy report, both aircraft were on deck when the destroyer attacked. I'm betting those two sonar images off the bow are the Seiran bombers.'

'Suits me fine if we don't have to get inside that coffin.' Dahlgren shook his head briefly, considering the scene in his head, then proceeded to strap on a well-worn lead weight belt.

When Dirk and Dahlgren were suited up in their dive gear, Delgado brought the *Grunion* back over the target position and threw out a small buoy tied to two hundred feet of line. The two black-suited divers took a giant step off the rear dive platform and plunged fin first into the ocean.

The cold Pacific water was a shock to Dirk's skin as he dropped beneath the surface and he paused momentarily in the green liquid, waiting for the thin layer of water trapped by the wet suit surface to match the warmth of his body heat.

'Damn, I knew we should have brought the dry suits,' Dahlgren's voice crackled in Dirk's ears. The two men wore full-face AGA Divator MK II dive masks with an integrated wireless communication system, so they could talk to each other while underwater.

'What do you mean, it feels just like the Keys,' Dirk joked, referring to the warm-water islands at the south end of Florida.

'I think you've been eating too much smoked salmon,' Dahlgren retorted.

Dirk purged the air out of his buoyancy compensator and cleared his ears, then flipped over and began kicking toward the bottom following the anchored buoy line. Dahlgren followed, tagging a few feet behind. A slight current pushed them toward the east, so Dirk compensated by angling himself against the flow as he descended, trying to maintain their relative position over the target. As they swam deeper, they passed through a thermocline, feeling the water temperature turn noticeably colder in just an instant. At 110 feet, the green water darkened as the murky water filtered the surface light. At 120 feet, Dirk flipped on a small underwater light strapped to his hood like a coal miner. As they descended a few more feet, the elongated, dark shape of the Japanese submarine suddenly grew out of the depths.

The huge black submarine lay quietly at the bottom, a silent iron mausoleum for the sailors who died on her. She had landed on her keel when she sank and sat proudly upright on the bottom, as if ready to set sail again. As Dirk and Dahlgren drew closer, they were amazed at the sheer size of the vessel. Descending near the bow, they could barely see a quarter of the ship before its bulk disappeared into the murky darkness. Dirk hovered over the bow for a moment, admiring the impressive girth, before examining the catapult ramp that angled down the center deck.

'Dirk, I see one of the planes over here,' Dahlgren said, pointing an arm toward a pile of debris lying off the port bow. 'I'll go take a look.'

'The second plane should be farther back, according to the sonar reading. I'll head in that direction,' Dirk replied, swimming along the deck.

Dahlgren quickly darted over to the wreckage, which he could easily see was the remains of a single-engine floatplane, dusted in a heavy layer of fine silt. The Aichi M6A1 Seiran was a sleek-looking monoplane specially designed as a submarine-launched bomber for the big I-boats. Its rakish design, similar in appearance to a Messerschmitt fighter, was made comical by the attachment of two huge pontoons braced several feet below the wing, which looked like oversized clown shoes extending beyond the fuselage. Dahlgren could see only a split portion of one pontoon, though, as the left float and wing had been sheared off by the charging American destroyer. The fuselage and right wing remained intact, propped up at an odd angle by the damaged pontoon. Dahlgren swam to the seafloor in front of the plane, studying the visible undercarriage and wing bottom of the bomber. Moving closer, he fanned an accumulation of silt away from several protrusions, revealing a set of bomb grips. The clasps that secured the bomber's payload were empty of armament.

Gliding slowly up the side of the fuselage, Dahlgren kicked over to the half-crushed cockpit canopy and wiped away a layer of silt from the glass enclosure. Shining his light inside, he felt his heart pound rapidly at the startling sight. A human skull stared up at him from the pilot's seat, the bared teeth seeming to smile at him in a macabre grin. Playing the light about the cockpit, he recognized a pair of deteriorated flying boots on the floorboard, a sizable bone remnant jutting out of one opening. The collapsed bones of the pilot still occupied the plane, Dahlgren realized, the flier having gone down with his ship.

Dahlgren slowly backed away from the aircraft, then called Dirk on the radiophone.

'Say, old buddy, I've got the business end of one of the floatplanes here, but it doesn't look like she had any weapons mounted when she sank. Airman Skully sends his regards, though.'

'I've found the remains of the second plane and she's clean as well,' Dirk replied. 'Meet me at the conning tower.'

Dirk had found the second bomber lying thirty yards away from the sub, flipped over on its back. The two large pontoons had been ripped off the Seiran bomber when the sub went under, and the plane's fuselage, with wings still attached, had fluttered down to the bottom. He could easily see that no ordinance was mounted on the undercarriage and found no evidence that a bomb or torpedo had fallen away when the plane sank.

Swimming back to the sub's topside deck, he followed the eighty-five-foot-long catapult ramp along the bow until reaching a large round hatch. The vertical hatch capped the end of a large twelve-foot-diameter tube, which was mounted at the base of the conning tower and stretched aft for more than one hundred feet. The airtight tube had been the hangar for the Seiran aircraft, storing the sectional pieces of the planes until they were ready for launching. Set back above the tubular section was a small platform containing triple-mounted 25mm antiaircraft guns, which still sat with their barrels pointed skyward waiting for an unseen enemy.

Instead of a large metal sail rising upward, Dirk

found a huge hole in the center of the *I-403*, the gaping remains of where the conning tower had been sheared off in the collision. A small school of lingcod swam around the jagged crater's edge, feeding on smaller marine life and adding a splash of color to the dark scene.

'Wow, you could drive your Chrysler through that hole,' Dahlgren remarked as he swam up alongside Dirk and surveyed the crater.

'With change to spare. She must have gone down in a hurry when the sail ripped off.' The two men silently visualized the violent collision between the two war vessels so many years before and imagined the agony of the helpless crew of the *I-403* as the submarine sank to the bottom.

'Jack, why don't you take a pass through the hangar and see if you can eyeball any ordnance,' Dirk said, pointing a gloved hand toward a gash along the top of the aircraft hangar. 'I'll go belowdecks and do the same.'

Dirk glanced at the orange face of his Doxa dive watch, a gift from his father on his last birthday. 'We've only got eight more minutes of bottom time. Let's be quick.'

'I'll meet you back here in six,' Dahlgren said, then disappeared with a kick of his fins through the gash in the hangar wall.

Dirk entered the gloomy crevice adjacent to the hangar, diving past a jagged edge of mangled and twisted steel. As he descended, he could make out the sub's unusual twin side-by-side pressured hulls, which ran lengthwise down the keel. He entered an open bay and quickly identified it as the remains of the control room, as evidenced by a large mounted helm's wheel, now covered in barnacles. An array of radio equipment was fixed to one side of the room while an assortment of mechanical levers and controls protruded from another wall and ceiling. Shining his light on one set of valves, he made out BARASUTO TANKU in white lettering, which he presumed operated the ballast tanks.

Kicking his fins gently, Dirk moved forward at a deliberate pace trying not to stir up sediment from the deck. As he passed from one compartment to the next, the submarine seemed to echo with the life from the Japanese sailors. Dining plates and silverware were strewn across the floor of a small galley. Porcelain sake vials were still standing in cabin shelves. Gliding into a large wardroom where officers' staterooms lined one side, Dirk admired a small Shinto shrine mounted on one wall.

He continued forward, cognizant of his dwindling bottom time but careful to take in all that his eyes could absorb. Moving past a maze of pipes, wires, and hydraulic lines, he reached the chief's quarters, near the forward part of the ship. At last, he approached his objective, the forward torpedo room, which loomed just ahead. Thrusting ahead with a powerful scissors kick, he advanced to the torpedo room entrance and prepared to pass in. Then he stopped dead in his tracks.

He blinked hard, wondering if his eyes were playing tricks on him. Then he turned off his light and looked through the hatch again. He was not imagining what he saw.

In the inky bowels of the rusting warship, entombed at the bottom of the sea for over sixty years, Dirk was welcomed by a faint but distinct flashing green light.

9

Dirk pulled himself through the hatch and into the pitch-black darkness of the torpedo room, save for the penetrating beam of light. As his eyes adjusted to the blackness, the flashing green light became clearer. It appeared to be a pair of tiny lights, situated at eye level, and fixed at the far side of the room.

Dirk turned his own light back on and surveyed the room. He was in the upper torpedo room, one of two torpedo bays the *I-403* had stacked vertically at the bow of the sub. Near the forward bulkhead, he could see the round chamber hatches for the four twenty-one-inch-diameter torpedo tubes. Lying in racks on either side of the room were six of the huge Type 95 torpedoes, large and deadly fish that were both more reliable and more explosive than the American counterpart during the war. Jumbled on the floor, Dirk shined his light on two additional torpedoes that had been jarred out of their racks when the submarine had slammed into the bottom. One torpedo lay flat on the floor, its nose angled slightly off bow from where it had rolled after hitting the deck. The second torpedo was propped on some debris near its tip, pointing its nose lazily upward. It was just above this second torpedo where the eerie green light flashed on and off.

Dirk floated over to the pulsating light, putting his face mask up close to the mystery beam. It was nothing more than a small stick-on digital clock wedged at the end of the torpedo rack. Fluorescent green block numbers flashed a row of zeroes, indicating an elapsed time that had run out more than twenty-four hours before. Days, weeks, or months before, it would be impossible to tell. But it certainly could not have been placed there sixty years earlier.

Dirk plucked the plastic clock and stuffed it in a pocket of his BC, then peered upward. His expended air bubbles were not gathering at the ceiling, as expected, but were trailing upward and through a shaft of pale light. He kicked up with his fins and found that a large hatch to the open deck had been wedged open several feet, easily allowing a diver access to and from the torpedo bay.

A crackly voice suddenly burst through his earpiece.

'Dirk, where are you? It's time to go upstairs,' Dahlgren's voice barked.

'I'm in the forward torpedo room. Come meet me on the bow, I need another minute.'

Dirk looked at his watch, noting that their eight minutes of bottom time had expired, then swam back down to the torpedo rack.

Two wooden crates were crushed beneath one of the fallen torpedoes, split open like a pair of suitcases.

Constructed of hardwood mahogany, the crates had amazingly survived the ravages of salt water and microorganisms and were in a minimal state of decay. He curiously noted that no silt covered the broken crates, unlike every other object he had seen on the submarine. Someone had recently fanned away the sediment to reveal the crates' contents.

Dirk swam over to the closest crate and looked inside. Like a half carton of eggs, six silver aerial bombs were lined up in a custom-fitted casemate. Each bomb was nearly three feet long and sausage-shaped, with a fin-winged tail. Half of the bombs were still wedged under the torpedo, but all six had been broken up by the torpedo's fall. Oddly, to Dirk, they appeared to be cracked rather than simply crushed. Running his hand over an undamaged section of one of the bombs, he was surprised to feel the surface had a glassy smoothness to the touch.

Kicking his fins gently, Dirk then glided over to the other crate and found a similar scene. All of the bomb canisters had been crushed by the falling torpedo in the second crate as well. Only this time, he counted five bombs, not six. One of the casings was empty. Dirk shined his light around and surveyed the area. The deck was clear in all directions, and no fragments were evident in the empty slot. One of the bombs was missing.

'Elevator, going up,' Dahlgren's voice suddenly crackled.

'Hold the door, I'll be right there,' Dirk replied,

glancing at his watch to see that they had overrun their bottom time by almost five minutes. Examining the smashed crates a last time, he tugged on one of the less mangled bombs. The ordnance slipped out of its case but fell apart into three separate pieces in Dirk's hands. As best he could, he gently placed the pieces into a large mesh dive bag, then, holding tight, he kicked toward the open hatch above. Pulling the bag through the hatch after him, Dirk found Dahlgren hovering above the sub's bow a few yards in front of him. Joining his dive partner, the two wasted no time in kicking toward their decompression stop.

Tracking their depth as they rose, Dirk flared his body out like a skydiver at forty feet to slow his ascent and purged a shot of air out of his BC. Dahlgren followed suit and the two men stabilized themselves at a depth of twenty feet to help rid their bodies of elevated levels of nitrogen in their blood.

'That extra five minutes on the bottom cost us another thirteen of decompression time. I'll be sucking my tank dry before thirty-eight minutes rolls around,' Dahlgren said, eyeing his depleted air gauge. Before Dirk could answer, they heard a muffled metallic clang in the distance.

'Never fear, Leo is here,' Dirk remarked, pointing at an object forty feet to their side.

A pair of silver scuba tanks with attached regulators dangled at the twenty-foot mark, tied to a rope that ascended to the surface. At the other end of the rope, Delgado stood munching a banana on the back deck of the *Grunion*, tracking the men's air bubbles and making sure they didn't stray too far from the boat. After hovering for a fifteen-minute decompression stop at twenty feet, the men grabbed the regulators affixed to the dangling tanks and floated up to ten feet for another twenty-five-minute wait. When Dirk and Dahlgren finally surfaced and climbed aboard the boat, Delgado acknowledged the men with just a wave as he turned the boat for landfall.

As the boat motored into the calmer waters of the Strait of Juan de Fuca, Dirk unwrapped the bomb canister fragments and laid them on the deck.

'No sign of one of these on the aircraft, or in the hangar?' Dirk asked.

'Definitely not. There was plenty of parts, tools, and other debris in the hangar, but nothing that looked like that,' Dahlgren replied, eyeing the pieces. 'Why would a canister crack open like that?'

'Because it's made of porcelain,' Dirk replied, holding a shard up for Dahlgren's closer inspection.

Dahlgren ran a finger over the surface, then shook his head. 'A porcelain bomb. Very handy for attacking tea parties, I presume.'

'Must have something to do with the payload.' Dirk rearranged the fragments until they fit roughly together, like pieces of a jigsaw puzzle. The payload armament had long since washed away in the sea, but several compartmentalized sections formed in the interior were clearly evident.

'Looks like different combustibles were to react together when detonated.'

'An incendiary bomb?' Dahlgren asked.

'Perhaps,' Dirk replied quietly. He then reached into the side pocket of his BC and pulled out the digital timer. 'Someone went to a fair amount of trouble to retrieve one of these bombs,' he said, tossing the timer over to Dahlgren.

Dahlgren studied the device, turning it over in his hands.

'Maybe it was the original owner,' he finally said with seriousness. Raising his arm with the timer in his palm, he showed Dirk the backside of the clock. In raised lettering on the plastic case was an indecipherable line of Asian script.

IO

Like a pack of hyenas fighting over a freshly killed zebra, the president's security advisers were biting and yipping at each other in a self-serving attempt to dodge responsibility over the events in Japan. Tempers flared across the Cabinet Room, situated in the West Wing of the White House.

'It's a breakdown of intelligence, clear and simple. Our consulates are not getting the intelligence support they need and two of my people are dead as a result,' the secretary of state complained harshly.

'We had no advance knowledge of an increase in terrorist activity in Japan. Diplomatic feeds from State reported that Japanese security forces were in the dark as well,' the deputy CIA director fired back.

'Gentlemen, what's done is done,' the president interjected as he attempted to light a large old-fashioned smoking pipe. Bearing the physical appearance of Teddy Roosevelt and the no-nonsense demeanor of Harry Truman, President Garner Ward was widely admired by the public for his common sense and pragmatic style. The first-term president from Montana welcomed spirited debate among his staff and cabinet but had a low tolerance for finger-pointing and self-serving pontification.

'We need to understand the nature of the threat and the motives of our opponent, and then calculate a course of action,' the president said simply. 'I'd also like a recommendation as to whether Homeland Security should issue an elevated domestic security alert.' He nodded toward Dennis Jimnez, sitting across the Cabinet Room conference table, who served as secretary of the homeland security department. 'But first, we need to figure out who these characters are. Martin, why don't you fill us in on what we know so far?' the president said, addressing FBI Director Martin Finch.

An ex-Marine Corps MP, Finch still sported a crew cut and spoke with the blunt voice of a basic training drill sergeant.

'Sir, the assassinations of Ambassador Hamilton and Deputy Chief of Mission Bridges appear to have been performed by the same individual. Surveillance video from the hotel where Bridges was killed exposed a suspect dressed as a waiter who was not known to be an employee of the hotel. Photographs from the video were matched to eyewitness accounts of an individual seen at the Tokyo area golf course shortly before Ambassador Hamilton was shot.'

'Any tie-in to the killing of the executive Chris Gavin and the SemCon plant explosion?' the president inquired.

'None that we have been able to identify, although there is a potential indicator in the note left with

Bridges's body. We are, of course, treating it as a related incident.'

'And what of the suspect?' the secretary of state asked.

'The Japanese authorities have been unable to make a match in their known criminal files, or provide a possible identification, for that matter. He was not a previously recognized member of the Japanese Red Army cell. He is apparently something of an unknown. The Japanese law enforcement agencies are cooperating fully in the manhunt and have placed their immigration checkpoints on high alert.'

'Despite no prior connection, there would seem to be little doubt that he is operating under the auspices of the Japanese Red Army,' the CIA deputy added.

'The note left with Bridges. What did it say?' asked Jimnez.

Finch rifled through a folder, then pulled out a typewritten sheet.

'Translated from Japanese, it says: "Be vanquished, American imperialists who soil Nippon with greed, or death will blow her cold, sweet breath to the shores of America. JRA." Classic fringe cult hyperbole.'

'What is the state of the Japanese Red Army? I thought they were essentially dissolved a number of years ago,' President Ward asked. Waiting for the reply, he tilted his head back and blew a cloud of cherry-scented tobacco smoke toward the paneled ceiling before Finch answered.

'As you may know, the Japanese Red Army is a fringe terrorist group that grew out of a number of communist factions in Japan during the seventies. They promote an anti-imperialist rant and have supported the overthrow of the Japanese government and monarchy by both legitimate and illegitimate means. With suspected ties to the Middle East and North Korea, the JRA was behind a number of bombings and hijackings, culminating in the attempted takeover of the U.S. embassy in Kuala Lumpur in 1975. They seemed to lose support in the nineties, and by 2000 the known leadership of the organization had been largely apprehended. Though many believed the organization was dead, indications of the group's stirrings have been seen again in the last two years. Published doctrines and active media reporting in Japan have provided a new sounding board, gaining more reception in the country's declining economic climate. Their message has focused on anti-American and anticapitalist tenets, rather than the anarchistic overthrow of the government, which has found a degree of support within a fragment of the population's youth. Oddly, there is no visible front man, or poster child, for the group.'

'I can endorse Marty's comments, Mr. President,' the deputy CIA director offered. 'Until the hits on our people, we've had no overt record of activity from these people in a number of years. The known leadership is behind bars. Quite frankly, we don't know who is now calling the shots.'

'Are we confident there is no Al Qaeda connection here?'

'Possible, but not likely,' Finch replied. 'The method of assassination is certainly not their style, and there has been no real radical Islamic presence visible in Japan. At this juncture, we have absolutely no evidence to suggest a link.'

'Where are we with the Japanese on this?' the president asked.

'We have an FBI counterterrorist team in-country working closely with the Japanese National Police Agency. The Japanese authorities are quite cognizant of the nefarious nature of these assassinations in their country and have assigned a large task force to the investigation. There is little more in the way of assistance we could ask of them that they haven't already offered up.'

'I have initiated a request through State to the Japanese Foreign Ministry for an update to their profile of high-risk aliens,' Jimnez interjected. 'We'll issue a border security alert watch, in coordination with the FBI.'

'And what are we doing elsewhere abroad to prevent any more target shooting?' the president asked, addressing the secretary of state.

'We have issued heightened security alerts at all of our embassies,' the secretary replied. 'We have also assigned additional security protection to our senior diplomats, and placed a temporary travel restriction for all State Department personnel within their host country. For the time being, our ambassadors abroad are under lock and key.'

'Any opinion that there is an imminent threat domestically, Dennis?'

'Not at this time, Mr. President,' the homeland security director replied. 'We've tightened our travel and immigration inspections on incoming traffic from Japan but don't feel it is necessary to raise the domestic security alert.'

'Do you concur, Marty?'

'Yes, sir. Like Dennis, all our indications suggest that the incidents are isolated to Japan.'

'Very well. Now what about the deaths of those two Coast Guard meteorologists in Alaska?' the president asked, drawing another puff on his pipe.

Finch rifled through some documents before responding. 'That would be the island of Yunaska in the Aleutians. We have an investigative team presently on site working with local officials. They are also looking at the destruction of a NUMA helicopter as a related incident. Preliminary indications are that the acts were the result of rogue poachers who used cyanide gas to subdue a herd of sea lions. We're trying to track down a Russian fishing trawler that was known to be fishing the local waters illegally. Officials on-site appear confident that they will apprehend the vessel.'

'Cyanide gas to hunt sea lions? There are lunatics all over this planet. All right, gentlemen, let's give it our all to find these murderers. Allowing our diplomatic representatives to be gunned down with-out repercussion is not the message I want to be giving the world. I knew Hamilton and Bridges. They were both good men.'

'We'll find them,' Finch promised.

'Make sure,' the president said, tapping his down-turned pipe bowl against a stainless steel ashtray for effect. 'I fear these characters have more up their sleeve than we realize and I want none of what they're selling.' As he spoke, a glob of burned tobacco plopped unceremoniously into the ashtray, and nobody said a word.

11

Although Keith Catana had been in South Korea only three months, he had already identified his favorite off-base watering hole. Chang's Saloon appeared little different from the dozen or so other bars of 'A-Town,' a seedy entertainment section on the fringe of Kunsan City that catered to the American servicemen stationed at Kunsan Air Force Base. Chang's skipped the loud blaring music that emanated from most of the other bars and offered a decent price for an OB beer, one of the local Korean brews. But perhaps more important, in Catana's eyes, Chang's attracted the best-looking working girls of A-Town.

Abandoned by two buddies who decided to pursue a group of American servicewomen headed to a dance club around the corner, Catana sat silently nursing his fourth beer, welcoming the early periphery of a warm buzz. The twenty-three-year-old master sergeant was an avionics specialist at the air base, supporting F-16 attack jets of the Eighth Fighter Wing. Located just a few minutes' flight time from the DMZ, his squadron stood in constant preparedness for an aerial counterstrike should North Korea initiate an invasion of the South.

Sentimental memories of his family back in Arkansas were suddenly jolted from his brain when the door to the bar flung open and in strolled the most stunning Korean woman Catana had ever laid eyes on. Four beers were not enough to deceive himself; she was a genuine beauty. Her long, straight black hair accentuated a delicate, almost porcelain-skinned face that featured a petite nose and mouth but stunningly bold black eyes. A tight leather skirt and silk top accentuated her small build but magnified a distorted symmetry created by her large, surgically enhanced breasts.

Like a tigress searching for prey, the woman surveyed the crowded bar from front to back before focusing on the lone airman sitting alone in a corner. With her sights locked, she swiveled her way over to Catana's table and smoothly slipped into the chair facing him.

'Hello, Joe. Be a friend and buy me a drink?' she purred.

'Glad to,' Catana stammered in reply. She was definitely in a different league from the normal A-Town hookers, he thought, and not the type that caters to enlisted servicemen. But who was he to argue? If the heavens intended to drop this creature in his lap on payday, then good fortune was indeed smiling his way.

It took only one quick beer before the harlot invited him back to her hotel room. Catana was pleasantly surprised that the woman didn't wrangle about price, or, in fact, mention it at all, he thought oddly.

She led him to a cheap motel nearby, where they walked arm in arm down its seedy hallway that was complete with red lights. At the end of the hall, the woman unlocked the door to a small, hot corner room. Sleep wasn't the major draw of the room, Catana could see, as evidenced by a condom machine mounted near the bed.

After closing the door, the woman quickly stripped off her top, then embraced Catana in a deep, passionate kiss. He paid little attention to a noise near the closet as he soaked in the warmth of the exotic woman, intoxicated by a combination of her beauty, the alcohol, and the expensive perfume she wore. His pleasurable delirium was suddenly jolted by a sharp jab to his buttocks, followed by a hot, searing pain. Whirling unsteadily around, he was shocked to find himself facing another man in the room. The stocky bald man grinned a crooked smile through his long mustache, his dark cold eyes seeming to penetrate right through Catana's skull. In his hands, he held a fully depressed hypodermic needle.

Pain and confusion overwhelmed Catana as his body suddenly went numb. He tried to raise his hands but his limbs were useless. Even his lips refused to cooperate with his brain in voicing a cry of protest. It took just a few seconds before a wave of blackness rolled over him and all feeling departed his senses.

It was hours later when the incessant pounding jarred him from a state of unconsciousness. The pounding was not in his head, as he first imagined, but came externally, from the motel room door. He noticed a warm stickiness enveloping him as he fought to clear the fog from his vision. Why the pounding? Why the wetness? The dimly lit room and cobwebs in his mind refused to reveal the mystery.

The banging ceased for a moment, then a loud blow struck the door, bashing it open with a flood of light. Squinting through the brightness, he saw a company of policemen storm into the room, followed by two men with cameras. As his eyes adjusted to the sudden infusion of light, he was able to notice what the wetness was around him.

Blood. It was everywhere: on the sheets, on the pillows, and smeared all over his body. But mostly it was pooled about the prone figure of the nude woman lying dead beside him.

Catana instinctively lurched back from the body in shock at the sight of the corpse. As two of the policemen pulled him off the bed and handcuffed his wrists, he cried out in horror.

'What happened? Who did this?' he said in a daze.

He looked on in shock as a third policeman pulled back a sheet partially covering the woman, fully exposing a body that had been brutally mutilated. To Catana's further bewilderment, he saw that the body was not that of the beautiful woman he had met the night before but rather was of a young girl whom he did not know.

Catana sagged as he was dragged out of the room amid a flurry of photographs. By noon that day, the story of the rape and savage murder of a thirteen-year-old Korean girl by a U.S. serviceman was a countrywide horror. By evening, it had become a national outrage. And by the time of the girl's funeral two days later, it was a full-blown international incident.

12

The high noonday sun shimmered brightly off the sapphire waters of the Bohol Sea, forcing Raul Biazon to squint as he gazed toward the large research vessel moored in the distance. For a moment, the Philippine government biologist thought the sun's rays were playing a trick on his eyes. No respectable scientific research ship could possibly be emblazoned in such a lively hue. But as the small weather-beaten launch in which he rode drew closer, he saw that there was nothing wrong with his vision. The ship was in fact painted a glistening turquoise blue from stem to stern, which made the vessel appear as if it belonged under the sea rather than bobbing atop it. Leave it to the Americans, Biazon thought, to escape the ordinary.

The launch pilot guided the worn wooden boat alongside a stepladder suspended over the side of the ship and Biazon wasted no time in leaping aboard. Speaking briefly to the pilot in Tagalog, he turned and scampered up the ladder and sprang onto the deck, nearly colliding with a tall brawny man who stood at the rail. With thinning blond hair and sturdy build, there was a Viking-like air about the man who was dressed in an immaculate white warm-weather captain's uniform.

'Dr. Biazon? Welcome aboard the *Mariana Explorer*. I'm Captain Bill Stenseth,' the man smiled warmly through gray eyes.

'Thank you for receiving me on such short notice, Captain,' Biazon replied, regaining his stance and composure. 'When a local fisherman informed me that a NUMA research vessel was seen in the region, I thought you might be able to offer some assistance.'

'Let's head to the bridge and out of the heat,' Stenseth directed, 'and you can fill us in on the environmental calamity you mentioned over the radio.'

'I hope that I am not interfering with your research work,' Biazon said as the two men climbed a flight of stairs.

'Not at all. We've just completed a seismic mapping project off Mindanao and are taking a break to test some equipment before heading up to Manila. Besides,' Stenseth said with a grin, 'when my boss says, "Stop the boat," I stop the boat.'

'Your boss?' Biazon inquired with a confused look.

'Yes,' Stenseth replied as they reached the bridge wing and he pulled open the side door. 'He's traveling on board with us.'

Biazon stepped through the door and into the bridge, shivering involuntarily as a blast of refrigerated air struck his perspiration-soaked body. At the rear of the bridge, he noticed a tall, distinguished-looking man in shorts and a polo shirt bent over a chart table studying a map.

'Dr. Biazon, may I present the director of NUMA, Dirk Pitt,' Stenseth introduced. 'Dirk, this is Dr. Raul Biazon, hazardous wastes manager with the Philippines Environmental Management Bureau.'

Biazon was shocked to find the head of a large government agency working at sea so far from Washington. But one look at Pitt and Biazon knew he wasn't the typical government administrator. Standing nearly a foot taller than his own five-foot-four frame, the NUMA chief carried a tan, lean, muscular body that showed few indications of having spent much time behind a desk. Though Biazon wouldn't know, the senior Pitt was nearly the spitting image of his son who carried the same name. The face was weathered and the ebony hair showed tinges of gray at the temples, but the opaline green eyes sparkled with life. They were eyes that had absorbed much in their day, Biazon gauged, reflecting an assorted mix of intelligence, mirth, and tenacity.

'Welcome aboard,' Pitt greeted warmly, shaking Biazon's hand with a firm grip. 'My underwater technology director, Al Giordino,' he added, jabbing a thumb over his shoulder toward the far corner of the wheelhouse. Curled up asleep on a bench seat was a short, thick man with dark curly hair. A light snore drifted from the man's lips with each breath of air that exhaled from his barrel-shaped chest. His powerful build reminded Biazon of a rhinoceros.

'Al, come join the party,' Pitt yelled across the bridge.

Giordino pried his eyes open, then popped instantly awake. He quickly stood and joined the other men at the table, showing no signs of slumber.

'As I told the captain, I appreciate your offer of assistance,' Biazon said.

'The Philippine government has always been supportive of our research work in your country's waters,' Pitt replied. 'When we received your radio call to help identify a toxic marine affliction, we were glad to help. Perhaps you can tell us a little more about the specifics of the outbreak.'

'A few weeks ago, our office was contacted by a resort hotel on Panglao Island. The hotel's management was upset because a large quantity of dead fish were washing up on the guest beach.'

'I could see where that would tend to dampen the holidaymakers' spirits,' Giordino grinned.

'Indeed,' Biazon replied sternly. 'We began monitoring the shoreline and have witnessed the fish kill growing at an alarming rate. Dead marine life is washing ashore along a ten-kilometer stretch of beach now, and growing day by day. The resort owners are all up in arms, and we, of course, are concerned about potential damage to the coral reef.'

'Have you been able to diagnose what is killing the fish?' Stenseth asked.

'Not yet. Toxic poisoning is all we can infer. We have sent samples to our departmental lab in Cebu for analysis but are still awaiting the results.' The look on Biazon's face revealed his dissatisfaction with the snail-paced response from the agency lab.

'Any speculation as to the source?' Pitt asked.

Biazon shook his head. 'We initially suspected industrial pollutants, which, regrettably, are an all too common source of environmental damage in my country. But my field team and I have scoured the impacted coastal region and failed to locate any heavy industrial businesses operating in the area. We also examined the coastline for obvious spillways or illegal dump sites but came up empty. It is my belief that the source of the kill originates at sea.'

'Perhaps a red tide?' Giordino said.

'We do experience toxic phytoplankton outbreaks in the Philippines,' Biazon said, 'though they are typically seen during the warmer late summer months.'

'It might also be some covert offshore industrial dumping,' Pitt replied. 'Where exactly is the impacted area, Dr. Biazon?'

Biazon glanced at the map, which showed Mindanao and the southern Philippine island groupings. 'Off the province of Bohol,' he said, pointing to a large round island north of Mindanao. 'Panglao is a small resort island located here, adjacent to the southwest coast. It's about fifty kilometers from our present position.'

'I can have us there in under two hours,' Stenseth said, eyeing the distance.

Pitt nodded toward the map. 'We've got a ship

full of scientists who can help find the answers. Bill, lay a course in to Panglao Island and we'll take a look.'

'Thank you,' a visibly relieved Biazon said.

'Doctor, perhaps you'd like a tour of the ship while we get under way?' Pitt offered.

'I'd like that very much.'

'Al, you care to join us?'

Giordino looked at his watch pensively. 'No, thanks. Two hours will be just enough time for me to finish my project,' he replied, easing himself back down on the bench seat and drifting rapidly back to sleep.

The *Mariana Explorer* cruised easily through a flat sea and arrived at Panglao Island in just over ninety minutes. Pitt studied an electronic navigational map of the area that was displayed on a color monitor as Biazon denoted a rectangular area where the fish kill was occurring.

'Bill, the current runs east to west through here, which would suggest that the hot zone is located at the eastern end of Dr. Biazon's box. Why don't we start to the west and work our way east into the current, taking water samples at quarter-mile increments.'

Stenseth nodded. 'I'll run a zigzag course, to see if we can gauge how far from shore the toxin is concentrated.'

'And let's deploy the side-scan sonar. Might as

well see if there's any obvious man-made objects involved.'

Dr. Biazon watched with interest as a towed sonar fish was deployed off the stern, then the *Mariana Explorer* began following a dot-to-dot path laid out on the navigation screen. At periodic intervals, a team of marine biologists collected seawater samples from varying depths. As the ship moved to the next position, the collected samples were sent down to the shipboard laboratory for immediate analysis.

On the bridge, Giordino tracked the signals from the side-scan sonar. The electronic image of the shallow seafloor revealed an interweaving mix of flat sand bottom and craggy coral mounts as the ship sailed over the fringes of a coral reef. In a short time, his trained eyes had already discerned a ship's anchor and an outboard motor lying beneath the well-traveled waters. As the monitor revealed each object, Giordino reached over and punched a MARK button on the console, which flagged the location for later assessment.

Pitt and Biazon stood nearby, admiring the tropical beaches of Panglao Island less than a half mile away. Pitt glanced down at the water alongside the ship, where he spotted a sea turtle and scores of dead fish floating belly-up.

'We've entered the toxic zone,' Pitt said. 'We should know the results shortly.'

As the research vessel plowed west, the concentration of dead fish in the water increased, then gradually fell away until the blue sea around them grew empty again.

'We're a half mile beyond Dr. Biazon's grid,' Stenseth reported. 'Judging by the water, it looks like we're well clear of the toxic zone.'

'Agreed,' Pitt replied. 'Let's stand by here until we see what kind of results the lab has found.'

As the ship ground to a halt and the sonar towfish was retrieved, Pitt led Biazon down a level into a teak-paneled conference room, followed by Giordino and Stenseth. Biazon studied the portraits of several famous underwater explorers which lined one wall, recognizing the images of William Beebe, Sylvia Earle, and Don Walsh. As they were seated, a pair of marine biologists clad in the requisite white lab coats entered the conference room. A short, attract-ive female, her brunet hair tied back in a ponytail, walked to a suspended viewing screen at the front of the room, while her male assistant began typing commands into the computer-driven projection system.

'We have completed an assessment of forty-four discrete water samples collected, which were analyzed using molecular separation of existing toxic mol-ecules,' she said in a clear voice. As she spoke, an image appeared on the screen behind her, similar to the navigation screen Biazon had noticed the ship tracking to earlier. A zigzag line punctuated by forty-four large dots ran parallel to an outline of the Panglao Island shoreline. Each dot was color-coded, though Biazon noted that most of them glowed green.

'The samples were measured for toxic content in parts per billion, with positive results occurring in fifteen of the samples,' the biologist stated, pointing to a row of yellow dots. 'As you can see from the chart, the concentration increases as the samples moved east, with the highest reading registered here,' she said, tracing past a few orange-colored dots to a lone red dot near the top of the map.

'So the source is from an isolated location,' Pitt said.

'The samples tested negative beyond the red point, indicating that it is likely of a concentrated origin spreading east with the current.'

'That would seem to dispel the red tide theory. Al, do the results mesh with anything we picked up on the sonar?'

Giordino walked over to the console and leaned over the operator's shoulder, typing in a quick series of commands. A dozen Xs suddenly appeared on the projection screen, overlaid at random points along the zigzag tracking line. Each X was lettered, beginning with A at the bottom, proceeding to L near the top.

'Al's "Dirty Dozen" hit list,' he smiled, retaking his seat. 'We ran over twelve objects that appeared man-made. Mostly chunks of pipe, rusty anchors, and the like. Three items appeared that could be suspected culprits,' he said, eyeing a sheet of handwritten notes.

'Mark C was a trio of fifty-five-gallon drums lying in the sand.'

Every eye in the room jumped to the X marked C on the overhead. The water samples on either side of the mark were all illuminated with green dots, which signified a negative test result.

'No toxins registered in the vicinity,' Pitt said. 'Next.'

'Mark F looks to be a wooden sailboat, perhaps a local fishing boat. She's sitting upright on the bottom with her mast still standing.'

This X was located adjacent to the first yellow dot. Pitt commented that it was still down current of the toxic readings.

'Strike two. But you're getting warmer.'

'My last mark is a little odd, as the image was just at the range of the sonar,' Giordino said, pausing with uncertainty.

'Well, what did it look like?' Stenseth asked.

'A ship's propeller. Looked like it was protruding from the reef. I couldn't make out any sign of the ship that went with it, though. Might just be a lone propeller that got bashed off against the reef. I tagged it at mark K.'

Every voice in the room fell silent as their eyes found the X marked K on the overhead screen. It was positioned right above the red dot.

'It would appear there's something more to it than just a propeller,' Pitt said finally. 'Leaking fuel from a submerged ship, or perhaps its cargo?'

'We did not detect abnormally high readings of petroleum compounds in the water samples,' the NUMA biologist stated.

'You never did tell us what you found,' Giordino said, raising a dark eyebrow at the biologist.

'Yes, you said you did identify toxins in the water, didn't you?' Biazon asked anxiously. 'What was it that you found?'

'Something I've never encountered in salt water before,' she replied, shaking her head slowly. 'Arsenic.'

13

The coral reef exploded with a rainbow of colors arranged in a serene beauty that put a Monet landscape to shame. Bright red sea anemones waved their tentacles lazily in the current amid a carpet of magenta-colored sea sponges. Delicate green sea fans climbed gracefully toward the surface beside round masses of violet-hued brain coral. Brilliant blue starfish glowed from the reef like bright neon signs, while dozens of sea urchins blanketed the seafloor in a carpet of pink pincushions.

Few things in nature rivaled the beauty of a healthy coral reef, Pitt reflected as his eyes drank in the assortment of colors. Floating just off the bottom, he peered out his faceplate in amusement as a pair of small clown fish darted into a crevice as a spotted ray cruised by searching for a snack. Of all the world's great dive spots, he always felt it was the warm waters of the western Pacific that held the most breathtaking coral reefs.

'The wreck should be slightly ahead and to the north of us,' Giordino's voice crackled through his ears, breaking the tranquility. After mooring the *Mariana Explorer* over the site of the maximum toxin readings, Pitt and Giordino donned rubberized dry suits with full faceplates to protect them from potential chemical or biological contamination. Dropping over the side, they splashed into the clear warm water that dropped 120 feet to the bottom.

The readings of arsenic in the water had been startling to everyone. Dr. Biazon reported that arsenic seepage had been known to occur in mining operations around the country and that several manganese mines operated on Bohol Island, but added that none was located near Panglao. Arsenic was also utilized in insecticides, the NUMA biologist countered. Perhaps an insecticide container was lost off a vessel, or intentionally dumped? There was only one way to find out, Pitt declared, and that was to go down and have a look.

With Giordino at his side, Pitt checked his compass, then thrust his fins together, kicking himself at an angle across the invisible current. The visibility was nearly seventy-five feet and Pitt could observe the reef gradually rising to shallower depths as he glided just above the bottom. His skin quickly began to sweat under the thick dry suit, its protective layer providing more insulation than was required in the warm tropical waters.

'Somebody turn on the air-conditioning,' he heard Giordino mutter, verbalizing his own sentiments.

With eyes aimed forward, he still saw no signs of a shipwreck, but noted that the coral bottom rose up sharply ahead. To his right, a large underwater sand dune boiled up against the reef, its rippled surface stretching beyond Pitt's field of vision. Reaching the coral uplift, he tilted his upper body toward the surface and thrust with a large scissors kick to propel himself up and over its jagged edge. He was surprised to find that the reef dropped vertically away on the other side, creating a large crevasse. More surprising was what he saw at the bottom of the ravine. It was the bow half of a ship.

'What the heck?' Giordino uttered, spotting the partial wreckage of the ship.

Pitt studied the partial remains of the ship for a moment, then laughed through the underwater communication system. 'Got me, too. It's an optical illusion. The rest of the ship is there, it's just buried under the sand dune.'

Giordino studied the wreck and saw that Pitt was right. The large sand dune that affronted the reef had built up partway into the crevasse and neatly covered the stern half of the ship. The current swirling through the crevasse had halted the onslaught of the sand at a point amidships of the wreck in a nearly perfect line, which gave the impression that only half a ship existed.

Pitt turned away from the exposed portion of the ship, swimming over the empty sand dune for several yards before it dropped sharply beneath him.

'Here's your propeller, Al,' he said, pointing down.

Beneath his fins, a small section of the ship's stern was exposed. The brown-encrusted skin curved down to a large brass propeller, which protruded from the sand dune like a windmill. Giordino kicked over and inspected the propeller, than swam up the sternpost several feet and began brushing away a layer of sand. From the curvature of the stern, he could tell that the ship was listing sharply to its port side, which was also apparent from the exposed bow section. Pitt floated over and watched as Giordino was able to expose the last few letters of the ship's name beaded onto the stern.

'Something MARU is the most I can get,' he said, struggling to trench into a refilling hole of sand.

'She's Japanese,' Pitt said, 'and, by the looks of the corrosion, she's been here awhile. If she's leaking toxins, it would have to be from the bow section.'

Giordino stopped digging in the sand and followed Pitt as he swam toward the exposed front of the ship. The vessel eerily emerged again from the sand dune at its main funnel, which jutted nearly horizontally, its top edged meshed into the coral wall. From its small bridge section and long forward deck, Pitt could see that the vessel was a common oceangoing cargo ship. He judged her length at slightly more than two hundred feet. As they swam over the angled topside, he could see that the main deck had vanished, its wooden planking disintegrated long ago in the warm Philippine waters.

'Those are some ancient-looking hoists,' Giordino remarked, eyeing a small pair of rusty derricks that reached across the deck like outstretched arms.

'If I had to guess, I'd say she was probably built in the twenties,' Pitt replied, kicking past a deck rail that appeared to be made of brass.

Pitt made his way along the deck until he reached a pair of large square hatch covers, the capstones to the ship's forward cargo holds. With the freighter's heavy list, Pitt had expected to find the hatch covers pitched off the storage compartments, but that wasn't the case. Together, the two men swam around the circumference of each hatch, searching for damage or signs of leakage.

'Locked down and sealed tight as a drum,' Giordino said after they returned to their starting point.

'There must be a breach somewhere else.'

Silently finishing his thought, Pitt slowly ascended until he could look down the curving starboard side and exposed hull. Surrounding the ship, the coral reef rose sharply on either side. Following his instincts, he swam down the starboard hull all the way to the partially exposed keel line, then moved slowly toward the bow. Kicking just a short distance, he suddenly halted. Before him, a jagged four-foot-wide gash stretched nearly twenty feet down the starboard hull to the very tip of the bow. The sound of whistling burst through his ears as Giordino swam up and surveyed the gaping wound.

'Just like the *Titanic*,' he marveled. 'Only she scraped herself to the bottom on a coral head instead of a chunk of ice.'

'She must have been trying to run aground on purpose,' Pitt surmised.

'Outrunning a typhoon, probably.'

'Or maybe a Navy Corsair. Leyte Gulf is just

around the corner, where the Japanese fleet was decimated in 1944.'

The Philippine Islands were a hotly contested piece of real estate in World War II, Pitt recalled. More than sixty thousand Americans lost their lives in the failed defense and later recapture of the islands, a forgotten toll that exceeded the losses in Vietnam. On the heels of the surprise attack at Pearl Harbor, Japanese forces had landed near Manila and quickly overrun the U.S. and Philippine forces garrisoned at Luzon, Bataan, and Corregidor. General MacArthur's hasty retreat was followed by three years of Japanese oppressive rule, until American advances across the Pacific led to the invasion of the southern island of Leyte in October 1944.

Just over a hundred miles from Panglao, the province of Leyte and its adjoining gulf was the site of the largest air/sea battle in history. Days after MacArthur and his invasion force landed on Leyte, the Japanese Imperial Navy appeared and successfully divided the American supporting naval force. The Japanese came within a hair of destroying the Seventh Fleet, but were ultimately turned back in a devastating defeat, losing four carriers and three battleships, including the massive battlewagon *Musashi*. The crippling losses finished the Imperial Navy's brief dominance in Pacific waters and led to the country's military collapse within a year.

The sea channels surrounding the southern Philippine islands of Leyte, Samar, Mindanao, and

Bohol were littered with sunken cargo, transport, and warships from the conflict. It would be no surprise to Pitt if the toxins were related to combat wreckage. Eyeing the gash in the cargo ship's hull, it was easy to presume that the vessel was a victim of war.

Pitt mentally envisioned the Japanese-flagged freighter under air attack, the desperate captain electing to run the ship aground in a perilous attempt to save the crew and cargo. Slicing into the coral reef, the bow quickly filled with water as the ship ricocheted off the sides of the crevasse. With a full head of steam, the ship literally drove itself over onto its port side. Whatever cargo the captain had tried to save lay hidden and dormant for decades to follow.

'I think we definitely hit the jackpot,' Giordino said in a morose tone.

Pitt turned to see Giordino's gloved hand pointing away from the hull and toward the adjacent reef. Gone was the vibrant red-, blue-, and green-colored corals they had witnessed earlier. In a fan-shaped pattern stretching around the ship's bow, the coral was uniformly tinted a dull white. Pitt grimly noted that no fish were visible in the area as well.

'Bleached dead from the arsenic,' he noted.

Turning back to the wreck, he grabbed a small flashlight clipped to his buoyancy compensator and ducked toward the gap in the hull. Edging his way slowly into the ship's underside, he flicked on the light and sprayed its beam across the black interior. The lower bow section was empty but for a mass of thick anchor chain coiled in a huge pile like an iron serpent. Creeping aft, Pitt moved toward the rear bulkhead as Giordino slipped through the gash and followed behind him. Reaching the bulkhead, Pitt panned his light across the steel wall that separated them from the forward cargo hold. At its lower joint with the starboard bulkhead, he found what he was looking for. The pressure from the outer hull's collision with the reef had buckled one of the plates on the cargo hold's bulkhead. The bent metal created a horizontal window to the cargo hold several feet wide.

Pitt eased up to the hole, careful not to kick up silt around him, then stuck his head in and pulled in the flashlight. A huge lifeless eye stared back at him just inches away, nearly causing him to recoil until he saw that it belonged to a grouper. The fifty-pound green fish drifted back and forth across the compartment in a slow maze, its gray belly pointing up toward the trail of Pitt's rising exhaust bubbles. Peering past the dead fish into its black tomb, Pitt's blood went cold as he surveyed the hold. Scattered in mounds like eggs in a henhouse were hundreds of decaying artillery shells. The forty-pound projectiles were ammunition for the 105mm artillery gun, a lethal field weapon utilized by the Imperial Army during the war.

'A Welcome-to-the-Philippines present for General MacArthur?' Giordino asked, peering in.

Pitt silently nodded, then pulled out a plastic-lined dive bag. Giordino obliged by reaching over and grabbing a shell and inserting it in the bag as Pitt sealed and wrapped it. Giordino then reached over and picked up another highly corroded shell, holding it just a few inches off the bottom. Both men looked on curiously as a brown oily substance leaked out of the projectile.

'That doesn't resemble any high-explosives powder I've ever seen,' he said, gingerly setting the weapon down.

'I don't think they are ordinary artillery shells,' Pitt replied as he noted a pool of brown ooze beneath a nearby pile of ordnance. 'Let's get this one back to the shipboard lab and find out what we've got,' he said, carrying the wrapped ordnance under his arm like a football. Gliding forward along the bow section, he slipped through the open hull and back into the bright sunlit water.

Pitt had little doubt that the armament was a lost World War II cache. Why the arsenic, he did not know. The Japanese were innovative in their weapons of war and the arsenic-laced shells might have been another device in their arsenal of death. The loss of the Philippines would have effectively spelled the end of the war for the Japanese and they may have prepared to use the weapons as part of a last-gasp measure against a determined enemy.

As they surfaced with the mysterious shell, Pitt felt a strange sense of relief. The deadly cargo that the ship carried so many years ago had never reached port. He was somehow glad that it had ended up sunk on the reef, never to be fielded in the face of battle.

PART TWO
Chimera

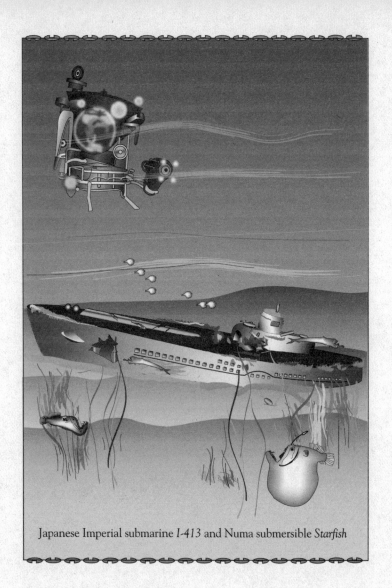

Japanese Imperial submarine *I-413* and Numa submersible *Starfish*

14

At fifty-five meters in length, the steel-hulled Benetti yacht was impressive even by Monte Carlo affluent standards. The custom-built Italian yacht's lush interior featured an array of marble flooring, Persian carpets, and rare Chinese antiques, which filled the cabins and salons with warm elegance. A collection of fifteenth-century oil paintings by the Flemish master Hans Memling dotted the walls, adding to the eclectic feel. The glistening maroon-and-white exterior, which featured a wide band of wraparound dark-tinted windows, was given a more traditional appearance, with inlaid teak decking and brass fittings on the outside verandas. The entire effect was a tasteful mix of old-world charm combined with the speed and function of modern design and technology. Always turning heads as it roared by, the vessel was an admired fixture on the Han River in and about Seoul. To the local society crowd, an invitation aboard was a highly desired mark of prominence, providing the rare opportunity to mingle with the boat's enigmatic owner.

Dae-jong Kang was a leading icon of South Korean industry and seemed to have his hands in everything. Little was known of the mercurial leader's early background, aside from his sudden appearance during the economic boom of the nineties as the head of a regional construction company. But upon his taking over the reins, the low-tech firm became a corporate Pac-Man, gobbling up companies in the shipping, electronics, semiconductor, and telecommunications industries in a series of leveraged buyouts and hostile takeovers. The businesses were all rolled under the umbrella of Kang Enterprises, a privately held empire entirely controlled and directed by Kang himself. Unafraid of the public spotlight, Kang mixed freely with politicians and business leaders alike, wielding additional influence on the board of directors of South Korea's largest companies.

The fifty-year-old bachelor held a veil of mystery over his private life, however. Much of his time was spent sequestered at his large estate on a secluded section of Kyodongdo Island, a lush mountainous outpost near the mouth of the Han River on the western Korean coast. There he dabbled with a stable of Austrian show horses or worked on his golf game, according to the few who had been invited inside the private enclave. More carefully hidden was a dark secret about the iconoclastic businessman that would have completely shocked his corporate cronies and political patrons. Unknown to even his closest associates, Kang had operated for over twenty-five years as a sleeper agent for the Democratic People's Republic of Korea, or North Korea, as it was known by the rest of the world.

Kang was born in the Hwanghae Province of North Korea shortly after the Korean War. At the age of three, his parents were killed in a railroad derailment, blamed on South Korean insurgents, and the infant boy was adopted by his maternal uncle. The uncle, a founding member of the Korean Workers' Party in 1945, had fought with Kim Il Sung and his anti-Japanese guerrilla forces based in the Soviet Union during World War II. When Kim Il Sung later rose to power in North Korea, the uncle was richly rewarded with a series of provincial government appointments, brokering himself into ever-more important spheres of influence until, ultimately, gaining a seat as an elite ruling member of the Central People's Committee, the top executive decision-making organization in North Korea.

During his uncle's ascension, Kang received a thorough indoctrination in the Korean Workers' Party dogma while obtaining the best state-sponsored education the fledgling country could offer. Recognized early as a fast learner who excelled at his studies, Kang was groomed as a foreign operative, with sponsorship from his uncle.

Blessed with a keen financial mind, commandlike leadership skills, and a ruthless heart, Kang was smuggled into South Korea at the age of twenty-two and set up as a laborer at a small construction company. With brutal efficiency, he quickly worked his way up to foreman, then arranged a series of 'accidental' work site deaths that killed the firm's president and top managers. Forging a series of ownership transfer documents, Kang quickly took control of the business within two years of his arrival. With secret direction and capital infusion from Pyongyang, the young communist entrepreneur slowly expanded his network of commercial enterprises over the years, focusing on products and services most beneficial to the North. Kang's forays into telecommunications provided access to Western network communications hardware valuable to the military's command and control systems. His semiconductor plants secretly built chips for use in short-range missiles. And his fleet of cargo ships provided the means for covertly transferring defense technology to the government of his homeland. The profits from his corporate empire that were not smuggled north in the form of Western goods and technology were spent bribing key politicians for government contracts or utilized for the hostile acquisition of other companies. Yet Kang's zealous appropriation of power and technology was almost peripheral to his primary objective, set forth by his handlers so many years before. Kang's mission, in the simplest of provisions, was to promote the reunification of the two Korean countries, but on North Korea's terms.

The sleek Benetti yacht slowed its engines as it

entered a narrow inlet off the Han River that wound snakelike into a protected cove. As the boat eased through the inlet, the pilot increased the throttle again, racing the boat smoothly across the calm waters of the interior lagoon. A yellow floating dock bobbed gently on the opposite side of the cove, which quickly grew larger in size as the yacht drew near. The big vessel stormed toward the dock, swinging parallel at just the last minute as its engines were cut. A pair of black-uniformed men grabbed the bow and stern lines and tied off the vessel as the pilot finessed her the last few feet to the dock. The shore crew quickly rolled a stepped platform against the yacht's side, the upper step matching the foot level of the first deck.

A cabin door popped open and three gray-looking men in dark blue suits stepped down onto the dock and instinctively peered up at the large stone structure perched above them. Jutting from a cliff that rose nearly vertically above the dock nestled an immense stone house that was half-carved into the crown of the bluff. Thick walls surrounded the house, lending a medieval look to the compound, although the house itself was clearly of Asian design, with a deep angular tiled roof capping the brownstone walls. The entire structure sat two hundred feet above the water, accessible by a steep set of stairs carved into the rock on one side. The three men noted that twelve-foot-high stone walls ran all the way down to the water's edge, ensuring a high degree of privacy. A tight-lipped guard standing at the dock's footing with an automatic rifle slung over his shoulder ensured even more.

As the men in suits made their way along the dock, a door opened from a small structure near the landing and out walked their host to greet them. There was no question that Dae-jong Kang had an imposing air about him. At an even six feet tall and weighing two hundred pounds, his physical mass was large by Korean standards. But it was his stern face and penetrating eyes that indicated a willful presence. Under the right circumstances, his piercing glare could almost cut a man in two. A practiced but insincere smile helped break down barriers when he needed to, but an icy-cold aloofness always lingered over him like a cloud. He was a man who reeked of power and was not afraid to use it.

'Welcome, gentlemen,' Kang said in a smooth voice. 'I trust your voyage from Seoul was enjoyable?'

The three men, all leading party members in the South Korean National Assembly, nodded in unison. The senior member of the political trio, a balding man named Youngnok Rhee, replied for the group: 'A trip down the Han River is a delight in such a beautiful boat.'

'It is my preferred means of commuting to Seoul,' Kang replied, implying the boredom he found flying in his private helicopter. 'Right this way,' he motioned toward the small building at the base of the cliff.

The politicians followed him obediently past a small security station and down a narrow passageway to a waiting elevator, the shaft of which had been carved directly into the cliff. The visitors admired an ancient painting of a tiger hung on the elevator's back wall as it rose rapidly to the main house. When the doors opened, the men stepped out into an expansive, ornately decorated dining room. Beyond an elegant mahogany dining table, floor-to-ceiling glass walls offered a breathtaking view of the Han River delta, where the grand river's waters emptied into the Yellow Sea. A sprinkling of worn sampans and small cargo boats dotted the horizon, fighting their way upriver toward Seoul with a supply of trade goods. Most of the boats clung to the south bank of the river, well away from the imaginary demarcation line with North Korea that ran down the river's center.

'An incredible view, Mr. Kang,' offered the tallest of the three politicians, a man named Won Ho.

'I enjoy it, for the vista encompasses both our countries,' Kang replied with intent. 'Please be seated.' He waved a hand as he spoke, then took a seat at the head of the table. A cadre of uniformed servants began shuttling in an array of fine wines and gourmet dishes, while the conversation among the seated men drifted toward politics. A medley of spicy fragrances filled the air as they dined on *daiji-bulgogi*, or pork marinated in a spicy garlic sauce, accompanied by *yachae gui*, an assortment of marinated vegetables. Kang played the gregarious host to his guests until they had comfortably imbibed, then he applied the knife.

'Gentlemen, it's high time we take seriously the effort to unify our two countries,' he spoke slowly, for effect. 'As a Korean, I know that we are one country in language, in culture, and in heart. As a businessman, I know how much stronger we could be economically in the global markets. The Sino-American threat, which has long justified the use of our countries as pawns to the superpowers, is no more. It is long past time that we throw off the shackles of foreign domination and do what is right for Korea. Our destiny is as one, and we should seize the opportunity now.'

'The goal of unification beats strongly in all our hearts, but the reckless leadership and military juggernaut of North Korea mandates that we tread with caution,' replied the third politician, a beady-eyed man named Kim.

Kang brushed aside the comment. 'As you know, I recently toured North Korea as part of a fact-finding trip sponsored by the Ministry of Unification. We found their economy to be in a moribund state, with food shortages widespread and rampant. The depleted economic state has taken a toll on the North Korean military as well. The military forces we witnessed appeared ill-equipped and extremely low in morale,' he lied.

'Yes, I can attest to their struggles,' Won Ho replied. 'But do you really think reunification would be a benefit to our own economy?'

'The northern provinces offer an abundance of

cheap labor that is readily accessible. We would immediately become more competitive on the world markets, as our average labor costs would diminish substantially. I have assessed the impact to my own enterprises and make no secret of the fact that my profits could be boosted dramatically. In addition, the northern province economies would provide a new, untapped consumption market that South Korean business is poised to serve. No, gentlemen, there is no question that unification would provide an economic windfall to all of us in the south.'

'There is still the issue of North Korea's hard-line contention in the matter,' Won Ho stated. 'We cannot simply achieve reunification unilaterally.'

'Yes,' Kim added. 'They have repeatedly insisted that the United States military presence be removed from our soil before reunification can be considered.'

'That is why,' Kang continued calmly, 'I am asking the three of you to support the resolution recently introduced in the National Assembly demanding the removal of all American military forces from South Korea.'

A stunned silence fell over the room as the three politicians digested Kang's words. Kang had brought them there for a reason, they knew, but the politicians had figured the corporate giant was seeking legislative tax relief or some other aid to his business empire. Not one of them expected a demand so risky to their political careers. The elder statesman Rhee finally cleared his throat and spoke deliberately.

'That particular resolution was introduced by radical elements in the assembly. There is little chance it would ever pass a full vote.'

'There is if the three of you came on record in support of it,' Kang replied.

'That's impossible,' Kim stammered. 'I cannot support weakening our military defense for the asking while North Korea continues to consign all its resources toward boosting its military might.'

'You can and you will. With the recent murder of the girl in Kunsan City by the American serviceman, there is a firestorm of animosity toward the American military from the mainstream populace. It is incumbent upon you to place pressure on our president to act and act now.'

'But the American forces are essential for our security. There are over thirty-five thousand troops stationed in our defense,' Kim argued before being cut off.

'May I remind you,' Kang hissed, his face contorting into an evil smirk, 'that I have paid and negotiated your way into the position that you hold today.' The controlled rage glowed from his eyes like burning embers.

Rhee and Won Ho slumped back in their chairs and nodded gravely, knowing their political futures were finished if knowledge of their graft over the years was ever released to the press. 'Yes, it will be done,' Won Ho said meekly.

Kim, however, appeared oblivious to Kang's rage.

Shaking his head, he replied firmly, 'I'm sorry, but I cannot support placing our country at risk of military defeat. I will not vote in favor of the resolution.' He turned and peered at his fellow politicians with a look of scorn.

The room fell silent again for several moments before the servants returned to clear away the dinner dishes. Kang leaned over and whispered something into the ear of one of the servants, who quickly paced back to the kitchen. Seconds later, a side door opened and two hulking security guards, attired in black from head to toe, entered the room. Without saying a word, they strode to either side of Kim's chair, grabbed his arms, and yanked the politician roughly to his feet.

'What is the meaning of this, Kang?' he cried.

'I will suffer your foolishness no more,' Kang replied coldly. With a wave of his hand, the two thugs muscled Kim to a veranda door that opened onto an outside balcony. Flailing and struggling hopelessly against the stronger men, Kim was dragged outside and to the edge of the balcony wall, which jutted over the face of the rock cliff. Obscenities burst from his mouth as he demanded to be let go but his pleas were ignored. As Rhee and Won Ho looked on in horror, the two men in black hoisted Kim up off his feet, then unceremoniously pitched his thrashing body over the wall.

Kim's screaming voice could be heard trailing away for several seconds as he plunged down the cliff wall. A faint thud signaled that his body had struck the beach landing below and his screaming suddenly ceased. Rhee and Won Ho turned ashen white as the two thugs calmly returned to the dining hall. Kang sipped at a glass of wine, then spoke to the security men in a nonchalant tone.

'Retrieve the body and take it to Seoul. Plant him on a street near his residence and make it look like a hit-and-run traffic accident,' he ordered.

As they left the room, Kang turned to the frightened politicians and asked with icy politeness, 'You will stay for dessert, won't you?'

Kang peered out the dining hall window and watched as Rhee and Won Ho anxiously boarded his yacht below. Kim's body, wrapped in a brown blanket, had been crudely dumped on the boat's stern deck and covered with a tarp but was readily distinguishable to the two shaken men as they climbed aboard. Observing the yacht as it cast off and began its fifty-mile trek upriver to Seoul, Kang turned as a man entered the room and approached. He had a scrawny build and greased-back black hair, with pale skin that seldom saw the light of day. His blue suit was well worn, and his choice of tie dated, but his white shirt was starched crisp. What Kang's administrative assistant lacked in panache he made up for in thrift and efficiency.

'Your meeting was a success?' the man asked Kang, with a dose of subservience.

'Yes, Kwan. Rhee and Won Ho are going to promote our initiative for the removal of U.S. forces through the National Assembly. It was unfortunate that we had to eliminate Kim, but it was apparent that he had lost his loyalty to us. His death will send a strong message to the other two.'

'A sensible decision. Sir, a courier from Yonan is arriving by boat this evening to receive the prototype missile guidance chip set that has passed final test at our semiconductor facility. Do you wish also to relay a briefing status?'

Like a foreign embassy in a hostile nation, Kang and his superiors in North Korea relied on couriers to funnel information, technology, and contraband out of the South. Although the Internet had become the spy's best friend when it came to dispatching information, there was still the need for one-on-one contact to transfer hard goods. An aged fisherman in a beat-up sampan, easily neglected by the Navy patrols, was the favored agent's disguise for crossing the DMZ to Kang's estate.

'Yes, we can report that a National Assembly vote will be brought forth on the expulsion resolution within the next several weeks, and that progress is being made on its passage. Our organized student protests are gaining momentum, and our media pay-offs will ensure continued press attention and coverage of the U.S. serviceman murder incident,' Kang said with a wry smile. 'Our external disruption plan is proving to be most effective. What remains to be seen is whether we can implement the chimera project quickly enough to maximize the Americans' strife. What is the latest from the biochemical laboratory?'

'The news is most promising. The lab team has completed their study of the test results from the Aleutian Islands and verified that the virus was successfully rejuvenated during flight release. In addition, dispersion of the virus through the mock-up missile-borne vapor mechanism covered a ground path larger than anticipated. The program engineers are confident that the full-scale deployment system already built will be operationally successful.'

'Providing we can generate sufficient quantities of the virus. It was most unfortunate that all but one of the canisters on the *I-403* submarine was destroyed.'

'An unforeseen circumstance. Since most of the recovered agent was utilized in the Aleutian test firing, very little was left available for laboratory growth purposes. Dr. Sarghov at the bio lab informs me it will take over three months to cultivate quantities necessitated by the program. For this reason, we have initiated your request to attempt recovery of the second Japanese armament stock.'

'A second Japanese submarine,' Kang muttered, picturing an Imperial Japanese submersible lying torpedoed on the ocean floor. 'An amazing intelligence discovery that there was not one but two submarines destroyed carrying such a virulent cargo. How soon before recovery operations commence?'

'The submarine must be located first. We have the *Baekje* en route to Yokohama to pick up a leased submersible that will be required for the deep-water recovery operation. Once on-site, we expect the survey to take approximately two days, and the entire recovery operation to be completed within ten days.'

'And Tongju?'

'He will meet up with the salvage ship in Yokohama and remain on board to lead security operations.'

'Very good,' Kang said, rubbing his hands together in satisfaction. 'Things are proceeding nicely, Kwan. The domestic pressures on the Americans will soon be very hot and the chimera project will be a sharp kick to their sides. We must soon prepare for the coming offensive and restoration of the country under our home flag.'

'You will hold a place of high honor in the new Korea,' Kwan stroked.

Kang looked again at the sweeping panorama to the north before him. The rolling hills of his native North Korea lay just across the Han River, stretching wide across the far horizon.

'It is time we regain our country,' he muttered softly.

Kwan started to leave the room, then stopped and turned.

'Sir, there is one other item that has cropped up related to the chimera project.'

Kang nodded at his assistant to proceed.

'The helicopter that was shot down in the Aleutians was operated by an American government research vessel from the National Underwater and Marine Agency. Our crew believed the pilot and crew were killed, which was initially confirmed by an Alaskan media report of a fatal helicopter crash. However, our U.S. field operations team monitoring the Americans' response to the test reported that the pilot, a special projects director named Pitt, and his copilot had in fact survived the crash.'

'That is of little consequence,' Kang replied irritably.

Kwan cleared his throat nervously. 'Well, sir, I had our team track the pilot upon his return to home port in Seattle. Two days after their return, the NUMA men were seen in a small survey boat headed for the region where the *I-403* is located.'

'What? That's not possible,' Kang belched with sudden anger, made visible by a large vein that throbbed on his forehead. 'How would they have any knowledge of our activities?'

'I do not understand it, either. They are undersea professionals. Perhaps our recovery operation was witnessed by others and they were simply monitoring the *I-403* for looters. Or perhaps it is just a coincidence. They may have been performing an engineering or archaeological assessment.'

'Perhaps. But this is no time to compromise the project. Have them both taken care of,' Kang directed.

'Yes, sir,' Kwan replied, backpedaling out of the room quickly. 'It will be handled at once.'

15

To the ancient Aztecs of central Mexico, it was known as the 'Great Leprosy.' The ghastly plague of death had appeared sometime after the arrival of Hernando Cortés and his troops in 1518. Some believe a rival conquistador named Narváez, sailing from Cuba, had carried the scourge. Whoever the carrier, the results proved horrific. When Cortés entered Mexico City after a four-month siege against the forces of Montezuma in 1521, he was shocked at what he found. Stacks upon stacks of dead, decaying bodies were piled high in homes, on the streets, everywhere the eye could see throughout the city. No casualties of battle, the dead were all victims of disease.

No one knows the origins of *Variola major*, but the deadly virus, better known as 'smallpox,' has left an expansive path of tragedy around the globe. Though smallpox epidemics have been recorded in civilizations as far back as the ancient Egyptians, history knows the disease best as the scourge of the Americas, leaving its deadliest mark on the highly susceptible natives of the western continents. Introduced to the New World by the crews of Christopher Columbus, smallpox wreaked havoc throughout the entire West Indies and virtually decimated the original Carib Indians who greeted Columbus on his first voyage west.

The Cortés/Narváez introduction of smallpox into Mexico is estimated to have killed nearly half of the three hundred thousand inhabitants of Mexico City in 1521. Cumulative deaths throughout the country from the highly contagious disease easily numbered in the millions. Similar devastation transpired in South America as well. When Pizarro landed in Peru in 1531 on his great quest for gold, the smallpox virus was already annihilating the Inca population. With his army of less than two hundred men, Pizarro would never have ransacked the Inca empire had the culture not been preoccupied with a chaotic struggle against the ravaging disease. More than five million Incas may have died from smallpox, which all but eradicated their entire civilization.

In North America, Native American tribes were not immune to the onslaught. Numerous tribes of river valley Mound Builders vanished altogether from smallpox, while the Massachusetts and Narragansett tribes were nearly wiped out. Estimates suggest that the population of the New World declined by ninety-five percent in the century following the arrival of Columbus, attributable primarily to smallpox.

The lethal virus didn't stop there, flaring up in sporadic epidemics that killed thousands more in Europe over the next two hundred years. Sinister military minds later made use of the disease as a tool of battle, to intentionally infect opposing forces. Historical allegations claim the British provided smallpox-infected blankets to warring Native American tribes in the 1760s, and employed similar tactics against American troops during the battle for Quebec during the Revolutionary War.

Primitive vaccinations were finally discovered in the early nineteenth century, using a related cowpox virus, which eventually provided some measure of control against the disease. Sporadic outbreaks and Cold War fears prompted routine smallpox vaccinations in the United States up until the nineteen seventies. In large part due to the World Health Organization's successful global battle against the disease, smallpox was declared completely eradicated in 1977. Save for a small research sample at the U.S. Centers for Disease Control, and an unknown quantity developed for military applications in the former Soviet Union, remaining worldwide stocks of the virus were completely destroyed. Smallpox was nearly a forgotten disease until the terrorist attacks in the early years of the new century raised the fear that a contagious virulent outbreak of any form was again a threat to be reckoned with.

The historical ravages of smallpox were of little concern to Irv Fowler at the moment. After mustering the strength to drive himself to the Alaska Regional Hospital emergency room, his only hopes were for a quiet room and an attractive nurse to help him recuperate from whatever form of killer flu was knocking him out. Even when a parade of somber-looking medical professionals kept marching by to have a look at him and then insisted he be wheeled into quarantine, he was feeling too weak to be alarmed. Only when a pair of masked doctors finally informed him that he had tested positive for smallpox did his mind begin to whir. Two thoughts came to mind before delirium washed over his brain again: Could he defy the thirty percent mortality rate? And who else had he infected?

16

'Dirk, I have some terrifying news.' The fear in Sarah's voice was palpable, even over the telephone.

'What's wrong?'

'It's Irv. He's sick in the hospital in Anchorage. The doctors say that he has contracted smallpox. I just can't believe it.'

'Smallpox? I thought that had all but been eliminated.'

'Practically speaking, it has. If the doctors are correct with the diagnosis, it will be the first documented case in the United States in thirty years. The medical authorities are keeping it quiet, though the CDC is rushing vaccination supplies to Alaska in case an outbreak develops.'

'How's he holding up?'

'He's at a critical juncture,' Sarah replied, nearly choking on the words. 'The next two or three days will be crucial to his outcome. He's in quarantine at Alaska Regional Hospital in Anchorage, along with three other people he has had close contact with.'

'I'm sorry to hear that,' Dirk said with genuine concern in his voice. 'Irv's a tough old bird, I'm sure he'll sail through without a hitch. Have you any idea how on earth he contracted smallpox?'

'Well,' Sarah replied, swallowing hard, 'the incubation period is approximately fourteen days. That would mean he became infected about the time we were on Yunaska . . . and aboard the *Deep Endeavor*.'

'He may have contracted it on our ship?' Dirk asked incredulously.

'I don't know. It was either on the ship or on the island, but it matters little now. The smallpox virus is remarkably contagious. We need to work fast to check everyone who was onboard the *Deep Endeavor* and isolate those infected. Time is critical.'

'What about you and Sandy? You were working and living together with Irv. Are you all right?'

'As CDC employees, Sandy and I were both vaccinated two years ago after concerns were first raised about smallpox as a potential bioterrorist threat. Irv was on loan to us from the state of Alaska's Department of Epidemiology and had not yet received his vaccination.'

'Can the crew of the *Deep Endeavor* still be vaccinated?'

'Unfortunately, it would do no good. The vaccine can be effective within a couple of days of exposure but becomes useless thereafter. It's a terrible disease, as once you've contracted it there is nothing that can be done to combat it until it has run its course.'

'I'll contact Captain Burch and we'll check on all the crew members as soon as possible.'

'I will be back from Spokane this evening. If you can assemble the crew, I can help the ship's doctor check each man for symptoms in the morning.'

'Consider it done. Sarah, I could use another favor from you as well. Okay if I pick you up in the morning?'

'Sure, that would be fine. And, Dirk . . . I pray that you are not infected.'

'Don't you worry,' he replied confidently. 'There's way too much rum in my blood to keep any bugs alive.'

Dirk immediately called Captain Burch, and, with Leo Delgado's help, quickly contacted each crew member who had sailed on the *Deep Endeavor*. To their relief, none of the men reported signs of illness, and all appeared at the NUMA field office the next morning.

As promised, Dirk picked up Sarah at her apartment early in the morning, electing to drive the big '58 Chrysler.

'My word, this is an enormous car,' Sarah declared as she climbed into the finned behemoth.

'It's the original definition of heavy metal,' Dirk grinned as he stoked the car out of the parking lot and drove toward the NUMA building.

Many of the *Deep Endeavor*'s crew greeted Sarah warmly when she arrived before the assembled group, and she noted to herself how the entire crew behaved more like close family members than coworkers.

'It is great to see my NUMA friends again,' she said, addressing the crew. 'As you may know, my associate Irv Fowler, who was on the ship with us, has been diagnosed with smallpox. The smallpox virus is highly contagious and it is critical that those infected be quickly isolated. I will need to know if any of you have suffered from the following symptoms since Irv, Sandy, and I left the *Deep Endeavor*: fever, headache, backache, severe abdominal pain, malaise, delirium, or rashes on the face, arms, or legs.'

One by one, she examined the apprehensive crew, taking temperatures and grilling each man or woman on signs of the deadly disease. Even Dirk and Captain Burch were subject to her checkup, after which Sarah gave a noticeable sigh of relief.

'Captain, just three of your crewmen are showing minor flulike signs of illness, which may or may not be preliminary symptoms of the virus. I request that these men remain isolated until we can complete their blood tests. Your remaining crew should avoid large public venues for at least a few more days. I would like to do a follow-up check at the end of the week, but it appears promising there has been no outbreak among the ship's crew.'

'That is good news,' Burch replied with audible relief. 'Seems odd to me that the virus did not spread easily through a confined ship.'

'Patients are most infectious after the onset of rash, which typically occurs twelve to fourteen days after exposure. Irv was well off the boat and working in Anchorage when he reached that stage, so it's possible that the virus had not spread while we were aboard. Captain, I would ensure that his stateroom on the *Deep Endeavor* is thoroughly sanitized, along with all linen and dining ware aboard the ship, just to be safe.'

'I'll see that it's taken care of right away.'

'It would appear that the source of the smallpox outbreak was on Yunaska,' Dirk speculated.

'I think so,' Sarah replied. 'It's a wonder that you and Jack were not exposed when you picked us up off the island.'

'Our protective gear may have saved us.'

''Thank God,' she said gratefully.

'It would seem that our mysterious friends on the fishing boat may have been dabbling with something even nastier than cyanide. Which reminds me . . . the favor I asked?'

Dirk led Sarah to the Chrysler, where he popped open the large trunk lid. Inside was the porcelain bomb canister from the *I-403*, carefully wrapped inside a milk crate. Sarah inspected the item with a quizzical look on her face.

'Okay, I give up. What is it?'

Dirk briefly explained his trip to Fort Stevens and the dive on the Japanese submarine.

'Can you have your lab identify any remaining residue? I have a hunch there may be something to it.'

Sarah stood silent a moment before speaking.

'Yes, we can have it examined,' she said in a serious tone. 'But it will cost you lunch,' she said, finally breaking into a wry smile.

17

Dirk drove Sarah to the state Public Health Lab on Fircrest Campus, where they carefully transferred the fragmented bomb casing into a small working lab room. After some chiding for bringing an explosive into the building, a jovial, slightly balding research scientist named Hal agreed to examine the fragment after the conclusion of a staff meeting.

'Looks like a long lunch is in order. Where shall we go?' Sarah asked.

'I know a quiet spot with a nice water view,' Dirk replied with a mischievous grin.

'Then take me away in the green machine,' she laughed, climbing into the turquoise Chrysler.

Dirk drove the car out of the laboratory's narrow parking lot, easing past a familiar-looking black Cadillac CTS that sat with its engine running. Exiting the campus grounds, he drove south past Seattle's bustling downtown, then turned west, following a road sign to Fauntleroy. Reaching the water's edge of Puget Sound, Dirk turned into the Fauntleroy Ferry Terminal, then steered the Chrysler up a loading ramp and onto the car deck of a waiting automobile ferry. As he parked the Chrysler amid several rows of tightly packed commuter cars, Sarah reached over and squeezed his hand tightly.

'A ferryboat snackbar? Donuts and coffee?' she inquired.

'I think we can do better than that. Let's go upstairs and look at the view.'

Sarah followed him up a stairwell that emptied onto the open upper deck, where they found a vacant bench facing the northern expanse of Puget Sound. A loud blast from the ferry's horn and a gentle nudge beneath their feet told them they were on their way, as two 2,500-horsepower diesel engines gently pushed the 328-foot vessel away from the dock.

It was a crystal clear day on the Sound, the kind that reminded local residents of why they endure the long, drizzly Pacific Northwest winters to call the area home. In the distance, the Cascade and Olympic mountain ranges sparkled along the horizon, almost shimmering against an azure blue sky so intense it felt close enough to touch. The Seattle downtown cut the skyline in a brilliant reflection of steel and glass, with the landmark Space Needle rising like a futuristic monolith from a George Jetson cartoon. Dirk pointed out a half-dozen other ferries plying their human cargoes about the harbor and watched as they dodged large freighters that cruised along the international shipping lanes.

It was only a fifteen-minute ride to their destination of Vashon Island, and when the boat's captain began aligning the ferry to dock Dirk and Sarah made their way back down to the Chrysler. As he held the door open for Sarah to climb into the passenger seat, Dirk glanced down the row of cars parked behind him. Sitting four spaces behind them, a black Cadillac sedan caught his eye. The same black Cadillac that had been parked with the motor running at the Public Health Lab. And, he now recalled, the same Cadillac that he had seen during his drive around Fort Stevens.

'I think I see a friend parked behind us,' Dirk said calmly to Sarah. 'Think I'll go back and say hello. I'll be right back.'

Strolling casually down the row of cars, he observed two Asian men sitting in the Cadillac staring directly at him. As he approached the driver's-side door, he suddenly leaned down and stuck his face into the open window.

'Excuse me, fellas, do you happen to know where the restroom is?' Dirk asked in a hick voice.

The driver, a heavyset goon with a bad crew cut, looked straight ahead, refusing to make eye contact, and slowly shook his head. Dirk looked for, and found, a slight protrusion under the man's coat near his left armpit, the telltale sign of a holstered weapon. Across the car's interior, the accomplice in the passenger seat showed none of the shyness of the driver. A skinny man with long hair and a stringy goatee glared back at Dirk with a menacing grin, a half-smoked cigarette dangling from his lips. On the floorboard between his feet was a large leather case, which concealed something more than a calculator and cell phone, Dirk surmised.

'Find your friend?' Sarah asked when he returned to the Chrysler.

'No,' Dirk replied, shaking his head. 'I was quite mistaken.'

A long blast from the ship's horn followed by two short blasts announced that the ferry was docking and moments later Dirk drove the Chrysler out of the covered car deck and into the bright sunshine. Crossing over the ferry ramp, he drove down a long pier, then turned out of the ferry complex and onto Vashon Island.

Situated on the lower end of Puget Sound, Vashon Island is a thirty-seven-square-mile scenic haven located just minutes from the congested hubbub of Seattle and Tacoma. Reachable only by boat, the island has maintained a quiet, rural tranquility far removed from its metropolitan neighbors. Strawberry and raspberry fields dot the lush wooded landscape, which is inhabited by a bohemian mix of farmers and computer intellectuals seeking a slower pace than that of city life.

Lowering the convertible top so that they could better enjoy the sights and smells of the landscape, Dirk drove south along the Vashon Highway, away from the ferry terminal at the northern tip of the island. Observing in his rearview mirror, he watched the black Cadillac exit the ferry terminal and fall in line behind him, maintaining a half-mile cushion behind the old car. They continued motoring south for several miles, past quaint cabins and farmhouses interspersed among thick groves of pine trees.

'This feels marvelous,' Sarah gushed, stretching her arms above her head and feeling the cool wind rush through her fingers. Dirk smiled to himself, having known too many women who despised riding in a convertible because it mussed up their hair. For him, driving fast in a convertible was like riding a storm out at sea or diving on an unexplored wreck. It was a little added serving of adventure that made life more fun.

Spotting a road sign marked BURTON, Dirk slowed and turned east off the highway, backtracking a short distance on a small side road that led to the tiny hamlet. They meandered past a small group of houses until the road petered out at the drive of a quaint Victorian inn situated right on the water. Built as a summer estate for a Seattle newspaper tycoon at the turn of the century, the three-story structure was agleam in pastel shades of green and lavender. Bright flowers sprouted in large pots and flower boxes were wedged everywhere, throwing a vast array of colors to the eye.

'Dirk, it's beautiful here,' Sarah beamed as he parked the car next to an ornate gazebo. 'How did you discover this place?'

'One of our scientists has a summer home on the island. Claims they have the best king salmon in the state here and I aim to find out.'

Dirk led Sarah to an intimate restaurant at one end of the lodge that continued the Victorian décor theme. Finding it nearly empty, they took a table next to a large picture window that faced east across the sound. After ordering a local Chardonnay, they admired the view across Quartermaster Harbor to a smaller island named Maury. To the southeast, they could see Mt. Rainier standing majestically in the distance.

'Reminds me a little of the Grand Tetons,' Sarah said, fondly recalling the craggy peaks of northwest Wyoming. 'I used to ride horses for miles around Lake Jackson at the base of the Tetons.'

'I bet you're a pretty fair downhill skier as well,' Dirk ventured.

'I banged up a few sets of skis growing up,' she laughed. 'How'd you know?'

'Jackson Hole is right around the corner. Skied it once a few years ago. Terrific snow.'

'I love it there,' Sarah gushed, her hazel eyes glistening. 'But I am surprised to hear that you have been to Jackson. I didn't think that a NUMA special projects director was allowed to leave sight of the ocean.'

It was Dirk's turn to laugh. 'Only on my annual vacation. The Gobi Desert happened to be booked that year,' he grinned. 'So tell me, how did a nice girl from Wyoming end up working at the Centers for Disease Control?'

'It's because I *am* a nice girl from Wyoming,' she

cooed. 'Growing up on my parents' ranch, I was always nursing a sick calf or mending a lame horse. My dad always said I was a softie, but I just loved being around animals and trying to help them. So I studied veterinary medicine in school, and, after bouncing around a few jobs, was able to snag the field epidemiologist job with the CDC. Now I travel the world preventing disease outbreaks and helping sick animals, and I even get paid for it,' she smiled.

Dirk could tell her compassion was genuine. Sarah had a warm heart that seemed to resonate through her. If not employed by the CDC, she would probably be off running a dog shelter or helping a wildlife rescue, with or without a paycheck. With her gazing at Dirk with tender eyes, he was glad she was here with him now.

A waiter appeared to spoil their intimacy, but brought a gourmet meal to the table. Dirk enjoyed a mesquite-grilled king salmon filet, while Sarah dined on Alaskan weathervane scallops she deemed so tender they melted in her mouth. After sharing a fresh raspberry cheesecake for dessert, they took a short stroll hand in hand along the water's edge. Dirk kept an eye out for the two men in the Cadillac, whom he finally observed parked a few blocks away in Burton.

'It's gorgeous here, but I guess we should be getting back,' Sarah said with disappointment. 'We should have the blood test results on your sick crewmen by now, and Hal probably has your bomb canister analysis completed.'

As they approached the car, she turned and hugged Dirk.

'Thanks for a lovely lunch,' she whispered.

'Kidnapping beautiful women in the afternoon is a specialty of mine,' he smiled, then took her in his arms and gave her a long passionate kiss. She responded by wrapping her arms around him, squeezing the back of his waist tightly.

Easing the car out of the parking lot, Dirk meandered slowly down the one-lane thoroughfare of Burton. He glared as he drove by the Cadillac parked in a side alley, the two men waiting for them to pass. As he watched in the rearview mirror, he was somewhat surprised to see the black sedan turn and follow immediately behind him. There was no more pretense of an invisible tail, Dirk thought, which was not a good sign.

The Cadillac followed behind until they reached the intersection of the Vashon Highway. As he stopped to turn, Dirk glanced again in his mirror. He could see the passenger with the goatee reaching down at his feet and pulling something out of the leather case.

A sick feeling hit him in his stomach and, without an instant's hesitation, he mashed down on the accelerator. With tires squealing, the Chrysler whipped onto the highway and sped north.

'Dirk, what are you doing?' Sarah asked with

a bewildered look as she was pushed back into the seat.

In an instant, the Cadillac screeched onto the highway behind them, sending a spray of gravel flying through the air. This time, the Cadillac was not intent on following behind the old Chrysler but nosed into the vacant oncoming traffic lane in order to pull alongside.

'Get down on the floor!' Dirk yelled at Sarah as he watched the black car approach in his side mirror. Confused but comprehending the tone in his voice, Sarah slipped down into the cavernous footwell of the Chrysler and rolled into a ball. Dirk eased off the accelerator and looked to his left as the Cadillac pulled rapidly alongside. The passenger window was rolled down and the young tough grinned sardonically at Dirk. Then he raised an Ingram Mac-10 submachine gun from his lap and leveled it at Dirk's head.

The gunman may have been younger but Dirk's reflexes were faster. By the time the killer's finger pulled the trigger, Dirk was already standing on the brakes. A short burst of fire ricocheted harmlessly across the hood of the Chrysler as it suddenly fell back of the speeding Cadillac in a cloud of burned rubber. The Chrysler's narrow tires screeched in protest as the wheels locked up for a moment before Dirk eased off the brakes. He paused a second, waiting for the Cadillac to react, then saw what he was waiting for. As the brake lights of the Cadillac lit up, he punched the push-button automatic transmission into second gear and stomped the accelerator to the floorboard.

A flood of raw gas charged down the throats of the Chrysler's twin four-barrel carburetors, spraying a gush of combustible fuel to the hungry 392-cubic-inch hemi motor. Packing over 380 horsepower, the Chrysler 300-D was the fastest and most powerful production car in the country in 1958. Showing no signs of its age, the big Chrysler got up and roared off down the road like a charging rhinoceros.

The would-be assassins were caught off guard by the suddenly accelerating Chrysler and swore at each other as the big green car shot by like an arrow. The gunman made an attempt to fire another burst but was too late with his aim, emptying the clip of the burp gun uselessly into the woods. With no oncoming traffic, Dirk cut to the left lane after passing the Cadillac, making it more difficult for the passenger-side gunman to aim his weapon.

'What's happening? Why are they shooting at us?' Sarah cried from the floor.

'Some relatives of our old pals in Alaska, I'm betting,' Dirk yelled over the roar of the engine as he upshifted into third gear. 'Been following us for some time now.'

'Can we escape?' Sarah asked with fear in her voice.

'We can hold our own on the straightaways, but they'll gain on us in the curves. If we can get close to the ferry landing and more people, they should back off,' he replied, hoping his words would hold true.

The Chrysler had opened a wide gap between the two cars, but the Cadillac was inching closer. A narrow bend in the road forced Dirk to ease off the gas slightly in order to keep the 4,500-pound colossus on the road, allowing the lighter and more nimble Cadillac to gain precious feet. The gunman, angry and undisciplined, began emptying a second clip in a rage, shooting wildly at the car. Most of the bullets zinged harmlessly into the Chrysler's trunk, creating a sievelike montage of small round holes. Dirk hunched low in the driver's seat and weaved the car randomly back and forth across the road to avoid presenting a stable target.

'How much farther?' Sarah asked, still hugging the carpeted floor.

'Just a couple of more miles. We'll make it,' Dirk replied, throwing a confident wink toward her.

But internally, Dirk cursed himself. He cursed that he had placed Sarah in such a position of danger and had not called for help earlier when he knew he was being followed. And he cursed that he was unarmed, having no weapon at his disposal to fight back with other than a nearly fifty-year-old car.

Like a vulture stalking its prey, the black Cadillac mimicked every move of the Chrysler, trying desperately to close the gap between the two speeding vehicles. As the cars entered a long straight stretch of the Vashon Highway, Dirk looked down and saw the speedometer needle tickling 125 miles per hour. A blue pickup truck approached from the opposite direction and Dirk eased into the right lane, holding the accelerator firmly to the floor. The Cadillac's driver, unduly intent on overtaking the Chrysler, didn't notice the rapidly approaching truck at first and swerved harshly to the right at the last second, braking reflexively in the slight panic. The move allowed the Chrysler to gain a few more precious feet of pavement and elicited a stream of profanities from the frustrated gunman.

But Dirk's temporary dominance was about to expire. The Vashon Highway began a series of curves and bends at the northern end of the island before it dropped down to the ferry terminal and the racing advantage turned from speed to road handling. Coming hard off the long straightaway, Dirk braked hard into a sweeping left curve, fighting vigorously to keep the big convertible on the road. The more agile Cadillac easily made up lost ground and was soon within a few yards of Dirk's bumper. Once more, he heard the sputter of machine-gun fire and ducked his head down low. A burst of fire shattered into the windshield in front of him, turning the glass into a maze of pockmarked cracks and holes. One round came in low and Dirk could feel it nearly graze his cheek as it whizzed by before smashing into the dashboard.

'I already shaved once today, you bastards,' he grumbled, his anger overcoming any feelings of fear.

As he flung the Chrysler into the next turn, the old-fashioned bias-ply tires screeched loudly, leaving a smoking black trail along the roadway. The gunman, having already exhausted two clips, began firing more cautiously to conserve his remaining ammunition. Waiting until the Chrysler entered a right turn, he then peppered the car with quick, point-blank bursts. Foolishly neglecting to shoot out the tires, he maintained his aim on the car's cockpit.

Inside, Dirk and Sarah were showered with a continuous deluge of broken glass, plastic, and metal shards as streams of bullets ripped into the interior. Dirk did his best to guide the car down the center of the road, glancing repeatedly at his side mirrors to ensure the Cadillac didn't accelerate alongside for a better kill shot. Several times he veered the Chrysler sharply to one side, nearly smashing the front end of the Cadillac before its driver backed down and maintained a five-foot buffer off his tail.

Dirk felt like a boxer in the ring, ducking and weaving his head and body up, down, and side to side in order to see the road while avoiding a rain of lead. He cringed while sliding the car through a right turn as he watched a ribbon of holes appear in a neat line down the hood. The burst punctured the radiator, sending a white plume of steam hissing out the grille and hood. Time was short now, he realized. Without coolant, the engine would overheat and seize up. He and Sarah would then be easy pickings.

As they approached the northern tip of the island,

he tried a last gambit. Approaching a narrow left turn ahead, Dirk eased into the center of the road and slowed slightly to pull the Cadillac in close. Then, with both feet on the pedal, he stomped on the brakes as hard as he could. Through the screaming tires and cloud of burned rubber, the Cadillac kissed the back of the Chrysler hard before its driver slammed on the brakes. But his gamble to decimate the front end of the Cadillac failed. The Chrysler's ancient drum brakes were no match for the Cadillac's four-wheel disc, antilock braking system, and the newer car nearly came to a stop while the big Chrysler was still skidding down the road. The Cadillac's driver realized the ploy and kept a healthy separation distance now. Dirk let off the brakes and jammed on the accelerator, hoping to keep making ground. There was little left he could do now.

The two cars had reached the top of the last rise on the northern section of the island. From there, the road gradually snaked downhill toward the water's edge, passing a few lanes of shops and houses before terminating at the ferry landing. Dirk noticed a small stream of cars beginning to dot the highway from the opposite direction, recent emigrants from a ferry stop, he surmised.

Despite the additional traffic on the road, the machine-gun firing from behind continued. The assassins had crossed the line and were bent on killing Dirk and Sarah regardless of who got in their way. Dirk gave Sarah a quick glance and forced a grin. Her soft eyes showed a mixture of both fear and trust. Trust that he would somehow find a way to save them. He gripped the steering wheel tightly, more determined than ever to shield her from harm.

But there were only seconds to act. The old Chrysler, which now resembled the remains of a B-2 bomber target, was clearly on its last legs. Smoke billowed from under the hood, accompanied by a throbbing melody of knocks and groans from the nearly spent motor. Sparks flew from beneath the frame, where a broken exhaust pipe scraped the pavement with a torturous grind. Even the tires had generated flat spots from the hard braking and thumped out of round. The temperature gauge, Dirk noted, had been firmly pegged in the red for several minutes now.

Above the roar, he could hear the blast of a ferry horn just ahead as they wound closer to the water. From behind, the squeal of the Cadillac's tires and the peppering sound of machine-gun fire rattled in his ears. The big Chrysler suddenly lurched as the hemi engine began to mortally overheat. Dirk's eyes raced over the landscape, searching for a sheriff's car, a bank that might employ an armed guard, any sort of help he might solicit as a last means of defense. But all he saw were quaint little bayside homes with small flower gardens.

Then, looking down the hill toward the approaching ferry terminal, he had a thought. Highly improbable, he figured, but at this point they had nothing to lose.

Sarah looked up and noticed a look of confident resolve suddenly appear on his face.

'What is it, Dirk?' she yelled above the din.

'Sarah, my dear,' he replied assuredly, 'I think our ship has come in.'

18

Larry Hatala watched as the final car in line, a pea green 1968 Volkswagen microbus, chugged up the ramp and onto the ferry. A thirty-year veteran of the Washington State Department of Transportation, the grizzled Vashon Island terminal attendant shook his head and smiled at the driver of the old hippie car, a bearded man in bandana and granny glasses. Once the VW was safely aboard the ferry, Hatala lowered a wooden orange-and-white signal arm that halted any pending traffic at the end of the pier. His work complete until the next boat arrived in thirty minutes, Hatala removed a weathered baseball cap and wiped his forehead with a sleeve, then threw a cheerful wave of the cap to a fellow employee on the departing ferry. A young man in a gray jumpsuit finished yanking a guardrail across the stern of the ferry, then returned Hatala's wave with a mock military salute. As the pilot let loose a deep blast from the air horn, Hatala untied a safety docking line and tossed the loose end across to the ferry, where his coworker neatly coiled it for the next stop.

The blast from the ferry horn had barely ceased echoing across the water when Hatala's ears detected an unusual sound. It was the wail of tires screeching violently on asphalt. Peering up the road, he could detect only a periodic flash through the trees of two cars roaring down the hill. The whine of revving engines and squealing tires grew closer, punctuated by a popping sound Hatala recognized from his Navy days as gunfire. Finally, the cars broke free of the trees as they neared the terminal, and Hatala stared in astonishment.

The big green Chrysler looked like a galloping dragon, complete with fire-breathing smoke and steam belching out of its grille. A black-haired man, hunched low in the seat, deftly kept the smoking behemoth on the road at speeds clearly too high for its means. Thirty feet behind, a sleek black Cadillac sedan followed in hot pursuit, a young Asian man dangling out the passenger window wildly firing an automatic weapon that did more damage to the trees bordering the road than to his intended target. To Hatala's complete horror, the green convertible spun into the ferry landing entrance and headed onto the pier.

By all rights, the old Chrysler should have up and died long before. A withering rain of fire had plastered the car in lead, cutting through wires, hoses, and belts, in addition to pasting the body and interior with myriad holes. Burning oil mixed with radiator fluid spewed from the red-hot motor that was nearly drained of fluids. But with an apparent heart of its own, the old Chrysler was not quite ready to give up, offering one last gasp of power.

'Dirk, where are we now?' Sarah asked, unable to see from her spot on the floor. A rackety sound of tires on wood told her they were no longer traveling on the highway.

'We have a boat to catch,' Dirk grimaced. 'Hang on tight.'

He could see a man waving his arms wildly at the end of the pier, some fifty yards ahead. Beyond the pier's edge, he could detect a churning in the water from the ferry's propellers as the boat began to pull away from the dock. It was going to be close.

Behind him, the Cadillac lost ground briefly, having nearly missed the turn when Dirk whipped onto the pier. The driver was doggedly determined to stay on Dirk's tail and accelerated hard, oblivious to the shortening pier and departure of the ferry. The gunman, too, was engrossed with the chase, intent on putting a bullet into the obstinate driver who had somehow avoided his previous blasts.

Dirk also kept his foot down hard on the accelerator, but for a different reason. He held his breath, hoping the Chrysler would hold together for just a few more seconds. Though the end of the pier was now just a few yards away, it seemed to take an eternity to reach it. Meanwhile, the ferry continued to inch farther into the sound.

A pair of boys bound for a fishing excursion at the end of the pier ran scrambling behind a piling as the two cars tore by, their poles sacrificed to the speeding machines when they jumped for cover. To

Dirk's surprise, the man at the end of the pier stopped waving and raised the orange-and-white traffic barrier, apparently realizing the futility of trying to stop the barreling mass of Detroit iron that was charging his way. As he roared by, Dirk nodded thanks at Hatala and threw him a jaunty wave. Hatala simply stared back, dumbfounded.

The Chrysler's hefty V-8 engine was now knocking like a pounding sledgehammer, but the old beast hung on and gave Dirk every last ounce of energy it could muster. The big convertible stormed up the ramp at the end of the pier and burst into the air like a cannon shot. Dirk gripped the steering wheel hard and braced for the impact as he watched a forty-foot ribbon of blue water pass beneath the car. Screams filled the air as shocked passengers on the rear of the ferry scrambled to avoid the path of the green monstrosity hurtling through space toward them. The momentum of the car and the angle of the ramp sent the Chrysler sailing through the air in an almost picture-perfect arc before gravity took hold and pulled the nose of the car down fast. But they had cleared the open water and would plunge down onto the ferry.

Just a few feet inboard on the open stern, the Chrysler's front wheels slammed down onto the deck, the tires immediately bursting from the force with a bang. A split second later, the rear wheels dropped down, smashing through a low railing just inches from the stern edge. A section of the handrail kicked up into a wheel well, where it became wedged as the full weight of the car crashed down. It proved to be a lifesaver. Rather than skidding wildly into the rows of cars parked on the auto deck, the wedged railing dug into the wooden deck like an anchor. The massive old car bounded twice, then skidded slowly to a stop just twenty feet from where it struck the deck, lightly smacking the pea green Volkswagen bus.

The black Cadillac did not fare as well. Just a few seconds behind, its driver saw too late that the ferry had left the dock. Too panicked to try to stop, the driver kept his foot down on the accelerator and soared off the pier in tandem with the Chrysler. Only by now, the ferry had moved beyond its path.

With the gunman screaming a bloodcurdling cry, the Cadillac soared gracefully into the sky before nosing hard into the stern of the ferryboat with a thunderous crash. The front bumper kissed the painted letters of the ferryboat's name, *Issaquah*, just above the waterline before the entire car crumpled like an accordion. A large spray of water flew up as the mangled wreckage of the car plopped into the water and sank to forty feet, carrying its crushed occupants to a watery grave.

In the Chrysler, Dirk shook off the daze of the impact and assessed their injuries. He felt a sprained knee and sore hip on himself as he wiped away a flow of blood from his lower lip, gashed open on the steering wheel. But otherwise all parts seemed to be working. Sarah looked up from the floor in a twisted angle, where she forced a smile through a painful grimace.

'I think my right leg is broken,' she said calmly, 'but otherwise I'm okay.'

Dirk lifted her out of the car and gently set her on the deck as a crowd of passengers crept in to offer assistance. In front of them, a door flung open on the VW bus and out popped its overage hippie driver, complete with ponytail and beer belly half-hidden under a tie-dyed Grateful Dead T-shirt. His eyes bulged as he surveyed the scene behind him. Smoke oozed from the smoldering wreckage of the Chrysler, tainting the air with the odor of burned oil and rubber. The car's metal skin was festooned with bullet holes from front to back, while broken glass and shreds of leather upholstery littered the interior. The front tires were splayed out from bursting on impact, while a metal guardrail poked out oddly from one of the rear wheel wells. A deep gash in the deck tailed back from the wreck like some sort of violent bread crumb trail. Dirk smiled weakly at the man as he wandered closer while surveying the scene.

Shaking his head, the old hippie finally quipped, 'Far out, man. I sure hope you have insurance.'

It took only a few hours for the authorities to commandeer a nearby work barge and position it off the ferry landing. Its twenty-ton crane easily hoisted the crushed Cadillac from the bottom and dumped it on the greasy deck of the old barge. A paramedic crew carefully extricated the mashed bodies from the vehicle and transferred them to the county morgue. Their cause of death was cited simply as blunt injury from motor vehicle accident.

At NUMA's request, the FBI interceded and opened a federal investigation into the incident. Initial attempts to identify the gunmen came up empty when no forms of ID were found on the bodies, and the Cadillac was discovered to be a stolen rental car. Immigration finally ascertained that the men were Japanese nationals who had entered the country illegally through Canada.

At the Seattle/King County morgue, the chief coroner shook his head in irritation as yet another investigator arrived to examine the bodies.

'Can't get any work done around here as long as we're holding these so-called Japanese gangsters,' he grumbled to an underling, as yet another pair of Feds left the storage facility.

The assistant medical examiner, an ex-Army doctor who had once been stationed in Seoul for a year, nodded in agreement.

'We might as well install a revolving door on the ice room,' he joked.

'I'll just be happy when the paperwork arrives to release them for transport back to Japan.'

'I hope that's their right home,' the assistant pathologist said, slowly sliding the bodies back into a refrigerated locker. 'If you ask me, I still say they look like a couple of Koreans.'

19

After twelve hours at Sarah's hospital bedside, Dirk finally convinced the doctors at Seattle's Swedish Providence Medical Center to release Sarah the following morning. Though a broken leg didn't normally warrant an overnight stay, the cautious medical staff was concerned about trauma from the accident and kept her there for observation. She was fortunate in that the break to her tibia, or shinbone, did not require any rods or screws to align. The doctors wrapped her leg in a heavy plaster cast and pumped her full of painkillers, then signed her release.

'Guess I can't take you dancing anytime soon,' Dirk joked as he pushed her out the hospital exit in a wheelchair.

'Not unless you want a black-and-blue foot,' she replied, grimacing at the heavy cast around her lower leg.

Despite insisting that she was well enough to work, Dirk took Sarah home to her stylish apartment in Seattle's Capitol Hill district. Gently carrying her to a leather couch, he propped her broken leg up on a large pillow.

'Afraid I've been called back to Washington,' he said, stroking her silky hair as she adjusted the pillows behind her back. 'Have to leave tonight. I'll make sure Sandy checks in on you.'

'I probably won't be able to keep her away,' she grinned. 'But what about the sick crew members of the *Deep Endeavor*? We need to find out if they are all right,' she said, struggling to rise from the couch. The drugs made her feel as if her mind and body were enshrouded in a coat of honey and she fought to remain lucid against the overwhelming desire to sleep.

'Okay,' he said, gently pushing her back down and bringing a portable phone to her. 'You get one phone call, then it's lights out for you.'

As she called the Public Health Lab, he checked to see that her kitchen was stocked with groceries. Peering into a scantly filled refrigerator, he idly wondered why unmarried women always seemed to have less food in the house than the single men he knew.

'Great news,' she called in a slurred voice after hanging up the phone. 'The tests on the sick crewmen all came back negative. No sign of the smallpox virus.'

'That is great news,' Dirk said, returning to her side. 'I'll let Captain Burch know before I leave for the airport.'

'When will I see you again?' she asked, squeezing his hand.

'Just a quick trip to headquarters. I'll be back before you know it.'

'You better,' she replied, her eyelids drooping low. Dirk leaned over and brushed her hair aside, then kissed her gently on the forehead. As he stood up, he could see that she had already fallen asleep.

Dirk slept soundly on his cross-country red-eye flight, popping awake well rested as the wheels of the NUMA jet touched down at Ronald Reagan Washington National Airport just after eight in the morning. An agency car was left waiting for him at the government terminal, and he drove himself out of the parking lot under a light drizzle. As he exited the airport, he cast a long glance toward a dilapidated-looking hangar situated off one of the runways. Though his father was out of the country, he still had the urge to visit the old man's hideout and tinker with one of his many antique autos stored there. Business before pleasure, he told himself, and wheeled the loaner car onto the highway.

Following the George Washington Memorial Parkway out of the airport, he drove north, passing the Pentagon on his left as he followed the banks of the Potomac River. A short distance later, he turned off the highway and angled toward a towering green glass building that housed the NUMA headquarters. Passing through an employee security gate, he pulled into an underground garage and parked. Opening the car trunk, he hoisted a large duffel bag over his shoulder, then rode the employees' elevator to the tenth floor, where the doors opened onto an elaborate maze of quietly humming computer hardware.

Established with a budget that would make a third

world dictator whimper, the NUMA Ocean Data Center computer network was a marvel of state-of-the-art computer processing. Buried within its massive data storage banks was the finest collection of oceanographic resources in the world. Real-time inputs of weather, current, temperature, and bio-diversity measurements were collected via satellite from hundreds of remote sea sites from around the world, giving a global snapshot of ocean conditions and trends at any given moment. Links to the leading research universities provided data on current investigations in geology, marine biology, and undersea flora and fauna research, as well as engineering and technology. NUMA's own historical reference library contained literally millions of data sources and was a constant reservoir of information for research institutes the world over.

Dirk found the maestro behind the vast computer network, sitting behind a horseshoe console munching a bear claw with one hand while tapping a keyboard with the other. To a stranger, Hiram Yaeger resembled a groupie from a Bob Dylan concert. His lean body was clad in faded Levi's and matching jeans jacket over a white T-shirt, complemented by a pair of scuffed cowboy boots on his feet. With his long gray hair tied in a ponytail, his appearance belied the fact that he lived in a high-end Maryland suburb with an ex-model wife and drove a BMW 7 Series. He caught sight of Dirk over a pair of granny glasses and smiled in greeting.

'Well, the young Mr. Pitt,' he grinned warmly.

'Hiram, how are you?'

'Not having smashed my car, nor destroyed an agency helicopter, I'd have to say I'm doing quite well,' he joked. 'By the way, has our esteemed director been advised of the loss of one of NUMA's flying assets?'

'Yes. Fortunately, with Dad and Al still over in the Philippines the bite was tempered somewhat.'

'They've had their hands full with a toxic spill they ran across near Mindanao, so your timing was good,' Yaeger said. 'So tell me, to what do I owe the pleasure of your visit?'

'Well,' Dirk hesitated, 'it's your daughters. I would like to go out with them.'

The color drained from Yaeger's thin boyish face for a moment as he took Dirk's proposal seriously. Yaeger's twin daughters, finishing their last year of private high school, were his pride and joy. For seventeen years, he had successfully scared away any male suitors who had the remotest inkling of touching his girls. God forbid the giddiness they'd show over the rugged and charismatic Dirk.

'You so much as mention their names around me and I'll have you off the payroll with a ruined credit rating that will take five lifetimes to fix,' Yaeger threatened.

It was Dirk's turn to laugh, chuckling loudly at Yaeger's vulnerable soft spot. The computer genius softened and grinned as well at Dirk's idle ploy.

'Okay, the girls are off-limits. But what I really want is a little time with you and Max before my meeting with Rudi later this morning.'

'Now, that I can approve,' Yaeger replied with a firm nod of the head. The bear claw now demolished, he applied both hands in a finger dance over the keyboard to conjure up his bionic confidante, Max.

No fellow computer programmer, Max was an artificial intelligence system with a virtual interface in the form of a holographic image. The brainchild of Yaeger to aid in researching voluminous databases, he had cleverly modeled the visual interface after his wife, Elsie, adding a sensual voice and saucy personality. On a platform opposite the horseshoe console, an attractive woman with auburn hair and topaz eyes suddenly appeared. She was dressed in a skimpy halter top that revealed her navel and a very short leather skirt.

'Good morning, gentlemen,' the three-dimensional image murmured.

'Hi, Max. You remember the younger Dirk Pitt?'

'Of course. Nice to see you again, Dirk.'

'You're looking good, Max.'

'I'd look better if Hiram would stop dressing me in Britney Spears outfits,' she replied with disdain, rolling her hands down her body.

'All right. Tomorrow it will be Prada,' Yaeger promised.

'Thank you.'

'Dirk, what is it that you'd like to ask Max?' Yaeger prompted.

'Max, what can you tell me about the Japanese efforts at chemical and biological warfare during World War Two?' Dirk asked, turning serious.

Max hesitated for a moment as the question generated a massive search through thousands of databases. Not just limiting it to oceanographic resources, Yaeger had wired the NUMA network into a diverse multitude of government and public information resources, ranging from the Library of Congress to the Securities and Exchange Commission. Sifting through the mass of information, Max consolidated the data points into a concisely summarized reply.

'The Japanese military conducted extensive research and experimentation into chemical and biological weaponry both during and preceding World War Two. Primary research and deployment occurred in Manchuria, under the direction of the occupying Japanese Imperial Army after they had seized control of northeast China in 1931. Numerous facilities were constructed throughout the region as test centers, under the guise of lumber mills or other false fronts. Inside the facilities, Chinese captives were subject to a wide variety of human experiments with germ and chemical compounds. The Qiqihar facility, under the command of Army Unit 516, was the largest Japanese chemical weapons research and test site, although chemical weapons manufacture actually took place on the Japanese mainland. Changchun, under Army

Unit 100, and the sprawling Ping Fan facility, under Army Unit 731, were the major biological warfare research and test centers. The facilities were in fact large prisons, where local criminals and derelicts were sent and used as test subjects, though few of the captives would survive their incarceration.'

'I've read about Unit 731,' Dirk commented. 'Some of their experiments made the Nazis look like Boy Scouts.'

'Allegations of inhuman experiments performed by the Japanese, particularly in Unit 731, are nearly endless. Chinese prisoners, and even some Allied prisoners of war, were routinely injected with an assortment of deadly pathogens, as their captors sought to determine the appropriate lethal dosage. Biological bombs were dropped on prisoners staked to the ground in order to test delivery systems. Many experiments took place outside the walls of the facilities. Typhoid bacilli germs were intentionally released into local village wells, resulting in widespread outbreaks of fever and death. Rats carrying plague-infected fleas were released in congested urban areas as a test of the speed and ferocity of infection. Children were even considered an acceptable target. In one experiment, local village children were given chocolates filled with anthrax, which they gratefully devoured, with horrifying side effects.'

'That's revolting,' Yaeger said, shaking his head. 'I hope the perpetrators paid for their crimes.'

'For the most part, they did not,' Max continued.

'Nearly to a man, those in charge of the chemical and biological army units avoided prosecution as war criminals. The Japanese destroyed much of the documentation, and the camps themselves, before their surrender. American intelligence forces, unaware of the extent of horrors, or, in some cases, seeking to obtain the results of the ghastly experiments, looked the other way at the atrocities. Many of the Imperial Army medical professionals who worked in the death camps went on to become respected business leaders in Japan's postwar pharmaceutical industry.'

'With blood on their hands,' Dirk muttered.

'No one knows for sure, but experts estimate that at least two hundred thousand Chinese died as a result of Japanese chemical and biological warfare activity during the thirties and forties. A large percentage of the casualties were innocent civilians. It was a wartime tragedy that has only recently received much attention from historians and scholars.'

'Man's inhumanity to man never ceases to amaze,' Yaeger said solemnly.

'Max, exactly what pathogens and chemicals did the Japanese work with?' Dirk asked.

'It might be easier to ask which agents they didn't experiment with. Their known research in bacteria and viruses ranged from anthrax, cholera, and bubonic plague to glanders, smallpox, and typhus, with experiments conducted in pretty much everything else in between. Among the chemical agents employed in weaponry were phosgene, hydrogen cyanide, sulfur mustard, and lewisite. It is unknown how much was actually deployed in the field, again due to the fact that the Japanese destroyed most of their records as they retreated from China at the end of the war.'

'How would these agents have been used on the battlefield?'

'Chemical agents, possessing a long shelf life, are perfectly suitable for munitions. The Japanese manufactured a large quantity of chemical munitions, mostly in the form of grenades, mortars, and a wide range of artillery shells. Thousands of these weapons were even left behind in Manchuria at the war's end. The Japanese biological delivery systems were less successful due to the sensitive nature of the arming agents. Development of a practical biological artillery shell proved difficult, so much of the Japanese effort at fabricating the release of biological agents was focused on aerial bombs. Known records seem to indicate that the Japanese scientists were never completely satisfied with the effectiveness of the bio bombs they developed.'

'Max, are you aware of the use of porcelain as a bomb-casing material for these chemical or biological agents?'

'Why, yes, as a matter of fact. Steel bombs generated excessive heat upon explosion that would destroy the biological pathogens, so the Japanese turned to ceramics. It is known that a variety of porcelain bomb canisters were tested in China as aerial delivery systems for the biological agents.'

Dirk felt a lump in his stomach. The *I-403* had indeed been on a mission of death with its biological bombs back in 1945. Fortuitously, the submarine had been sunk, but was that, in fact, the last of its failed mission?

Yaeger broke his concentration. 'Max, this is all new history to me. I had no idea the Japanese actually used chemical and biological weapons in battle. Were they ever employed outside of China, against American forces?'

'The Japanese deployment of chemical and biological weapons was primarily restricted to the Chinese theater of war. Limited instances of their usage were also reported in Burma, Thailand, and Malaysia. My data sources show no recorded use of bio/chemical agents in battle with Western Allied forces, perhaps due to Japanese fear of reprisal. It is suspected that chemical weapons would have been employed in defense of the homeland, had an invasion of Japan been necessary. Of course, your father's discovery proves that chemical munitions were to be stockpiled in the Philippines for possible deployment in defense of the islands.'

'My father's discovery?' Dirk asked. 'I don't understand.'

'I'm sorry, Dirk, let me explain. I received a toxin assessment from the *Mariana Explorer* taken from an ordnance sample recovered by your father and Al Giordino.'

'You've completed your database search on the arsenic sample already? I thought you said you wouldn't have that completed until after lunch,' Yaeger asked the hologram.

'Sometimes, I can just be brutally efficient,' she replied, throwing her nose in the air.

'What's the connection?' Dirk asked, still confused.

'Your father and Al traced a toxic arsenic leak to an old cargo ship that apparently sank on a coral reef near Mindanao during World War Two. The arsenic was leaking from a shipment of artillery shells carried in the ship's hold,' Yaeger explained.

'One-hundred-five-millimeter shells, to be precise,' Max added. 'Ammunition for a common artillery gun used by the Japanese Imperial Army. Only the contents weren't arsenic, per se.'

'What did you find?' Yaeger asked.

'The actual contents were a mixture of sulfur mustard and lewisite. A popular chemical munitions concentrate from the thirties, it acts as a fatal blistering agent when released as a gas. Lewisite is an arsenic derivative, which accounts for the toxic readings found in the Philippines. The Japanese produced thousands of mustard/lewisite shells in Manchuria, some of which were deployed against the Chinese. Some of these old buried chemical munitions are still being dug up today.'

'Was the Japanese Navy connected with the deployment of these weapons?' Dirk asked.

'The Japanese Imperial Navy was actively involved

with chemical weapons production at its Sagami Naval Yard, and was believed to have had four additional storage arsenals at Kure, Yokosuka, Hiroshima, and Sasebo. But the Navy possessed only a fraction of the estimated 1.7 million chemical bombs and shells produced during the war, and no records indicate they were ever used in any naval engagements. The biological weapons research was funded through the Imperial Army and, as I mentioned, centered in occupied China. A primary conduit for the research activity was the Army Medical School in Tokyo. It is unknown whether the Navy had any involvement through the medical school, as the college was destroyed by wartime bombing in 1945.'

'So no wartime records exist that show chemical or biological weapons were ever assigned onboard Navy vessels?'

'None that were publicly released,' Max said, shaking her holographic head. 'The bulk of the captured Japanese wartime records, including those of the Navy Ministry, were consigned to the National Archives. As a gesture of goodwill, most of the documents were later returned to the Japanese government. Only a fraction of the records were copied, however, and even a smaller portion have ever been translated.'

'Max, I'd like to explore the Naval Ministry records for information on the mission of a particular Japanese submarine, the *I-403*. Can you determine whether these records might still exist?'

'I'm sorry, Dirk, but I don't have access to that portion of the National Archives' data records.'

Dirk turned to Yaeger with an arched brow and gave him a long, knowing look.

'The National Archives, eh? Well, that should be a lot less dangerous than tapping into Langley,' Yaeger acceded with a shrug.

'That's the old Silicon Valley hacker I know and love,' Dirk replied with a laugh.

'Give me a couple of hours and I'll see what I can do.'

'Max,' Dirk said, looking at the transparent woman in the eye, 'thank you for the information.'

'My pleasure, Dirk,' she replied seductively. 'I'm happy to be at your service any time.'

Then, in an instant, she vanished. Yaeger already had his nose against a computer monitor, fingers flying over a keyboard, completely engrossed in his subversive mission at hand.

At promptly ten o'clock, Dirk entered a plush executive conference room, still carrying the large duffel bag over his shoulder. Thick azure carpet under his feet complemented the dark cherrywood conference table and matching wood paneling on the walls, which were dotted with ancient oil paintings of American Revolutionary warships. A thick pane of glass stretched the length of one wall, offering a bird's-eye view of the Potomac River and the Washington Mall across the water. Seated at the table, two stone-faced men in dark suits listened attentively as a diminutive man in horn-rimmed glasses discussed the *Deep Endeavor*'s recent events in the Aleutian Islands. Rudi Gunn stopped in midsentence and popped to his feet as Dirk entered the room.

'Dirk, good of you to return to Washington so quickly,' he greeted warmly, his bright blue eyes beaming through the thick pair of eyeglasses. 'Glad to see your ferry landing injuries were minor,' he added, eyeing Dirk's swollen lip and bandaged cheek.

'My companion broke her leg, but I managed to escape with just a fat lip. We fared a little better than the other guys,' he said with a smirk, 'whoever they were. It's good to see you again, Rudi,' he added, shaking the hand of NUMA's longtime assistant director.

Gunn escorted him over and introduced him to the other two men.

'Dirk, this is Jim Webster, Department of Homeland Security special assistant, Information Analysis and Infrastructure Protection,' he said, waving a hand toward a pale-skinned man with cropped blond hair, 'and Rob Jost, assistant director of Maritime and Land Security, Transportation Security Administration, under DHS.' A rotund, bearish-looking man with a flush red nose nodded at Dirk without smiling.

'We were discussing Captain Burch's report of your rescue of the CDC team on Yunaska Island,' Gunn continued.

'A fortunate thing we happened to be in the area.

I'm just sorry we weren't able to reach the two Coast Guardsmen in time.'

'Given the apparently high levels of toxins that were released near the station, they really didn't have much of a chance from the beginning,' Webster said.

'You confirmed that they died from cyanide poisoning?' Dirk asked.

'Yes. How did you know? That information hasn't been made public.'

'We recovered a dead sea lion from the island, which a CDC team in Seattle examined after we returned. They found that it had been killed by cyanide inhalation.'

'That is consistent with the autopsy reports for the two Coast Guardsmen.'

'Have you uncovered any information on the boat that fired at us, and presumably released the cyanide?'

After an uncomfortable pause, Webster replied, 'No additional information has been obtained. Unfortunately, the description provided matches a thousand other fishing boats of its kind. It is not believed to have been a local vessel, and we are now working with the Japanese authorities to investigate leads in their country.'

'So you believe there is a Japanese connection. Any ideas on why someone would launch a chemical attack on a remote weather station in the Aleutians?'

'Mr. Pitt,' Jost interrupted, 'did you know the men who tried to kill you in Seattle?'

'Never saw them before. They appeared to be

semiprofessionals, more than just a pair of hired street hoods.'

Webster opened a file on the table before him and slid over a crinkled photograph in the form of a small postcard. Dirk silently looked at the black-and-white image of a hardened Japanese woman of fifty glaring violently into the camera lens.

'An homage card of Fusako Shigenobu, former revolutionary leader of the JRA,' Webster continued. 'Found it in the wallet of one of your would-be assassins after we fished them out of the sound.'

'What's the JRA?' Dirk asked.

'The Japanese Red Army. An international terrorist cell that dates to the seventies. Believed to have been broken up with the arrest of Shigenobu in 2000, they appear to have staged a deadly resurgence in activity.'

'I've read that the prolonged weakness in Japan's economy has spawned renewed interest in fringe cults by the Japanese youth,' Gunn added.

'The JRA has attracted more than a few bored youths. They have claimed responsibility for the assassinations of our ambassador to Japan and deputy chief of mission, as well as the explosion at the SemCon plant in Chiba. These were all very professional hits. The public outrage, as you are no doubt aware, is straining our relations with Tokyo.'

'We suspect the JRA may have been behind the cyanide attack on Yunaska, as a prelude to a more deadly strike in a major urban area,' Jost added.

'And also behind the smallpox infection of the Yunaska scientist Irv Fowler,' Dirk stated.

'We have not established that link,' Webster countered. 'Our analysts suspect that the scientist may have contracted the disease in Unalaska, from a local Aleut. Japanese authorities do not believe the JRA is sophisticated enough to obtain and disperse the smallpox virus.'

'I might think otherwise,' Dirk cautioned.

'Mr. Pitt, we are not here to gather your conspiracy theories,' Jost remarked in a belittling tone. 'We are just interested in learning what two JRA agents were doing in the country and why they tried to kill a NUMA diver.'

'That's special projects director,' Dirk replied as he hoisted the duffel bag up onto the conference table. Then, giving it a strong shove, he pushed the bag across the table in the direction of Jost. The arrogant transportation security director scrambled to hoist a cup of coffee out of the way before the bag slid up against his chest.

'Your answer is in there,' Dirk stated brusquely.

Webster stood and unzipped the bag as Jost and Gunn looked on intently. Carefully wrapped in foam padding was a large section of the bomb canister that Dirk had recovered from the *I-403*. The silver-porcelain casing was split open, revealing a segmented interior, with several empty compartments positioned beneath a small nose tip component.

'What is it?' Gunn asked.

'A sixty-year-old dirty bomb,' Dirk replied. He then retold the story of the World War II attack on Fort Stevens, his discovery of the submarine, and the retrieval of the bomb canister.

'An ingenious weapon,' Dirk continued. 'I had the epidemiology lab in Washington test for trace elements, to see what was armed in the payload section.'

'It's made of porcelain,' Webster noted.

'Used to protect biological agents. The nose cone had a simple timed explosive, designed to detonate at a prespecified altitude to disperse the main payload armament. As you can see, it would have been a pretty small charge. Enough to shatter the porcelain casing but not damage the payload with undue heat or pressure.'

Dirk pointed to the interior payload compartments, which were cigar-shaped and stretched nearly to the tail fins.

'It's not clear whether the payload agents were mixed together during flight or upon detonation. But the bomb could obviously carry multiple compounds. The contents might be one or more biological agents with a booster, or a combination of biological or chemical agents. The CDC lab was only able to find a trace chemical agent in one of the compartments on this particular bomb.'

'Cyanide?' Gunn asked.

'None other,' Dirk replied.

'But why utilize more than one payload?' Webster queried.

'To ensure a specific kill zone, and perhaps divert attention. Let's say cyanide was combined with a biological agent. The cyanide gas would have a high lethality in a concentrated area only, whereas the biological agent would create gradual problems over a larger region. Cyanide gas also dissipates quickly, so attack survivors would reenter the drop zone unaware of a secondary danger. But that's just speculation. It's possible the canister design was for a different intent, to strike with a mixture of several chemical agents or biological agents that would produce a higher lethality in combination.'

'So what additional agents were on this bomb?' Gunn asked.

Dirk shook his head slowly. 'That, we don't know. The lab technicians were unable to detect any remaining trace elements from the other compartments. We know that the reason for using porcelain was to house biological agents, but the Japanese experimented with all kinds of organisms, so it could be anything from bubonic plague to yellow fever.'

'Or smallpox?' Gunn asked.

'Or smallpox,' Dirk confirmed.

Jost's face glowed beet red. 'This is a preposterous fantasy,' he grumbled. 'The history lesson is interesting but irrelevant. A modern terrorist group salvaging weapons off a World War Two submarine? A nice story, but how are your biological viruses going to survive under the sea for sixty years, Mr. Pitt? We know the Japanese Red Army. It's a small, tight-knit organization with limited sophistication. Political assassination and planted explosives are within their means. Deep-sea salvage and microbiology are not.'

'I have to agree with Rob,' Webster added in a muted tone. 'Although the cyanide canister is an interesting coincidence with the Yunaska attack, the fact is that cyanide is a compound readily obtainable from many sources. You've admitted that there is no traceable evidence supporting the smallpox source. And we don't know for sure if the missing bomb canister on the sub was lost somewhere else on the vessel or was even loaded on board in the first place.'

Dirk reached over to the duffel bag and unzipped a side pocket, pulling out the still-blinking digital timer he'd found in the torpedo room. 'Maybe you can at least find out where this came from,' he said, handing it to Webster.

'Could have been left behind by a sport diver,' Jost noted.

'A sport diver with a possessive disposition, apparently,' Dirk remarked drily. 'I've been shot at twice now. I don't know who these characters are, but they take their game seriously.'

'I assure you, we have a full investigation under way,' Webster stated. 'I'll have our lab in Quantico reanalyze the bomb casing and take a look at the timer. We will find the perpetrators who caused the death of the two Coast Guardsmen.' The words were firm, but the hollow tone in his voice revealed his lack of confidence in the outcome.

'We can offer a safe house for you, Mr. Pitt, until we have made an apprehension,' he added.

'No, thanks. If these people are who you say they are, then I should have nothing more to fear. After all, how many JRA operatives can they have in the country?' Dirk asked with a penetrating glare.

Webster and Jost looked at each other in unknowing silence. Gunn jumped in diplomatically.

'We appreciate your investigation into the loss of our helicopter,' he said, gently ushering the men to the door. 'Please keep us advised as to any new developments, and, of course, NUMA will be happy to assist in any way we can.'

After they left the room, Dirk sat silently shaking his head.

'They've hushed up the Yunaska incident because they are getting so much flak for the unsolved assassinations in Japan,' Gunn said. 'Homeland Security and the FBI are stymied and are relying on the Japanese authorities to make a break in the case. The last thing they want to admit, on top of that, is that the smallpox case was part of the attack, with just one victim and no terrorists.'

'The evidence may be weak, but there is no reason to foolishly ignore an attack on our own soil,' Dirk stated.

'I'll speak to the admiral about it. The director of the FBI is an old tennis partner of his. He'll make sure it doesn't get brushed under the carpet.'

They were interrupted by a knock on the door, followed by the lean face of Yaeger poking in.

'Sorry to intrude. Dirk, I have something for you.'

'Come in, Hiram. Rudi and I were just plotting the overthrow of the government. Was Max able to access the National Archives' secure records?'

'Does McDonald's have golden arches?' Yaeger replied, feigning insult.

Gunn gave Dirk a sideways glance, then shook his head in amusement. 'If you guys get caught on a security breach, do me a favor and blame it on your father, will you?'

Dirk laughed. 'Sure, Rudi. What did you find, Hiram?'

'The Naval Ministry records were somewhat limited. It's a shame that most all of the original documents were returned to the Japanese government in the fifties. The available records in the archives are, of course, written in Japanese, using a variety of dialects, so I had to set up several translation programs before I could initiate a scan.'

Yaeger paused and poured himself a cup of coffee from a large silver urn before continuing.

'As it is, you are in luck. I found a log of operations orders from the Japanese Sixth Fleet covering the last six months of 1944.'

'Including the *I-403*?' Dirk asked.

'Yep. Its mission of December 1944 evidently had high importance. It was approved by the fleet admiral himself. The actual sailing order was short and sweet.'

Yaeger pulled a sheet of paper from a thin folder and read aloud. '"Proceed northerly route to Pacific West Coast, refueling Amchitka (*Morioka*). Initiate aerial strike with *Makaze* ordnance earliest practicable. Primary Target: Tacoma, Seattle, Vancouver, Victoria. Alternate Target: Alameda, Oakland, San Francisco. With the emperor's blessing."'

'That's a pretty ambitious target list for just two planes,' Gunn remarked.

'Think about it, though,' Dirk said. 'The cities are concentrated enough all to be reached on a single flyover. Two or three biological bombs per city would wreak deadly havoc, if that's in fact what they were. Hiram, you said the ordnance was referred to as *Makaze*. St. Julien Perlmutter found mention of the same term. Any information on what they were?'

'I was curious about that myself,' Yaeger replied. 'I found that the literal translation was "evil wind" or "black wind." But there was no additional information in the official naval records.'

Yaeger paused and sat back in his chair with a knowing look.

'Well, did you find anything else?' Gunn finally goaded.

'It was Max, actually,' Yaeger replied proudly. 'After exhausting the National Archives' data, I had her search the public databases in the U.S. and Japan. In a Japanese genealogy database, she hit pay dirt, locating an obscure diary from a sailor who served aboard the *I-403* during the war.' Holding a printout up to his face, he continued. 'Mechanic First Class Hiroshi Sakora, Imperial Navy Air Corps, was a lucky devil. He came down with appendicitis while the sub was crossing the Pacific on its fateful voyage in December of 1944 and was transferred off the boat and onto the refueling ship in the Aleutian Islands. All his shipmates, of course, went on to perish when the sub was sunk off Washington State.'

'And he made mention of the *I-403*'s mission?' Dirk asked.

'In vivid detail. It turns out that the young Mr. Sakora, in addition to his aircraft mechanic duties, was also in charge of aerial ordnance for the submarine's airplanes. He wrote that before they left port on their final voyage, an Army officer named Tanaka brought aboard an unusual type of aerial bomb that was to be used on the mission. The shipboard morale became very high, he added, when the crew learned they were to make an attack on the United States. But there was much mystery and speculation about the unknown weapon.'

'Did he identify what it was?' Gunn pressed.

'He tried to, but working with the fellow Tanaka was difficult. "A gloomy, overbearing, obstinate taskmaster," he wrote about the officer. Typical Army-Navy rivalry, I suppose, plus the submariners didn't like his being a last-minute addition to the sailing crew. At any rate, he pressed Tanaka for information, but to no avail. Finally, just before he fell ill and was transferred off the sub in the Aleutians, he wriggled the information out of one of the pilots. The pilot, so the story goes, shared some sake with Tanaka and was able to pry the secret payload out of him. It was smallpox.'

'Good God, so it's true!' Gunn exclaimed.

'Apparently so. He wrote that the payload was a freeze-dried virus, which was to be detonated and dispersed at altitude above the most concentrated population points of each city. Within two weeks, an outbreak of smallpox was expected all along the West Coast. With a thirty percent mortality rate, the deaths would have been staggering. The Japanese figured the resulting panic would allow them to negotiate a peace settlement on their terms.'

'The threat of more smallpox bombs on our home soil might very well have changed the resolve of many people to finish the war,' Gunn speculated.

An uneasiness crept over the room as the three considered how history may have played out differently had the *I-403* successfully completed its mission. Their thoughts then turned to the possibility of a more current threat.

'You mentioned that the virus was freeze-dried. So they must have had the ability to store the virus for long periods and then rejuvenate it,' Dirk commented.

'Necessary for a long sea voyage,' Yaeger added. 'According to Max, the Japanese had difficulty in keeping the viruses alive in their munitions for any length of time. They ultimately perfected a way of freeze-drying the virus, for easier handling and longer storage, until the need for activation when deployed. Insert a little H_2O and you're in business.'

'So the virus could still be a viable danger, even after sixty years at the bottom of the sea,' Gunn remarked. 'I guess that answers Jost's question.'

'There's no reason the smallpox wouldn't survive in freeze-dried form if the canisters hadn't cracked during sinking. Since they're made of porcelain, the canisters could survive intact for centuries under-water,' Dirk said. 'Might also explain the various interior segments to the bomb. A compartment with water was needed to rejuvenate the virus.'

'Perhaps it was more fortunate than we know that all but one of the canisters were demolished on the *I-403*,' Gunn remarked.

'That still leaves one canister unaccounted for,' Dirk replied.

'Yes, as well as the other mission ordnance,' Yaeger added.

Dirk and Gunn looked at each other. 'What other mission?' Gunn asked incredulously.

'The *I-411*.'

Yaeger felt their eyes boring right through him.

'Didn't you know?' he asked. 'There was a second submarine, the *I-411*. It, too, was armed with the *Makaze* ordnance and was sent to attack the eastern seaboard of the United States,' Yaeger said quietly, realizing he had just dropped a bomb of his own.

20

It had been a long day for Takeo Yoshida. A crane operator for the Yokohama Port Development Corporation, Yoshida had toiled since six in the morning loading an aged Iberian freighter with container after container of Japanese consumer electronics bound for export. He had just secured the last of the metal containers onto the ship's deck when a radio crackled in the crane's control cabin.

'Yoshida, this is Takagi,' the deep voice of his foreman grumbled. 'Report to Dock D-5 upon completion with *San Sebastian*. A single loading for the vessel *Baekje*. Takagi, out.'

'Affirmed, Takagi-san,' Yoshida answered, holding his disdain under his breath. Just twenty minutes to go on his shift and Takagi gives him a last-minute assignment across the shipyard. Securing the crane, Yoshida walked eight hundred yards across the Honmoku Port Terminal toward Dock D-5, cursing Takagi's name with each step he took. As he approached the end of the pier, he glanced beyond at the waters of the bustling port of Yokohama, where a constant stream of commercial ships jockeyed into position for loading and unloading.

With three hundred meters of waterfront, container terminal D-5 was big enough to handle the largest cargo ships afloat. Yoshida was surprised to find the vessel tied to the dock was not the typical jumbo containership awaiting a load of industrial cargo but a special-purpose cable ship. Yoshida even recognized the *Baekje* as having been built in the nearby Mitsubishi Heavy Industries shipyard. At 436 feet long and with a beam of 133 feet, the stout vessel was designed to lay fiber-optic cable on the seafloor while withstanding the turbulent seas of the North Pacific. With a modern-appearing superstructure and white paint that still glistened, Yoshida could tell that it had not been many years since the high-tech ship slid into Yokohama Bay for the first time. She sported a Korean flag above the bridge mast and a blue lightning bolt across the funnel, which Yoshida recalled was the signature of a Kang Enterprises vessel. Short on Korean history, the crane operator did not know that her name, *Baekje*, represented one of the early Korean tribal kingdoms that dominated the peninsula in the third century A.D.

A pair of dockworkers was securing cables beneath an oblong object on the bed of a large flatbed truck when one of the men turned and greeted Yoshida as he approached.

'Hey, Takeo, ever fly a submarine before?' the man yelled.

Yoshida returned a confused look before realizing that the object on the back of the truck was a small white submersible.

'Takagi says our shift is over once we get it aboard,' the man continued, displaying a missing front tooth as he spoke. 'Lay it aboard and let's go get some Sapporos.'

'Is she secure?' Yoshida asked, waving a hand at the submersible.

'All ready,' the second man replied eagerly, a young kid of nineteen who Yoshida knew had just started work on the docks a few weeks before.

A few yards away, Yoshida noticed a stocky bald man with dark eyes surveying the scene near the ship's gangway. A menacing quality lingered over the man, Yoshida thought. He'd been in enough scrapes in the nearby shipyard bars to recognize which men were legitimate tough guys and which were pretenders. This man was no pretender, he judged.

Shifting thoughts to the taste of a cold Sapporo beer, Yoshida climbed up a high ladder into the cab of the adjacent container crane and fired up its diesel motor. Adeptly working the levers like a concert pianist tickling the ivories, he expertly adjusted the movable boom and sliding block until satisfied, then dropped the hook and block quickly toward the ground, halting it dead center a few inches above the submersible. The two dockworkers quickly slipped a pair of cables over the hoist hook and gave Yoshida the thumbs-up sign. Ever so gently, the crane operator pulled up on the hoist line, the thick cable drawing tight as it wrapped around a drum behind the cab. Slowly, Yoshida raised the twenty-four-ton submersible to a height of fifty feet, hesitating as he waited for its twisting motion to halt before swinging it over to a waiting pad on the *Baekje*'s rear deck. But he never got the chance.

Before it could be seen, and almost before it physically started, Yoshida's experienced hands could feel something wrong through the controls. One of the cables had not been properly secured to the submersible and the tail suddenly slipped down and through a loop in the cable. In an instant, the rear of the sub lunged down and the white metal capsule hung vertically at a grotesque angle, clinging precariously to the single cable wrapped around its nose. Yoshida didn't breathe, and, for a moment, it looked like the dangling submersible would stabilize. But before he could move it an inch, a loud twang burst through the air as the lone securing cable snapped. Like a ton of bricks, the submersible dropped straight to the dock below, landing on its tail with an accordionlike smash before plopping over on its side in distress.

Yoshida grimaced, already thinking of the grief he would suffer at the hands of Takagai, as well as the reams of insurance paperwork he would be forced to fill out. Thankfully, no one was hurt on the dock. As he climbed down from the crane's cab to inspect the damage, Yoshida glanced at the bald man on the gangway, expecting to see a seething fury. Instead, the mysterious man looked back at him with a cold face of stone. The dark eyes, however, seemed to pierce right through him.

The Shinkai three-man submersible was heavily mashed on one end and clearly inoperable. It would be shipped back to its home at the Japanese Marine Science and Technology Center for three months' worth of repairs before it would be seaworthy again. The two dockworkers did not fare as well. Though not fired, Yoshida noticed that the two men did not show up for work the next day, and, in fact, were never seen or heard from again.

Twenty hours later and 250 miles farther to the southwest, an American commercial jetliner touched down at Osaka's modern Kansai International Airport and taxied to the international gate. Dirk stretched his six-foot-four frame as he exited the plane, relieved to be free from the cramped airline seating that only a jockey would find comfortable. Passing quickly through the customs checkpoint, he entered the busy main terminal crowded with businessmen hustling to catch their flights. Stopping briefly, it took just a momentary scan of the terminal before he picked out the woman he was looking for from the mass of humanity.

Standing nearly six feet tall with shoulder-length flaming red hair, Dirk's fraternal twin sister Summer towered like a beacon in a sea of black-haired Japanese. Her pearl gray eyes glistened and her soft mouth broke into a grin as she spotted her brother and waved him over to her.

'Welcome to Japan,' she gushed, giving him a hug. 'How was your flight?'

'Like riding in a sardine can with wings.'

'Good, then you'll feel right at home in the cabin berth I scraped up for you on the *Sea Rover*,' she laughed.

'I was afraid you wouldn't be here yet,' Dirk remarked as he collected his luggage and they made their way to the parking lot.

'When Captain Morgan received word from Rudi that we were to terminate our study of pollutants along the eastern coast of Japan to assist in an emergency search-and-recovery mission, he wasted no time in responding. Fortunately, we were working not far off Shikoku when we got the call so were able to reach Osaka this morning.'

Like her brother, Summer had possessed a deep love of the sea since childhood. After obtaining a master's degree in oceanography from the Scripps Institute, she'd joined her brother at NUMA following a uniting with their father, who now headed up the undersea organization. As headstrong and resourceful as her sibling, she'd gained respect in the field with her knowledge and hands-on abilities, while her attractive looks never failed to turn heads.

Leading Dirk past a row of parked cars, Summer suddenly stopped in front of a tiny orange Suzuki subcompact parked by itself.

'Oh, no, not another knee-crusher,' Dirk laughed as he surveyed the tiny vehicle.

'A loaner from the Port Authority. You'll be surprised.'

After carefully wedging his gear into the minuscule hatchback, Dirk opened the left-side door and prepared to pretzel himself into the passenger seat. To his amazement, the interior of the right-hand-drive car proved roomy, with a low sitting position creating ample headroom for the two six-footers. Summer jumped into the driver's seat and threaded their way out of the parking lot and onto the Hanshin Expressway. Heading north toward downtown Osaka, she accelerated the little Suzuki hard, zipping in and out of traffic, for the twelve-kilometer drive to the city's port terminal. Exiting the expressway, she turned the car into the Osaka South Port Intermodal Terminal and down a side dock before pulling up in front of the *Sea Rover*.

The NUMA research vessel was a slightly newer and larger version of the *Deep Endeavor*, complete with matching turquoise paint scheme. Dirk's eyes were drawn to the stern deck, where a bright orange submersible called the *Starfish* sat glistening like a setting sun.

'Welcome aboard, Dirk,' boomed the deep voice of Robert Morgan, the master of the *Sea Rover*. A bearded bear of a man, Morgan resembled a muscular version of Burl Ives. The jovial captain held an amazing array of seagoing experience, having commanded everything from a Mississippi River tugboat to a Saudi Arabian oil tanker. Having salted away a healthy retirement sum from his commercial captain days, Morgan joined NUMA for the pure adventure of sailing to unique corners of the globe. Deeply admired by his crew, the skipper of the *Sea Rover* was a highly organized leader who possessed an acute attention to detail.

After storing Dirk's bags, the threesome adjourned to a starboard-side conference room whose porthole windows offered a serene view of Osaka Harbor. They were joined by First Officer Tim Ryan, a lanky man with ice blue eyes. Dirk grabbed a cup of coffee to regain alertness after his long flight while Morgan got down to business.

'Tell us about this urgent search-and-recovery mission. Gunn was rather vague with the details over the satellite phone.'

Dirk recapped the Yunaska incident and the recovery of the *I-403*'s bomb canister and what had been learned of the sub's failed mission.

'When Hiram Yaeger reviewed the Japanese naval records in the National Archives, he discovered a near-duplicate operations order that was issued to a second submarine, the *I-411*. It had the same mission, only to cross the Atlantic and strike New York and Philadelphia instead of the West Coast.'

'What became of the *I-411*?' Summer asked.

'That's what we're here to find out. Yaeger was unable to uncover any definitive information on the *I-411*'s final whereabouts, other than that she failed to appear for a refueling rendezvous near Singapore and was presumed lost in the South China Sea. I contacted St. Julien Perlmutter, who took it a step further and found an official Japanese naval inquiry which placed the loss in the middle of the *East* China Sea sometime during the first few weeks of 1945. Perlmutter noted that those facts matched up to a report from the American submarine *Swordfish* that she had engaged and sunk a large enemy submarine in that region during the same time frame. Unfortunately, the *Swordfish* was later destroyed on the same mission so the full accounting was never documented. Their radio report did provide an approximate coordinate of the sinking, however.'

'So it's up to us to find the *I-411*,' Morgan said matter-of-factly.

Dirk nodded. 'We need to ensure that the biological bombs were destroyed when the submarine went down, or recover them if they are still intact.'

Summer stared out one of the porthole windows at a skyscraper in distant downtown Osaka. 'Dirk, Rudi Gunn briefed us about the Japanese Red Army. Could they have already recovered the biological weapons from the *I-411*?'

'Yes, that's a possibility. Homeland Security and the FBI don't seem to think the JRA has the resources to conduct a deep-water salvage operation and they're probably right. But, then, all it would take is money, and who's to say how well funded they, or an associate terrorist group, may be. Rudi agrees that we better make sure one way or the other.'

The room fell silent as all minds visualized a cache of deadly biological bombs sitting deep below the ocean's surface and the consequence if they fell into the wrong hands.

'You've got the best ship and crew in NUMA at your disposal,' Morgan finally said. 'We'll get her done.'

'Captain, we've got a pretty large search area on our hands. How soon can we be under way?' Dirk asked.

'We'll need to top off our fuel supplies, plus two or three of the crew are still ashore obtaining additional provisions. I expect we can be under way in six hours,' Morgan said, glancing at a wall chronometer.

'Fine. I'll retrieve the search coordinates and provide them to the ship's navigator right away.'

As they exited the conference room, Summer tugged at Dirk's elbow.

'So what did the data from Perlmutter cost you?' she chided, knowing the gourmet historian's penchant for culinary blackmail.

'Nothing much. Just a jar of pickled sea urchins and an eighty-year-old bottle of sake.'

'You found those in Washington, D.C.?'

Dirk gave his sister a pleading look of helplessness.

'Well,' she laughed, 'we do have six more hours in port.'

21

'But, Dae-jong, opening the gates to the North is not going to provide me a usable, skilled labor pool,' the CEO of South Korea's largest auto manufacturer asserted before taking a puff on a large Cuban cigar.

Sitting across a mahogany cocktail table, Dae-jong Kang shook his head politely as a long-legged waitress brought a second round of drinks to the table. Their conversation halted while the young Chaebel Club waitress placed their drinks in front of them. The club was a private enclave for Korea's super rich and powerful, a secure and neutral meeting place where huge deals were hammered out over kimchi and martinis. The aristocratic club was appropriately housed on the hundredth floor of the world's tallest building, the recently completed International Business Center Tower located in western Seoul.

'You must consider the lower labor wages. Retraining costs would be minor and recouped in no time. My staff has analyzed the prospects and told me I could save twenty million dollars a year in labor costs alone if we could draw on manpower from North Korea at their current equivalent wage rate. I can only imagine what your potential auto-manufacturing savings would be. Suppose instead of expanding your Ulsan manufacturing facility, you built an entirely new plant in the northern province of Yanggang. How would that improve your competitiveness on the world markets, not to mention open access to the northern consumers?'

'Yes, but it is not so easy for me. I have unions to contend with, as well as capital budget constraints. I certainly can't throw people out on the street at Ulsan and rehire workers from the North at half the price. Besides, there's a whole mind-set that we'll need to contend with if we bring on the northern worker. After all, no socialist state was ever admired for its devotion to quality output.'

'Nothing that a dose of retraining and a taste of capitalistic wages wouldn't quickly solve,' Kang countered.

'Perhaps. But, face it, there is no consumer market for automobiles in the North. The country is an economic mess, and the average man on the street is primarily concerned with putting a meal on the table. The disposable income just isn't there to aid my industry.'

'Yes, but you are looking at the present, not the future. Our two countries are on an inescapable collision course toward unification, and those that are prepared today will reap the riches tomorrow. You had the vision to expand your manufacturing presence to India and the United States and now you are a major player in the auto industry. Have the vision of a unified Korea and help place our homeland at the forefront of world leadership.'

The auto exec blew a large puff of blue cigar smoke toward the ceiling as he contemplated Kang's words. 'I can see the wisdom in your thinking. I'll have my strategy office look into it, perhaps work up some contingencies. I'm not sure I have the stomach for dealing with the political issues and approvals, with both the North and South Korean governments, to establish a presence in the North just yet,' he hedged.

Kang set down his vodka gimlet and smiled. 'I have friends and influence in both governments that can come to your aid when the time is right,' he replied with understatement.

'Most gracious of you. And there is something I can do for you, my good friend, in return?' the exec replied with a smirk.

'The resolution in the National Assembly to expel the U.S. military from our soil is gaining momentum,' Kang answered. 'Your support of the resolution would sway a good deal of political opinion.'

'The embarrassing news incidents with the American military personnel are admittedly making things touchy in some areas of our business. However, I am not convinced the security concerns regarding an American force withdrawal are unfounded.'

'Of course they are,' Kang lied. 'The American presence promotes aggression from the North. Their removal will only stabilize relations between our countries and allow our ultimate reunification.'

'You really think it's the right thing to do?'

'It could make us very rich men, Song-woo,' Kang replied.

'We already are,' the auto executive laughed as he snuffed out his cigar in a porcelain ashtray. 'We already are.'

Kang shook hands good-bye with his fellow industrialist, then took a quick ear-popping elevator ride a hundred floors down to the lobby of the sprawling business center. An accompanying bodyguard attired in black spoke into a handheld radio, and, seconds later, a red Bentley Arnage RL limousine pulled up to the curb to collect them. As Kang rode silently in the leather-bound backseat, he allowed a sense of self-congratulation to overtake him.

The plan of events was going better than expected. The staged murder of a young girl by the American airman had caused widespread outrage across the country. Mothers were staging numerous protests outside of American military bases, while a mob of loud and riotous college students had marched on the U.S. embassy. Kang's corporate administrative staff had orchestrated an intense letter-writing campaign that bombarded a score of local politicians with demands to oust the foreign armed forces. And Kang's extortion of several National Assembly leaders had initiated the political resolution that South Korea's president would soon have to contend with.

Now he was working the business leadership community, which had the real clout with both the media and the members of the National Assembly.

The North Korean leadership in Pyongyang was doing their part in the deception by talking up reunification on every public front. As a goodwill gesture signaling improved relations, they temporarily lifted a majority of the travel restrictions to the north. With additional fanfare, they announced that an army armored division was being pulled back from the DMZ in a peaceful move, though failed to admit that they were just being repositioned a short distance away. Facts to the contrary, a peaceful and friendly front was being promoted in the spirit that a Madison Avenue ad exec would admire.

The Bentley drove into downtown Seoul, turning through the gates of a nondescript low-rise glass building marked with a small sign, stating simply: KANG ENTERPRISES – SEMICONDUCTOR DIVISION. The luxury car continued past a crowded parking lot, then down a small alleyway that led to the back of the building and the shoreline of the Han River. The driver stopped in front of a private dock, where Kang's Italian motor yacht was tied up. A servant welcomed Kang and his bodyguard aboard as the engines were started, and, before he had entered the main cabin, the yacht was cast off for its commute back to Kang's estate.

Kang's assistant, Kwan, bowed as the tycoon entered a small interior cabin he used as a working office aboard the boat. As was his tradition, Kwan provided daily briefings to his boss, either on board the yacht or at the estate, at the end of each work-day. A pile of two-page briefing reports that bested the intelligence reports of many Western leaders lay stacked on the table. Kang quickly scanned the assorted briefings, which detailed everything from forecast quarterly earnings at his telecom subsidiary, to military exercises of the South Korean army, to personal profiles of which politician was cheating on his wife. Items related to subversive activities or from protected sources were printed on a special orange paper that dissolved when immersed in water and were destroyed immediately after Kang's viewing.

After addressing a number of business issues, Kang rubbed his eyes and asked, 'What have we heard from Tongju on the *Baekje*?'

Kwan's face visibly paled. 'We have a problem with the marine equipment for the recovery operation,' he replied tentatively. 'The Japanese submersible we leased was damaged while being transported to the *Baekje*. It was the fault of some careless dockworkers.'

Kwan watched as a vein stood out on Kang's temple and began throbbing violently. The anger rose quickly in the man but came out in a control-led hiss.

'This bungling must stop! First we lose two of our agents in America on a simple assassination attempt and now this. How long before repairs to the damage can be completed?'

'At least three months. The Shinkai is out,' Kwan said quietly.

'We have a timetable to adhere to,' Kang replied with agitation. 'We're talking days, not months.'

'I have initiated a complete search of available submersibles in the region. The other potential Japanese deep-water submersible is undergoing a refit, and all the Russian vessels are currently operating in Western waters. The nearest available submersible that is suitable for the recovery is a Ukrainian vessel currently operating in the Indian Ocean. It will take three weeks to have her on-site, however.'

'That is too late,' Kang mumbled. 'The momentum we have built in the National Assembly for the referendum is peaking. There will be a forced vote within a few weeks. We must act before then. I need not remind you that we had committed to strike during the G8 assemblage,' he said, his eyes simmering with anger.

An anguished silence filled the room. Then Kwan ventured to speak.

'Sir, there may be another option. We were told that an American scientific research vessel has been operating in Japanese waters with a deep-sea submersible. I was able to track the vessel down earlier today as it was taking on fuel in Osaka. It is a NUMA ship, fully capable of deep-water recovery.'

'NUMA again?' Kang mused. His face pinched up as he contemplated the successful foundation he had laid for the project and the potential risk of delay. Finally, he nodded his head at Kwan.

'It is imperative that we initiate the recovery as soon as possible. Obtain the American submersible, but do it quietly and without incident.'

'Tongju is there to lead the operation,' Kwan replied confidently. 'At your instructions, he will proceed. He will not fail us.'

'See to it,' Kang replied, his dark eyes boring through Kwan with seething intolerance.

22

Six-foot swells carrying caps of white foam atop their shoulders pushed and prodded at the *Sea Rover*, causing her decks to roll gently with the undulating seas. A high-pressure front was slowly moving out of the East China Sea, and Captain Morgan noted with satisfaction that the strong southerly winds had gradually softened since they had entered the sea located southeast of the Japanese mainland the night before. As Morgan watched from the bridge, a gray dawn slowly washed the research ship in a bath of muted light. Near the rising and falling bow, he spotted a solitary figure standing at the rail scanning the horizon. A wavy patch of black hair could be seen fluttering in the wind above the upturned collar of his navy blue foul-weather jacket.

Dirk breathed in a deep lungful of the sea air, tasting the damp saltiness of it on his tongue. The ocean always invigorated him, both physically and mentally, the blue vastness providing a tranquil tonic that allowed him to think and act more clearly. Not one capable of working behind a desk, he was addicted to the outdoors, flourishing when at one with what Mother Nature had to offer.

After watching a pair of gulls arc lazily above the ship in search of a morning meal, he made his way aft and climbed up to the elevated bridge. Morgan thrust a steaming mug of coffee into his hand as he entered the ship's control room.

'You're up early,' the captain boomed, a jovial grin on his face even at the early hour of the day.

'Didn't want to miss out on any of the fun,' Dirk replied, taking a long draw at the coffee. 'I figured we would be approaching the search area shortly after dawn.'

'Pretty near,' Morgan said. 'We're about forty minutes from the *Swordfish*'s reported position where she sank the Japanese sub.'

'What's the depth here?'

A young helmsman in a blue jumpsuit eyed the depth monitor and crisply announced, 'Depth 920 feet, sir.'

'Looks like territory for a deep-water AUV search,' Dirk said.

'I'll have Summer wake up Audry and get her ready for work,' Morgan replied with a grin.

Audry was the variant of an Autonomous Underwater Vehicle, which the NUMA scientists who built her had instead dubbed 'Autonomous Underwater Data Recovery Vehicle.' A state-of-the-art self-propelled sensing unit, Audry contained a side-scan sonar, a magnetometer, and a sub-bottom profiler, all packaged into a torpedo-shaped casing that was simply dropped over the side of the ship. The combined sensors provided the capability to seismically map the seafloor for natural or man-made objects, as well as peer beneath the seabed for buried anomalies. The fish-shaped sensor could skim above the seafloor at a depth of five thousand feet, propelled by a powerful battery pack, which eliminated the need for a lengthy and cumbersome tow cable.

As the *Sea Rover* approached the search area, Dirk assisted Summer in downloading the search parameters into Audry's navigation computer.

'We'll use the side-scan sonar only so we can run wider search lanes,' Dirk instructed. 'If the *I-411* is out there, we ought to be able to see her sitting up off the bottom.'

'How large a search grid?' Summer asked as she tapped instructions into a laptop computer.

'We have only a rough fix from the *Swordfish*, so we'll likely have plenty of ground to cover. Let's set the initial search grid at five by five miles.'

'That's still within range of the data relay system. I'll do a quick systems check, then we should be ready to deploy.'

As Audry's software program was reconfigured, the *Sea Rover* dropped a pair of self-positioning transducers into the water at either end of the search grid. With built-in GPS satellite receivers, the transducers would relay underwater navigational guidance to Audry that would enable the vehicle to run a precise back-and-forth grid pattern several dozen feet above the seafloor. Audry in return would upload packets of data to the transducers at periodic intervals, detailing the sonar's search results.

'Ready with the winch,' a crewman's voice shouted.

Dirk gave the thumbs-up signal, then he and Summer watched as the eight-foot-long, lemon-colored survey vehicle was lifted out of a rack on the rear deck and lowered over the side railing into the water. A white plume of spray from the tail indicated that Audry's small propeller was churning, then the grips from the winch were let go. Lunging like a thoroughbred out of the gates at Santa Anita, the torpedo-shaped vehicle surged down the length of the *Sea Rover* before submerging under a wave and into the depths.

'Audry has some legs on her,' Dirk noted.

'She's undergone a recent modification and is now capable of running her surveys at a speed of 9 knots.'

'At that pace, she may not give me much time for my favorite part of the search.'

'What's that?' Summer asked, a quizzical look on her face.

'Why, having a beer and a peanut butter sandwich while waiting for the results,' he grinned.

While Audry motored back and forth down neat imaginary lanes a hundred feet above the seafloor, Summer monitored the vehicle's progress on a computer display aboard the *Sea Rover*. At twenty-minute intervals, a digital data upload was wirelessly transmitted from the transducers to the ship, where further electronic processing converted the binary data bits into a graphical image of the sonar readings. Dirk and Summer took turns scanning through the images of the seabed, searching for linear or angular shapes that might signify a shipwreck.

'Looks like a pepperoni pizza,' Dirk mused as he studied the rock-strewn bottom, seeing odd-shaped boulders that threw off round shadows against the flat backdrop.

'Don't tell me you're hungry again,' Summer replied, shaking her head.

'No, but I bet Audry is. What kind of mileage does she get on a tank of battery acid?'

'The batteries for high-speed operation are only designed to last eight hours. We never run her past seven hours, though, to make sure she has enough juice to propel herself from deep water to the surface. She's been in the water now about six hours,' Summer said, glancing at her watch, 'so we'll need to call her back for a battery change within the next hour.'

A pop-up window suddenly appeared on the computer screen, signaling receipt of the latest data upload.

'Only one more file to go till we've covered the first search box,' Dirk remarked, standing up from his computer console chair and stretching his arms. 'I better identify the boundaries of the next search grid. Can you take a look at the next data feed?'

'Sure, I'll just go ahead and find it for you,' Summer joked as she took his seat and typed a string of commands into the keyboard. A new set of images appeared on the screen, a five-hundred-meter swath of ocean bottom scrolling from top to bottom, which resembled the aerial view of a hard-packed dirt road through the desert. Summer had adjusted the color images in a golden hue so that the occasional rock or mound on the bottom cast a brown-tinted shadow. She studied the monitor closely, watching the same monotonous sea bottom glide by. Suddenly, a dark smudge appeared on the top right side of the screen and grew larger as the readings rolled down. The smudge was a shadow, she quickly realized, created by a long tubular shape that was crisply defined in a dark shade of russet.

'My word, there it is!' she squealed, surprised at her own voice.

A small crowd gathered around Summer as she replayed the image at a slow speed several times. The distinct outline of a submarine was clearly evident, complete with an upright conning tower that cast a long shadow to one side. The image roughened near one end of the vessel, but Summer measured the object at well over three hundred feet.

'Sure looks like a submarine, and a big one,' she said, not sure whether to trust her eyes.

'That's our baby,' Dirk said confidently. 'Looks just like the image we scanned of the *I-403*.'

'Nice work, Summer,' Morgan offered as he approached the commotion.

'Thanks, Captain, but Audry did all the work. We

better pull her aboard before she makes her way to China.'

Summer typed in a new handful of commands and a signal was relayed from the transducers to the underwater vehicle. In a matter of seconds, Audry terminated the search pattern and propelled herself upward, where she broke the water's surface a quarter mile away from the *Sea Rover*. Summer, Dirk, and Morgan watched as a retrieval team in a rubber Zodiac scooted over to the idling yellow sensor and clamped it to the gunwale. The team slowly made their way back alongside the research ship, where Audry was hoisted out of the water and replaced in her cradle on the stern deck.

As the second of the two transducers was hoisted back aboard, Dirk admired a large exploration vessel that was inching past them a mile away, a Japanese flag wafting off its high bow platform.

'Cable-laying ship,' Morgan said, catching Dirk's gaze. 'She followed us out of the Inland Sea.'

'She's a beauty. Doesn't appear to be in any hurry,' Dirk said, noting the vessel's slow speed.

'Must be operating under a daily billing rate contract,' Morgan laughed, then turned his attention to ensuring the transducers were securely aboard.

'Maybe,' Dirk replied, smiling, but a vague caution tugged at the recesses of his mind. He shook off the feeling and refocused his thoughts on the task at hand. It was time to take a look at the *I-411* up close and personal.

23

The crew of the *Sea Rover* wasted no time in making preparations to investigate the submerged target. Captain Morgan brought the ship around and positioned it directly above the target, using the GPS coordinates identified by Audry. Computerized side thrusters on the research vessel were activated and the *Sea Rover* was parked in place, constantly self-adjusting its position against the wind and current with the thrusters to remain fixed within a few inches of the designated mark.

On the aft deck, Dirk, Summer, and First Officer Ryan carefully walked through a predive checklist for the *Starfish*. Specifically designed for deep-water scientific exploration, the *Starfish* was a high-tech submersible capable of operating in depths up to two thousand meters. Resembling a giant translucent ball on a forklift, the *Starfish* carried two operators in a six-inch-thick reinforced acrylic bubble that offered a panoramic view of the sea. Wedged into a bright orange supporting buttress, the see-through sphere was filled with myriad sensors, still and video cameras, and coring devices. Four sets of adjustable thrusters were mounted behind and beneath the bubble, which provided the sub with a high degree of maneuverability. Adding to the functionality were a pair of steel articulating arms mounted on either side of the bubble, which could be used for collecting samples and manipulating the multiple data analysis devices. Since the right mechanical arm was larger in size than the left, the whole submersible took on a crablike appearance when operating on the seafloor.

'I think we're set,' Summer said, eyeing the last item on her clipboard. 'You ready to get wet?'

'Only if I get to drive,' Dirk grinned back.

Clad in aqua-colored NUMA jumpsuits, the two siblings threaded their way into the tiny chamber through a hatch in the rear. Though cramped inside, Dirk and Summer sat comfortably in a pair of padded captain's chairs, which faced out the front of the acrylic bubble. Dirk slipped on a communications headset and spoke to First Officer Ryan.

'This is *Starfish*,' he said, checking the system. 'Ready when you are, Tim.'

'Prepare for deployment,' Ryan's voice rang back.

An overhead boom reeled up a thick cable attached to the submersible by a pair of eyelets, raising the underwater vessel straight into the air and suspending her three feet above the deck. As the *Starfish* hung floating in the air, Ryan pushed a button on a side console and the deck suddenly split open beneath the submersible, sliding on rollers to either side of the deck. Exposed beneath the dangling submersible was the pale green water of the East China Sea. Ryan hit another switch and a circular band of underwater floodlights burst on, outlining the perimeter of the large moon pool cut into the *Sea Rover*'s rear hull section. A large meandering grouper was caught illuminated by the sudden flash of light and quickly bolted from beneath the odd hole in the ship's hull. The orange submersible was slowly dropped through the hole and into the water, the lifting cable released after Dirk confirmed that all systems were operational aboard the *Starfish*.

'Cable is released,' Ryan's voice announced over Dirk's headset. 'You are free to swim. Happy hunting, guys.'

'Thanks for the drop,' Dirk answered. 'I'll honk the horn when we get back from the store.'

Dirk tested the thrusters one last time as Summer opened a ballast tank, allowing a flood of salt water to fill the chamber. Negative buoyancy was quickly achieved and the submersible began slowly dropping into the depths.

The pale green water gradually dissolved to brown, then faded to an inky black as the *Starfish* sank deeper. Summer flicked on a switch and a powerful bank of xenon arc lights illuminated their path, though there was little to see in the murky water. Dependent on gravity to reach the bottom, it took about fifteen minutes to make the nearly thousand-foot descent to the seafloor. Despite the frigid water temperatures outside, the occupants soon became warm from the electronic equipment churning about them in the insulated acrylic and Summer finally turned on an air-conditioning unit to keep themselves cool. Attempting to make the time go faster, Dirk rehashed a few of Jack Dahlgren's stale jokes while Summer brought her brother up to date on the sea pollutant survey taken off Japan's eastern coast.

At nine hundred feet, Summer began tweaking the buoyancy level to slow their descent and avoid smacking hard on the bottom. Dirk noticed the water visibility had cleared, though the seas were devoid of much life at that depth. Gradually, through the murk, he eyed a familiar dark shape looming up beneath them.

'There she is. We're right on her.'

The shadowy black superstructure of the *I-411*'s conning tower reached out to them like a tiny sky-scraper as the *Starfish* descended amidships of the giant submarine. Much like he had found with the *I-403*, Dirk observed that the *I-411* was sitting upright on the bottom, tilted at just a fifteen-degree angle. Surface encrustation was much less severe than on the *I-403* and the big sub looked as if she had been underwater only a few months, not years. Dirk activated the *Starfish*'s thrusters and backed away slightly from the approaching vessel while Summer adjusted their buoyancy to remain neutral at 960 feet, just even with the submarine's deck.

'She's enormous!' Summer exclaimed as her eyes took in the sub's huge girth. Even with *Starfish*'s bright lights, she could see only a portion of the entire vessel.

'Definitely not your run-of-the-mill World War Two U-boat,' he replied. 'Let's see where she got hit.'

Maneuvering the thrusters, Dirk propelled the submersible along a path down the starboard flank of the submarine, gliding just a few feet above its rounded topsides. Circling around the stern, Summer pointed out the tips of the *I-411*'s two giant bronze propellers poking out of the muddy bottom. Moving forward along the port side, they traveled about fifty feet before a huge gash appeared at the waterline.

'Torpedo hit number one,' Dirk called out, eyeing the fatal impact from one of the *Swordfish*'s torpedoes. He positioned the *Starfish* so that its lights shined into the irregular opening. Inside, a circular mass of twisted and jagged metal shined back at them, like the open jaws of an iron-toothed shark. Turning and moving forward again, the submersible crept along the silent wreck another thirty feet before a second opening appeared.

'Torpedo hit number two,' Dirk said.

Unlike the first gash on the port flank, the second hole was oddly centered higher up, along the edge of the topside deck, almost as if the explosive force had been delivered from above.

'You're right, this must have been the second torpedo impact,' Summer speculated. 'The stern must have already dropped under from the first hit, and the sub rolled back from the initial recoil when the second torpedo hit her here.'

'Pretty good firing from the *Swordfish*. They must have caught her at night, while she was running on the surface.'

'Is that the aircraft hangar?' Summer asked, pointing to a large tubular appendage that ran lengthwise along the rear deck to the conning tower.

'Yes. Looks like it was blasted open in the explosion,' he said as they glided over toward the opening. A twenty-foot section of the hangar adjacent to the deck had simply disappeared in the carnage. Under the beam of the floodlights, they could see a three-bladed aircraft propeller mounted on the backside of the hangar wall as they floated outside peering in. Applying power to the thrusters, Dirk turned the vehicle and zoomed forward, gliding past the *I-411*'s conning tower with its multiple gun platforms still in place. The *Starfish* proceeded down the forward deck before turning and hovering off the bow near one of the large diving planes, which sprouted off the submarine like a giant wing.

'That concludes the scenic portion of the tour,' Dirk said. 'Let's see if we can find out what she carried.'

'We better check in with the gang upstairs first,' Summer said, slipping on her communications headset and pushing the TRANSMIT button.

'*Sea Rover*, this is *Starfish*. We've found the Easter Bunny and are proceeding to hunt for the eggs.'

'Roger,' Ryan's voice crackled back. 'Be careful with the basket.'

'I think he's more concerned about his submersible than he is about us,' Dirk deadpanned.

'A typical man,' Summer mused, shaking her head. 'Places emotional feelings on inanimate mechanical objects.'

'I'm sure I don't know what you're talking about,' Dirk replied facetiously.

As he spoke, he gently guided the *Starfish* above the submarine's bow section, studying the forward deck. After several minutes, he spotted what he was looking for.

'There's the forward hatch to the upper torpedo room. If they followed suit with the *I-403*, that's where the biological ordnance would have been loaded and stored.'

Dirk maneuvered the *Starfish* in front of the hatch before setting the submersible down onto the deck of the *I-411* and killing the thrusters.

'How's your breaking and entering skills?' he asked of Summer.

Unlike on the *I-403*, the forward hatch was closed and battened tight by a flush-mounted wheel. Summer activated a joystick control hidden in the armrest of her chair and powered the hydraulics to the submersible's right retractable arm. As she manipulated the controls, the metal appendage sprang from the side of *Starfish* and extended forward in a clumsy stretch. Slowly she dropped the arm down toward the hatch, adjusting the toggle control with short flips to maneuver the device. With the precision of a surgeon, she opened the clawlike hand and dropped it down to the hatch, wedging the fingers into the open slots of the hatch wheel on the first attempt.

'Nicely done,' Dirk admired.

'Now, if she'll just open,' Summer replied. With the flick of a second toggle control, the articulated grip of the mechanical claw began to twist. Dirk and Summer both pressed their faces to the bubble window, intent on seeing the wheel turn. But the seal that had been locked for sixty years didn't budge. Summer tried toggling the grip back and forth a half-dozen more times but to no avail.

'So much for my hydraulic grip,' she finally muttered.

'Keep a hold on the wheel,' Dirk instructed. 'We'll try a little leverage.'

In an instant, he powered up the thrusters and lifted the *Starfish* a few inches off the deck. With Summer gripping the hatch wheel with the claw, Dirk applied full reverse thrust and tried to break the seal with the momentum of the entire submersible. The wheel held tight, so he began rocking the *Starfish* forward and backward, trying to get a quick burst of leverage against the hatch.

'I think you're going to rip the arm off,' Summer cautioned.

With silent determination, he kept trying. On the next tug, he observed a barely perceptible movement in the wheel. Another blast and the seal broke at last, the wheel jerking a quarter spin.

'That's showing it who's boss,' Summer said.

'Just don't tell Ryan that his baby's right arm is now a few inches longer than it used to be,' Dirk smiled.

Hovering over the hatch, Summer was quickly able to spin the locking wheel to its stops with the articulated claw. Dirk then backed the *Starfish* away, and, with Summer holding on, the hatch finally swung up and open. Repositioning the submersible in front of the opening, they peered into the hole but could see nothing but a black void.

'I guess this is a job for *Snoopy*. You have the controls,' Summer said.

Dirk pulled out a laptop control module and pressed the POWER ON button. A row of lights lit up green as the unit was activated. 'Ready, go fetch,' he murmured while pressing a toggle switch that engaged a tiny thruster.

From an external cradle tucked beneath the acrylic bubble popped out a small tethered Remote Operated Vehicle. No larger than an attaché case, the tiny ROV was little more than a self-illuminated video camera wedged against a small set of electronic thrusters. Able to probe and prod into tight spaces, *Snoopy* was an ideal tool for exploring the deep and dangerous niches of a submerged wreck.

Summer watched as *Snoopy* sprang into view and quickly ducked into the open hatch amid a spray of small bubbles. Dirk punched another console button and a live video feed from the ROV appeared on a color monitor. Watching the monitor to steer, he guided the vehicle around the now-familiar torpedo room. *Snoopy* skirted down one row of torpedoes, where the camera showed all five of the huge steel fish still resting in their racks. Circling to the other side of the bay, a duplicate scene was replayed on the opposite side of the torpedo room. The *I-411* was clearly not anticipating battle when the *Swordfish* surprised and sank her.

But Dirk wasn't interested in torpedoes. Methodically, he drove *Snoopy* to the prow of the torpedo room, then systematically swept the ROV back and forth across the bay, slipping a few feet toward the stern with each pass until he was satisfied that every square foot had been viewed.

'No sign of the canisters or their crates. But there is a second torpedo room below where they could have been stored.'

'Can you get *Snoopy* down there?' Summer asked.

'There's a floor hatch for loading the torpedoes, but I don't think *Snoopy* is going to lift that open. I may know of another route.'

Scanning the room with *Snoopy*'s camera lens eye, he spotted the rear hatch door that led to the chief's quarters. The hatch door was still open and Dirk maneuvered the ROV through it a few seconds later.

'Over there,' Summer said, motioning to a corner of the monitor. 'There's a ladder that looks like it leads to the deck below.'

Dirk danced the ROV around a mass of debris

and down an open hatchway in the floor. Dropping down to the deck below, *Snoopy* sniffed out the doorway to the lower torpedo room and entered the second bay of warheads. Though slightly smaller due to the more tapered sides of the submarine's hull, the bay was an exact duplicate of the torpedo room above it. And just as they had seen once before, the camera showed all ten of the deadly Type 95 torpedoes resting peacefully in their racks. Though near the limit of the self-coiling tether that provided *Snoopy* its power, Dirk carefully maneuvered the ROV around the full confines of the room. The camera showed a full complement of torpedoes in the bay but nothing else. The empty room glared back at them vacantly.

'It would appear,' Summer said, shaking her head with disappointment, 'that there are no eggs to be had.'

24

As Dirk carefully guided the small ROV back to the *Starfish*, he began whistling the old Stephen Foster standard 'Swanee River.' Summer looked at her brother with abashed curiosity.

'You seem awfully happy, given that the biological bombs are missing in action,' she said.

'Sister, we may not know where they are, but we sure know where they ain't. Now, if it was me, I'd want to keep those eggs close to the hen.'

Summer took a second to digest the comments, then her face brightened slightly.

'The deck hangar? Where the aircraft are stored?'

'The deck hangar,' Dirk replied. 'And the *Swordfish* was even kind enough to leave the door open for us.'

Once *Snoopy* was secure in its cradle, Dirk activated the main thrusters and the *Starfish* shot off down the deck of the submarine toward the second torpedo blast. The detonation hole was easily large enough to allow the *Starfish* to drop into the interior, but the 11.5-foot diameter of the hangar was just fractionally too tight to allow any room for the submersible to maneuver any farther. Dirk studied the gash in the aircraft hangar before inching the *Starfish* into the opening. The deck had been blasted away in pockmarked sections, leaving step-through holes that led into the dank bowels of the submarine. Dirk slowly guided the *Starfish* lower until he spied firm decking near the forward edge of the gap that was large enough to support the submersible. Out of the corner of his eye, he noticed that the airplane propeller they detected earlier was hanging just to his right. He gently eased lower until the *Starfish*'s supporting skids tapped onto solid decking.

As he powered off the *Starfish*'s thrusters, a momentary silence filled the submersible. Together, they peered down the enclosed hangar that stretched in front of them like an endless tunnel. Then the quiet was broken by a muffled metallic clunk that rang through the water.

'Dirk, the propeller!' Summer shouted, pointing out the bubble window toward the right.

The mounting bracket that held the spare three-bladed Seiran bomber propeller had long ago corroded in the salt water yet against all reason had somehow maintained sufficient integrity to hold the heavy blade onto the wall for sixty years. Not until the stirred waters from the *Starfish*'s thrusters blasted against it did it decide to give up its mission and crumble from the wall in a rusty glob of dust. As the bracket fell away, the heavy propeller dropped straight to the deck, landing on the tips of its lower two blades with a clang.

But the show wasn't over. They watched in helpless fascination as the propeller fell forward, its upper blade skimming just in front of the *Starfish*'s bubble window, inches from Summer's face. It appeared to move in slow motion as the force of the water suspended the movement of the steel blades. A secondary clang echoed through the water as the blade and nosepiece hit home, the entire assembly dragging across the submersible's right robotic arm and falling onto the front skid plates. A cloud of brown sediment rose and obscured their vision for a moment, then, as the water cleared, Summer noticed a small trail of dark fluid rising up in front of them, as if the *Starfish* were bleeding.

'We're pinned,' Summer gasped, eyeing the heavy propeller lying across the front skids.

'Try the right arm. See if you can lift the blade up and I'll try and back us out,' Dirk directed as he powered up the thrusters.

Summer grasped the joystick and toggled it back to raise the arm. The metallic appendage began to rise briefly, then fell away limp. She repeatedly toggled the joystick control back and forth but there was no response.

'No good,' she said calmly. 'The blade must have cut the hydraulics. The right arm is as good as amputated.'

'That must have been the fluid we saw. Try the left arm,' Dirk replied.

Summer configured a second joystick and applied power to the submersible's left mechanical arm. Working the controls, she tried stretching the arm across the viewing window and down to the fallen propeller. Since the left arm was both smaller and shorter than the right arm, it allowed for less maneuverability. After several minutes of bending and twisting the arm in various configurations, she finally worked the claw to a position where she could grab the edge of the propeller blade.

'I've got a grip, but it's at an awkward angle. I don't think I'll be able to exert enough pressure,' she said.

Pushing at the controls, her words fell true. The arm attempted to pull the propeller up but nothing budged. Several further attempts met with the same result.

'Guess we'll have to barge our way out,' Dirk replied, gritting his teeth.

Applying full-throttle power to the thrusters, he tried to elevate the *Starfish* and slip back and away from the fallen propeller. The electronic thrusters hummed and vibrated violently as they clawed at the water with all their might, but the weight of the propeller was just too great. The submersible sat still as a rock while its thrusters beat the water madly, kicking up a dirty cloud of silt around them. He adjusted the thrusters forward and backward, trying to rock their way out, but it was no use. After several fruitless attempts, Dirk shut off the thrusters and waited for the brown cloud to settle.

'We'll just needlessly burn up our batteries if we continue to try and slide out,' he said dejectedly. 'We just don't have enough thrust to pull ourselves away from the prop.'

Summer could see the wheels churning in her brother's head. It wasn't the first time she had been trapped underwater with Dirk and she felt reassurance knowing that he was with her. Just months before, they had nearly died together off Navidad Bank when their undersea research habitat had rolled into a crevasse from the force of a killer hurricane. Only the last-second arrival by her father and Al Giordino had saved them from a slow death by asphyxiation. But this time, her father and Giordino were a thousand miles away.

Out of the murky darkness, voices of the past began to whisper. The long-dead crew of the *I-411* seemed to call out to Dirk and Summer to join them in a cold, watery grave a thousand feet under the sea. The silent black sub exuded a morbid sense that sent a shiver up Summer's spine. The stirred waters around them calmed and they could peer again into the depths of the hangar. She could not help but dwell on the fact that they were lodged in an iron tomb for dozens of brave Imperial Navy sailors. Forcing the macabre image from her mind, she tried to refocus her attention on the logical demands of their situation.

'How much time do we have left?' Summer asked, the desperation of their situation beginning to sink in.

Dirk glanced at a row of gauges to his side. 'We're

fine until the scrubbers give way to the loss of battery power. It'll be lights out in about three hours, then another hour or so for the air to go. We better contact the *Sea Rover*.' His voice was muted but matter-of-fact.

Summer activated the communication system and called Ryan on the *Sea Rover* but was met with silence in return. After several additional attempts, the receiver crackled in her earpiece.

'*Starfish*, this is *Sea Rover*. We do not copy, please repeat, over,' came a faint and fuzzy call from Ryan.

'Our com signal must be blocked by the submarine's bulkheads,' Dirk said. 'We can hear them, but they can't hear us.'

'I'll keep trying in case they can pick up sporadic signals.'

Summer continued calling for another ten minutes, speaking in a loud, clear voice, but received only the same frustrating reply from Ryan.

'It's no use. They can't hear us. We're on our own,' Summer finally conceded.

Dirk began flipping switches on the console, shutting down all nonessential electronics in order to conserve battery power. His hand came to the controls that powered *Snoopy* and he hesitated.

'Any objection to taking *Snoopy* for a walk?'

'We came here to explore the hangar, so we might as well finish the job. We still need to determine if the biological weapons are aboard or if there's any evidence they've been removed.'

'My thoughts exactly,' Dirk said as he powered up

the tiny ROV. Grasping the controls, he worked the vehicle out of its cradle and over the fallen propeller, then elevated it to eye level in front of the *Starfish*. Ahead lay the long dark shaft of the hangar stretching into the gloom toward the conning tower. He quickly toggled the ROV's thrusters forward and *Snoopy* sailed into the darkened hangar.

Both their eyes shifted from observing the illuminated ROV out the viewing bubble to watching *Snoopy*'s field of vision on the color monitor as it moved away from the submersible. The hangar appeared empty at first, but, as *Snoopy* moved forward, silt-covered objects began to materialize. The camera lens glided up to a large encrusted mound positioned on a platform to one side, beyond which several large cabinets protruded from the hangar walls.

'A spare aircraft engine,' Dirk remarked as he aimed *Snoopy*'s eyes at the long metal block.

'I'll bet those are storage bins for other spare parts and mechanic's tools,' Summer added, pointing at the image of the cabinets.

'No doubt there's a floor jack in there somewhere,' Dirk lamented, knowing there was no way of retrieving any tools that might aid their escape.

Slowly he led *Snoopy* down the cavernous hangar before nearly driving the ROV into a grouping of thin metal sheets hanging vertically. Backing up the camera, Dirk identified the structure as the tail assembly of an airplane, with the tip of the vertical stabilizer folded down, as well as both horizontal stabilizers. Swinging *Snoopy* ahead and to the side, they could clearly see it was part of the fuselage of an Aichi M6A1 Seiran floatplane.

'Wow,' Summer murmured, impressed by both the size and condition of the twin-seat bomber. 'Hard to believe they could fold up a plane and slide it in here.'

Dirk led *Snoopy* alongside the fuselage for a side view of the craft. The camera showed that the wings were still attached to the fuselage but folded back toward the tail like the wings on a duck. Faintly visible beneath the silt, they could still make out the familiar red Japanese 'meatball' insignia painted on the wingtips.

'It's still amazing to me that they could store, launch, and retrieve aircraft from a submarine,' Summer pondered.

'Just roll the fuselage out onto the forward deck, raise the tail stabilizers, bolt on the wings and floats, and launch it off the catapult. A trained crew of four men were capable of assembling and launching a plane in under thirty minutes.'

'I guess it's a good thing these big Sen Toku boats weren't around earlier in the war,' Summer replied.

Dirk kept *Snoopy* nosing forward through the hangar. Gliding past the fuselage, the cameras revealed a pair of the plane's giant pontoons strapped to a wooden pallet on the deck. A blast from the ROV's thrusters dusted a layer of silt and mud off one of the pontoons, exposing a forest green paint scheme on the topsides and a shark gray tone on the pontoon's belly. A similar camouflage paint pattern would be found on the wings and fuselage.

Once past the pontoons, the hangar grew empty for several feet as the ROV passed through a separate open compartment. Like its beagle namesake, *Snoopy* sniffed along, gingerly examining each silt-covered object or debris item carefully via the touch of Dirk's fingers. A set of low-slung racks gradually grew out of the darkness on either side of the hangar holding what Dirk immediately recognized as torpedoes. Four of the metallic fish rested in each rack, aerial torpedoes that at thirteen hundred pounds each were much smaller than the massive submarine-launched torpedoes found belowdecks.

Dirk and Summer stared at the monitor, straining to see evidence of additional armament. But no other weaponry was visible. Dirk turned and noticed Summer peering at her watch, grimly cognizant of each minute that passed.

'Let's keep going. There should be at least one more plane in here,' Dirk said, trying to keep her mind off the inevitable. The ROV again moved through a vacant compartment before emerging into the next hangar section. Seconds later, the tail and fuselage of a second Seiran bomber emerged into view, complete with folded wings. Just beyond was its matching pair of floats, strapped to the deck by cables. An assortment of wall-mounted tool bins followed and then twenty feet of empty space. *Snoopy* finally bumped up against the giant round hatch door that led to the submarine's forward deck.

'Well, that's it,' Dirk said solemnly. 'We've covered the length of the hangar and no sign of any aerial bombs other than the torpedoes.'

Summer said nothing for a moment, subconsciously biting her lower lip in dejection. 'Well . . . there was no indication of a forced entry anywhere, nor did the silt appear to have been disturbed anytime recently. Perhaps they were destroyed in the torpedo blast?'

'Could be. There's still a small section of hangar behind us we could take a look at.'

Dirk quietly steered *Snoopy* back toward the submersible, reeling in its dangling electronic power cable while it progressed. The cockpit fell silent as brother and sister contemplated their predicament. Dirk silently cursed their bad luck and failure to locate the aerial bombs. As the ROV passed the second plane's fuselage and approached the first plane's set of pontoons, a quizzical look fell over Summer's face.

'Dirk, hold it there for a second,' she said quietly, focusing on the monitor.

'What is it?' he asked while neutralizing the position of the ROV.

'Look at the pontoons. Do you notice anything different?'

Dirk studied the monitor for a moment, then shook his head.

'The pair at the end of the hangar were cabled directly to the deck,' Summer said. 'But these two have a platform under each of them.'

He looked at the images and his brow furrowed. Each of the pontoons sat balanced on a square-shaped platform roughly two feet high.

Dirk eased the ROV around and alongside the base of one of the pontoons, then positioned it next to the platform. Spinning the ROV around, he applied the thrusters hard for a few seconds to try and blow away the encrusted sediment. He repositioned the ROV, then waited for the resulting cloud of sediment to subside. Peering through the murk, they could clearly see an exposed section of the platform. It was a hardwood crate built from what appeared to be mahogany. Dirk carefully studied the entire platform.

'By God, that's got to be it.'

'Are you sure?' Summer questioned.

'Well, I can't say what's inside, but the exterior is the same construction and dimension as the bomb canister crates that I found smashed open on the *I-403*.'

Dirk surveyed the crate from all angles, then confirmed that a matching crate was wedged beneath the second pontoon. Summer made a notation on the video files, documenting the exact location in the hangar where the crates were found. Pitt observed that each crate appeared to be held in place by the force of the pontoon, which was securely tied to the hangar deck by a half-dozen thick steel cables that crisscrossed the top of each float.

'Nice eye, Summer. You get a beer for that catch.'

'Make mine a bottle of Martin Ray Chardonnay,' she replied with a half smile. 'I'm just glad we know where they are now.'

'It's going to take someone a little more doing to get these out of here.'

'Us too, for that matter,' Summer replied glumly.

The wheels in Dirk's mind were still churning to compute an escape plan as he guided the ROV back toward the submersible. He lost concentration when *Snoopy*'s bright underwater lights approached and shined brilliantly into the submersible's cockpit. Blinded in the glare, he instinctively steered the ROV down toward the hangar deck as he brought it closer to the *Starfish*. But as it approached, the ROV suddenly hung suspended, failing to move the last few feet to its cradle.

'Dirk, *Snoopy*'s umbilical is caught on something,' Summer noticed, pointing out the bubble window.

Dirk followed her guide and could see in the murkiness that the ROV's cable had snagged on some sort of debris lying on the hangar deck, about twenty feet in front of them.

'I'm surprised we even made it so far through this obstacle course,' he replied.

Reversing direction, he backed up the ROV until the cable straightened from its grasp around what looked to be a small engine sitting in a tubular frame three feet off the ground.

'A gas-powered compressor, I bet,' he said, noticing a pair of decayed hoses connected to one end of the motor.

'What's with the big handle?' Summer asked, eyeing a large metal rod protruding from one side of the block. A round, shovel-type grip was attached to the end.

'It has an old mechanical starter. Kind of like pulling the rope on a lawn mower, only pumping the handle cranks the motor over. I saw a Swiss-made compressor on a dive boat once that had the same setup.' Dirk stared at the handle for a moment, not moving the ROV.

'You're going to bring *Snoopy* home?' Summer finally asked.

'Yes,' he replied with a sudden gleam in his eye. 'But first he's going to help get us out of here.'

On board the *Sea Rover*, nervous apprehension was creeping over the captain and crew. It had been nearly ninety minutes since they last communicated with the *Starfish* and Morgan was anxiously preparing to call in an emergency rescue. The *Sea Rover* was not carrying a backup submersible, and the nearest NUMA submersible was at least twelve hours away.

'Ryan, let's contact the Navy's Deep Submergence Unit. Notify them of our situation and request the ETA on a deep-water rescue vehicle,' Morgan barked, silently dreading the thought.

If Dirk and Summer were in real trouble, he knew they had only a matter of minutes, not hours. Their chances of rescue would be as slim as a dime.

25

'Okay, Summer, hold the take-up reel.'

Dirk had positioned *Snoopy* near the top of the hangar ceiling a few feet past the compressor when he gave the command to Summer. She pressed a button on the console that stopped an automatic spool from reeling in the ROV's power cable. Dirk gently moved the ROV back toward the compressor, watching the cable slacken beneath it. Like an anaconda coiling about its prey, he carefully manipulated the ROV in a circular motion above the compressor, letting the slack cable wrap loosely around the protruding handle. After dancing the ROV around and around several times, he successfully engineered five loops about the handle, which he tightened by drawing the ROV up and away.

'Okay, activate the take-up spool and I'll pull with *Snoopy*.'

'That compressor must weigh three hundred pounds. Even underwater, you'll never budge it,' Summer replied, wondering if her brother had lost his mind.

'It's not the compressor I'm after, it's the handle.'

Toggling the ROV's controls, he increased the power to *Snoopy*, now pointed in the direction of the submersible. The ROV surged forward until its power cord tightened around the metal handle. Its small thrusters churning the water, the little ROV fought to move forward but could not muster enough force to budge the handle. Then Summer joined in, reeling in the other end of the cable with the automatic take-up spool until the cord went taut around the base of the handle. Though both ends of the handle were now being yanked at, it was the lower end snagged by Summer that did the trick. The boxed end of the metal bar slid off the sprocketed knuckle that turned the flywheel and the whole handle slipped free of the compressor, gliding through the water toward the *Starfish*. Dirk carefully dragged it in a horizontal position, so as not to lose his coiled grip, and gently tugged it to the front of the submersible.

'I don't think Ryan is going to appreciate how you're treating his ROV,' Summer said with feigned concern.

'I'll buy him a new one if this works.'

'And what exactly is it that you have in mind?' Summer asked, still not sure of his intent.

'Why, just a little bit of leverage, my dear sister. If you'd be so kind as to grab my newfound crowbar with the left mechanical arm, you'll see what I mean.'

Dirk guided the ROV close to the left side of the *Starfish*, towing the handle with it. Summer then activated the controls of the left mechanical arm and opened its clawlike hand. Working in unison, they brought the two devices together until Summer could securely snatch one end of the handle with the vise-strong claw. Dirk then slackened the ROV cable and slowly backed *Snoopy* away, unraveling the cable off the free end of the bar. Once clear, he activated the cable spool up and returned *Snoopy* to the *Starfish*, securing the ROV in its cradle.

'For a beagle, *Snoopy* makes for a pretty good retriever,' Summer remarked.

'Let's see now if our mechanical arm can make for a good floor jack,' Dirk replied.

His eyes studied a row of battery ampere gauges on the submarine's control panel. They had spent more than an hour operating the ROV and their power level had been drained to barely thirty percent. Time was running short if they were to have any hope of making it back to the surface on their own.

'Let's do this on one try. Purging tanks,' he said, pushing a pair of buttons that pumped water out of the ballast tank in order to increase buoyancy. He then powered up the main thrusters to the submersible. Summer had meanwhile brought the mechanical arm around the front of the *Starfish* to its full dexterity and studied the position of the wedged propeller. It would have to be lifted and pushed forward slightly for them to pry themselves away, but there was little space to work the handle in. After leaning the handle against one of the skids and shortening her grip, she was able to work eight inches of the metal bar under the tip of the fallen propeller.

'Ready,' she said tentatively, wiping a sweaty palm

on her pant leg. Dirk was also sweating profusely, as the cramped cockpit had grown hot once the air-conditioning was shut down to conserve power.

'Pry us out of here,' Dirk said, his hand at the ready on the thruster controls. With tense anticipation, Summer gently shifted the controls that raised the mechanical arm. Where the hydraulic power of the arm was insufficient to lift the arm on its own, the added leverage of the metal handle prying against the deck was just enough to budge it. Creeping ever so slowly, the propeller blade rose an inch, then two, then a few more. Dirk could feel the rear of the submersible tilt off the deck slightly from the added buoyancy. When Summer had safely jimmied the blade above the height of the front skids, he slammed the power controls to maximum reverse thrust.

There was no immediate blast of power or sky-rocketing acceleration by the *Starfish* but rather just a slight jerk as it backed tail first off the deck. The submersible slid up and away from the grasp of the propeller as the blade slipped down the compressor handle and clanged back to the hangar deck just inches in front of the *Starfish*'s skids.

'Nicely done, sis. What do you say we go get some fresh air?' Dirk said, adjusting the thrusters to raise the *Starfish* up and out of *I-411*'s hangar.

'I'm with you,' Summer replied with obvious relief.

Almost the second they cleared the walls of the hangar deck, the deep voice of Ryan blew loudly through communication earphones.

'*Starfish*, this is *Sea Rover*. Do you read, over,' came a monotonous tone that had obviously been repeating the phrase a thousand times over in the last few hours.

'This is *Starfish*,' Summer responded. 'We read you loud and clear. Have initiated ascent, please stand by for recovery.'

'Roger, *Starfish*,' Ryan replied in a suddenly excited pitch. 'You have some folks worried up here. Do you need assistance?'

'Negative. We just stubbed our toe down here. All is well; we'll be topside shortly.'

'Copy that. Standing by for recovery.'

Their ascent time, aided by controlled positive buoyancy, was slightly quicker than their descent, and in ten minutes they could make out the glowing bright lights of the *Sea Rover*'s moon pool. The faint outline of the ship appeared as the submersible drew closer and Dirk tweaked the *Starfish*'s thrusters with what little remaining power he had to guide them to the center of the glowing ring of beacons. Dirk and Summer both let out a silent sigh of relief as they popped through the hole in the ship's bottom and bobbed to the surface of the pool. Morgan, Ryan, and a half-dozen crew members ringed the moon pool and watched intently as the *Starfish* was plucked from the water by a hoist and lowered gently to the deck. Dirk powered down the submersible as Summer opened the rear hatch and the two climbed out for a grateful breath of fresh air.

'We were afraid you got lost down there,' Morgan smiled, then looked quizzically at the compressor handle that was still lodged in the grip of the left mechanical arm.

'That's our walking stick,' Summer explained. 'We took a walk where we ought not to have gone and had a little trouble getting back out.'

'Well,' Morgan asked, unable to refrain from the other concern on his mind, 'what did you find?'

'Two cartons of eggs waiting to be delivered,' Dirk said with a grin.

The *Sea Rover*'s crew worked feverishly to repair the *Starfish*'s mechanical arm and replenish the submersible's drained batteries while Dirk, Summer, and Morgan formulated a salvage strategy. Reviewing the video footage recorded by *Snoopy*, they calculated the exact position in the sub's hangar where the bomb crates were situated. Studying the video closely, they determined that the hangar's bulkhead walls were constructed in ten-foot sections.

'We should be able to cut through the original seams and lift out a ten-foot piece of bulkhead alongside the pontoons,' Dirk said, tapping a frozen video image with a pencil. 'The *Starfish* is eight feet wide, so that should give us enough room to maneuver close and remove the bombs with the mechanical arms.'

'We're fortunate in that the currents around the wreck are only about 1 to 2 knots, so we'll be able to work unimpeded by the seas. It will still take us a couple of dives, though,' Summer added.

'Ryan can alternate dives with you two,' Morgan said. 'Why don't you grab a few hours' rest while we turn the submersible around and prepare for some cutting?'

'You don't have to ask me twice,' Summer yawned in reply.

Her sleep was short-lived, however, when Dirk woke her three hours later and they prepared for another dive. With a fresh set of batteries, the *Starfish* was released again and they made their slow descent to the submarine. The submersible hovered off the side of the hangar facing the blast hole, then slowly moved sideways toward the conning tower. At six-foot intervals, measured by the width between the two semiextended mechanical arms, Dirk would push the submersible forward and scratch a measuring mark on the encrusted surface with the left claw. At the tenth interval, or sixty feet from the torpedo gash, he scratched a rough X on the side of the hangar.

'This is where we cut,' he said to Summer. 'Let's see if we can find the seams.'

Dragging one of the claws along the surface of the hangar, Dirk thrust the submersible sideways, leaving a long scratch along the wall. Moving back and closely examining the scarred section, which bled a dirty rust and gold, they quickly found an exposed vertical crease, representing the seam where two plates of the watertight hangar were welded together. As expected, another vertical seam was found ten feet away. While the *Starfish* hovered, Summer scraped away at the seams, using the claw like a knife, exposing the weld lines. When she was finished, a square outline in the shape of a garage door had been etched on the hangar.

'So much for the easy part,' Dirk said. 'You ready to cut?'

'Pop these on and let's get started,' Summer replied, handing him a pair of welder's protective glasses while donning a pair herself. Taking control of both mechanical arms, she reached into a basket mounted on the front skid pad and with the right claw retrieved an electrode holder, connected via a reinforced line to a 230-amp DC power source inside the submersible. With the left claw, she attached an iron oxide nonexothermic cutting rod into the electrode holder and flicked on the power. Unlike a typical underwater cutting rod, which required a supply of oxygen to fuel the burn, the iron oxide rods simply required a power source to generate a super-heated cutting arc. The less complicated design was more practical for welding at remote underwater depths. The electrical surge popped through to the end of the rod, igniting a brilliant arc of yellow light that flared from the tip, burning at several thousand degrees.

'Let's start at the top right corner and work down,' Summer directed. Dirk maneuvered the submersible to the corner seam and held it stationary while

Summer extended the right mechanical arm toward the hangar wall until the high-temperature flame flared against the surface. With the *Starfish* suspended against a light current, Summer applied the heat from the arc to cut through the sixty-year-old plating weld. Progress was measured in inches, as the swaying of the submersible undermined the cutting efficiency. But, gradually, a surgical line appeared on the hangar wall, which lengthened as Dirk slid the *Starfish* down the seam. After fifteen minutes, the electrode rod burned down to the stub. Summer shut off the electrical power and replaced the electrode, then powered it up again and continued cutting. The tedious process continued until a fine cut was made around the entire perimeter seam of the hangar wall. With just a few inches to go, Summer worked the free mechanical claw into an open gap and grabbed onto the panel. She then cut the last of the seam, then yanked with the secured claw. The cut section broke free and fell back onto the main deck of the submarine with a swirling cloud of sediment.

Dirk backed the *Starfish* away and waited for the water to clear before moving up to their newly created entryway. As he maneuvered back in, he could see that they had measured perfectly. The pair of aircraft pontoons sat directly in front of the opening, the wooden crates sitting just below. He crept the submersible in as close as he could get, bumping the hangar ceiling a time or two before setting it down on the deck near a large protruding iron loop.

Through the circular eyelet ran several cables, which secured the nearest pontoon to the deck while the submarine was in motion.

'Let's torch those cables, then figure out a way to slide that pontoon out of the way,' he suggested.

Summer reignited the underwater torch and quickly cut through the first of three steel-braided cables. The corroded lines disintegrated quickly under the flame of the cutting rod and she soon ate through the second cable. She was surprised when the pontoon lurched slightly as the second cable fell away. When the third cable cut free, she was shocked to see the pontoon rise gracefully off the deck and float to the top of the twelve-foot hangar ceiling.

'It's still holding air,' she blurted.

'Compliments to the engineers who built her. That will make our job a little easier,' Dirk replied as he maneuvered the *Starfish* alongside the wooden crates. Summer grabbed control of both mechanical arms and gently danced their claws over one of the containers. Manipulating the metal fingers, she grasped the top lid on either side and lifted the arms up. The once durable hardwood lid rose like a damp pancake before it split in two as Summer tried to place it off to one side.

'So much for the boxed set,' Dirk said drily.

Inside, however, they could see the bonanza. Six silver-porcelain aerial bombs sat secure and intact, aligned in a neat row. Dirk and Summer looked at each other with a profound sense of relief.

'Guess it's our lucky day after all,' Summer said triumphantly. 'They're still here, safe and sound.'

Dirk carefully inched the *Starfish* closer to the crate as Summer prepared for the harrowing prospect of removing the fragile bombs from their disintegrating case.

'Be gentle, sis. Remember, they're made of glass,' he cautioned.

Summer hardly needed the warning as she manipulated the mechanical arms with great caution. Working with the nearest bomb, she gently slid the canister away from the others, then gingerly worked the claws underneath either end. Moving with patient deliberation, she lifted the bomb up and away, then set it into a padded mesh box that had been hastily attached to the front of the submersible. Confident that the canister was stable, she moved the arms back and retrieved the next bomb in the crate. Lifting and laying it next to the first snugly in the box, she grasped its tail fin with one claw, then snatched the fin of the first bomb with the other claw and locked both arms in place.

'Bombardier to pilot. Ready for takeoff,' she said. Fearful of damaging dangerous cargo, two bombs would be all that the *Starfish* would safely transport at a time.

The submersible made a slow ascent to the surface, where the bombs were carefully unloaded and stored in a makeshift container that the ship's carpenter had hurriedly constructed.

'Two down, ten to go,' Dirk reported to Morgan and Ryan. 'Both crates are readily accessible with the mechanical arms, so, if the second batch is intact, we should be able to recover all twelve canisters.'

'The weather is holding,' Morgan replied. 'If we work through the night at the same pace, we should have the recovery operation complete by morning.'

'I'm all for that,' he replied with a grin. 'With all these dives, I'm beginning to feel like a yo-yo.'

Less than a mile away, Tongju peered at the NUMA vessel through a pair of high-powered marine binoculars. For nearly forty minutes, Kang's personal executioner studied the *Sea Rover*, making careful mental notes on passageways, stairwells, hatches, and other elements of the ship that he could detect in the distance. At last satisfied with his observations, the bald assassin entered the *Baekje*'s bridge and walked into a small side anteroom. A pug-faced man with short-cropped hair sat in a wooden chair intently studying a set of ship plans. He stiffened slightly as Tongju entered the room.

'Sir, the assault team has studied the plans to the NUMA research vessel that was relayed by the Kang Shipping corporate office. We have formulated an assault and seizure strategy and are prepared to commence at your direction.' Ki-Ri Kim spoke in a clipped, blunt tone that could be expected from a former special operations commando of the Korean People's Army.

'From the bits of underwater communication that we have been able to intercept, it appears that they have located the weapons and are in the process of retrieving them from the seabed,' Tongju said in a quiet voice. 'I have notified the captain that we will be launching the operation tonight.'

A broad grin fell over the commando's face before he uttered the single word 'Excellent.'

'As we formulated,' Tongju continued, 'I will lead Team A to capture the starboard and bow sections and you will lead Team B to take the port and stern sections. Have the men assembled for a final briefing at 01:00. We will commence the strike at 02:00.'

'My men will be ready. They are curious to know, however, if we will be expecting any resistance?'

Tongju snarled a confident reply. 'None whatsoever.'

Shortly after midnight, the *Starfish* bobbed to the surface of the moon pool, its bright orange frame reflecting golden rays through the water from the blazing underwater lights. Dirk and Summer stood watching on the deck as the submersible was hoisted from the water and parked gently on a platform. A pair of technicians working the graveyard shift rolled a portable hoist to the submersible's front skids and began the delicate process of removing the two porcelain bombs wedged into the mesh basket.

Dirk walked around and helped open the *Starfish*'s rear entry hatch and lent a hand as Ryan and an engineer named Mike Farley corkscrewed their way out of the cramped compartment.

'Nice work, Tim. That makes a total of eight. I take it you accessed the second case without any problems?' Dirk asked.

'Piece of cake. We cut the cables on the second pontoon and she floated out of the way like the first. Mike deserves the credit, though. He operates those mechanical arms like a surgeon.'

A likable, soft-spoken man who smiled constantly, Farley grinned modestly. 'The second crate fell apart like it was made of mashed potatoes. But all six bombs were lying there intact. We snatched the first two, and the remaining four are readily accessible. Be mindful of the current, though, it seems to have picked up since our last dive.'

'Thanks, Mike, will do.'

Dirk proceeded to help the technician crew change the batteries on the *Starfish*, then methodically worked through the predive checklist, ensuring that all on-board systems were operating properly. Shortly after 1 A.M., he and Summer squeezed back into the sub-mersible and were released into the moon pool for another dive to the *I-411*. They relaxed in their slow descent, saying little to each other. The around-the-clock, repetitive dives were beginning to take their toll, casting a veil of fatigue over them. But Dirk was enlivened by the fact they were recovering the bombs intact and would soon find out what biological agent they contained.

Summer let out a wide yawn. 'Wish I was back in my bunk snoozing like the rest of the crew,' she murmured. 'We'll have the last two dives complete before everyone even wakes up.'

'Look on the bright side,' Dirk smiled. 'We'll be first in line for breakfast.'

26

They came out of the darkness like muted demons, gliding across the water in silence. Black-clad men in black rubber boats dashing across a blackened sea. Tongju led the assault from the first boat, accompanied by five gritty-looking and heavily armed commandos, while Kim followed behind in a second boat with a similar contingency. Together they raced toward the *Sea Rover* in rubber Zodiacs propelled by high-power electric motors, beefed-up versions of the trolling motors used by lake fishermen to cruise quietly. Only, these boats were capable of running at 30 knots, emitting just a barely detectable hum. Running in the dead of night, the only audible evidence of their presence were the waves smacking against their semirigid hulls.

On board the *Sea Rover*, the helmsman on watch glanced at a sweeping radarscope on the bridge, observing the large smudge of a ship off the starboard bow. The large cable ship that had stood a mile off the *Sea Rover* since they arrived on-site was still sitting parked in the same position. He watched as a pair of faint white smudges appeared against the screen's green background periodically, positioned somewhere between the two ships. Too faint for a vessel this far from shore, he reckoned. More likely some cresting waves registering on the equipment.

The two rubberized cresting waves throttled back as they approached within a hundred meters of the NUMA ship, creeping the remaining distance at a slow crawl. Tongju brought his boat alongside the starboard flank of the *Sea Rover* and waited momentarily while Kim's craft skirted around the ship's stern and eased up on the port side. In unseen unison, a pair of rubber-coated grappling hooks sailed up from the sea on either side of the ship, catching secure grips around the *Sea Rover*'s lower-deck railing. Narrow rope ladders trailing off the grappling hooks provided the means of entry. In orderly unison, the commandos quickly scrambled up the swaying lines.

On the port deck, a sleepless marine biologist was taking in the night sky when he heard something strike the ship. A pronged hook materialized around the railing just a few feet away. Curious, he bent over the side to look down the trailing rope just as a black-capped head emerged from the other side. In mutual surprise, the two men banged heads together with a crack. The startled scientist fell back, groping for words to cry out, but, in an instant, the commando was on deck, brandishing an assault rifle. The rifle stock caught the unfortunate biologist across the jawbone and the man crumpled in an unconscious heap.

The two commando teams assembled independently, then moved forward along the deck, intent on subduing the bridge and radio room first before any calls for help could be sent. Silently creeping through the sleeping ship, their 2 A.M. raid found the vessel ghostly quiet.

On the bridge, the *Sea Rover*'s helmsman and second officer were sipping coffee while discussing college football. Without warning, Tongju and two of his men burst through the starboard wing door, aiming their weapons at the men's faces.

'Down on the deck!' Tongju yelled in clear English. The second officer quickly dropped to his knees, but the helmsman panicked. Dropping his coffee, he bolted for the port wing in a futile attempt at escape. Before Tongju or his men could cut the man down, one of Kim's commandos appeared in the doorway, striking the man in the chest with his assault rifle, then kicking him in the groin for good measure. The helmsman withered to the deck, groaning in agony.

Scanning the bridge, Tongju saw that the adjacent communications bay was empty and nodded at one of the commandos to stand guard over the equipment. He then walked toward the door to the captain's cabin situated off the back of the bridge. With a silent nod, he ordered one of his men to charge in.

Morgan was asleep in his bunk when the commando burst into his cabin, flicked on the light, and leveled his AK-74 assault rifle at the captain's head. The salty captain awoke immediately and sprang out of bed clad in T-shirt and boxers, bullying toward the man with the gun.

'What's this all about?' he barked, storming his

way toward the bridge. The startled commando hesitated in the doorway as the burly captain bore toward him. With a nearly invisible flick of his arm, Morgan knocked the muzzle of the firearm away from his chest and toward the ceiling, then, with his free right hand, shoved the commando out the door with the strength of a barreling freight train. The shocked commando went sprawling across the bridge, falling on his backside and sliding with a thud into the forward bulkhead.

The commando was still sliding across the deck when Tongju leveled his Glock 22 semiautomatic pistol and fired a single shot at Morgan. The .40 caliber slug ripped into and through Morgan's left thigh, throwing a spray of blood onto the wall behind him. Morgan cursed as he grabbed his leg before crumpling to the deck.

'This is a United States government vessel,' he hissed defiantly.

'It is my ship now,' Tongju replied coolly, 'and any more insolence from you, Captain, and I shall place the next bullet into your skull.' To emphasize his words, he stepped forward and flung his right leg toward the kneeling captain, the heel of his black boot striking Morgan high on the cheekbone and sending him sprawling flat to the deck. The proud captain slowly gathered himself back to his knees and stared quietly at his captor, eyes burning with hatred.

Unable to warn his fellow shipmates, Morgan could only watch helplessly as the small team of intruders took over his ship. Little resistance was met elsewhere on the vessel as the commandos rounded up the sleeping crew at gunpoint. Only in the engine room did a brawny machinist's mate surprise one of the commandos, crushing a pipe wrench through his skull. The machinist was quickly subdued by gunshots from another assailant, but the wounds would not prove lethal. Sporadic gunfire began to resonate throughout the ship as the commando teams worked through the *Sea Rover*. In less than twenty minutes, the assault team had achieved their objective and taken control of the 350-foot research vessel.

Tim Ryan and Mike Farley were in the undersea operations control room monitoring the current dive of the *Starfish* when a pair of commandos burst in on them. Ryan could only mutter a 'What the hell?' over the underwater communications system before he was yanked away from the control station at gunpoint with Farley in tow.

Like sheep led to the slaughterhouse, the shipboard crew was herded in groups of three and four to the rear deck of the *Sea Rover*. Astern of the moon pool was a recessed cargo hold where the submersible and other equipment was stored when not in use. Under Kim's direction, the hold's heavy steel hatch cover was winched off with one of the *Sea Rover*'s cranes. The frightened captives were then forced down a steel ladder into the dark, cavernous bay.

Tongju approached Kim on the rear deck with a bound and limping Morgan in tow, another commando prodding the captain forward with the barrel of his assault rifle.

'Report?' Tongju asked bluntly.

'All objectives achieved,' Kim reported proudly. 'One casualty in the engine room, Ta-kong, but all ship's compartments are now secure. We've transferred all the captives to the stern hold. Jin-chul reports that eight units of ordnance have been located intact in the ship's auxiliary laboratory,' he added, nodding toward a wiry commando standing next to a prefabricated structure across the deck. 'The submersible is currently deployed in recovery of additional ordnance.'

'Very well,' Tongju replied with a rare smile that revealed a set of heavily yellowed teeth. 'Contact the *Baekje*. Tell her to tie up alongside and prepare for transfer of the ordnance.'

'You won't get far,' Morgan growled, spitting out a mouthful of blood as he spoke.

'But, Captain,' Tongju replied with an evil smirk, 'we already have.'

A thousand feet beneath the *Sea Rover*, Summer was carefully placing the tenth aerial bomb into the makeshift holding tray alongside the ninth canister she had plucked from the bottom just moments before. She again secured both bombs with the mechanical arms, then turned to Dirk when she was finished.

'Ten down, two to go. You may take us home now, Jeeves.'

'Yes, m'lady,' he replied in a Cockney accent, then he actuated the submersible's thrusters and backed out of the tight confines of the hangar. As they cleared the deck of the *I-411*, Summer radioed up to the *Sea Rover*'s control room.

'*Sea Rover*, this is *Starfish*. Have secured the next batch and are preparing to ascend with the goods, over.'

The call was returned with silence. She tried calling several more times as they started their ascent but again received no response from the surface.

'Ryan must be asleep at the wheel,' Dirk said.

'Can't blame him,' Summer replied while suppressing a yawn. 'It is two-thirty in the morning.'

'I just hope the guy on the crane is awake,' he smirked.

As they neared the surface, they spotted the familiar glow of the moon pool lights and maneuvered the *Starfish* into the center of the ring, where they bobbed gently to the surface. Dirk and Summer paid scant attention to the shadowy figures on the deck as the clank of the main hoist was dropped and attached to the submersible and they began to power down its electronic equipment. It was only when they were jerked roughly out of the water and swung wildly to the stern deck, nearly colliding with the port bulkhead, that they realized something was amiss.

'Who the hell's working the crane?' Summer cursed as they were set down harshly on the deck. 'Don't they know we've got two bombs aboard?'

'It sure ain't the Welcome Wagon,' Dirk said drily as he stared out of the bubble window.

Directly in front of them, an Asian man in a black paramilitary outfit stood holding an automatic pistol to the stomach of Captain Morgan. Dirk looked beyond the man's long Fu Manchu mustache and crooked yellow teeth splayed in an evil grin and focused on the eyes. They were cold, black eyes that portrayed a menacing air of utter indifference. They were, Dirk knew, the eyes of an experienced killer.

Summer gasped at the sight of Morgan. A make-shift bandage was wrapped about his left thigh but failed to cover the rivulets of dried blood that was splattered down his leg. His cheekbone was bruised and swollen to the size of a grapefruit, and his eye had already begun to blacken. More dried blood ran from his mouth and onto his shirt. Yet the crusty captain stood unflinching, his lack of fear so prominent that Summer failed to notice he was still wearing a pair of boxer shorts.

A pair of commandos suddenly jumped in front of the *Starfish*'s acrylic bubble, waving their AK-74s about wildly in a show for Dirk and Summer to exit the submersible. The gun muzzles were quickly poked in their faces as they climbed out of the submersible and were marched over to Morgan and Tongju.

'Mr. Pitt,' Tongju said in a low voice. 'Good of you to join us.'

'I don't believe I've had the pleasure of your acquaintance,' Dirk replied sarcastically.

'A humble servant of the Japanese Red Army whose name is unimportant,' Tongju replied with feigned graciousness, bowing his head slightly.

'I didn't realize there were still any of you fruitcakes left outside of jail.'

Tongju just held his grin, not moving a facial muscle. 'You and your sister have fifteen minutes to replenish the submersible's batteries and prepare to retrieve the final two ordnance,' he said calmly.

'They are both damaged and in pieces,' Dirk lied, his mind racing to compute a plan of action.

Tongju calmly raised the Glock pistol aimed at Morgan's side and held the muzzle to the captain's right temple. 'You have fourteen minutes, at which time I shall kill your captain. Then I will kill your sister. And then I will kill you,' he said coldly, his lips parting in a self-satisfying grin.

Dirk could feel the blood racing through his veins as he glared at the madman in anger. Then the delicate touch of Summer's hand on his shoulder dispelled any thoughts of rash action.

'Come on, Dirk, we haven't much time,' she said, guiding him to a wheeled cart that had been rolled out with replacement batteries for the submersible. Morgan looked at Dirk and nodded in concurrence. Fighting the feeling of total helplessness, he reluctantly began transferring the batteries to the *Starfish*, all the while keeping one eye glued to the commando leader.

As they prepped the submersible for a last dive,

the final remnants of the ship's crew were marched by and forced into the rear hold at gunpoint. Summer grimly noted the frightened look on two lab analysts as they were prodded roughly down the hatchway.

Working quickly, Dirk and Summer replaced the submersible's power supply in just over twelve minutes. There would be no time for the standard postoperation and predive system checks normally performed before the submersible was returned to the water. They would have to hope the *Starfish* was operational for one more dive.

Tongju walked over in a measured clip and glared up at the two Americans, who both towered over him.

'You will promptly retrieve the remaining ordnance and return to the vessel without any nonsense. You have ninety minutes to complete your dive successfully or there will be severe consequences.'

'If I were you, I think I'd be worrying about the consequences from our military forces for pirating a government ship,' Summer spat angrily.

'There will be no consequences,' Tongju replied, smiling thinly, 'for a ship that no longer exists.'

Before Summer could respond, Tongju spun on his heels and walked away, replaced by two commandos who stepped forward with their assault rifles drawn and aimed.

'Come on, sister,' Dirk muttered. 'There's no use arguing with a psychopath.'

*

Dirk and Summer threaded themselves back into the *Starfish*, then were roughly jostled into the air by the crane operator. As they were prepared to be let go, Dirk watched through the acrylic bubble as Morgan was roughly manhandled to the stern hold and forcefully pitched down into the container. A commando on a stern deck crane hoisted up the massive steel hatch and positioned it over the rear hold before lowering it in place. Secured over the hold, the hatch imprisoned the entire ship's crew in darkness below.

With a violent splash, the *Starfish* was crudely dropped into the moon pool a second later and released from the ship's cable.

'He means to sink the *Sea Rover*,' Dirk said to Summer as they began their slow descent to the bottom.

'With the entire crew locked in the hold?' she asked, shaking her head in disbelief.

'I think so,' he said somberly. 'Unfortunately, there's not much we can do in the way of calling for help.'

'Our underwater communication system won't do any good, and any surface calls we might try wouldn't have the range to reach anybody in this region except a few Chinese fishermen.'

'Or the cable ship that is evidently supporting these characters,' he added, shaking his head.

'Our intelligence heads apparently underestimated this Japanese Red Army,' Summer said. 'Those guys didn't look like a rogue band of ideological extremists with dynamite strapped to their backs.'

'No, it's apparent they are well-trained military professionals. Whoever's running their operation is obviously skilled and well funded.'

'I wonder what they intend to do with the bombs?'

'An attack in Japan would figure. But there's obviously more to this Japanese Red Army than meets the eye, so I wouldn't want to wager on what their intent is.'

'I guess we can't worry about that for now. We've got to figure out a way to save the crew.'

'I counted eight commandos, and there was no doubt a few more on the bridge and elsewhere on the ship. Too many to overpower with a couple of screwdrivers,' Dirk said, examining the contents of a small toolbox mounted behind his seat.

'We'll need to quietly get some of the crewmen out of the hold to help us. If we had enough people, maybe we could overpower them.'

'I don't relish the thought of going unarmed against an AK-74, but there might be a chance in numbers. Getting the lid off that storage hold is the problem. I'd need a couple of uninterrupted minutes on the stern crane, but I don't think our friends in black would be too obliging.'

'There must be another way out of that hold,' Summer wondered.

'No, unfortunately, there isn't. I'm sure it matches the *Deep Endeavor*, where it was designed strictly as a storage hold and is blocked off from any entry amidships by the moon pool.'

'I thought Ryan had run a power cable down there once from someplace other than the open hatch cover.'

Dirk thought hard for a moment, trying to jog his memory. After a long minute, a light finally clicked on.

'You're right. There's a small venting hatch that opens on the bulkhead just aft of the moon pool. It's really more of an air vent, designed to release the buildup of noxious gases if chemicals are stored in the hold. I'm pretty sure a man could squeeze through it. The problem for Morgan and the crew is that it's sealed and locked from the outside.'

'We've got to figure out a way to unlock it,' Summer willed.

Together, they worked through several contingency plans, finally settling on an order of attack based on their opportunities once aboard the *Sea Rover*. It would take timing, skill, and a dose of daring to pull off. But mostly it would take luck.

27

Dirk and Summer fell silent as their minds conjured up gruesome images of the *Sea Rover* sinking with all hands, their friends, and coworkers trapped in the airtight hold. Then the specter of the *I-411* suddenly rose up in the blackness before them and they washed the images from their minds. With the clock ticking, they went about their business of retrieving the final two canisters of death.

Dirk maneuvered the submersible into the hangar as before, setting the *Starfish* down within easy reach of the remaining ordnance. As Summer began manipulating the mechanical arms by sight through the acrylic bubble, Dirk observed the video camera feed on the monitor, which recorded every moment of the recovery. He watched while Summer gently lifted the first canister and was placing it in the recovery basket when he suddenly powered up *Snoopy* and grabbed the remote vehicle's controls. In an instant, he nudged the ROV out of its cradle just a few inches, then spun the tiny machine around until its nose was pressed against the submersible's skid plates and applied full thrusting power. The tiny ROV went nowhere, but its water jets stirred up a thick cloud of muck and sediment in front of the *Starfish*. In a flash, the water visibility went to zero amid a cloud of brown.

'What are you doing?' Summer demanded, freezing the mechanical arm controls.

'You'll see,' he said, although there was nothing to see at all. After reaching over and fidgeting with Summer's controls for a moment, he then powered down the ROV's thruster. It took two minutes for the seawater to clear enough that Summer could proceed with seizing the final canister.

'You want to try that trick again?' she asked after depositing the bomb into the basket.

'Why not?' he replied, hitting the ROV thruster again and stirring up another muddy cloud for the camera.

Once the water cleared and both canisters were pinned into the basket, Dirk edged the submersible away from the submarine and they began their slow ascent. Halfway to the surface, they traded positions, squirming over one another so that Summer controlled the submersible's movements while Dirk manned the controls of both mechanical arms.

'Okay, take us on up,' Dirk instructed. 'As soon as they drop us onto the deck, I'll need you to create a diversion.' While he spoke, he worked the left mechanical arm away from its locked position on the weapons basket and flexed it straight out to its full extension so that it poked out from the *Starfish* like a lance.

Summer trusted her brother's instincts implicitly,

and had little time to argue anyway. The ringed lights of the moon pool soon came into view. Summer steered the *Starfish* to the center of the opening, then they broke surface with a rush of bubbles and foaming seawater. A metallic clank was heard as the lifting hook was attached to the submersible and the diminutive vessel was yanked from the water. Summer peered out at Tongju and a half-dozen other commandos as the submersible swung through the air. Her brother, she noted, was intently watching their forward progress while gently adjusting the mechanical arm's position. When they were crudely dropped to the deck by the inexperienced crane operator, she saw Dirk jam the arm controls all the way forward. The metal claw bounced forward along the deck as they stopped, coming to a halt near the rear bulkhead. Four feet off to the side was the small, sealed venting hatch that led to the storage hold.

'Our boy on the crane came through,' Dirk muttered. 'We're in the ballpark.'

'I guess it's showtime,' Summer replied with a nervous look.

Moving quickly, she stripped out of her NUMA jumpsuit, revealing a lean body that was clad in a skimpy two-piece bathing suit covered by a large T-shirt. Reaching under the shirt, she unhooked her bathing top and let it fall to the floor, then grabbed the loose base of her T-shirt and tied a knot with the material just above her navel. The tightened shirt clearly revealed the shapely contour of her full breasts and midriff. Dirk helped open the escape hatch, then quickly returned to the manipulator arm controls as Summer burst out of the submersible.

Tongju was busy talking to the crane operator with his back toward the submersible when Summer crawled out. Seeing him turned away, she hurriedly approached the nearest commando, who stood glaring at her exposed features with a leer. His leer turned to shock as Summer shouted at the top of her lungs, 'Get your hands off me, creep!'

Her words were followed by an open-hand slap to the man's face that nearly sent him sprawling. If her bikini and tight shirt hadn't already attracted everyone's attention, then her decking one of their fellow commandos suddenly brought every eye on the ship upon her.

Every eye except Dirk's. Capitalizing on the commotion, he powered the mechanical arm to its full lateral reach, just barely stretching its extended claw to the bulkhead vent hatch. Grabbing the lockdown handle with the claw, he nudged it to the unlocked position and pulled on it just a hair, to ensure the hatch would open. Quickly letting go, he eased the arm back alongside the *Starfish*, then powered it down. Scampering out the submersible's entry hatch, he stood casually in back of the submersible as if he'd been there all along.

'What is this all about?' Tongju hissed as he approached Summer, his Glock pistol drawn and aimed at her midsection.

'This pervert tried to assault me,' Summer screeched, jerking a thumb toward the slack-jawed commando. Tongju let fly a stream of obscenities until the confounded gunman shrank like a wilting violet. The commando leader then turned back to Summer and Dirk, who now stood behind his sister.

'You two, back in the submersible,' he commanded in English, the muzzle of his Glock pointing the way.

'Jeez, a guy can't even stretch his legs around here,' Dirk complained as if it were his biggest concern at the moment. As they made their way back into the submersible, they noticed for the first time that the Japanese cable-laying ship was heaving to alongside the *Sea Rover*. Though little longer than the NUMA vessel, the Japanese ship had a much higher superstructure and seemed to tower over the *Sea Rover*. The *Baekje* was hardly alongside a minute before a huge crane on her stern deck swung over the *Sea Rover*'s side rail trailing a cable with an empty pallet that spun lazily in the breeze. From inside the submersible, they watched as the pallet was dropped to the deck beside them. A trio of black-clad commandos then rolled several storage containers out of the *Sea Rover*'s auxiliary laboratory and secured them to the pallet. Each container, they knew, held one of the biological bombs encased in a cushioned sheath.

The *Baekje*'s crane operator quickly transferred the pallet back and forth several times in the predawn darkness until all of the bomb containers were aboard the Japanese ship. The empty pallet then became a bus, ferrying the commandos to the ship a handful at a time. From belowdecks, a black-clad gunman appeared and conversed briefly with Tongju. Dirk noticed Tongju break into a thin smile, then pointed toward the submersible and barked out an order. The cable hook was released from the pallet and attached to the *Starfish*.

'Guess we're changing rides,' Dirk commented when the cable was pulled taut.

This time the submersible was hoisted smoothly into the air. Dirk rapidly jabbed the mechanical arm out and rapped three times on the rear bulkhead with the claw before being pulled up and off the deck. He and Summer watched the *Sea Rover* fall away beneath them as they were carried over the water and deposited on a high stern deck of the *Baekje*. Climbing out of the submersible, they were welcomed by a pair of armed thugs, who prodded them toward the ship's railing with their guns.

'I've had about enough of the assault rifle hospitality,' Dirk muttered.

'I bet they feel naked when they don't have a gun in their hands,' Summer replied.

From their vantage point, they watched as the remaining commandos were ferried over on the pallet, Tongju riding with the last batch.

'Dirk, is it my eyes or is the *Sea Rover* sitting lower in the water?' Summer asked with alarm in her voice.

'You're right,' he agreed, studying the ship. 'They

must have opened the sea cocks. She's listing a little to starboard as well.'

The pallet carrying Tongju swung to the deck and the commando leader jumped off, landing lightly on his feet. He immediately approached the two captives.

'I suggest you say good-bye to your ship,' he said without feeling.

'The crew is trapped in the hold, you murderous swine!' Summer cried out.

Charged by emotion, she took a lunging step toward Tongju in anger. The trained killer reacted instinctively, launching a vicious right kick to Summer's midsection, sending her sprawling backward. But his trained reflexes were not swift enough to ward off the unexpected quickness of Dirk, who sprang forward and threw a solid left hook just as Tongju regained his footing. The crushing blow landed on Tongju's right temple, sending him dropping to one knee, where he teetered on the verge of blacking out. The nearby gunmen immediately jumped on Dirk, one of them ramming an assault rifle into his stomach as two others held back his arms.

Tongju gradually regained his senses and rose to his feet, then stepped purposely over to Dirk. Thrusting his face close to Dirk's chin, he spoke in a calm voice dripping with menace.

'I shall enjoy watching you die in the manner of your shipmates,' he said, then brusquely turned and walked away.

The remaining commandos roughly herded Dirk and Summer down a side stairwell and along a narrow corridor before shoving them into a small cabin berth. The cabin door was slammed shut behind them and locked from the outside, where two men remained on guard.

Dirk and Summer quickly shook off the pain from their blows. Staggering past two twin beds wedged into the tiny cabin, they pressed their faces against a small porthole on the outside bulkhead.

'She's lower in the water,' Summer observed with dread in her voice.

Through the porthole, they could see the *Sea Rover* still floating alongside the *Baekje*, the seawater creeping inexorably closer to the tops of her gunwales. No sign of life appeared on the decks, and the big research vessel had all the appearance of a listing ghost ship. Dirk and Summer searched for signs of movement aft of the moon pool but saw nothing.

'They've either relocked the vent hatch or Morgan can't get to it,' Dirk cursed.

'Or he doesn't know it exists,' Summer whispered.

Beneath their feet, they heard then felt an increased rumbling as the *Baekje*'s engines were engaged and the big cable ship slowly pulled away from the sinking NUMA vessel. The predawn light had yet to edge over the black night sky and it took just a few minutes before the sight of the *Sea Rover* fell away into a fuzzy grouping of twinkling lights.

Dirk and Summer strained to watch the NUMA

ship as the *Baekje* increased speed and distance. The twinkling lights eventually dissolved beneath the horizon until they could see nothing more of their ship and comrades.

28

'Sir, we seem to have lost all contact with the *Sea Rover*.'

Rudi Gunn looked up slowly from his desk. His bespectacled blue eyes bore into the NUMA field support analyst standing nervously before him.

'How long ago?' Gunn probed.

'Our communications link fell nonresponsive a little over three hours ago. We continued to receive a digital GPS position update, which showed they were still fixed on-site in the East China Sea. That signal was lost approximately twenty minutes ago.'

'Did they issue a distress call?'

'No, sir, none that we received.' Despite ten years of service with the agency, the analyst displayed obvious discomfort at being the bearer of bad news to senior management.

'What about the Navy vessel? They were assigned an escort.'

'Sir, the Navy rescinded their frigate escort before *Sea Rover* left port in Osaka due to an exercise commitment with the Taiwanese Navy.'

'That's just great,' Gunn exclaimed in frustration.

'Sir, we've requested satellite imagery from the National Reconnaissance Office. We should have something within the hour.'

'I want search and rescue craft in the air now,' Gunn barked. 'Contact the Air Force and Navy. See who's got the closest resources and get them moving. Quick!'

'Yes, sir,' the young man replied, nearly jumping out of Gunn's office.

Gunn mulled over the situation. NUMA research ships had the latest in satellite communications equipment. They wouldn't just disappear without warning. And the *Sea Rover* had one of the most experienced and competent crews in the NUMA fleet. Dirk must be right, he feared. There must be a powerful operation that was pursuing the biological bombs on board the *I-411*.

With a foreboding sense of dread, Gunn picked up his telephone and buzzed his secretary.

'Darla, get me the vice president.'

Captain Robert Morgan was not a man to go down easy. Shaking off his shattered femur and broken cheekbone as if they were a sprain and a scratch, he quickly took order of his shaken crew after being unceremoniously tossed into the confined storage hold. Seconds after his arrival, the heavy steel hatch cover was slammed down above them, the crash of the massive lid thrusting the compartment into complete darkness. Frightened whispers echoed off the steel walls while the dank air hung thick with the odor of diesel fuel.

'Don't panic,' Morgan bellowed in response to the murmurs. 'Ryan, are you in here?'

'Over here,' Ryan's voice rang back from a corner.

'There should be a spare lightweight ROV secured in the rear. Find some batteries and see if you can't get the lights rigged,' he ordered.

A dim light suddenly glowed in the back of the hold, the narrow beam of a portable flashlight clasped in the paw of the *Sea Rover*'s chief engineer.

'We'll get it done, Cap'n,' growled the Irish-tinged voice of the engineer, a red-haired salt named McIntosh.

Ryan and McIntosh located the spare ROV in a storage cradle, and further rummaging under the faint light produced a stockpile of battery packs. Ryan proceeded to cut one end of the ROV's power cable and spliced several internal lines to the battery pack terminals. Once he configured a complete circuit, the ROV's bright xenon lights burst on in a blinding shower of blue-white luminescence. Several crew members standing near the ROV's lights squinted their eyes shut tight at the sudden surge of light in the blackened hold. Under the bath of light, Morgan was able to examine his shipboard crew and the onboard team of scientists, which he noted were huddled in small groups throughout the hold. A mix of confusion and fear was reflected in the faces of most of the men and women.

'Nice work, Ryan. McIntosh, move those lights across the hold, please. Now, then, is anybody hurt?' the captain said, ignoring his own severe injuries.

A quick tally revealed a score of cuts, bumps, and

bruises. But aside from the wounded machinist and a broken leg suffered by a geologist when he fell into the hold, there were no other serious injuries.

'We're going to get out of this,' Morgan lectured confidently. 'These goons just want the items we've been salvaging off the Japanese submarine. Chances are, they'll let us out of here just as soon as they've smuggled the materials off to their ship,' he said, internally doubting his own words. 'But, just in case, we'll figure out a way to pop the lid on our own. We've certainly got plenty of manpower to do it with. McIntosh, swing that light around again, let's see what we've got to work with around here.'

McIntosh and Ryan picked up the portable ROV and walked it toward the center of the hold, then slowly turned it in a 360-degree circle, the bright beams spraying an arc of light over the people and objects in its path. As a storeroom for the *Starfish*, the hold resembled a large electronic parts bin. Coils of cabling hung from the bulkheads, while spare electronic components were stored in multiple cabinets mounted on the aft wall. Racks of test equipment lined one side of the hold, while at the forward end of the bay a sixteen-foot Zodiac inflatable boat sat on a wooden cradle. Off to one corner, a half-dozen fifty-five-gallon drums of gasoline were wedged alongside two spare outboard motors. Ryan held the light shining on the drums for several minutes, illuminating a series of iron rungs that ran up the bulkhead and under an overhang in back of the drums.

'Captain, there's a venting hatch located up those rungs that opens up onto the aft moon pool deck,' Ryan said. 'It locks from the deck side, but there's a chance it may have been left open.'

'One of you men there,' Morgan barked at a trio of scientists huddled near the drums. 'Climb up that ladder and see if the hatch is unlocked.'

A barefoot oceanographer clad in blue pajamas jumped at the captain's request and scampered up the metal rungs, disappearing into a narrow vent shaft that was carved through the overhang. A few moments later, he climbed back into view, his feet now sensitive to the crude ladder steps.

'It's locked solid, Captain,' he said with disappointment.

McIntosh suddenly piped up from the center of the hold.

'Cap'n, I think we can construct a couple of spars from the wooden supports underneath that Zodiac,' he said, pointing an arm toward the rubber boat. 'With six or eight men on each, we ought to be able to prod up a corner of the main hatch.'

'Poke it off with a couple of big chopsticks, eh? That, indeed, might work. Go to it, McIntosh. You men over there, help get that Zodiac off its stand,' he growled at a party assembled near the boat.

Limping over, he grabbed hold of the boat's bow and helped muscle it off the wooden stands and onto the deck. Several men assisted McIntosh in dissecting the support cradle and laying out its separate pieces while the ship's carpenter assessed how to reassemble the material into several spars.

While they worked, they could hear the muffled voices of the commandos on deck and the whirring and clanking of the *Baekje*'s crane as it loaded and hoisted away the *I-411*'s ordnance. At one point, the faint echo of machine-gun fire was heard emanating from a distant part of the ship. A short time later, Morgan detected the sound of the *Starfish* being hoisted out of the moon pool and dropped to the deck, followed by the shrieking cry of a woman's voice he knew to be Summer's. The activity above them grew quieter after some banging on the bulkhead above their heads. Eventually, the humming of the cranes and the sporadic voices fell silent. As it became evident that the commandos had left the ship, Morgan quietly wondered about the fate of Dirk and Summer. His thoughts were suddenly jarred by the rumble of the *Baekje*'s engines vibrating through the hold as the cable ship pulled away from *Sea Rover*.

'How are we coming along, McIntosh?' he asked loudly to mask the sound of abandonment, although he could clearly see the progress in front of him.

'We've two spars together and are close to completing a third,' the chief engineer grunted. At his feet were three uneven-looking wooden poles, roughly ten feet in length. Each was constructed of three separate pieces of timber, crudely indented at either end with a hammer and screwdriver and fitted together in a notched tongue-and-groove fashion.

Metal sheeting cannibalized from a test rack was hammered around the joints for stability and finished off in a wrapped layer of the handyman's favored duct tape.

As McIntosh sifted through the remaining pieces of scrap wood, a sudden rushing noise drifted up from the bowels of the ship. In a few minutes, the sound doubled in intensity, resembling the rumbling waters of a turbulent stream. McIntosh stood slowly and addressed the captain in a somber, matter-of-fact voice.

'Sir, they've opened the sea cocks. They mean to sink her.'

Several unseen voices gasped in horror at McIntosh's words and numerous cries of 'No!' echoed through the hold. Morgan ignored them all.

'Looks like we'll have to make do with three spars,' the captain replied calmly. 'I need seven men on each pole. Let's get them up now.'

A rush of men moved forward and grabbed the spars as the first drops of seawater began trickling into the hold through a half-dozen small bilge drains mounted flush on the hold's deck. Within minutes, they were sloshing around in ankle-deep water as the men positioned the ends of the spars against the forward corner of the hatch, next to the entry ladder. On the top step, a man stood with a two-foot-high triangular block of timber, his job to insert it under the open hatch lid and keep it wedged open.

'Ready . . . lift!' Morgan shouted.

In unison, the three teams of men pressed the tips of their spars against the hatch cover eight feet over their heads and pushed up with all their might. To everyone's surprise, the hatch cover burst open several feet, letting in a spray of muted light from the deck lights, before its weight shifted and the heavy cover slammed back down.

The forlorn man at the top of the ladder froze an instant before trying to insert the block wedge and was too late. The hatch crashed down about his head as he tried to shove the wedge into the open gap, the lip nearly taking off the fingers of his right hand. The shaken man took a deep breath, then nodded at Morgan that he was okay to try again.

'All right, let's give it another try,' Morgan commanded as water now swirled about his knees, the salt water stinging his open leg wound. 'One . . . two . . . three!'

A loud crack ripped through the hold as the top joint on one of the spars broke clean in two, the loose section falling into the water with a splash. McIntosh waded over and examined the damaged end piece, finding the grooved joint had broken completely off.

'Not good, sir,' he reported. 'Will take some time to repair.'

'Do what you can,' Morgan barked. 'Let's continue with two spars . . . Heave!'

The remaining men shoved at their spars but it was a lost cause. There was no way of getting enough manpower behind the two spars to apply enough leverage. Additional men crowded in to try and help, but there was simply not enough room to put more hands on the timbers and push. Twice the men strained with the additional force and were able to pry the hatch open a few inches, but it was not nearly enough to block it so that a man could escape. The surging seawater was now up to Morgan's waist and he could see in the faces of the crew that the terror of drowning was about to incite panic in the hold.

'One more try, men,' he urged on while somewhere in the back of his own mind he morbidly calculated the estimated duration it took for a man to drown.

With adrenaline pumping, the men jammed the two spars against the hatch cover one last time with all their might. This time, they seemed to find their strength and the lid began to creak up. But just as they pressed their leverage, another crack echoed through the hold. A second spar splintered at the joint and the hatch cover clanged back shut.

Somewhere in a darkened corner a voice blurted out, 'That's it, we're finished.'

It was enough for a trembling cook standing near the gasoline drums to lose his nerve.

'I can't swim, I can't swim!' he cried out as the water level inched up his chest.

In a frightened panic, he grabbed onto the iron rungs that ran to the vent hatch and scurried up into the shaft. Reaching the top rung in darkness, his frenzied terror continued and he began pounding on the small round hatch cover with his fists, crying to be let out. In a state of complete shock, he suddenly felt the hatch give way under his hands and drift open. With his heart pounding in disbelief, he squirmed through the hatch and stood on the deck beside the moon pool dumbfounded. It took nearly a full minute before his racing pulse began to slow and he regained composure over his senses. Realizing that he wasn't going to die just yet, he scrambled back into the hatch and down the ladder a few steps, then shouted into the hold at the top of his lungs.

'The hatch is open! The hatch is open! This way, everybody!'

Like an army of angry fire ants, the panicked crew swarmed to the ladder, crushing one another to escape. By now, most of the crew were treading water or clinging to the bulkheads, while a few drifted about the hold clinging to the now-floating rubber Zodiac. The small ROV also drifted freely, casting its bright lights in a surreal glow about the hold.

'Ladies first,' Morgan shouted, deferring to the traditional rule of the sea.

Ryan, who stood near the ladder on his toes chin high to the water, tried to restore order amid the chaos.

'You heard the captain. Ladies only. Back off, you,' he growled at a pair of male biologists clamoring to get up the ladder. As the female crew members rapidly scurried up the vent and out the hatch, Ryan succeeded in maintaining some semblance of order with the dozens waiting their turn. Across the hold, Morgan could see that the water level was rising too fast. There was no way everyone was going to get out in time, assuming the ship didn't suddenly sink from under their feet to begin with.

'Ryan, get up that ladder. See if you can get the main hatch off,' Morgan ordered.

Ryan didn't take time to answer, following a ship's nurse up the ladder as fast as his legs would carry him. Squirming through the hatch and falling to the deck, he was shocked at what his eyes beheld. In the early dawn light, he could see that the *Sea Rover* was sinking fast by the stern. Seawater was already washing over the sternpost, while the bow poked up toward the sky at better than a twenty-degree angle. Scrambling to his feet, he saw a young assistant communications officer helping others move to a higher level on the ship.

'Melissa, get to the radio room and issue a Mayday,' he shouted, running past her.

He climbed a short stairwell to the rear hatch, his eye catching the sparkle of a light in the far distance to the north, the cable ship heading off over the horizon. Jumping up onto the hatch, he allowed himself a second to let out a brief sigh of relief. The rising waters off the stern had not yet lapped over the edge of the hatch nor had inundated the aft crane. In their haste, the commandos had even left the crane's hook-and-boom assembly attached to the hatch.

Sprinting to the crane, he hopped into the cab and fired up its diesel engines, immediately shoving the hand controls to raise the boom. With unbearable slowness, the boom gradually rose into the air, lifting the massive hatch cover up with it. Ryan wasted no time rotating the boom a few feet to starboard before jumping out of the cab, leaving the hatch cover dangling in the air.

Rushing to the edge of the hold, he found more than thirty men bobbing in the water fighting for their lives. The water level had already risen to within a foot of the hatch. Another two minutes, he figured, and the men would have all drowned. Reaching his arms in, he began tugging and grabbing at the men one by one, yanking them up and out of the hold. With those on deck helping, Ryan had every man out within a matter of seconds. He ensured that he personally eased the final man out of the water, Captain Morgan.

'Nice work, Tim,' the captain winced as he wobbled to his feet.

'Sorry that I didn't personally check the vent hatch in the first place, sir. We could have gotten everyone out sooner had we known it was actually unlocked.'

'But it wasn't. Don't you get it? It was Dirk who unlocked it. He knocked on the door for us but we forgot to answer.'

A look of enlightenment crossed Ryan's face. 'Thank God for him and Summer, the poor devils.

But I'm afraid we're not out of the woods yet, sir. She's going down fast.'

'Spread the word to abandon ship. Let's get some lifeboats in the water, pronto,' Morgan replied, stumbling up the inclining deck toward the bow. 'I'll see about sending a distress.'

As if on cue, Melissa the communications officer came scrambling across the deck half out of breath.

'Sir,' she gasped, 'they've shot up the communications system . . . and satellite equipment. There's no way to send a Mayday.'

'All right,' Morgan replied without surprise. 'We'll deploy our emergency beacons and wait for someone to come looking for us. Report to your lifeboat. Let's get everybody off this ship now.'

While heading to assist with the lifeboats, Ryan now noticed that the *Starfish* was missing. Slipping into the auxiliary lab, he found that the recovered bomb canisters had been neatly removed, dissolving any doubts about the reason for the assault.

After their ordeal in the storage hold, an unusual calmness fell over the crew as they abandoned ship. Quietly and in composed order, the men and women quickly made their way to their respective lifeboat stations, glad to have a second chance at life despite the fact their ship was sinking beneath their feet. The advancing water was proceeding rapidly up the deck and two lifeboats closest to the stern were already flooded before they could be released from their davits. The assigned crew was quickly dispersed to other boats, which were being launched to the water in a torrid frenzy.

Morgan hobbled up the sloping deck, which was now inclined at a thirty-degree angle, till reaching the captain's boat, which sat loaded and waiting. Morgan stopped and surveyed the ship's decks a last time, like a gambler who had bet, and lost, the farm. The ship was creaking and groaning as the weight of the salt water filling its lower compartments tugged at the vessel's structural integrity. An aura of sadness enveloped the research ship, as if it knew that it was too soon for it to be cast to the waves.

At last confident that all the crew were safely away, Morgan threw a sharp salute to his vessel, then stepped into the lifeboat, the last man off. The boat was quickly winched down to the rolling sea and motored away from the stricken ship. The sun had just crept over the horizon and cast a golden beam on the research ship as it struggled for its last moments. Morgan's lifeboat was just a few yards away from the *Sea Rover* when her bow suddenly rose sharply toward the sky, then the turquoise ship slipped gracefully into the sea stern first amid a boiling hiss of bubbles.

As the ship slipped from view, its traumatized crew was overcome by a solitary sensation: silence.

29

'Something's rotten in Denmark.'

Summer ignored her brother's words and held a small bowl of fish stew up to her nose. After uninterrupted confinement for most of the day, the heavy door of their cabin had burst open and a galley cook wearing a white apron entered with a tray containing the stew, some rice, and a pot of tea. An armed guard watched menacingly from the hallway as the food was set down and the nervous cook quickly left without saying a word. Summer was famished and eagerly surveyed the food as the door was bolted back shut from the outside.

Taking a deep whiff of the fish stew, she wrinkled her nose.

'I think there's a few things rotten around here as well,' she said.

Moving on to the rice, she drove a pair of chopsticks into the bowl and began munching on the steamed grains. At last bringing relief to her hunger pangs, she turned her attention back to Dirk, who sat gazing out the porthole window.

'Aside from our crummy lower-berth cabin, what's bugging you now?' she asked.

'Don't quote me on this, but I don't think we're headed to Japan.'

'How can you tell?' Summer asked, scooping a mound of rice into her mouth.

'I've been observing the sun and the shadows cast off the ship. We should be heading north-northeast if we were traveling to Japan, but it appears to me that our course heading is more to the northwest.'

'That's a fine line to distinguish with the naked eye.'

'Agreed. But I just call 'em as I see 'em. If we pull into Nagasaki, then just send me back to celestial navigation school.'

'That would mean we're heading toward the Yellow Sea,' she replied, picturing an imaginary map of the region in her head. 'Do you think we're sailing to China?'

'Could be. There's certainly no love lost between China and Japan. Perhaps the Japanese Red Army has a base of operations in China. That might explain the lack of success the authorities have had in tracking down any suspects in Japan.'

'Possibly. But they'd have to be operating with state knowledge or sponsorship, and I would hope they'd think twice before sinking an American research vessel.'

'True. Then again, there is another possibility.'

Summer nodded, waiting for Dirk to continue.

'The two Japanese hoods who shot up my Chrysler. A forensics doctor at the county morgue thought that the men looked Korean.'

Summer finished eating the rice and set down the bowl and chopsticks.

'Korea?' she asked, her brow furrowing.

'Korea.'

Ed Coyle's eyes had long since grown weary of scanning the flat gray sea for something out of the ordinary. He nearly didn't trust his eyes when something finally tugged at the corner of his vision. Focusing toward the horizon, he just barely made out a small light in the sky dragging a wispy white tail. It was exactly what the copilot of the Lockheed HC-130 Hercules search-and-rescue plane had been hoping to see.

'Charlie, I've got a flare at two o'clock,' Coyle said into his microphoned headset with the smooth voice of an ESPN sportscaster. Instinctively, he pointed a gloved hand at a spot on the windshield where he'd seen the white burst.

'I got her,' Major Charles Wight replied with a slight drawl while peering out the cockpit. A lanky Texan with a cucumber-cool demeanor, the HC-130's pilot gently banked the aircraft toward the fading smoke stream and slightly reduced airspeed.

Six hours after departing Kadena Air Base in Okinawa, the search-and-rescue pilots had started wondering whether their mission was a wild-goose chase. Now they crept to the edge of their seats, wondering what they would find in the waters beneath them. A grouping of white dots slowly appeared on the distant horizon, gradually growing larger as the aircraft approached.

'Looks like we've got us some lifeboats,' Wight stated as the specks grew into distinguishable shapes.

'Seven of them,' Coyle confirmed, counting the small boats stretched in a line. Morgan had rounded up all the lifeboats and lashed them together, bow to stern, in order to keep the survivors together. As the Hercules flew in low over them, the crew of the *Sea Rover* waved wildly in response and let out a collective cheer.

'Roughly sixty heads,' Coyle estimated as Wight brought the plane around in a slow circle. 'They look to be in pretty good shape.'

'Let's hold the PJs, drop an emergency medical pack, and see if we can initiate a sea pickup.'

The PJs were three medically trained pararescue jumpers in the back of the plane ready to parachute out of the HC-130 at a moment's notice. Since the crew of the *Sea Rover* appeared in no imminent danger, Wight opted to withhold their deployment for the time being. A loadman at the back of the Hercules instead lowered a big hydraulic door beneath the tail and, at Coyle's command, shoved out several emergency medical and ration packs, which drifted down to the sea suspended from small parachutes.

An airborne communications specialist had meanwhile issued a distress call over the marine frequency. Within seconds, several nearby ships answered the call, the closest being a containership bound for Hong

Kong from Osaka. Wight and Coyle continued to circle the lifeboats for another two hours until the containership arrived on the scene and began taking aboard survivors off the first lifeboat. Satisfied they were now safe, the rescue plane took a final low pass over the castaways, Wight waggling the wingtips as he passed. Though the pilots could not hear it, the tired and haggard survivors let out a robust cheer of thanks that echoed across the water.

'Lucky devils,' Coyle commented with satisfaction.

Wight nodded in silent agreement, then banked the Hercules southeast toward its home base on Okinawa.

The large freighter had let go a welcoming blast of its Kahlenberg air horn as it glided toward the lifeboats. A whaleboat was lowered to guide the shipwreck victims around to a lowered stairwell near the stern, where most of the *Sea Rover*'s crew climbed up to the high deck. Morgan and a few other injured crewmen were transferred to the whaleboat and hoisted up to the containership's main deck. After a brief welcome and inquiry by the ship's Malaysian captain, Morgan was rushed down to the medical bay for treatment of his wounds.

Ryan caught up with him after the ship's doctor had tended to the NUMA captain's leg and confined him to a bunk next to the crewman with the broken leg.

'How's the prognosis, sir?'

'The knee's a mess but I'll live.'

'They do amazing things with artificial joints these days,' Ryan encouraged.

'Apparently, I'll be finding that out in an intimate way. Beats a peg leg, I guess. What's the state of the crew?'

'In good spirits now. With the exception of Dirk and Summer, the *Sea Rover*'s crew is all aboard and accounted for. I borrowed Captain Malaka's satellite phone and called Washington. I was able to speak directly with Rudi Gunn and informed him of our situation after briefing him on the loss of the ship. I let him know that our recovered cargo, along with Dirk, Summer, and the submersible, is believed aboard the Japanese cable ship. He asked me to express his thanks to you for saving the crew and promised that the highest levels of the government will be activated to apprehend those responsible.'

Morgan stared blankly at a white wall, his mind tumbling over the events of the past few hours. Who were these pirates that had attacked and sunk his ship? What was their intent with the biological weapons? And what had become of Dirk and Summer? Not generating any answers, he simply shook his head slowly.

'I just hope it won't be too late.'

30

After sailing north for a day and a half, the *Baekje* gradually arched its bow around toward an easterly heading. Landfall was spotted at dusk, and the ship waited until dark before creeping into a large harbor amid a hazy fog. Dirk and Summer surmised that they had, in fact, sailed to Korea and correctly guessed that they were in the South's large port city of Inchon, based on the number of internationally flagged freighters and containerships they passed entering the port.

The cable-laying ship moved slowly past the wide-spaced commercial docks that busily loaded and unloaded huge containerships around the clock. Turning north, the *Baekje* crept past an oil refinery terminal, snaking around a rusty tanker ship before entering a dark and less developed corner of the harbor. Drifting past a decrepit-looking shipyard housing scores of decomposing hulks, the ship slowed as it approached a small side channel that ran to the northwest. A guard hut with a small speedboat alongside stood at the entrance to the channel, beneath a rusting sign that proclaimed, in Korean: KANG MARINE SERVICES — PRIVATE.

The *Baekje*'s captain maneuvered the ship gently into the channel and proceeded several hundred yards at a slow creep before rounding a sharp bend. The channel fed into a small lagoon, which was dwarfed by a massive pair of covered docks that sat at the opposite end. As if pulling a car into the garage, the *Baekje*'s captain inched the ship into one of the cavernous hangars that towered a solid fifty feet above the ship's forecastle. The ship was tied off under a field of bright halogen lamps that hung from the ceiling, while a large hydraulic door quietly slid shut behind them, completely concealing the vessel from outside eyes.

A crane immediately swung over and a half-dozen crewmen began unloading the ordnance containers, which were lowered to the dock under Tongju's supervision. Once the bomb canisters were stacked on the deck in an orderly pyramid, a large white panel truck backed down the dock to the cargo. Another group of men, wearing powder blue lab coats, carefully loaded the weapons into the back of the truck, then drove away from the ship. As it turned a corner at the end of the dock, Tongju could see the familiar blue lightning bolt emblazoned on the side of the truck, beneath the words KANG SATELLITE TELE-COMMUNICATIONS CORP.

Kim approached as Tongju watched the truck exit the hangar through a guarded doorway.

'Mr. Kang will be quite pleased when he learns that we have recovered all of the ordnance,' Kim stated.

'Yes, though two of the twelve are worthless. The

submersible pilots cracked open the last two shells and released the armament into the water. An accident, they claim, due to a loss of visibility in the water.'

'An inconsequential loss. The overall mission was quite successful.'

'True, but there is still a difficult operation ahead of us. I am taking the prisoners to Kang in order for him to interrogate them. I trust that you will administer to the ship preparations satisfactorily,' he stated rather than asked.

'The reconfiguration of the vessel, as well as the replenishment of fuel and provisions, will begin immediately. I will ensure that the ship is ready to depart the minute our cargo is reloaded.'

'Very well. The sooner we get to sea, the better our chances of success.'

'We have surprise on our side. There is no way we can fail,' Kim said confidently.

But Tongju knew otherwise. Taking a long puff on a lit cigarette, he considered the element of surprise. It could indeed mean the difference between life and death.

'Let us just hope that our deception endures,' he finally replied thoughtfully.

Belowdecks, Dirk and Summer were roughly roused from their cabin cell, a thick-necked guard first handcuffing their wrists behind their backs before shoving them out of the room. They were marched at gunpoint to a gangway leading off the ship, where Tongju stood watching with a sneer on his face.

'It was a lovely cruise. You never did show us where the shuffleboard court was located, however,' Dirk said to the assassin.

'Now, be honest,' Summer piped in. 'The food didn't exactly warrant a five-star rating.'

'The American sense of humor is hardly amusing,' Tongju grunted, his cold eyes showing that he was not the least bit entertained.

'By the way, what exactly is the Japanese Red Army doing in Inchon, Korea?' Dirk asked bluntly.

A barely perceptible arch crossed Tongju's brow.

'Most observant, Mr. Pitt.' Then, ignoring his captives further, he turned to Thick Neck, who cradled an AK-74 leveled at the pair.

'Take them to the high-speed launch and lock them in the forward berth under guard,' he barked, then turned on his heels and marched to the bridge.

Dirk and Summer were marshaled down the gangplank and across the dock to a smaller side slip, where a sleek-looking motor yacht was tied up. It was a thirty-one-meter South Pacific marine high-speed catamaran, painted a teal blue. Designed and built for passenger ferry service, it had been refitted as a fast oceangoing personal luxury yacht. Equipped with four-thousand-horsepower diesel engines, the luxury cat could cruise along at speeds over 35 knots.

'Now, this is more my style,' Summer commented

as they were prodded aboard and locked in a small but plushly appointed center berth.

'No windows this time. Guess Mr. Hospitality didn't like your Inchon crack,' Summer added as she curled her way into a small salon chair, her hands still cuffed behind her back.

'Me and my big mouth,' Dirk replied. 'At least we now have a rough idea of where we are.'

'Yes . . . right in the middle of deep kimchi. Well, if we got to go, at least we get to go first class,' she said, admiring the walnut paneling and expensive artwork adorning the walls. 'These guys certainly have some deep pockets for a second-rate terrorist organization.'

'Apparently, they have some friends at Kang Enterprises.'

'The shipping company?'

'A large conglomerate. We've seen their commercial freighters around for years. They're also involved in some other high-tech businesses as well, though I'm only familiar with their shipping division. I met a guy in a bar once who worked as an oiler on one of their ships. He told me about their enclosed repair and storage facility in Inchon. Never seen anything like it. There's supposedly a dry dock at one end, and the place is chock-full of state-of-the-art equipment. The cable ship had the Kang trademark blue lightning bolt on the funnel. This has to be the place.'

'Glad to see all that time you spent as a barfly is finally paying off,' Summer quipped.

'Research. Strictly research,' he smiled.

Summer suddenly turned serious. 'Why would a South Korean business be mixed up with the JRA? And what do they want with us?'

Her words were interrupted by the throaty roar of the catamaran's diesel engines as they were fired up astern of their cabin.

'I guess we'll soon find out.'

Tongju crossed over and boarded the catamaran as the ropes were cast off, the fast boat burbling along the dockage at a crawl. The huge hangar door slid to the side again, allowing the catamaran to exit the enclosed building. As they slipped through the doorway, Tongju glanced back at the big cable ship towering over them.

An army of workmen was already crawling about the *Baekje* like a swarm of bees. A heavy-duty crane was removing the giant cable-laying wheel from the stern deck, while teams of painters resprayed the topside decks. Elsewhere, construction crews were cutting the superstructure in some areas while adding compartments and bulkheads in other places. A work detail hung over the fantail, rebeading and painting the ship's name, while another team painted the funnel a golden yellow. In just a matter of hours, the entire ship would be transformed to another vessel that even the trained eye would have trouble detecting. It would be as if the cable ship *Baekje* never existed.

The fiery bantam marched through the executive corridors of NUMA's headquarters as if he owned the building, which, in fact, he essentially did. Admiral James Sandecker was a revered figure throughout the halls, offices, and laboratories of NUMA, the legacy of his founding the agency with a handful of scientists and engineers several decades before. Though diminutive in size, his blazing blue eyes and bright red hair with matching goatee simply advertised the burning intensity with which he operated twenty-four hours a day.

'Hello, Darla, you're looking stunning today,' he said graciously to the forty-something secretary typing on a computer. 'Is Rudi in the executive conference room?'

'Good to see you again, Admiral,' the woman beamed as her eyes roved to a pair of Secret Service agents struggling to keep up with the fast-moving chief. 'Yes, Mr. Gunn is waiting for you inside. Please go right in.'

Though still regarded as the Admiral by his NUMA comrades, the rest of the world knew him as Vice President Sandecker. Despite a lifelong aversion to the subversive world of Washington politics,

Sandecker was persuaded by President Ward to fill the shoes of the vice presidency when the elected veep unexpectedly died in office. Sandecker knew the president to be a man of honor and integrity who would not force his second-in-command to remain a wallflower. The fiery admiral immediately broke the mold of past vice presidents. Far from being a figurehead and emissary for state funerals, Sandecker held a strong position in the administration. He vigorously spearheaded defense and security reforms, increased the funding and focus of government-sponsored scientific research, and led the point for environmental conservancy initiatives and all matters relating to the seas. At his bullying, the administration successfully strong-armed a worldwide ban on whaling by all industrialized nations, as well as implementing a host of tough penalties and sanctions on ocean polluters.

Sandecker burst through the door to the conference room, immediately hushing the group of NUMA officials deliberating the loss of the *Sea Rover*.

'Thanks for coming over, Admiral,' Gunn said, jumping up and showing his boss to the head of the table.

'What's the latest information?' Sandecker asked, dispensing with the usual around-the-table pleasantries.

'We've confirmed that the *Sea Rover* has, in fact, been sunk after being attacked in the East China Sea by a small armed force that infiltrated the vessel.

Miraculously, the crew escaped from a locked storage hold minutes before the ship went under. They were able to make it into the lifeboats, where they were later spotted by an Air Force search-and-rescue plane. A nearby freighter was alerted, and they have since been picked up. The freighter and crew are en route to Nagasaki as we speak. All but two of the crew have been accounted for.'

'She was boarded by force?'

'A stealth commando team of unidentified nationality got aboard her at night and took over the ship without a struggle.'

'That's Bob Morgan's ship, isn't it?'

'Yes. The old goat apparently put up a fight and took a gunshot wound to the leg during the struggle. I spoke with Ryan, his exec, who told me that he's expected to pull through in good shape. According to Ryan, the boarders claimed to be with the Japanese Red Army. They made their escape in a cable-laying ship bearing the Japanese flag.'

'Odd choice of attack ship,' Sandecker mused. 'I take it they absconded with the biological bombs that had been recovered from the *I-411*?'

'Ryan confirmed as much. They had nearly completed the recovery operation at the time of the attack. The *Starfish* was missing when the crew escaped from the hold, and Ryan believes it was hoisted onto the attack ship, perhaps with the submersible's missing pilots.'

'I'll call the State Department and request an

immediate dragnet from the Japanese naval resources.' Sandecker pulled an enormous Dominican Republic cigar out of his breast pocket and lit the green stogie, sending a thick plume of smoke toward the ceiling. 'Shouldn't be too difficult to peg a cable ship when she slips into port.'

'I've alerted Homeland Security, who is working along those same lines. They don't seem to believe the Japanese Red Army has the skill or technology to create a domestic threat with the weapons but are now looking at possible ties to Al Qaeda and a few other terrorist organizations.'

'I wouldn't bet against it,' Sandecker replied drily as he rolled the cigar between his thumb and forefinger. 'I'll brief the president this afternoon. Someone is going to damn well pay for destroying an American government vessel,' he snarled, his eyes ablaze.

The inhabitants of the conference room nodded in collective agreement. Though a large organization, there was a close-knit sense of family within the agency and an act of terror against fellow colleagues halfway around the world was still felt strongly by those at home.

'We share your sentiments, Admiral,' Gunn replied quietly.

'By the way, the two crewmen that are missing?' Sandecker asked.

Gunn swallowed hard. 'Summer and Dirk Pitt. Presumed abducted with the *Starfish*.'

Sandecker stiffened in shock. 'Good Lord, not them. Does their father know?'

'Yes. He's in the Philippines with Al Giordino trying to contain an underwater environmental hazard. I spoke with him by satellite phone and he understands that we are doing everything we can right now.'

Sandecker leaned back in his leather chair and gazed at the cloud of blue cigar smoke drifting above his head. God have mercy on the fool that would harm that man's offspring, he thought.

Seven thousand miles away, the blue catamaran ripped across the west coastal waters of Korea like a top fuel dragster running the traps. Summer and Dirk were nudged and rocked in their luxury confinement as the speedy yacht tore through the swells at almost 40 knots. A pair of Korean fishermen in a rickety sampan cursed vehemently as the cat stormed perilously close by, the powerful boat's wake washing waves over the sides of the tiny fishing boat.

After two hours of hard running, the catamaran turned inland and slowed its speed as it threaded its way through the sprinkling of small islands that dotted the mouth of the Han River. The pilot maneuvered the boat upriver another hour until spotting the semihidden channel that curled into Kang's Kyodongdo Island lair. Passing through the inlet that he knew was monitored by hidden video cameras, the pilot guided the catamaran across the cove to the floating dock at the base of the sheer-walled compound. Inching to a stop, the blue catamaran was tied up astern of Kang's gleaming white Benetti yacht.

Dirk and Summer remained locked in their cabin as Tongju strode off the craft and rode the elevator up the cliff to Kang's private enclave. Kang sat in his cherrywood-paneled executive office with Kwan, studying the financial statements of a radio component manufacturer that he intended to acquire via hostile takeover. He looked up slowly when Tongju entered and bowed.

'Captain Lee of the *Baekje* has sent word that your mission was a success,' Kang stated through tight lips, offering no hint of satisfaction.

Tongju nodded slightly. 'We acquired the ordnance after it was salvaged by the American vessel. Ten of the devices were still intact and have been determined to be usable,' he continued, neglecting to mention that Dirk had sabotaged the other two canisters.

'More than a sufficient quantity to proceed with the operation,' Kang replied.

'The weapon scientists aboard the *Baekje* were most pleased. The devices were immediately transferred to the biological research laboratory upon our arrival at Inchon. The lab chief assured me that the necessary refinement and containment will be complete within forty-eight hours.'

'At which time I trust the *Baekje*'s reconfiguration will be complete?'

Tongju nodded in reply. 'She will be ready to set sail on time.'

'Schedule is critical,' Kang continued. 'The mission must be achieved ahead of the National Assembly referendum vote.'

'As long as there is no delay with the ordnance, we will be ready,' Tongju assured him. 'The shipyard workers had already made impressive progress by the time we departed the dock facility.'

'We cannot tolerate another miscalculation,' Kang said coldly.

Tongju squinted slightly, unsure of his boss's meaning. Ignoring the comment, he continued speaking.

'I have brought two of the captives from the American vessel with me. The pilots who operated their submersible. One of them is the man responsible for the death of our two agents in America. I thought perhaps you might wish to entertain him personally,' he said, placing a sinister emphasis on the word *entertain*.

'Ah, yes, the two missing crew members from the NUMA ship.'

'Missing crew members?'

Kwan stepped forward and thrust a news story gleaned from the Internet into Tongju's hands.

'It is all over the news,' Kwan said. 'Research vessel sunk in East China Sea; all but two saved,' he quoted from a headline in *Chosun Ilbo*, Korea's largest newspaper.

Tongju's face went pale but he didn't move a muscle. 'That is impossible. We sank the vessel with the crew sealed in a storage hold. They could not have all escaped.'

'Escape they did,' Kang said. 'A passing freighter picked up the crew and took them to Japan. Did you not watch the ship go under?'

Tongju shook his head. 'We were anxious to return with the salvaged material at the earliest possible moment,' he said quietly.

'It is being reported that the ship suffered an accidental fire on board. Apparently, the Americans are afraid of publicizing yet another terrorist incident,' Kwan said.

'As well as revealing the true nature of their presence in the East China Sea,' Kang added. 'Perhaps the lack of media reporting will temper their investigation into the incident.'

'I am confident that we maintained our false identity. My assault team was of mixed ethnicity and only English or Japanese was spoken while on the American ship,' Tongju replied.

'Perhaps your failure to dispose of the crew was not a bad thing,' Kang stated with a slight glare. 'It will further embarrass the Japanese and keep the American intelligence effort focused on Japan. They will, of course, be searching for the *Baekje*. The sooner she can be put back to sea, the better.'

'I will provide a continuous update from the shipyard,' Tongju replied. 'And the two Americans?'

Kang perused a leather-bound schedule book. 'I am traveling to Seoul for an engagement with the minister of unification this evening and shall return tomorrow. Keep them alive until then.'

'I shall give them a last supper,' Tongju replied without humor.

Kang ignored the comment and stuck his nose back into a stack of financial documents. Taking the clue, the assassin turned and departed Kang's office without making a sound.

32

A half mile from the Inchon enclosed dock where *Baekje* was undergoing its cosmetic refit, two men in a dingy pickup truck slowly circled a nondescript shipyard building. Empty pallets and rusting flatbed carriers littered the grounds around the windowless structure, which was marked by a faded KANG SHIP-PING COMPANY sign perched over the main entrance. Dressed in worn coveralls and grease-stained baseball caps, the two men were part of a heavily armed undercover security team numbering two dozen strong who patrolled the supersecret facility around the clock. The dilapidated exterior of the building hid a high-tech engineering development center filled with the latest supercomputing technology. The main and upper floors were dedicated to developing satellite payloads for Kang's satellite communications business. A small team of crack engineers worked to incorporate concealed eavesdropping and reconnaissance capabilities into conventional telecommunication satellites that were sold for export and launched by other regional governments or commercial companies. Hidden in the basement, and heavily guarded, was a small microbiology laboratory whose very existence was known by only a handful of Kang employees. The small cadre of scientists who worked in the lab had mostly been smuggled in from North Korea. With their families still living in the northern provinces, and forceful patriotic mandates placed upon them, the microbiologists and immunologists had little choice in accepting the nature of their work with hazardous biological agents.

The *I-411*'s deadly bombs had been quietly transferred into the lab, where an ordnance expert had assisted the biologists in separating the powdery smallpox virus from the sixty-year-old compartmentalized aerial bombs. The viruses had been freeze-dried by the Japanese, allowing the pathogens to remain inert for storage and handling. The smallpox-laden bombs were designed to maintain their deadly efficacy for the duration of the submarine's voyage until hydrogenated upon deployment. Over sixty years later, their porcelain casings had repelled all destructive effects from decades of submersion. The aged bomb payloads were still every bit as potent as when they were loaded.

Placing samples of the cream-colored powder into a biosafe container, the biologists carefully initiated a controlled reconstitution of the viruses using a sterile water-based diluent. Under a microscopic eye, the dormant, block-shaped microorganisms could be seen waking from their long slumber and bouncing off each other like bumper cars as they resumed their lethal state. Despite the long period of dormancy, only a small percentage of the viruses failed to rejuvenate.

The research lab was run by a highly paid Ukrainian microbiologist named Sarghov. A former scientist with Biopreparat, the old Soviet Union civilian agency that fronted the republic's military biological weapons program, Sarghov had taken his knowledge of bio-weapon genetic manipulation and sold his skills in the marketplace to the highest bidder. Though he never desired to leave his homeland, his stock as a budding scientific leader in the agency was tarnished when he was caught in bed with the wife of a polit-buro member. Fearing for his life, he made his way through Ukraine to Romania, where he hopped a Kang freighter in the Black Sea. A hefty bribe to the ship's captain led him to higher contacts in the company, where his scientific skills were recognized and soon put to illicit use.

With ample resources, Sarghov quietly compiled a high-tech DNA research laboratory stocked with the equipment and tools necessary for a skilled bioengi-neer to splice, dice, isolate, or recombine the genetic material of one microorganism to another. In the confines of Sarghov's secret laboratory, a smorgas-bord of dangerous bacterial and viral agents was littered about the facility, the seeds he cultivated to create a garden of death. But he still felt impotent. His stock was a commoner's cache of easily acquired agents, such as the hepatitis B virus and tuberculosis mycobacterium. Potentially lethal agents in their own right, they were nothing like the deadly Ebola, small-pox, and Marburg viruses he had worked with during his days at the Russian facility in Obolensk. Sarghov's feverish attempts at creating a knockout killer agent with the resources at hand had failed. He felt like a boxer with one hand tied behind his back. What he needed and desired was a truly lethal pathogen, one from the A-list.

His gift to evil science came from an unexpected source. A North Korean agent in Tokyo had infiltrated a government records disposal center and intercepted a cache of classified Japanese documents. Expecting to find a bonanza of current Japanese security secrets, the agent's handlers in Pyongyang were angered to find that the records were old World War II classified documents. Included in the heist were reports relating to Imperial Army experiments with biological weapons, records that were to be destroyed for fear of embarrassing the government. A sharp intelligence analyst stumbled upon the Imperial Army's involvement with the final missions of the *I-403* and *I-411*, however, and Sarghov was soon on his way to his own supply of *Variola major*.

In the Frankenstein world of genetic engineering, biologists have found it a daunting task to create an entirely new organism from scratch. But manipulating existing microorganisms through deliberate mutation, then prompting their reproduction to useful quantities, has been an ongoing art since the seventies. Laboratory-formulated agricultural crops that are resistant to pestilence and drought have been a major societal benefit of such bioengineering, along with the more controversial creation of superdeveloped livestock. But the dark side of genetic surgery has always been the potential creation of a new strain of virus or bacteria with unknown, and possibly catastrophic, consequences.

For a man of his propensity, Sarghov was not content simply to regenerate the supply of smallpox. He had much more up his sleeve. With help from a Finnish research assistant, Sarghov acquired a sample of the HIV-1 virus, the most common source of acquired immune deficiency syndrome. Delving into the HIV-1 viral makeup, Sarghov synthesized a key genetic element of the horrifying AIDS virus. Taking his freshly reconstituted batch of smallpox virus, the scientist attempted to grow a new mutated bug, integrating the highly unstable HIV-1 virus. Boosted by the synthetic element that acted to stimulate recombination, mutant viruses were soon cultivated and then reproduced in mass. The result was a new microorganism that contained the attributes of both individual pathogens. Microbiologists sometimes refer to the process as a 'chimera.' Sarghov's chimera combined the highly contagious lethality of smallpox with the immunitive destroying abilities of HIV-1 into one deadly supervirus.

Reproducing the mutant pathogen in large quantities from scratch was a time-consuming process despite the ferocity of the virus. Limited by Kang's schedule, Sarghov maximized the quantities as best he could, then freeze-dried the resulting mutant viruses much as the Japanese had years before. The crystallized supervirus was then mixed into the larger stores of freeze-dried smallpox virus from the aerial bombs, creating a diversified toxic compound. The entire batch was processed and refined a second time with boosters that would accelerate the rejuvenation process.

The now easily disseminated mixture was delicately packed into a series of lightweight tubular containers resembling the insert to a roll of paper towels, which were then stacked on a gurney and transported out of the lab. The packaged viral amalgamate was rolled upstairs to the satellite payload assembly bay, where a team of mechanical engineers took over, inserting the tubes into larger stainless steel cylinders that encapsulated a hydrogenation tank and fittings. The process was repeated under bright floodlights several times over until five of the large cylinders were assembled and placed into large shipping crates. A forklift arrived and loaded the crates onto the same white Kang panel truck that had delivered the ordnance, now making a return trip to the covered dock with a highly revitalized form of the weapon.

Sarghov grinned in delight, knowing a large payday was coming his way. His exhausted team of scientists had met the mark, verifying that the ancient smallpox virus still packed a lethal punch, then boosting its strength to murderous proportions. In less than forty-eight hours, Sarghov's biologists had processed the sixty-year-old virus into an entirely new killer, the likes of which the world had never seen before.

33

'What do you mean the ship has yet to materialize?' Gunn rasped in dismay.

The section chief of the FBI's International Terrorism Operations, a compact man named Tyler, opened a file on his desk and perused the contents as he spoke.

'We've had no information on the whereabouts of the cable ship *Baekje*. The Japanese National Police Agency has been monitoring shipping traffic in every port in the country, physically checking every ship that remotely resembles the description offered by your NUMA crew. They've come up empty so far.'

'Have you checked ports outside of Japan?'

'An international notice has been posted with Interpol, and it is my understanding that the CIA has been asked to provide inputs at the request of the vice president. At this time, no confirming information has been received. There's a million places she could be hiding, Rudi, or she could have been scuttled herself.'

'What about satellite imagery of the site where *Sea Rover* was sunk?'

'Bad timing there, unfortunately. With the recent

flare-up of political tensions in Iran, the National Reconnaissance Office has repositioned several of its high-resolution imaging resources to the Middle East. The East China Sea is one of many dead spots right now that is only covered by periodic scans from non-geosynchronous satellites. Which all means that the *Baekje* could move five hundred miles between covering passes. I'm waiting for the historical images from the last few days but have been told not to be too hopeful.'

Gunn's anger softened as he realized that the slightly balding G-man in the starched white shirt was a competent professional doing the best with the resources he had available. 'Any headway on the ship's history?' he asked.

'Your man Hiram Yaeger gave us a good head start on that one. Yaeger was the one who tentatively identified the ship as the *Baekje*, based on a worldwide review of ship registries through his NUMA computer bank. Apparently, there are less than forty known cable-laying ships of the size and configuration reported by your NUMA rescued crew. We narrowed the list down to twelve that were owned or leased in the Asia Pacific region and the *Baekje* came up missing in action.' The FBI man paused as he leafed through the folder before extracting a white sheet that carried the blurred markings of a fax copy across its header.

'Here we are, details of the vessel. Cable-laying ship *Baekje*, 445 feet long, gross tonnage of 9,500.

Built by the Hyundai Mipo Dockyard Company, Ltd., Ulsan, South Korea, in 1998. Owned and operated by Kang Shipping Enterprises, Inchon, South Korea, from 1998 to 2000. Since 2000, ship has been under lease to the Nippon Telegraph and Telephone Corporation, Tokyo, Japan, for cable-laying services in and around the Sea of Japan.'

Setting the folder down, he stared straight into the eyes of Gunn.

'NTT's operating lease expired six months ago, at which time the *Baekje* sat unutilized in a Yokohama dock. Two months ago, representatives from NTT renegotiated a one-year lease of the ship and took possession of the vessel with their own crew. Port records show she was unaccounted for during a five-week period, then appeared briefly back in Yokohama approximately three weeks ago. She was believed sighted in Osaka, where she apparently tailed the *Sea Rover* to the East China Sea.'

'Was the ship seized from NTT?'

'No. NTT officials were shocked to learn that their name was on a revised lease agreement for the vessel since their fiber-optic cable route had been completed. The NTT corporate representatives that leased the ship were, in fact, impostors who buffaloed the Kang Shipping agents. The Kang people produced the paperwork, everything looked legitimate to them, though one representative thought it odd at the time that the NTT people were providing their own crew, which they had not done in the past. The

Kang Shipping people are apparently scrambling to file an insurance claim on the vessel now.'

'Sounds like there must have been some inside information somewhere. Any known links between the Japanese Red Army and Nippon Telegraph and Telephone?'

'None that we've established yet, but we're looking into it. NTT's executives are cooperating fully and seem eager to clear their name from a possible connection. Official corporate sponsorship looks un- likely, so the Japanese authorities are focusing on a possible employee faction somewhere within the company.'

Gunn shook his head discouragingly. 'So we've got a four-hundred-foot ship that has vanished into thin air, a U.S. government vessel that has been sunk, and an empty list of suspects. Two of my people have been kidnapped, possibly murdered, and we have no idea where to even look for them.'

'We're frustrated, too, Rudi, but we'll get them eventually. Sometimes, these things just take time.'

Time, Gunn thought. Just how much time did Dirk and Summer still have, if any at all?

The hot shower felt delicious. Summer let the steam- ing water pelt her body for more than twenty minutes before finally willing herself to turn off the shower control knobs and reach for a towel. It had been nearly four days since her last bout with cleanliness, she mentally calculated, rerunning over in her mind the events of the last few days. Stepping from the marble-tiled shower, she dried herself with a fluffy towel, then wrapped the fabric around her body, tucking the loose end under an armpit. Before her stretched an immense marble counter with double sinks and gleaming gold fixtures set beneath an expansive beveled mirror that stretched to the high ceiling. You had to give these unsmiling thugs some credit, she thought. Someone around here has taste.

After an uncomfortable night's sleep in the motor yacht, where she and her brother took turns sleeping on the twin bed with their hands cuffed behind their back, a trio of armed guards marched them ashore in the morning. Peering at the massive residence perched on the stone bluff above them, Dirk remarked, 'Kind of reminds you of the Berghof, doesn't it?' The stone structure with the commanding view over the Han River did bear a passing resemblance to Hitler's vacation lair in the German Alps. The image was made all the more complete with the surrounding array of blackshirted henchmen.

Prodded to the rock-enveloped elevator, they rode up to an interior corridor level beneath the main quarters and were escorted to a pair of guestrooms. In rough English, a guard barked, 'Prepare for dining with Mr. Kang, two hour.'

While Summer showered, Dirk surveyed his plushly decorated adjoining room for a potential means of escape. The windowless rooms were dug into the face of the cliff, the only entry or exit being the corridor hall, where two armed guards stood in front of each room's open door. If they were going to make an escape, it probably wasn't going to happen here, he figured.

As Summer dried her wet hair, she briefly became lost in the luxury and allowed herself to enjoy the surroundings. She sniffed at an array of exotic lotions and perfumes aligned on the marble counter, settling on an aloe vera body lotion and a lilac-scented fragrance. A rack of silk clothing stood in the corner, a conspicuous offering for female guests. Running her fingers through the brightly colored collection of petite-sized robes and dresses, she spotted a flaming red pullover dress with matching short jacket that looked like it might fit. Squirming into the silk dress, she eyed herself in the mirror and admired the results. A little tight in the bust, but a fair representation of a china doll, albeit tall and red-haired, she thought, smiling at the reflected image. Finding an assortment of shoes at the foot of the rack, she rummaged through a dozen pairs before finding a black set of low-heeled flats that fit. Wedging the shoes on, she cursed as a thumbnail cracked while tugging at a heel. Instinctively, she rummaged through the bathroom counter, bypassing combs and brushes before discovering one of a woman's essentials: an emery board. Not a cheap cardboard version, the metal file sported a small flat porcelain handle. Admiring the tiny tool, she absently stuck it in a side pocket after smoothing her thumbnail. An instant later, a pounding at the room door indicated her interval of private luxury was over.

Exiting the room into the corridor at gunpoint, Summer found Dirk standing casually with two rifle muzzles pointed at his back. He looked at his sister in the stunning silk dress and let fly a wolf whistle.

'I'm afraid we've only got a few rats to guide your chariot tonight, Cinderella,' he joked, jerking his thumb in the direction of the two guards behind him.

'I see you've decided to stick with the Mr. Goodwrench look,' she countered, observing that he wore the same grease-and-sweat-stained NUMA jumpsuit he'd worn since they were abducted.

'Afraid my available wardrobe was a little on the short side,' he said, pulling the cuffs of his jumpsuit up to midcalf range for emphasis. 'Never did care much for the Alfalfa sartorial look.'

The four guards grew annoyed with their chattering and forcefully guided them to the elevator, where they rode silently up one floor. The doors opened on Kang's impressive dining room, with the broad vista shimmering through the picture windows. Kang sat at the head of the dining table, quietly reviewing the contents of a leather-bound folder, while Tongju stood erect off his left shoulder. The Korean magnate looked the part of an industrial captain, attired in a custom-fitted navy blue suit from an expensive Hong Kong tailor, with complementary maroon silk tie. His steely slate eyes darted toward the elevator briefly, then returned to the documents before him, his face a mask of cold austerity.

Dirk and Summer were escorted to the table, where their eyes briefly drank in the scenic riverscape view through the window before settling on their captor host. They both mentally noted how the cove below was fed by a narrow winding inlet that led to the wide river in the distance. Standing before the table, Summer felt a chill run up her spine as Tongju shot her a lascivious look, while Kang peered up coldly. Her minor gaiety at being clean and finely dressed withered away in the palpable presence of evil. She suddenly felt foolish in the silken outfit and subconsciously clasped her hands in front of her waist in nervous fear. But her anxiety diminished after she glanced over at Dirk.

If her brother felt any fear, he didn't show it. Dirk stood tall with his chin thrust out defiantly, yet carried a bored-with-it-all look on his face. He seemed to enjoy peering down with derision at Tongju, who stood nearly ten inches shorter. The assassin paid no heed and instead spoke directly to his boss.

'The submersible operators from the NUMA vessel,' he said with a touch of disdain.

'Dae-jong Kang,' Dirk retorted, ignoring Tongju, 'CEO of Kang Enterprises.'

Kang nodded slightly, then motioned for Dirk and Summer to sit down. The guards eased back to a side wall, where they kept a vigilant watch over the two captives, while Tongju slid into a chair opposite Dirk.

'Mr. Pitt here was responsible for the death of our two men in America,' Tongju said, his eyes narrowing on Dirk.

Dirk nodded in mute satisfaction. It was as he suspected, the clear connection between the salvage efforts on both Japanese submarines, as well as the murder attempt on Vashon Island.

'A small world,' Kang replied.

'Too small for mass murderers like you,' Summer hissed in a low voice, her anger taking rise.

Kang ignored the comment. 'A pity. The men in Seattle were among Tongju's top agents.'

'A tragic accident, really,' Dirk replied. 'You must learn to recruit employees with better driving skills,' he added, his cold glance at Tongju met by an equally frigid stare back.

'Fortuitous indeed, as we otherwise may have lost your generous assistance in salvaging the *I-411*,' Kang said. 'I am most curious as to what led you to the submarines.'

'Luck, mostly. I discovered that an earlier Japanese submarine had launched a few cyanide shells at the Oregon coast and wondered if someone had recovered some similar shells and used them in the Aleutians. It wasn't until I dove on the *I-403* and discovered the remains of the aerial biological bombs that it became evident that there was something more afoot.'

'A shame that the bombs were damaged during the vessel's sinking,' Kang said. 'They would have been much easier to recover than those from the *I-411*.'

'But you did recover one bomb canister intact, which you discharged in the Aleutian Islands.'

Kang showed a hint of surprise at Dirk's remark. 'Of course,' he replied. 'Rather interesting how the Japanese combined a chemical and biological agent in one weapon. Our test release revealed that the efficacy of the biological agent was hampered by the dual release, although the chemical component was more potent than we anticipated.'

'Potent enough to kill two U.S. Coast Guardsmen,' Summer commented.

Kang shrugged. 'How did you come to have such a focus with the death of two sailors in the Aleutians? Were you there?'

Summer shook her head in silence. Then Dirk spoke up.

'I was piloting the helicopter that your "fishing trawler" shot down.'

Kang and Tongju looked at each other with suspicious eyes. 'You are rather a resilient man, Mr. Pitt,' Kang finally stated.

Before he could respond, a side door swayed open and two men in white waiter's jackets glided over to the table hoisting large silver trays above their shoulders. A colorful array of seafood dishes was spread before each place setting, followed by a glass of Veuve Clicquot champagne. Dirk and Summer, having not eaten a full meal in days, calmly attacked the food as the probing conversation continued.

'Your government . . . is rather displeased with the Japanese, I suspect,' Kang prodded.

'Your shady activities under the guise of the Japanese Red Army was a clever ruse but uncovered for what it was by my government. Your two flunky hit men were easily traced to Korea,' Dirk lied, grinning at Tongju. 'I suspect the authorities will be banging on your door any minute now, Kang.'

A brief look of agitation on Kang's brow suddenly softened. 'A commendable effort. But the truth is that the two men had no idea themselves who their employer was. No, I think it is apparent that you know nothing of our intent.'

'The long-standing animosity of Korea toward Japan for their many years of brutal colonization is well known,' Dirk said, continuing the pretext. 'It would be no surprise to expect the warped minds possessing these type of weapons to use them on a historical adversary, which in your case is the Japanese.'

A thin smile crossed Kang's lips and he sat back in his chair with satisfaction, less from the meal than from Dirk's words.

'A nice bluff, Mr. Pitt. The fact that your NUMA vessel was neither armed nor escorted during the salvage operation tells me that your country did not think much of your discovery on the *I-403*. And your presumptive guess as to the operative use of the biological weapons is quite off the mark.'

'What exactly is your . . . intended use of the weapons?' Summer stammered.

'Perhaps your own country,' Kang teased as the color drained from Summer's face. 'Or perhaps not. That is neither here nor there.'

'The smallpox vaccine is readily available in the United States in quantities sufficient to vaccinate the entire population,' Dirk countered. 'Tens of thousands of health workers have already been inoculated. A release of the smallpox virus might create a minor panic, at best. Certainly, there's not much risk of creating an epidemic.'

'Certainly a release of *Variola major*, or common smallpox, would register only a small nuisance. But your vaccinations would be useless against a chimera.'

'A "chimera"? Of Greek lore? A monster – part lion, part goat, and part serpent?'

'Indeed. Another monster, if you will, would be a hybrid mix of virulent agents combined into a single organism that maintains the lethal components of each element. A biological weapon against which your vaccinations would be laughably impotent.'

'But, in God's name, why?' Summer cried.

Kang calmly finished his meal and set his napkin on the table, folding it into neat thirds before speaking.

'You see, my country has been divided against itself since your incursion in the fifties. What you Americans fail to understand is that all Koreans dream of the day when our peninsula is united as one nation. Constant interference from outside meddlers will keep us from achieving that dream. Just as the presence of foreign military forces on our soil creates an impediment to the day when unification becomes a reality.'

'The American military presence in South Korea ensures that the dream of unification will not be realized at the point of a North Korean bayonet,' Dirk replied.

'South Korea no longer has the stomach for a fight, and the military power of North Korea offers the leadership and stabilizing force necessary to restore order during reunification.'

'I don't believe it,' Summer muttered to Dirk. 'We're having lunch with a cross between Typhoid Mary and Joseph Stalin.'

Kang, not understanding the remark, continued speaking. 'The young people of South Korea today have had their fill of your military occupation and abuses to the citizenry. They are not fearful of unification and will help pave the way for a speedy resolution.'

'In other words, once the U.S. military is removed the forces of North Korea will march south and unify the country by force.'

'Absent the U.S. defensive forces, military estimates suggest that eighty percent of the South Korean Peninsula can be overrun within seventy-two hours. Casualties will be necessary, but the country will be unified under Workers' Party rule before the United States, Japan, or any other outside interfering force has the opportunity to react.'

Dirk and Summer sat in stunned silence. Their fears of a terrorist plot using the Japanese smallpox had been well founded, but they had no suspicion of the magnitude at stake: no less than the overthrow of the Republic of Korea in conjunction with the wholesale death of millions of Americans.

'I think you may be underestimating the resolve of the United States, particularly in the face of a terrorist attack. Our president has shown no hesitation in applying swift and fearsome retribution,' Dirk said.

'Perhaps. But retribution against whom? The pattern of events all still points to a Japanese source . . .'

'The Japanese Red Army again,' Dirk interjected.

'The Japanese Red Army. You see, there simply are no other likelihoods. Your military, intelligence, and political resources will be focused entirely on Japan while, at the same time, we will be mandating through our government the removal of all U.S. military personnel from the Korean Peninsula within thirty days. Your country's knee-jerk media will be in a frenzy over the epidemic casualties and so focused on finding a culprit in Japan that the American military expulsion from Korea will be a minor news item until well after the fact.'

'The intelligence community will ultimately see past the Red Army façade and trace the actions back to you and your communist pals up north.'

'Perhaps. But how long will that take? How long has it been for your government to solve the 2001 anthrax killings in your own capital? When and if that day should come, emotions will no longer be running high. It will all be a "moot point," as you say.'

'Killing millions of people and calling it "moot"?' Summer injected. 'You are sick.'

'How many of my countrymen did you kill in the fifties?' Kang retorted with a flash of anger in his eyes.

'We left plenty of our own blood on your soil,' Summer replied, glaring back at Kang.

Dirk peered across the table at Tongju, whose dark eyes were narrowly focused on Summer. The assassin was not accustomed to people speaking belligerently to Kang, and most certainly not a woman. While his face remained expressionless, a piqued intolerance oozed from his gaze.

'Aren't you overlooking your own business interests?' Dirk said to Kang, deflecting the tone. 'Your industrial profits won't continue to accrue if the almighty state Workers' Party suddenly takes the reins.'

Kang smiled weakly. 'You Americans, always the capitalists at heart. As it is, I have already arranged the sale of half my holdings to a French conglomerate, with payment in Swiss francs. And when my homeland is reunited, who better to help manage the state control of South Korea's industrial resources than myself?' he said arrogantly.

'A tidy arrangement,' Dirk replied. 'A pity there won't be a nation around that will be interested in purchasing the ill-gotten goods of a totalitarian regime.'

'You forget China, Mr. Pitt. A huge market in and of itself, as well as a friendly conduit for funneling goods to the world markets. There will, of course, be a business interruption during the transfer of power, but output will quickly recover. There is always a demand for inexpensive, quality products.'

'Sure,' Dirk said sarcastically. 'Name me one quality consumer product that ever came out of a communist country. Face it, Kang, you're on the losing end of a new global authority. There's no longer room for warped despots who screw their own countrymen for personal wealth, military might, or grand delusions of greatness. You and your buddies in the north might have a few laughs along the way, but, at the end of the day, you'll all be steamrolled by a concept foreign to you called "freedom."'

Kang sat stiffly for a moment, a long look of annoyance settling over his face. 'Thank you for the civics lesson. It has been a most enlightening meal. Good-bye, Miss Pitt, good-bye, Mr. Pitt,' he said coldly.

With a glance to the side wall by Kang, the guards were instantly upon them, pulling the two to their feet. Dirk had thoughts of grabbing a dinner knife off the table and having a go at the guards but was dissuaded when he saw Tongju pointing a Glock pistol at his chest.

'Take them to the river cave,' Kang barked.

'Thanks for the warm hospitality,' Dirk muttered at Kang. 'I look forward to returning the privilege.'

Kang said nothing, nodding at the guards instead, who forcibly pushed the pair toward the elevator. Dirk and Summer glanced at each other with a knowing look. Their time was short now. If they were to make it out of Kang's grasp alive, they would have to act soon.

The immediate problem was Tongju and his Glock 22. Any resistance would be futile while the assassin kept his gun aimed at them, as there was little doubt he would use it without hesitation. Tongju followed the four guards as they herded Dirk and Summer to the elevator, his pistol still drawn. As the doors slid open, two pairs of hands shoved them forcefully to the rear of the elevator. Tongju barked something in Korean, and then, to Dirk's relief, remained standing in the dining hall with one of the guards, a menacing look of satisfaction on his face as the elevator doors slid shut.

The elevator was cramped with five bodies in it, which would work to their advantage. Dirk glanced at Summer and nodded ever so slightly, his sister acknowledging the silent message with a quick wink. She immediately grabbed her stomach and groaned, leaning forward as if she were about to vomit. The nearest guard, a chunky man with a shaved head, took the bait and bent down slightly toward Summer. Like a cat mistakenly pouncing onto a hot stove, she suddenly sprang her body upright, jerking her knee into the man's groin with all the might she could muster. The man's eyes nearly burst out of their sockets as her knee hit home and he doubled over in agony, a shriek of pain quivering from his lips.

Summer's move was all Dirk needed to neutralize guard number two. As all three guards' attention turned initially to Summer, he launched an uppercut that connected squarely on the man's jaw, nearly lifting him out of his shoes. Dirk watched from inches away as the man's eyes rolled to the back of his head and he slumped to the floor unconscious.

Guard number three took a small step back as the fighting broke out and attempted to raise the muzzle of his rifle at Dirk. Summer reacted by grabbing the shoulders of the man she'd kneed and shoving his hunched-over body toward the standing guard. The still-groaning bald man swayed heavily into his taller accomplice with just enough force to offset the other man's balance. It was enough time to allow Dirk to step over the fallen guard and let go a left cross that landed a glancing blow on the gunman's temple. The dazed guard tried to counter with a braced karate kick, but Dirk's right fist was already there, mashing solidly into the man's larynx. The guard's face turned blue as he fought to take in air and he dropped to his knees, grabbing his throat with both hands. Dirk grabbed the man's assault rifle and swung it around viciously, striking the stock against the face of the guard struggling with Summer. The blow threw the man against the back of the elevator, where he slid to the floor unconscious.

'Nice work, Smokin' Joe,' Summer praised.

'Let's not wait for round two,' Dirk gasped as the elevator descent slowed beneath their feet. He checked that the safety on the assault rifle was turned off, then prepared to leap out of the elevator as the doors opened. Only there was no where to go.

As the doors slid open, the muzzles of three AK-74s were thrust in, the compensators at the end of the gun barrels poking into their faces. A security guard sitting at a bank of television monitors had witnessed the fracas in the elevator over closed-circuit video and quickly dispatched a cadre of guards in the vicinity.

'Saw!' the guards yelled in Korean, their meaning perfectly clear. Dirk and Summer froze in their tracks, wondering what degree of hair triggers existed on the assault rifles pointed their way. Dirk gently dropped his rifle to the ground, detecting a stirring in the elevator behind him. Too late, he turned to see the third guard staggering from the elevator while swinging the butt of his rifle toward his head. He tried to duck but the gun handle was too far along its way toward the top of his skull, where it collided with a thump.

For an instant, he saw a blinding light and shining stars, and, through the fog, an odd glimpse of Summer's feet. But that soon gave way to a fading darkness that turned to black as the curtain closed and he crumpled to the ground in a limp heap.

34

A throbbing jolt of pain shooting down from the top of his skull to the tip of his toes was the first evidence sent to his brain that he was still alive. As consciousness slowly seeped back to Dirk, his mind performed a physical inventory, denoting via neural signals which parts of the body were deviating from their normal state. Pain signals from his wrists, arms, and shoulders began registering as if they were pulling at a great weight, but were easily outclassed by the agonizing pangs from his head. More confusing to his senses was the feeling from his feet and legs that he was standing in a bucket of water. As the shroud of fog gradually lifted, he opened his eyes to a wet, dark, and gloomy cave.

'Welcome back to the land of the living,' Summer's voice echoed through the gloomy cavern.

'You didn't happen to get the license number of the truck that hit me?' he said groggily.

'Yes, but I'm pretty sure he wasn't carrying insurance.'

'Where the hell are we?' Dirk asked, his mind beginning to register the concepts of time and space.

'A side cavern, just off Kang's floating dock. That cool water nibbling at your navel is the River Han.'

The bucket of water he thought he was standing in was in fact a cavern full of rising river water. His vision now cleared, Dirk could see through the murky light that Summer was spread-eagled and handcuffed to two large barge anchors. Large weights rather than actual anchors, they were nothing more than a three-foot-square block of concrete. The white blocks were slickened with a decade's coating of pale green algae, with a rusty iron mooring ring protruding from the top. Dirk saw that there were nearly a dozen of the weights aligned in a row across the floor of the cavern. He and Summer stood adjacent to each other, their arms stretched wide with each wrist handcuffed to adjoining blocks.

Dirk's eyes wandered about the dim cavern. In the fading dusk light that filtered through the mouth of the cave, he could see the distinct line on the wall that he was looking for. It was the high-water mark, which he noted uncomfortably ran two feet above their heads.

'Death by slow drowning,' he said.

'Our Fu Manchu friend, Tongju, was most insistent,' Summer replied grimly. 'He even prevented one of the guards from shooting you so that we could wallow down here together.'

'I must remember to send him a thank-you card.' Dirk looked down and saw that the water was now sloshing around his rib cage.

'Water's rising pretty fast.'

'We're near the mouth of the Han River, so there's

plenty of tidal surge at work.' Summer gazed fearfully at her brother. 'I'd estimate that the water level has risen over a foot in the last hour.'

Seeing the despair in his sister's eyes, Dirk's mind engaged in high gear to determine a means of escape. 'We have another hour and a half, tops,' he calculated.

'I just remembered something,' Summer said, crinkling her brow. 'I've got a small nail file in my side pocket. Might be like trying to kill a pterodactyl with a flyswatter, but it might help.'

'Sure, toss it over,' Dirk replied.

'This one mooring ring looks pretty mangy,' she said, tugging at her left wrist. 'If I could just get one hand free.'

'Maybe I can help.' Dirk slid his legs toward Summer, leaning his torso at an angle along the concrete blocks for support. Raising one leg, he slid his foot along until the sole of his shoe met up with the face of the protruding iron. Applying as much pressure as he could, he pressed his weight hard against the top of the metal ring.

Nothing happened.

Shifting his foot so that his heel was against the ring, he pushed once more. This time, the ring bent a fraction toward Summer. Jamming his weight repeatedly against the stanchion, he gradually forced the ring to bend over nearly ninety degrees.

'Okay, I'll need your help in pushing it back upright,' he said. 'Let's try it on the count of three.'

Slipping his foot to the backside of the ring, he

counted to three, then pulled his leg toward him. Summer pushed with her manacled hand and they gradually shoved the ring back to its original vertical position.

'Well, that was fun,' Dirk said while resting his leg. 'Let's try it again.'

For twenty minutes, they toggled the ring back and forth, the movement gradually becoming easier as the tensile strength of the old iron weakened. With a last strong kick by Dirk, the ring finally snapped off its concrete base, freeing Summer's left arm. She immediately twisted her hand around and dug into the small side pocket of her silk jacket and produced the porcelain-handled nail file.

'I've got the file. Should I try on the handcuff itself or the mooring ring?' she asked.

'Go for the ring. Even though it's thicker, it will be much softer to cut through than the hardened stainless steel handcuffs.'

Using the small file like a hacksaw, Summer began grinding away at the base of the mooring ring. Working the file with any degree of accuracy beneath the murky river water and fading cavern light would have been a Herculean task for most, but Summer's extensive diving experience gave her a leg up. Years of exploring and excavating historic shipwrecks in foul visibility had heightened her sense of touch to the extent that she could nearly tell more about a wreck from her hands than by her eyes.

With some measure of hope, she felt the file cut

rapidly through the outer layer of the rusty ring. Her confidence waned when the blade met up with the hardened inner core of the iron ring and progress slowed to a snail's pace. The rising water was now level with her chest and the pending urgency unleashed a surge of adrenaline. Summer worked the blade back and forth as fast as she could muster underwater, gaining ground millimeter by millimeter. Taking quick breaks from sawing, she placed her hands on the iron ring and pushed and pulled it to weaken the metal. Alternating sawing and prodding with an intermittent gulp or two of river water, she at last broke through the ring and freed herself.

'Got it,' she exclaimed with victory.

'Mind if I borrow that file?' Dirk asked calmly, but Summer had already kicked and swum her way over and begun cutting into the ring grasping his right hand. As she worked the file, she mentally noted that it had taken her roughly thirty minutes to cut through the first ring and that the water level was now nearly to their shoulders. The water was rising faster than she anticipated and would be well above Dirk's head in less than an hour. Despite aching fingers and limbs, she rubbed the file ferociously against the iron.

Dirk, waiting patiently as Summer filed away, began whistling the old 1880s tune 'While Strolling Through the Park One Day.'

'That's not helping,' Summer gasped, then smiled to herself at the silly tune. 'Now I won't be able to get that ridiculous song out of my head.'

Sure enough, he quit whistling, but the tune kept replaying over and over in her head. She was surprised to find it became a good sawing mantra that provided a rhythm to her hand movements.

While strolling through the park one day, . . .

With each syllable, she applied a cutting stroke to the iron, creating an efficient sawing cadence.

. . . in the merry merry month of May.
I was taken by surprise by a pair of roguish eyes.
In a moment my poor heart was stole away.

The water level had now crept up over her chin and she found herself taking in gasps of air, then submerging briefly to keep the file clawing in one spot. Dirk was beginning to strain to keep his face out of the water while applying alternating tugs and shoves on the ring as Summer sawed tirelessly on. A muffled metallic ting finally echoed beneath them as the ring broke loose under their combined pressure.

'Three down, one to go,' Summer gasped, taking in a lungful of air after being submerged for several seconds.

'Let me give you a breather,' Dirk said, grabbing the file from Summer with his free hand. The release of his right hand gave him a few extra inches of breathing room, but it was not enough to file the last mooring ring without submerging. Taking a deep breath, he ducked under the surface and began filing rapidly on the ring that held down his left wrist. After thirty seconds, he bobbed to the surface, sucked in some fresh air, and plunged back under. Summer stretched her cramped fingers, then swam to Dirk's left side and waited for him to surface. Like a pair of tag team wrestlers trying to floor Hulk Hogan, they passed the file back and forth and ducked underwater, attacking the iron ring with muscle and fervor.

As the minutes wore on, the water level in the cavern crept higher and higher. Each time Dirk surfaced for a gasp of air, he felt himself stretching farther and farther to raise his mouth and nose above water. The handcuff shackle on his left wrist dug into his flesh as he instinctively yanked hard to escape the clutch of the massive barge weight.

'Save your strength for getting out of here,' he told his sister as the inevitable truth drew closer that they were running out of time. Summer said nothing as she grabbed the file out of his hand and plunged back beneath the surface. Dirk half-floated with his head tilted back, his face just barely out of the water, drawing a few deep breaths. He could feel the water wash over his face in ripples and stretched for one last deep breath before pulling himself under. Grasping Summer's wrist, he pulled the file out of her hand and began a last furious rush at cutting through the iron. Feeling the gouge with his thumb, he could tell that they had cut only a third of the way through. There was just too far to go.

The seconds felt like hours as Dirk made a final effort to break free. He could feel his heart beating like a bass drum as it struggled to pump oxygen into his depleted blood. In the murkiness, he could feel that Summer was no longer by his side. Perhaps she had finally taken his advice and sought escape. Or perhaps she just couldn't bear to be with him during his final gasp of life.

He paused from filing for a second to try pushing his weight against the ring. He could generate little leverage, however, and the iron ring held firm. Again, to the file he went, making furious strokes with the flimsy metal blade. His ears began pounding with each beat of his heart. How long had he been holding his breath now? A minute, two minutes? It was difficult to remember.

Light-headedness fell over him as spots began to creep into his vision. He exhaled what remaining air was left in his lungs and fought the temptation to open his mouth and gulp in. His heart pounded stronger and it became a mental fight against succumbing to panic. A light current seemed to push him away from the mooring ring, but his hand muscle grasped the file tightly in a death grip. A white veil was being drawn across his vision and a distant voice inside was telling him to let go. As he fought a last battle with the voice, his ringing ears detected a deep thump and then a strange vibration rippled up his arm and through his body just before his mind tumbled into a dark and empty void.

35

Summer knew that they were at least twenty minutes from filing through the iron ring and that there would have to be another way to free her brother. Abandoning Dirk, she dove to the cavern floor, searching and groping for another tool or device, anything that would help break the manacle. But the flat, sandy bottom yielded nothing, just the row of mooring weights, one after the other. Kicking ahead with one hand guiding along the blocks of concrete, she touched a large chunk of concrete that had broken off one of the weights when it had been dropped too close to another. Gliding beyond the debris, she reached the last block, where she felt something flat and squishy like soggy leather fall away in her hand. A harder piece beneath it was narrow and curved, which she identified as the sole of a boot. A stick leaned against it, which she started to grab, then let go in horror. It was no stick, she could tell, but the femur bone of a skeleton that was still wearing the boot. Another victim of Kang's savagery, the corpse had long ago been left chained to the anchor. Recoiling, she turned to swim back toward Dirk and bumped her head square into the fallen chunk of concrete. The broken piece was roughly square shaped, weighing about ninety pounds. She surveyed the block with her hands to get around it, then hesitated. It might be the answer, she decided, and was the best she could do under the circumstances.

Kicking up for a quick breath of air, she dove back down and muscled the block off the floor and up to her chest. On dry land, she would have struggled mightily to lift the heavy weight, but underwater the block was more yielding. Moving quickly, she shuffled down the row of weights to her brother, fighting to keep the chunk balanced. Feeling rather than seeing Dirk, she turned and backed into her brother, pushing his body away from the block that held his left wrist. She noted apprehensively that his body gave way rather limply, unlike his normal stonelike stature.

Lining herself up with the mooring weight as best she could, she took a step and lunged forward, throwing herself and the broken chunk of concrete at the iron ring. In a slow-motion haze, Summer floated through the water with a slight ripple before the effects of gravity took over. But her timing was perfect. In the fraction of a second before her forward momentum was replaced by sinking gravity, the concrete chunk hit home on the iron ring. An audible clang, muffled by the water, told Summer that she was on target as she let go of the block. The rusty mooring ring, weakened just enough by the frantic filing, succumbed to the weight of the blow and snapped neatly off the anchor.

Summer immediately grabbed Dirk's arm and felt

down to the wrist, which now dangled loosely. In a burst, she pushed her brother to the surface, took a deep breath of air herself, then towed his limp body to a small rock ledge, pulling him up and out of the water. She knelt by his side to administer CPR when his body suddenly stirred, his head turning to one side. With a groan, he expunged a small flood of water from his mouth and replaced it with a heaving lungful of air. Rising unsteadily to his elbows, he turned to Summer and gasped, 'I feel like I drank half the river. Remind me to stick to bottled water next time.'

The words barely gurgled out of his mouth when he leaned over and retched a second time, then sat up and rubbed his left wrist. Eyeing his sister, he was pleased to see she appeared unharmed and in good spirits.

'Thanks for pulling me out,' he said. 'How did you finally get the ring off?'

'I found a loose chunk of concrete and flung it against the stanchion. Thankfully, I didn't take your hand off in the process.'

'Much obliged for that,' he muttered, shaking his head.

After catching their breath, they rested for nearly an hour, slowly regaining their strength as Dirk purged the remaining water from his lungs, inhaled moments before Summer broke the iron grip that had nearly drowned him. What little sunlight that earlier wafted through the mouth of the cavern had long since vanished with nightfall, leaving them prone in the cave in near-total blackness.

'Do you know the way out of here?' Dirk asked once he felt fit to move.

'The mouth of the cave is less than fifty meters away,' Summer said, 'just a short distance to the east is Kang's dock.'

'How'd we get in here in the first place?' he asked.

'A small skiff. I forgot that you slept through the scenic portion of the cruise.'

'Sorry I missed it,' Dirk replied, rubbing a small gash on the top of his head. 'We'll have to borrow a boat from Kang if we want to get off this rock. There was a small speedboat tied up behind his floating palace when we came in and docked. Maybe it's still there.'

'If we can untie it from the dock and drift it out into the cove undetected before starting it up, it may buy us some more time.' Summer shivered as she spoke, her body feeling the effects of the cool river dousing.

'Back in the water, I'm afraid. You know the way out, so lead on.'

Summer ripped the side seam of the silk dress up to her hip to allow more freedom for swimming, then slipped back into the cool murky water. Dirk followed as they swam and groped their way along the narrow winding cavern, moving toward a pale gray circular patch of light that faintly shimmered against the surrounding darkness. The murmur of distant voices gave them a momentary pause as they approached the cave's exit. Swimming around a tight bend, the oval mouth of the cavern opened up before them, the night sky twinkling with starlight while the glittering reflection of Kang's dockside floodlights danced about the water's surface. Dirk and Summer swam silently out of the cavern entrance to a small rock outcropping a few yards away. The algae-slickened boulders afforded a safely concealed vantage point from which they could observe the dock and adjacent grounds.

For several minutes, they hung quietly against the rocks, studying the moored boats and shoreline for signs of movement. There were three boats tied up to the floating dock that ran parallel to the shore. Just as Dirk recalled, a small green patrol speedboat was wedged between Kang's large Italian luxury yacht and the high-speed catamaran on which they had arrived. No signs of life were visible on any of the three boats, which were all tied up in a row bow to stern. Dirk knew that a small live-aboard crew would be present on the larger vessel.

A lone sentry finally emerged in the distance, walking slowly along the shoreline. As he passed under a floodlight, Dirk could clearly see the glint of an assault rifle slung under the man's shoulder. Casually, the guard strode out onto the dock and alongside the three boats, pausing for several minutes near the large yacht. Growing bored, he strode back down the dock and onto shore, advancing along a stone walkway toward the estate elevator, where he deposited himself in a small security station at the base of the cliff.

'That's our man,' Dirk whispered. 'As long as he stays in that hut, his view of the speedboat is overshadowed by the larger boats.'

'Now's the time to steal it, before he makes the next round.'

Dirk nodded and the two of them pushed away from the rocks and began swimming silently toward the dock. He kept an eye on the guardhouse while mentally computing how long it might take to hot-wire the speedboat's ignition in the dark if the keys weren't conveniently left in the boat.

They swam well away from the dock, so as not to arouse suspicion until they were directly offshore of the speedboat, then slowly worked their way in toward it. With handcuffs still clasped to their wrists, their swimming motions felt clumsy, but they quietly kept their hands under the water as they stroked.

Furtively approaching the dock, they were blocked from view of the guardhouse until they reached the stern of the boat, where they again had a view of the shore. The guard was still in the security hut, where he could be seen sitting on a stool reading a magazine.

Using hand motions, Dirk directed Summer to remove the boat's stern line while he would swim forward and take care of the bowline. Moving along the boat's hull, he felt the looming presence of Kang's yacht towering over him as he crossed the smaller boat's bow. Stretching to grab the mooring line in order to pull himself to the dock, he suddenly heard a sharp click directly above him and he froze still in the water. A spark of yellow light erupted briefly, and, in the glow, he could see the ruddy face of a guard lighting a cigarette on the fantail of Kang's yacht no more than ten feet away.

Dirk didn't move a muscle, steadying himself with one hand clasped on the speedboat's prow, careful not to disturb the quietly lapping water. He watched patiently as the red ember of the cigarette rhythmically flared like a crimson beacon as the guard inhaled on the tobacco. Dirk found himself holding his breath, not for himself but for Summer, whom he hoped would avoid detection at the stern of the boat. The guard fully enjoyed his smoke, pulling at it for ten minutes before flinging the butt over the railing. The burning stub landed in the water just three feet from Dirk's head, extinguishing with a hiss.

Waiting until he heard the padded sound of footsteps move away from the railing, Dirk ducked underwater and swam toward the rear of the speedboat. Surfacing just astern of the boat's propeller, he found Summer waiting with an impatient look on her face. Dirk shook his head at her, then quietly pulled himself up the rear transom of the speedboat and peered toward the pilot seat. In the darkness, he could just barely make out the dashboard ignition, which winked back at him void of a key. He slunk back into the water and looked at Summer, then reached for the loose mooring line in her hands.

She was surprised when he ducked underwater for a minute, then surfaced empty-handed, expecting that he was going to retie the line to the dock. Instead he pointed offshore. Summer followed his finger and began swimming silently away from the boat. When they were safely out of earshot, they stopped and rested.

'What was that all about?' Summer asked with a tinge of annoyance.

Dirk described the guard positioned on the stern of Kang's yacht. 'There wasn't much chance without the starter key. As close as the boats are together, he'd have seen or heard me trying to rummage around hot-wiring the ignition. Chances are, there's a guard or two on the catamaran as well. I think we're going to have to settle for the skiff.'

The small skiff that Kang's thugs had used to ferry Dirk and Summer into the cavern was pulled up onto the shore, adjacent to the dock.

'That's awfully close to the guardhouse,' Summer noted.

Dirk looked ashore, spotting the guard still sitting in the guardhouse, about twenty meters from the skiff. 'Stealth it will be,' he said confidently.

Kicking back toward shore, they swam widely around the docked boats and approached the rocky beach from the east side. When their feet touched bottom, Dirk had Summer wait in the water while he crept slowly to the shoreline.

Inching his way out of the water, he crawled snakelike on his belly toward the boat, which was wedged between two rocks about twenty feet from the water. Using the boat as a shield between him and the guardhouse, he burrowed alongside the wooden skiff until he could peer over the side. A spool of line, coiled on the front bench and tied to a small bow cleat, caught his eye. Reaching over the gunwale, he unfastened the line and pulled the coil to his chest, then burrowed backward over the loose pebble beach to the boat's stern, which faced the water. Running his hand along the top of the transom, he felt a bolt-hole for attaching an outboard motor and ran one end of the line through, tying it securely.

Scurrying on his belly back into the water, he played out the line until he reached the end of its fifty-foot length. Summer swam over and they huddled together, hunched over in four feet of water with just their heads poking above the surface.

'We'll reel it in like a marlin,' Dirk whispered. 'If anybody gets wise, we can duck back behind those rocks by the cavern,' he said, tilting his head toward the protruding boulders nearby. Placing Summer's hands on the line, he leaned back in the water and gradually began applying tension to the line. Summer tightened her grip and then threw her weight onto the line as it drew taut.

The small boat jumped easily from its perch, emitting a jarring grind as its hull scraped across its rocky berth. They quickly eased off the line and stared toward the guardhouse. Inside, the guard still had his nose stuck in the magazine, impervious to the noise made by the boat. They quietly took up the slack and continued to reel the boat toward them a foot at a time, stopping periodically to ensure they had not attracted any attention. Summer held her breath as the boat approached the water's edge, letting out a long sigh when they tugged it fully into the water, the scraping sound at last ceasing.

'Let's tow her out a little farther,' Dirk whispered, winding the towline over his shoulder and kicking toward the center of the cove. When they were a hundred meters from the shoreline, he tossed the line into the boat and pulled himself over the side, then grabbed Summer's hand and pulled her aboard.

'Not exactly a Fountain offshore powerboat but I guess she'll do,' he said, surveying the interior of the small boat. Spying a pair of oars under the bench seat, he popped the shafts into the side oarlocks and dipped the blades into the water. Facing the stern of the skiff, with Kang's compound illuminated in the background, he pulled heavily on the oars, propelling the small boat swiftly into the center of the cove.

'It's about a mile to the main river channel,' Summer estimated. 'Maybe we can find a friendly South Korean naval or Coast Guard vessel on the river.'

'I'd settle for a passing freighter.'

'Sure,' Summer replied. 'Just as long as it doesn't have a Kang Enterprises lightning bolt on the funnel.'

Glancing toward the shoreline, Dirk suddenly detected a movement in the distance and squinted to better see across the water. As his eyes focused, he grimaced slightly.

'I'm afraid it's not going to be a freighter offering us the first lift,' he said as his knuckles tightened their grip on the oars.

The dockside guard had grown bored with his magazine and decided to patrol the moored boats once again. A fellow guard stationed on Kang's yacht was from a neighboring province and he loved to harass the man about the lack of attractive women in his home region. Walking toward the dock, he at first failed to take notice of the empty beach, but then tripped as he stepped onto the dock ramp. Grabbing the side rail to steady himself, his eyes fell to the ground nearby, detecting the scarred indentation of a boat that had been dragged across the pebbly beach. Only, the boat was gone.

The embarrassed guard quickly radioed his discovery to the central security post and, in an instant, two heavily armed guards came running from the shadows. After a brief but heated exchange, several flashlights were produced, their yellow beams rapidly waved in a chaotic frenzy about the water, rocks, and sky in a frantic search for the missing skiff. But it was the guard on the stern of Kang's yacht who located the two escapees. Shining a powerful marine spotlight across the water of the cove, he pinpointed the small white boat lurching across the waves.

'Not a good time to be in the limelight,' Summer

cursed as the rays of the distant searchlight fell over them. The clattering burst of an assault rifle rattled across the water, accompanied by the whistling of bullets that raced harmlessly over their heads.

'Get down low in the boat,' Dirk commanded his sister as he pulled harder on the oars. 'We're out of accurate firing range but they could still get off a lucky shot.'

The small skiff was just midway across the cove and Dirk and Summer would be sitting ducks for a gunman in Kang's speedboat, which could be on them in a matter of seconds. Dirk silently hoped and prayed that nobody would notice the boat's stern line as they rushed to chase after them.

On shore, one of the guards had already jumped into the green speedboat and started the motor. Tongju, awakened by the gunfire, burst out of his cabin on the catamaran and began barking inquiries at one of the guards.

'Take the speedboat. Kill them if you have to,' he hissed.

The two other guards scrambled into the speed-boat, one of them casting off the bowline as he jumped aboard. In the rushed moment, none of the men noticed that the stern line was dropped over the outboard side. The pilot saw only that the lines to the dock cleat were free. As the boat drifted clear of the dock, he jammed it into gear and pushed the throttle all the way to its stops.

The green boat surged forward for a split second,

then mysteriously stopped dead in its tracks. The engine continued to scream with a whine, churning at high rpm, but the boat sat drifting lazily. The confused pilot pulled back on the throttle, unsure of what was causing the lack of forward motion.

'Idiot!' Tongju screamed from the deck of the catamaran with uncharacteristic emotion. 'Your stern line is caught in the propeller. Put someone over the side to cut it free.'

Dirk's handiwork had paid off. Diving under the speedboat, he had tightly wrapped the stern line around the propeller and its exposed shaft, clogging its ability to spin freely. The heavy hand of the pilot on the throttle had only served to wind the line tighter, spinning it up and into the driveshaft coupling in a laborious mess. It would take a diver twenty minutes to cut and yank free the mass of coiled rope embedded in the driveline.

Realizing the speedboat's predicament, Tongju burst into the cabin of the catamaran's pilot.

'Start the engines. Get us under way immediately,' he barked.

The groggy pilot, clad in a pair of red silk pajamas, nodded sharply and made his way quickly to the wheelhouse.

Three-quarters of a mile away, Dirk grunted as he pulled another stroke of the oars, his heart pounding fiercely. His shoulder and arm muscles began to burn from the strenuous effort to propel the skiff faster, and even his thigh muscles ached from pushing against the oars. His tired body was telling himself to slow the pace but his mental will pushed to keep rowing with all his strength. They had gained a few precious minutes by sabotaging the speedboat, but Kang's men still had two more boats at their disposal.

In the distance, they could hear the deep muffled exhaust of the catamaran as its engines were started and revved. As Dirk rowed in a controlled rhythm, Summer helped guide him through the inlet they approached at the far end of the cove. Kang's compound and boats suddenly drifted from view as they began threading their way through the S-curved inlet.

'We've got maybe five minutes,' he exhaled between strokes. 'You up for another swim?'

'I can't exactly glide through the water like Esther Williams with these,' she said, holding up the two handcuffs that dangled from her wrists, 'but I can certainly do without another dose of Kang's hospitality.' She knew better than to ask whether Dirk was up for a strenuous swim. Despite his exhausted state, she knew her brother was like a fish in the water. Growing up in Hawaii, they swam in the warm surf constantly. Dirk excelled at marathon swimming and routinely swam five-mile ocean legs for pleasure.

'If we can make it to the main channel, we may have a chance,' he said.

The inlet grew dark as they made their way past the first bend and the lights of Kang's compound became shielded by the surrounding hills. The otherwise still night was broken only by the faraway sound of the catamaran's four diesel engines, which they could detect were now throttled up. Like a machine himself, Dirk rhythmically tugged at the oars, smoothly dipping the blades in and out of the water in a long, efficient stroke. Summer acted as coxswain, offering subtle course changes to guide them through the channel in the shortest route possible while offering periodic words of encouragement.

'We're coming up on the second bend,' she said. 'Pull to your right and we should clear the inlet in another thirty meters.'

Dirk continued his even stroke, easing off the left oar with every third pull to nose the bow into and through the bend. The beating drone of the catamaran's engines grew louder behind them as the speedy boat ripped across the cove. Though his limbs ached, Dirk seemed to grow stronger with the approach of their adversary, propelling the small boat even faster through the flat water.

The ebony darkness softened around them as they rounded the last bend of the inlet and rowed into the expansive breadth of the Han River. Patches of starry lights twinkled across the horizon, shining from small villages scattered along the river and hillsides. The faint lights were the only clue to the river's width, which stretched nearly five miles across to the opposite shore. In the late hour of the night, traffic on the river was almost nonexistent. Several miles downstream sat a handful of small commercial freighters, moored for the night while waiting to traverse the

Han to Seoul at first daylight. A brightly illuminated dredge ship was slowly making its way upstream nearly across from Dirk and Summer but was still some four miles away. Upriver, a small vessel with an array of multicolored lights appeared to be moving down the center of the river at a slow pace.

'Afraid I don't see any passing water taxis,' Summer said, scanning the dark horizons.

As Dirk tried to row toward the center of the river, he could feel the current pushing them downstream. The river's flow was aided by an outgoing tide that pulled at the remains of the Han River as it dispersed into the dusky waters of the Yellow Sea. He eased off the oars for a moment to survey their options. The dredge ship looked appealing, but they would have to fight the crosscurrent to reach it, which would be near impossible once they took to the water. Peering downriver, he spotted a small cluster of yellow lights on the opposite shore twinkling fuzzily through the damp air.

'Let's try for the village there,' he said, pointing an oar in the direction of the lights, which were about two miles downstream. 'If we swim directly across the river, the current should carry us pretty close.'

'Whatever entails the least swimming.'

Unbeknownst to both was the fact that the Korean demarcation line ran through this section of the Han River delta. The twinkling lights downriver were not a village at all but a heavily garrisoned North Korean military patrol boat base.

Any further contingency planning was suddenly dashed by the abrupt roar of the high-speed catamaran as it burst out of the inlet. A pair of bright spotlights flared from beside the wheelhouse, sweeping back and forth rapidly across the water. It would be only seconds before one of the beams fell on the small white skiff heading across the river.

'Time to exit stage right,' Dirk said, swinging the boat around so that the bow pointed downstream. Summer quickly slipped over the side followed by Dirk, who hesitated a moment, flinging a pair of life jackets out away from the boat before he rolled into the water.

'Let's angle across and slightly upriver to put as much distance as possible between us and the drifting boat,' he said.

'Right. We'll surface for air at the count of thirty.'

The clatter of machine-gun fire suddenly tore through the night air while a seamlike spray of bullets slapped into the water a few yards in front of them. One of the spotlights had found the skiff and a guard opened fire as the catamaran raced toward it.

In unison, Dirk and Summer ducked under the water, kicking down to a depth of four feet before angling into the current. The powerful flow of the river made them feel like they were swimming in place as they inched their way toward midriver. Gaining ground upriver was hopeless as the current overpowered them, but it pushed them downstream at a much slower pace than the drifting skiff.

The deep pulsations of the catamaran's diesel engines resonated through the water and they could feel the boat as it approached the skiff. Counting time with each breaststroke, Dirk hoped that Summer would not get separated from him in the darkness. Swimming at night in the black water, their only indication of direction was the tug of the river's current. As he approached the count of thirty, he eased slowly to the surface, breaking the water with barely a ripple.

Just ten feet away, Summer's face emerged from the water and Dirk could hear her breathing deeply. Glancing briefly at each other, then back toward the skiff, they quickly gulped a deep swallow of fresh air and resubmerged, kicking back into the river current for another count of thirty.

The quick glimpse Dirk made toward the skiff was a reassuring one. Kang's catamaran had barreled in on the skiff from upriver with guns blazing and was now creeping up close to assess the damage. No one on board had bothered to look across the river, assuming that Dirk and Summer were still in the boat. In their brief time in the water, they had already established a separation of nearly a hundred meters from the skiff.

As the catamaran approached the drifting boat, Tongju ordered his gunmen to cease firing. There was no sign of the two escapees, whom Tongju expected to find sprawled dead in the bottom of the bullet-ridden boat. Looking down from the upper deck of the catamaran, Tongju cursed to himself as they pulled alongside and shined a light into the skiff. The small boat was completely empty.

'Search the surrounding water and shoreline,' he ordered crisply. The catamaran circled around the skiff while the spotlights were splayed across the water, all eyes peering intently into the darkness. Suddenly, a gunman on the bow of the catamaran yelled out.

'There, in the water . . . two objects!' he cried, pointing an arm off the port bow.

Tongju nodded at the words. This time they are finished, he thought with ruthless satisfaction.

36

After their fourth submerged interval, Dirk and Summer reunited on the surface and took a moment to rest. Fighting their way across the current, they had distanced themselves from the skiff by almost four hundred meters.

'We can swim on the surface for the time being,' Dirk said between deep breaths. 'Give us a chance to see what our friends are up to.'

Summer followed her brother's lead and rolled onto her back, kicking into a backstroke that allowed them to watch the distant catamaran as they moved farther across the river. Kang's boat was idling near the skiff, its spotlights circling the immediate area around them. Shouting erupted from the catamaran and the boat suddenly raced downriver a short distance. Gunfire exploded again for a moment, then ceased as the boat stopped in the water.

Tongju had raced the catamaran toward the two objects spotted floating on the water and watched with disdain as his gunmen blasted away at the empty life vests that Dirk had tossed into the water. The boat idled around the life jackets for several minutes, waiting for the two escapees to surface in case they were hiding submerged nearby, before resuming the search. Dirk and Summer struggled toward midriver as they watched the catamaran begin making a wide-circle search around the skiff and life jackets. With each loop around the still-drifting skiff, the catamaran's pilot enlarged the circle in an ever-expanding spiral.

'Won't be too many more minutes before they work their way up and out our direction,' Summer lamented.

Dirk scanned the watery horizon. They had worked their way about a mile into the river but were still barely a quarter of the way across the vast waterway. They could turn back and try for the nearest shoreline, but that would entail crossing the path of the advancing catamaran. Or they could continue with their original plan of traversing the river toward the lights on the opposite shore. But fatigue was beginning to creep up on them, hastened by their long immersion in the cool water. Another three-mile swim would be a tall order, made more difficult by the repeated submergings they would have to perform to avoid Kang's boat. Whether they could in fact survive the game of cat and mouse with Tongju and his gunmen would be uncertain at best.

But there was a third option. The small vessel with the colored lights that they had earlier noticed upriver was approaching on a nearby path about a half mile away. In the darkness, Dirk had trouble identifying the boat, but it appeared to be a wooden sailing vessel of some kind. A small red sail, revealed under the white mast light to be square shaped in dimension, was raised near the bow, but the boat didn't appear to be moving much faster than the current.

Dirk gauged the path of the boat and swam another hundred yards toward the center of the river, then stopped. Summer swam past before realizing her brother had halted.

'What gives? We need to keep going,' she whispered after swimming back to him.

Dirk nodded downriver toward the catamaran. The sleek vessel had arced well out into the river as it circled downstream. He mentally calculated the trajectory of the yacht if it held its current circular course.

'They'll be within sight of us on the next upriver pass,' he said quietly.

Summer could see he was right. The bright beams of the searchlights would shine upon their position on the next loop. They would have to remain submerged for several minutes to guarantee their concealment.

Dirk took a quick glance upriver. 'Sister, I think it's time for Plan B.'

'Plan B?' she asked.

'Yes, Plan B. Stick out your thumb and start hitchhiking.'

The large wooden sailboat creaked lazily down the river, its foremast sail and a small auxiliary motor pushing it along just 3 knots faster than the current.

As the vessel crept closer, Dirk could see that it was a three-masted Chinese junk of about twenty-five meters in length. Unlike most dilapidated sailing boats in this part of the world, the junk appeared to be maintained in pristine condition. A string of multicolored Chinese lanterns hung gaily from bow to stern, lending a partylike atmosphere to the boat. Constructed entirely of rich teakwood, the highly varnished surfaces seemed to glisten under the swaying overhead lamps. Somewhere belowdecks, a pair of stereo speakers blared out an orchestral tune, which Dirk recognized as a Gershwin melody. Yet despite the festive atmosphere, there was not a soul to be seen on deck.

'Ahoy! We're in the water. Can you help?'

Dirk's muted shout went unanswered as the junk approached. He repeated the call, careful not to draw attention from the catamaran, which had completed a downstream turn and was now headed upriver. Swimming closer to the moving junk, Dirk thought he detected a shadowy movement on the stern, but, again, there was no response to his call for help. He tried a third time, failing to notice as he spoke that the muffled drone of the junk's motor audibly raised a note.

The junk's golden teak hull began gliding past Dirk and Summer, an ornately carved dragon on the prow eyeing them maliciously in the water less than ten feet from the starboard beam. Like a phantom in the night, the junk slipped by strangely impervious to the voices calling from the water. As the stern and rudderpost floated past, Dirk abandoned hope of rescue from the junk and angrily wondered whether the pilot was asleep, drunk, or both.

Peering toward the slowly approaching catamaran, he was startled by a sudden splash in the water near his head. It was an orange plastic float tied to a coil of rope, trailing back to the stern of the junk.

'Grab hold and hang on tight,' he instructed his sister, making sure Summer had a strong grip on the line before grasping it himself. As the line quickly drew taut, the force of the junk sailing faster than the river momentarily jerked them underwater. With a face full of water, they were dragged along the river's surface like a fallen water-skier who forgot to let go of the towline. Dirk slowly began pulling himself up the line hand over hand as his legs flailed out behind him. Reaching the high, blunt stern of the junk, he shimmied up the rope almost vertically until reaching the stern railing. A pair of hands emerged from the darkness, grabbing about his lapels and forcefully yanking him over the railing and onto the deck.

'Thanks,' Dirk muttered, paying little heed to a tall figure in the shadows. 'My sister is still on the line,' he gasped, standing and grabbing the line at the stern rail and pulling at it. The tall man stepped up behind him and clasped the line, throwing his weight into it with Dirk. Together, they hoisted Summer up the railing like a gigged flounder until she flopped over the railing and onto the deck in a soggy heap. A high-pitched bark erupted from across the deck and, in an instant, a small black-and-tan dachshund raced over to Summer and began licking her face.

'Dark night for a swim, don't you think?' the stranger said in English.

'You're American,' Dirk stated with surprise.

'Ever since being born in the Land of Lincoln,' came the reply.

Dirk studied the man beside him for the first time. He stood six-foot-three, nearly matching his own height, though he carried a good twenty pounds more heft. A wave of unruly white hair and a matching goatee indicated that he was at least forty years his senior. The man's blue-green eyes, which seemed to twinkle with mischief under the hanging lights, touched a nerve with him. He felt as if he was looking at an older version of his own father, he finally decided.

'We're in great danger,' Summer injected, rising to her feet. She scooped up the small dog as she stood and rubbed its ears briskly, which produced a sharp wag of its tail. 'Our research vessel was sunk by these murderers and they mean to kill us,' she said, nodding downriver toward the catamaran that was circling slowly in their direction.

'I heard the machine-gun fire,' the man replied.

'They intend to make another deadly attack. We need to alert the authorities,' she pleaded.

'Thousands of additional lives are at risk,' Dirk added somberly.

The white-haired man perused the odd pair up and down. Summer, soaked but elegant still in her ripped silk cocktail dress, appeared an unusual companion for Dirk, who was battered and bruised in a shredded blue jumpsuit. Neither attempted to conceal the handcuff shackles that dangled from their wrists.

A slight grin fell across the man's lips. 'I guess I'll buy it. We better hide you belowdecks until we get past that cat. You can stay in Mauser's cabin.'

'Mauser? How many people are aboard?' Dirk asked.

'Just me and that fellow who's kissing your sister,' he replied. Dirk turned to see the small dachshund happily licking the water off Summer's face.

The junk's owner quickly led them through a bulkhead door and down a flight of steps that led to a tastefully decorated stateroom.

'There's towels in the bath and dry clothes in the closet. And here, this will warm you up.' He grabbed a bottle sitting on a side table and poured them each a glass of the clear fluid. Dirk downed a shot quickly, tasting a bitter flavor from the smooth liquor that clearly packed a high alcohol content.

'Soju,' the man said. 'A local rice brew. Help yourself while I try to get us past your friends in the cat.'

'Thank you for helping us,' Summer replied appreciatively. 'By the way, my name is Summer Pitt, and this is my brother, Dirk.'

'Pleased to meet you. My name is Clive Cussler.'

*

Cussler returned to the junk's exposed wheel and slipped the engine into gear, tweaking the throttle slightly higher while nosing the bow farther toward midriver. It took only a few minutes before the catamaran approached from downstream, pulling alongside and washing the junk in a flood of spotlights. Cussler slipped on a conical straw peasant's hat and hunched his tall frame low at the wheel.

Through the glare of the lights, he could see several men pointing automatic weapons at him. As the catamaran crept to within inches of the port beam, an unseen man on the bridge barked a question across through the boat's PA system. Cussler replied by shaking his head. Another command echoed across from the catamaran as the spotlights bounced about the junk. Cussler again shook his head, wondering whether the waterlogged coil of rope and wet pairs of footprints across the deck would be detected. For several long minutes, the catamaran held steady at the junk's side as if waiting to board. Then, with a sudden blast of its engines, the catamaran roared away, resuming its river search closer to shore.

Cussler guided the junk down the last vestiges of the Han River until its waters were swallowed by the Yellow Sea. As the sea-lanes opened and the potential for nearby water traffic fell away, Cussler punched a handful of electronic controls at the helm. Hydraulic winches began to whir as lines were pulled and yards were raised, pulling the traditional red, square-shaped lugsails of a classic junk to the peak of the main- and mizzenmasts. Cussler manually tied off the out haul lines and then powered off the small diesel motor. The old junk now leaped through the waves under the graceful power of its sails.

'You've got a beautiful vessel,' Dirk said, emerging from belowdecks dressed in jeans and a polo shirt. Summer followed him onto the deck, clad in an oversized pair of coveralls and a man's work shirt.

'The standard Chinese merchant ship that dates back almost two thousand years,' Cussler replied. 'This one was built in Shanghai in 1907 for a wealthy tea trader. She's made entirely from a hard teakwood called "Takien Tong." She's extremely durable and surprisingly seaworthy.'

'Where did you find her?' Summer asked.

'A friend of mine found her abandoned in a Malaysian boatyard and decided to refurbish her. Took him six years to complete the job. After he grew bored with sailing, I traded him a few antique cars for her. Plan to cruise the Asian Pacific in her. Started in Japan and am going to work my way down to Wellington.'

'You sail her by yourself?' Summer asked.

'She's been modified with a strong diesel engine and hydraulic lifts for the lugsails, which are linked to a computerized automatic pilot. She's a breeze to manage, and can, in fact, sail herself.'

'Do you have a satellite phone aboard?' Dirk asked.

'Afraid not. A ship-to-shore radio is the best I can offer you. I didn't want any phone calls or Internet messages bothering me on this cruise.'

'Understandable. Where are you headed, and, for that matter, where are we located now?' he asked.

Cussler pulled out a marine navigation chart and held it under the weak light of the helm console. 'We're entering the Yellow Sea about forty miles northwest of Seoul. I take it you aren't interested in staying aboard till Wellington?' he grinned, running an index finger across the chart. 'How about Inchon?' he continued, tapping the map. 'I can drop you there in about eight hours. I believe there's a U.S. Air Force base located somewhere near there.'

'That would be great. Anywhere we can find a phone and get ahold of someone at NUMA head-quarters.'

'NUMA,' Cussler said, mulling over the word. 'You're not from that NUMA ship that sank south-west of Japan?'

'The *Sea Rover.* Yes, we are. How did you know about that?' Summer asked.

'It was all over CNN. I saw them interview the captain. Told how the crew was rescued by a Japanese freighter following an explosion in the engine room.'

Dirk and Summer stared at each other in disbelief.

'Captain Morgan and the crew are alive?' she finally blurted.

'Yes, that was the fellow's name. I thought he said the whole crew was rescued.'

Summer retold the story of their attack on the ship and abduction by Kang's men and their uncertainty over the fate of their crew members.

'I suspect there's more than a few people out there looking for you,' Cussler said. 'You're safe for now. There's some sandwiches and beer in the galley. Why don't you two grab a bite and get some rest. I'll wake you when we reach Inchon.'

'Thank you. I'll take you up on that,' Summer replied, heading belowdecks.

Dirk lingered a moment, standing at the rail and watching the first glimmer of daybreak attempt to paint the eastern horizon. As he contemplated the events of the past three days, a hardened resolve surged through his exhausted body. By some miracle, the *Sea Rover*'s crew had survived the sinking of the NUMA research ship. But Kang still had blood on his hands, and the stakes were now dramatically higher. If what Kang had told them was true, then millions of lives were at risk. The madman would have to be stopped, he knew, and quick.

PART THREE
Sea Launch

Sea Launch platform *Odyssey* and airship *Icarus*

37

June 16, 2007
Long Beach, California

Though it was a cool, damp Southern California morning, Danny Stamp could feel the sweat beginning to drip from his underarms. The veteran engineer was as nervous as a teenager on prom night awaiting his first make-out session. But as those who knew him could affirm, he always felt this way when his baby was on the move.

No diaper-clad infant, his baby today was a 209-foot Zenit-3SL liquid-fuel rocket that was in the delicate process of being transferred to its launch platform. The roundish and slightly balding launch vehicle director peered purposefully over the railing of a large ship's superstructure as the $90 million rocket he was responsible for inched into view below his feet. As the huge white cylinder rolled slowly out of its horizontal berth on a centipedelike cradle, Stamp's eyes were drawn to the large blue letters emblazoned on the rocket's housing that read SEA LAUNCH.

Incorporated in the nineteen nineties, Sea Launch was an international commercial venture formed to provide rocket-launch services geared primarily for satellite telecommunications operators. The American aerospace giant Boeing was the prime founder, signing on to handle launch operations as well as integrating the customer's satellite payloads into the rocket housing. Turning swords into rubles, a pair of Russian companies joined the consortium by providing the actual rockets, or 'launch vehicles,' as they are known in the parlance. Ex-military rockets that once carried nuclear warheads, the Zenits were tried-and-true launch vehicles that were perfectly suited to commercial applications. But it was a Norwegian firm, Kvaerner, that provided perhaps the most unique asset to the venture. Starting with a used North Sea oil platform, the Oslo firm constructed a self-propelled floating launchpad that could be positioned for launching in almost any ocean waters of the world.

Though an interesting selling point, practicality dictates that there is only one area on the globe worth launching from and that is the equator. For a geosynchronous satellite, which remains in a fixed relative orbital position following the earth's rotation, there is no more direct path to orbit than from the equator. Less rocket fuel burned in pushing a satellite to orbit can allow for a heavier satellite payload. Satellite owners, seeking to maximize revenues from their multimillion-dollar investments, can thus add more capacity to their satellites or additional operating fuel to extend the satellite's life. Integrating the satellites into the launch vehicle in Long Beach, then sailing the rocket to the equator for launch had grown from an intriguing idea to an efficient business model in the high-stakes, high-risk game of commercial space operations.

A handheld Motorola radio fastened to Stamp's belt suddenly cackled with static. 'Rollout complete. Ready for crane hook-up,' barked the unseen voice. Stamp paused and studied the Zenit rocket, which protruded from the ship's stern like a stinger on a wasp. In an unusual bid for flexibility, the Sea Launch team actually assembled the rocket and its payload in the bowels of a custom-fitted ship named the *Sea Launch Commander*. Officially known as the 'Assembly and Command Ship,' the 660-foot cargo-designed vessel contained myriad computer bays on its upper deck, as well as a mission operations command center, which directed the complete launch operation at sea. On the lower deck was a cavernous assembly compartment that housed the Zenit rocket components. Here, an army of white-smocked engineers and technicians bolted together horizontally the segmented Russian rocket sections utilizing a rail system that ran nearly the length of the ship. Once the rocket assembly was complete, the mission satellite was encapsulated into the upper-section payload fairing and then the entire launch vehicle was rolled at a snail's pace out the stern of the *Sea Launch Commander*.

'Proceed with hookup. Transfer when ready,' Stamp spoke into the radio with a slight Midwestern accent. He glanced up at a huge crane system built onto the edge of the towering launch platform. A pair of tilted M-shaped trusses extended off one end of the platform, dangling several lines of thick cable. The floating platform, christened *Odyssey*, had been positioned just aft of the *Sea Launch Commander*, its crane system hanging directly above the prone rocket. The crane's winch lines were silently dropped down to the launch vehicle, where teams of engineers in hard hats attached the cables to a series of slings and lift points along the length of the rocket.

'*Sea Launch Commander*, this is *Odyssey*,' a new voice blared through Stamp's radio. 'Ready to transfer launch vehicle.'

Stamp nodded to a short fellow standing beside him, a bearded man named Christiano who captained the *Sea Launch Commander*. Christiano spoke into his own radio.

'This is *Commander*. Proceed with transfer at will. Good luck, *Odyssey*.'

Seconds later, the cable lines drew taut and the horizontal rocket was lifted slowly off its cradle. Stamp held his breath as the Zenit rocket was hoisted high into the air until it hung suspended far above the decks of the *Commander*. The unfueled rocket was just a fraction of its launch weight, so the process was akin to lifting an empty beer can. But Stamp couldn't help feeling nervous watching the huge rocket dangling in midair above him.

After a tantalizingly slow rise to the top of the launch platform, the crane operations crew activated the movable winch and the launch vehicle was tugged horizontally into an environmentally controlled hangar on *Odyssey*'s high deck. Once the tip of the rocket had cleared the hangar doors, the entire launch vehicle was gently nestled down into a wheeled cradle. When the floating platform reached the designated launch site, the cradle device would roll the rocket out of its hangar and tilt it up on end for firing.

'Launch vehicle secure. Well done, gentlemen. The beers are on me tonight. *Odyssey* out.'

Stamp visibly relaxed, a broad grin spreading across his face. 'Piece of cake,' he said to Christiano as if the outcome was never in doubt.

'Looks like we'll make the scheduled launch date in seventeen days after all,' Christiano replied as he watched the empty launch vehicle cradle slide back into the ship's lower-deck hangar. 'The long-range weather forecast is still looking favorable. After final checks and fueling, the *Odyssey* can depart in four days and we'll follow in the *Commander* forty-eight hours later after additional spares and provisions are put aboard. We'll easily catch up with her before reaching the launch site.'

'A good thing, too,' Stamp said with relief. 'There's a penalty clause in the customer contract that's a killer if we are late to launch.'

'Nobody could have predicted the dockworkers' strike would delay receipt of the Zenit rocket components by fifteen days,' Christiano said, shaking his head.

'The launch vehicle team did a heckuva job making up lost schedule. I'm not looking forward to seeing the overtime charges but the team must have set a record for assembly and integration. Even with our paranoid customer shielding the mission payload from everyone.'

'What's so terribly secretive about a broadcast television satellite?'

'Search me,' Stamp said, shrugging his shoulders. 'Typical Asian reticence, I guess. The whole operation doesn't make sense to me. They've got a relatively lightweight satellite that they could have easily launched off the Chinese Long March rocket for a couple of million dollars less than our fees.'

'Angst with the Chinese isn't an unusual sentiment in the Far East.'

'True, but usually overlooked when it comes to dollars and cents. Perhaps it's due to the head of the telecommunications firm. He's apparently a real maverick.'

'He owns the company outright, doesn't he?' Christiano asked, his eyes searching skyward trying to recall.

'Yep,' Stamp replied. 'Dae-jong Kang is one rich and powerful man.'

*

Kang leaned back in the padded leather chair of his cherrywood study and listened intently as a pair of engineers from his Inchon facility provided a technical briefing. Tongju sat silently at the back of the room, his dark eyes scrutinizing the men out of habit. One of the engineers, a slight, disheveled man with glasses and a deeply receding hairline, spoke to Kang with a raspy voice.

'As you know, the Koreasat 2 satellite was delivered to the launch provider's facility approximately three weeks ago, where it was encapsulated inside the payload fairing, or nose cone section, of the Zenit rocket. The entire launch vehicle has since been loaded onto the self-propelled launch platform, which is preparing for departure to the equator.'

'There have been no security lapses?' Kang asked, throwing a cold glance toward Tongju.

The engineer shook his head. 'We've had our own security team protecting the satellite around the clock. The Sea Launch team suspects nothing. By all external appearances, the satellite is designated for television broadcast services. Now that the satellite is enshrouded in the rocket housing, there is little chance of suspicion.' The engineer swallowed a sip of coffee from an overflowing mug, spilling a few drops of the hot liquid on the sleeve of his worn checkered sport coat. The brown stain matched a similar pattern of spots on his tie.

'The aerosol device ... it was verified as operational?' Kang asked.

'Yes. As you know, we made a number of modifications from the small-scale model that was tested in the Aleutian Islands. There is no longer a dual agent capability, as the deployment of the cyanide mixture was eliminated from the mission. Plus, the system was redesigned with removable canisters that will allow us to arm the payload with the bioagent just hours before launch. And, of course, it is a much higher volume system. The Aleutian test model, you may recall, carried less than five kilograms of bio-chemical compound, while the satellite vehicle will deploy 325 kilograms of the chimera agent after hydrogenation. Before the satellite was encapsulated at the Sea Launch facility, we conducted a final late-night test under secure conditions. The test results were flawless. We are confident the aerosol system will operate as designed over the target.'

'I do not expect any failures from our equipment,' Kang stated.

'The launch operation will be the most critical phase of the mission,' the raspy-voiced engineer continued. 'Lee-Wook, have we obtained the necessary command and control data to proceed with an independent launch?'

The second engineer, a younger, greasy-haired man with a broad nose, was clearly intimidated by Kang's presence.

'There are two primary components to the launch process,' Lee-Wook replied, stuttering slightly. 'The first is positioning and stabilizing the floating launch platform, then erecting, fueling, and preparing the rocket for launch. We have obtained the Sea Launch operating procedures for these steps,' he said, neglecting to mention the cash bribes involved, 'which our team has reviewed and practiced thoroughly. In addition, we have obtained the services of two Ukrainian launch specialists formerly employed by Yuzhnoye, the manufacturer of the Zenit rocket. They are assisting with trajectory and fueling computations and will be on hand to assist with the mechanical preparations.'

'Yes, I am aware of the enticements required to obtain them,' Kang replied with distaste. 'I believe the Russians could teach the West a thing or two about capitalistic extortion.'

Lee-Wook ignored the comment and continued speaking, his stutter finally under control. 'The second critical component is the actual launch initiation and flight control. During a normal launch at sea, the Sea Launch assembly and command ship performs these controls. For our launch, this duty will be handled by the *Baekje*. We have refitted the ship with the necessary communications equipment and computer hardware required to execute the launch and flight control,' Lee-Wook said, his voice almost at a whisper. 'Our last input has been the software that monitors, tracks, and commands the launch vehicle. The actual launch from the floating platform is a highly automated process, so the software plays a critical role. There are several million lines of software code that support the launch, telemetry, and tracking phases.'

'Have we re-created the necessary software for our mission?'

'It would have required many months to write and test the software on our own. We were fortunate in that all of these software programs are contained within the databases of the assembly and command ship. As the payload customer, our team has had almost unlimited access to the ship for the last three weeks while the Koreasat 2 satellite was being integrated with the launch vehicle. Once on board, our systems team found it relatively easy to breach the vessel's mainframe computers and acquire the software code. Under the nose of their computer experts, we downloaded copies of the software and, over a four-day period, transmitted the code by satellite link direct from the Sea Launch vessel to our laboratory at Inchon.'

'But I was told the *Baekje*, or *Koguryo* as she is now called, left port a day ago.'

'We have already transferred a portion of the program to the shipboard computers and will download the remaining software while the ship is in transit via satellite.'

'And you have determined the optimal flight path to achieve maximum dispersal of the agent?' Kang asked.

'We can theoretically launch uprange of the target as far as four thousand kilometers away; however, the probability of accurately striking the target is quite small. There is no guidance system for the suborbital payload, so we are relying on wind, thrust, and launch positioning to reach the strike zone. Utilizing normal Pacific wind conditions, our Ukrainian engineers have determined that positioning the launch platform approximately four hundred kilometers uprange of the target will maximize the accuracy of delivery. Adjusting for atmospheric conditions at the time of launch, we can expect the payload to fall to earth within a five-kilometer radius.'

'But the aerosol system will be activated well before that,' the first engineer injected.

'Correct. At an elevation of six thousand meters, the aerosol, or payload system, will be activated. This will occur shortly after the nose cone fairing has been discarded during flight. In its descent, the payload system will be traveling nearly eight kilometers down-range for every one kilometer of descent. A vapor trail of the armed agent will thus be dispersed along a forty-eight-kilometer-long corridor.'

'I would have preferred that the launch not take place so close to the North American mainland,' Kang said with a wrinkled brow, 'but if the accuracy of the mission dictates such then so be it. The flight trajectory will be controlled by the rocket burn?'

'Precisely. The Zenit-3SL is a three-stage rocket designed for pushing heavy payloads into high orbit. But our desired maximum altitude is less than fifty kilometers, so we will not fuel the second and third stages and will short-fuel the first stage. We can terminate the burn at any time, which we will program to do at slightly over a minute into the flight. As the launch vehicle coasts in flight to the east, we'll initiate separation of the payload section from the rocket boosters, then release the payload housing. The mock satellite will deploy the aerosol system automatically and disperse the agent until impact.'

'Are we positive the American missile defense systems pose no risk?'

'The American antiballistic system is still in its infancy. It is geared toward intercontinental ballistic missiles that are launched from thousands of miles away. They will have no time to react. Even if they did, their intercept missiles would arrive after we have initiated separation. They might harmlessly destroy the rocket boosters at best. No, sir, there will be no stopping the payload deployment once we have launched.'

'I am expecting the countdown to occur while the G8 leaders are in the target area,' Kang stated bluntly.

'Weather permitting, we have scheduled the launch to coincide with the pre-summit assembly in Los Angeles,' the engineer said nervously.

'I understand that you will see things through from Inchon?'

'The telecommunications lab is in constant communications with the *Koguryo* and will be monitoring the launch live. We of course will be advising the shipboard crew during the countdown preparations. I trust that you will be able to join us in viewing the launch?'

Kang nodded. 'As my schedule permits. You have done exceptional work. Bring the mission to success and you will bring high honor to the Central People's Committee.'

Kang nodded again, indicating that the briefing was over. The two engineers glanced at each other, then bowed to Kang and quietly shuffled out of the study. Tongju rose from his seat and stepped to the front of the large mahogany desk.

'Your assault team is in place?' Kang asked his quiet enforcer.

'Yes, they remained aboard ship in Inchon. With your indulgence, I have arranged for a company jet to fly me to an abandoned Japanese airstrip in the Ogasawara Islands, where I will rejoin the vessel for the operation.'

'Yes, I expect you to lead the assault phase.' Kang paused for a moment. 'We have come a long way in implementing our plan of deception to risk failure now,' he said sternly. 'I will hold you responsible for the continued secrecy of our operation.'

'The two Americans . . . they surely drowned in the river,' Tongju replied in a hushed tone, catching Kang's drift.

'There is little they know or could prove even if they somehow survived. The difficulty lies in main-taining the deception once the mission succeeds. The

Japanese must be painted as the responsible party, with no recourse.'

'Once the strike is made, the only physical evidence will be aboard the *Koguryo*.'

'Precisely. Which is why you must destroy the ship after the launch.' Kang spoke as if he were asking for a napkin at a cocktail party.

Tongju arched a brow. 'My assault team will be on the ship, as well as your many satellite telecommunications experts?' he questioned.

'Regrettably, your team is expendable. And I have already ensured that my top satellite engineers are remaining in Inchon during the operation. It is the way it must be, Tongju,' Kang said, showing a rare hint of empathy.

'It will be done.'

'Take these coordinates,' Kang said, passing an envelope across the desk. 'One of my freighters bound for Chile will be waiting at that position. Once the launch is initiated, have the captain sail the *Koguryo* to within sight of the freighter and scuttle her. Take the captain and two or three men, if you wish, and make your way to the freighter. Under no condition must the *Koguryo* be apprehended with the crew aboard.'

Tongju nodded in silence, accepting the mass murder assignment without question.

'Good luck,' Kang said, rising and escorting him to the door. 'Our homeland is counting on you.'

After he left, Kang returned to his desk and stared

up at the ceiling for a long while. The wheels were in motion now. There was nothing more he could do but wait for the results. Eventually, he pulled out a file of financial reports and began methodically calculating his next quarter's expected profit.

38

The G8 Summit meeting is a forum that was created by former French president Giscard d'Estaing in 1975. Designed as a conference for the leaders of the major industrialized nations to come together and discuss global economic issues of the day, the summit is by tradition restricted to heads of state only. No controlling advisers or staff members are allowed, just the top world leaders thrown together once a year in a private and informal setting. Though the meetings occasionally result in little more than a prized photo op, the agendas have expanded beyond global economics over the years to include issues of world health, the environment, and combating terrorism.

Having recently passed a major global warming legislative package, the president of the United States was anxious to promote his environmental protection initiatives on a world stage as host of the next summit. Following in the tradition of recent nation hosts, President Ward had selected the scenic and tranquil setting of Yosemite National Park as the site of the summit. The remote location, he knew, would deter the usual throng of urban protesters. But in an out-of-character bow to the worldwide *amour* with

Hollywood, he had agreed to host a pre-summit reception at a posh Beverly Hills hotel the day before, to be attended by the current crop of top movie actors and film industry moguls. Not surprisingly, the invitation was accepted by each of the leaders of Japan, Italy, France, Germany, Russia, Canada, and the United Kingdom, rounding out the complete G8 membership ranks.

What the president and his security advisers had no way of knowing was that the G8 reception in Beverly Hills was ground zero for Kang's missile payload.

Adverse weather, unforeseen mechanical problems, a thousand and one things could throw off the timetable, Kang knew. But the goal was set. Make a successful strike while the major leaders of the free world were assembled and the shock value would be incalculable. Even without striking the assembled G8 leaders, the terror from the planned attack would rock the world.

Arcing across the sky from an unseen launch position in the Pacific Ocean, the aerosol dispenser would be timed to activate as the payload crossed landfall. Commencing its release over the beachfront of Santa Monica, the payload would dump its deadly agent in a swath across northern Los Angeles, streaking over the mansions of Beverly Hills, the film studios of Hollywood, and on past the suburban enclaves of Glendale and Pasadena. Passing over the Rose Bowl, the viral canisters would finally run dry and the empty payload would plunge to an obliterating impact somewhere in the San Gabriel Mountains.

The light mist settling to the ground would be innocuous to the people on the street. Yet over the next twenty-four hours, the dispersed viruses would remain alive and highly contagious, even in its low concentrated dose. Through the hustle and bustle of L.A.'s main tourist corridor, the unseen viruses would latch onto unsuspecting victims, without discriminating among men, women, or children. Rejuvenated by their living hosts, the viruses would silently launch their internal cellular attacks. Like a quietly ticking time bomb, there would be no initial clues or symptoms of infection during the following two-week incubation period. Then, suddenly, a frightening horror would strike.

At first, it would appear as a small trickle of people staggering to their doctor's office complaining of fever and body aches. Quickly, the numbers would swell, soon swamping hospital emergency rooms throughout Los Angeles County. With the disease having been eradicated for over thirty years, health professionals would be slow to identify the culprit. When the diagnosis of smallpox was finally made and the extent of the outbreak realized, pandemonium would ensue. A frenzied media would fan the hysteria as more and more cases were diagnosed. County hospitals would be mobbed by the thousands as every hypochondriac with a headache or elevated fever rushed to see a physician. But that would be just the tip of the iceberg for health officials. As thousands of new smallpox cases suddenly appeared, the health facilities would be woefully unprepared to provide the primary treatment for smallpox victims: quarantine. Without an adequate ability to isolate confirmed cases, the epidemic would grow exponentially.

Kang's scientists had conservatively estimated that twenty percent of the people exposed to the released vapor would succumb to infection. With over eighteen million people in the Los Angeles metropolitan area, even the narrow swath of the payload's flight path would expose two hundred thousand people to the germ, infecting some forty thousand. The real expansion would come two weeks later, as those initially infected would have spread the contagious germs unknowingly during their first few days of illness. Medical experts had modeled a tenfold explosion in smallpox cases from those first exposed. In a month's time, nearly half a million people in Southern California would be fighting the lethal disease.

Fear would spread faster than the smallpox infection itself, made more shocking by the vision of the president and other G8 world leaders fighting the lethal disease. As the epidemic gained strength, cries of help from citizens, health care workers, and the media would quickly overwhelm the federal government. Federal authorities would assure the nation that all would be safe, as sufficient smallpox vaccinations were on hand to inoculate the entire national population. The Centers for Disease Control would deliver the vaccinations to local health authorities to quickly counter the spreading scourge. But to those already exposed to the virus, the vaccinations would come too late to be of any help. And to many who received the vaccination, it would turn out to be useless as well.

For to the horror of health care and public officials, the veracity of the chimera virus would suddenly come to life. By virtue of its recombinant strength, the killer bug would prove itself largely immune to the U.S. stockpiled smallpox vaccinations. With the death toll mounting, distressed health officials and scientists would scramble to develop an effective vaccination that could be mass-produced, but that would take months. In the meantime, the viral plague would begin sweeping across the country like a tidal wave. Tourists and travelers from Los Angeles would unknowingly carry the live virus to points all over the nation, sparking new outbreaks in a thousand different cities. As the vaccinations were found to be ineffective, authorities would resort to the last available means of stopping the epidemic: mass quarantine. Public assemblies and gatherings would be banned in a desperate attempt to halt the viral storm. Airports would close, subways halted, and buses parked as mandatory travel restrictions would be imposed. Businesses would be forced to furlough employees while local governments curtailed their services to avoid debilitating their entire workforce.

Rock concerts, baseball games, and even church gatherings would all be canceled in fear of sparking new outbreaks. Those who would venture out for food or medicine would only do so clad in rubber gloves and surgical masks.

The economic impact to the country would be devastating. Wholesale industries would be forced to shut down overnight. Furloughed and laid-off workers would spike unemployment rates to double that of the Great Depression. The government would teeter on insolvency as tax revenues would dry up while the demand for food, medical, and social services would explode. In a few short weeks, the national output would fall to the level of a third world country.

A further crisis would ensue in defending the national security. The highly contagious disease would rip through the armed forces, infecting thousands of soldiers and sailors living in close quarters. Entire army divisions, air wings, and even naval fleets would be incapacitated, reducing the effective military force to a paper tiger. For the first time in nearly two centuries, the country's ability to defend itself would be seriously endangered.

In the civilian population, health facilities and morgues would be stretched beyond their breaking point. The number of sick and dying would quickly reach a critical mass, overwhelming available resources. Despite operating around the clock, the country's available crematories would rapidly be overrun with the dead. Like a scene from Mexico City at the conquest of Cortés, stacks of dead bodies would accumulate in overwhelming numbers. Makeshift crematories would hastily be assembled to burn the dead in mass, reproducing the ancient funeral pyres of old.

In homes and apartments, citizens would be forced to live like incarcerated prisoners, afraid to mingle with neighbors, friends, or even close relatives for fear of risking infection. Rural inhabitants would fare best, but in the major cities few families would be spared the affliction. The diseased would be carefully quarantined while family members burned sheets, towels, clothing, furniture, and anything else that might have caught an ambient germ.

The lethal virus would take a deadly toll across all ages and races. But hardest hit would be working adults, forced to expose themselves to greater risk of infection in order to provide food for their families. With millions of adults lying dead, the raging disease would create an immense class of orphaned children across the land. In a terrible replay of Western Europe after World War I, an entire generation would nearly be lost, vanished in just a few months' time. Only a SARS-like containment of infected travelers, after being alerted by the initial U.S. outbreaks, would prevent the scourge from decimating other countries in a similar fashion.

To those infected, the disease would wreak a rapid and horrifying progression of agony. Following the two-week incubation period, a burning rash would emerge on the infected after the initial onset of fever, starting in the mouth and spreading to the face and body. The stricken would be highly contagious at this stage, where face-to-face contact, or even shared clothes and bedding, would easily spread the disease. Over the course of three or four days, the rash would expand and painfully develop into hard raised bumps. The mass of horrid-looking skin lesions, produced with the sensation of a hot torch to the skin, would then gradually dry and scab over. For two to three more weeks, the afflicted would battle the body-morphing disease until all of the scabs had fallen away and the last risk of transmission subsided. All the while, the sick would be forced to fight it alone, as smallpox has no cure once the virus is unleashed in the body.

The survivors, if lucky, would be left with just the telltale pitted scars on their skin as a constant reminder of their ordeal. Less fortunate survivors would end up blind as well. The one-third of infected persons who lost the fight would die a painful death, as their lungs and kidneys slowly shut down under the viral onslaught.

But the horror would not end there. For still hidden in the smallpox outburst was the specter of HIV. Slower acting and less detectable but all the more deadly, the HIV attributes not only made the chimera virus resistant to the smallpox vaccine but continued a viral path of destruction in the surviving victims. Thriving in an already weakened immune system, the virus would surge through the victims, destroying and altering cells in a barbaric invasion. While most HIV victims succumb to its debilitating effects in the course of a decade, the chimera would attain lethality in just two to three years. Like a satanic roller coaster, yet another wave of death would surge across the country, striking down the poor souls who had overcome the initial bout with smallpox. While the smallpox pandemic would claim a thirty percent mortality rate, the HIV death rate would hover near ninety percent. An already shocked and numbed nation would face a death pall the likes of which had never been seen in its history before.

By the time the chimera ran its course, tens of millions would lie dead in the U.S., with untold more around the world. Not a family would go unscathed by its black touch and not a soul would live free from the fear of a lethal biological shadow in the doorway. Amid the initial unfolding of the scourge, few would pay concern to political disturbances around the world. And, on the far side of the globe, when the old ally of South Korea was overrun by its totalitarian neighbor to the north there would be little response from the devastated nation aside from a feeble cry of protest.

39

The Chinese junk looked like an antiquated relic amid the modern freighters and containerships swarming about Inchon Harbor. Cussler carefully threaded the high-sterned sailing vessel through a maze of mid-morning commercial traffic before easing into a small public marina that was nestled between two large cargo docks. An odd assortment of beat-up sampans and expensive weekend sailboats encircled the marina as he motored the teak junk to a transit dock and tied up. He gave a quick knock on the spare cabin door to wake its slumbering occupants, then brewed a large pot of coffee in the galley as a marina employee refilled the junk's fuel tank.

Summer staggered out into the sunshine of the aft deck holding the dachshund in her arms as Dirk followed a few steps behind, trying to suppress a yawn. Cussler threw a mug of coffee in their hands, then ducked belowdecks for a moment before emerging with a hacksaw in his grip.

'Might be a good idea to off-load those handcuffs before going ashore,' he grinned.

'I'll be only too happy to dispose of these bracelets,' Summer concurred, rubbing her wrists.

Dirk peered around the neighboring boats, then

turned to Cussler. 'Anybody follow us in?' he asked.

'No, I'm quite sure we arrived alone. I kept a keen watch, and zigzagged our course a few times just to be sure. Nobody seemed intent on following us. I bet those boys are still cruising up and down the Han River looking for you two,' he laughed.

'I sure hope so,' Summer said with a shudder, stroking the small dog's ears for comfort.

Dirk picked up the hacksaw and began cutting into the shackle on Summer's left wrist. 'You saved our lives back there. Is there anything we can do to repay you?' he asked while gliding the saw blade evenly across an edge of the handcuff.

'You don't owe me anything,' he replied warmly. 'Just stay out of any more trouble and let the government take care of those hoodlums.'

'Can do,' Dirk replied. After efficiently sawing through both of Summer's shackles, he relaxed while she and Cussler took turns cutting through his handcuffs. When the last shackle fell free, he sat up and downed the last of his coffee.

'There's a phone in the marina restaurant you can use to call the American embassy, if you like. Here, take some Korean won. You can use it to make the call and buy a bowl of kimchi,' Cussler said, passing Summer a few purple-colored bills of the national currency.

'Thanks, Mr. Cussler. And good luck on your voyage,' Dirk said, shaking the man's hand. Summer leaned over and kissed the old sailor on the cheek.

'Your kindness was overwhelming,' she gushed, then patted the dog good-bye.

'You kids take care. Be seeing you.'

Dirk and Summer stood on the dock and waved good-bye as the junk eased out into the harbor, smiling as Mauser barked a final farewell from the bow deck. They made their way up a set of well-worn concrete steps and entered a faded yellow building that was a combination marina office, sundry store, and restaurant. The walls were draped in the traditional lobster trap and fishing net motif that sufficed for interior decorating in a thousand seafood restaurants around the world. Only, this one smelled like the nets were hung up while still dripping wet with salt water.

Dirk found a phone on the wall in back and, after several failed attempts, completed a connection to NUMA headquarters in Washington. The NUMA operator required only minimal convincing before patching the call through to Rudi Gunn's home line, despite the late hour on the East Coast. Gunn had just dropped off to sleep but answered the phone on the second ring and nearly flew out of bed when he heard Dirk's voice. After several minutes of animated conversation, Dirk hung up the phone.

'Well?' Summer asked.

Dirk glanced toward the smelly restaurant with a look of adventure. 'I'm afraid it's time to take the man up and sample some kimchi while we wait for a ride,' he replied, rubbing his stomach with hunger.

*

The hungry pair downed a Korean breakfast of hot soup, rice, tofu flavored with dried seaweed, and the omnipresent side dish of fermented vegetables, kimchi, which nearly blew smoke out of their ears from the spiciness. As they finished their meal, a bulky pair of U.S. Air Force security police strode sternly into the restaurant. Summer waved the two men over and the senior of the two men confirmed their identity.

'I'm First Sergeant Bimson, Fifty-first Fighter Wing Security Forces. This is Staff Sergeant Rodgers,' he continued, nodding to his partner. 'We have orders to escort you to Osan Air Base without delay.'

'The pleasure will be all ours,' Summer assured him as they stood and left the marina restaurant, following the airmen to a government sedan parked outside.

Though Seoul was actually a shorter distance to Inchon than Osan Air Base, Gunn had elected to take no chances with their safety, ordering their transport to the nearest military base. The airmen drove south from Inchon, winding through mountainous hills and past flooded rice paddies before entering the sprawling complex of Osan, which started life as a lone airfield constructed during the Korean War. The modern base now hosted a large contingent of combat-ready F-16 fighter jets and A-10 Thunderbolt II attack planes, deployed in the forward defense of South Korea.

Entering the main gate, they traveled a short distance to the base hospital, where a fast-talking colonel greeted Dirk and Summer and led them to a medical examination room. After a brief checkup and treatment of Dirk's wounds, they were allowed to clean up and then given a fresh set of clothes. Summer laughed that the baggy military fatigues provided did nothing for her figure.

'What's our travel situation?' Dirk asked of the colonel.

'There's an Air Mobility Command C-141 bound for McChord Air Force Base leaving in a few hours that I'm holding a pair of first-class seats on. Your NUMA people have arranged a government aircraft to transport you from McChord to Washington, D.C., after you arrive. In the meantime, you are welcome to rest here for a bit, then I'll take you by the officers' club, where you can grab a hot meal before jumping on that twenty-hour plane ride stateside.'

'Colonel, if we have the time I'd like to contact an in-country Special Ops unit, preferably Navy, if that's at all possible. And I'd like to make a phone call to Washington.'

The Air Force colonel's face turned up indignantly at Dirk's mention of the word *Navy*. 'There's only one Navy base in the country and that's just a small operations support facility in Chinhae near Pusan. I'll send over one of our Air Force S.O. captains. As I think about it, there are SEALs and UDTs running in and out of here all the time. He ought to be able to help you out.'

Two hours later, Dirk and Summer climbed aboard a gray Air Force C-141B Starlifter with a large contingent of GIs headed stateside. As they settled into their seats in the windowless transport jet, Dirk found an eye mask and a pair of earplugs in the seat back in front of him. Donning the sleep aids, he turned to Summer and said, 'Please don't wake me till we're over land. Preferably, land where they don't serve seaweed for breakfast.'

He then pulled down the eye mask, stretched out flat in the seat, and promptly fell fast asleep.

40

The fire was minuscule by most arson standards, burning less than twenty minutes before it was brought under control. Yet the targeted damage had been carefully calculated with a precise outcome in mind.

It was two in the morning when the fire bells sounded aboard the *Sea Launch Commander*, jolting Christiano from a deep sleep in his captain's cabin. In an instant he was on the bridge, alertly checking the ship's fire control monitors. A graphic image of the ship showed a single red light on the ship's lower topside deck.

'Conduit room on the shelter deck, just forward of the launch control center,' reported a dark-haired crewman manning the bridge watch. 'Automated water mist system has been activated.'

'Cut all electrical power except for emergency systems to that part of the ship,' Christiano ordered. 'Notify the port fire station that we require assistance.'

'Yes, sir. I have two men en route to the conduit room and am awaiting their report.'

While at port, the *Commander* carried only a skeleton marine crew aboard around the clock, few of whom had any degree of firefighting training. A rapidly spreading fire could easily gut the ship before sufficient help arrived, Christiano knew. The captain looked out a bridge window, half-expecting to see smoke and flames erupting from the ship but there were none. The only indication of fire was the acrid odor of burned electrical components that wafted through his nostrils and the distant shriek of a port fire truck rumbling toward the pier. His attention turned toward a handheld radio clipped to the crewman's belt as a deep voice suddenly rasped through the bridge.

'Briggs here,' the radio crackled. 'The fire is burning in the conduit room but does not appear to have spread. The computer hardware bay is okay, and the FM-200 gas system has been activated there to prevent combustion. It doesn't look like the fire suppression system was triggered in the conduit room, but if we can get some extinguishers on her before she spreads I think we can contain it.'

Christiano grabbed the radio. 'Do what you can, Briggs, help is on the way. Bridge out.'

Briggs and a fellow mechanic he had pressed into fire duty found a smoking rage billowing from the conduit room. No bigger than a large walk-in closet, the room housed power connections between the ship's electrical generator output and the myriad computers aboard the vessel that supported payload processing and launch operations. Briggs leaned into the bay and quickly emptied two fire extinguishers, then stood back a moment to see if the smoke would lessen. A cloud of acrid blue haze rolled out of the room, the noxious fumes it carried filtered by Briggs's respirator. His assistant passed him a third fire extinguisher and this time Briggs burst into the fiery room, directing the carbon dioxide spray at the remaining flames he could see flickering through the billows of dark smoke. His extinguisher empty, he quickly danced out of the room and caught his breath before peering in again. The room was pitch-black, with the beam of his flashlight reflecting only smoke. Satisfied that the flames were doused and not likely to reignite, he stepped into a side hallway and radioed the bridge.

'The fire is extinguished. Briggs out.'

Though the flames were extinguished, the damage had been done. It would take another two hours before the melted mass of wire, cabling, and connectors stopped smoldering and the Port of Long Beach Fire Department declared the ship safe. The pungent smell of an electrical fire hung over the ship like a cloud, refusing to go away for days. Danny Stamp arrived at the ship shortly after the fire crew left, the launch director having been summoned by Christiano. Sitting with the captain in the adjacent launch control center, he shook his head as he listened to the damage assessment from the *Sea Launch Commander*'s computer operations manager.

'You couldn't have picked a worse place for a

fire to break out,' the systems man said, his face tinted red in frustration. 'Literally every launch ops computer on the ship runs through that room, as well as most of the test and tracking monitors. We'll have to rewire the whole works. It's a complete nightmare,' he said, shaking his head.

'What about the actual hardware?' asked Stamp.

'Well, if you want to call that the good news, there was no damage to any of our hardware resources. I was really concerned with the potential for water damage, but, thankfully, our own crew put down the flames before any hoses were let loose on board.'

'In order to go operational, then, we're just talking about restringing the hardware. How long will that take?'

'Oh, man. We've got to rebuild the conduit room, order and obtain a couple miles of cable, some of it custom application, and restring the whole system. That would take three or four weeks at best under normal circumstances.'

'Our circumstances are a pending launch with significant delay penalties. You've got eight days,' Stamp replied, staring hard into the eyes of the computer manager.

The frazzled man nodded his head slowly, then got up to leave the room. 'Guess I've got to get a few people out of bed,' he muttered while slipping out through a side door.

'Do you think he can do it?' Christiano asked once the door had closed shut.

'If it can be done, then he'll get us close.'

'What about the *Odyssey*? Do we hold her in port until the damage to the *Commander* is repaired?'

'No,' Stamp said after mulling over the question. 'The Zenit is loaded and secured aboard the *Odyssey*, so we'll send her out as planned. We can still make the equator with the *Commander* in half the time the platform will take to get there. And there's no harm in having the *Odyssey* wait on station a few days if we're a little late getting out. That's just more opportunity for the platform crew to prep for the launch.'

Christiano nodded, then sat silently in thought.

'I'll notify the customer of our revised plans,' Stamp continued. 'I'm sure I'll have to do a Kabuki dance to keep them calm. Do we know the cause of the fire yet?'

'The fire inspector will take a look first thing in the morning. Everything points to a short, probably some defective cable couplings.'

Stamp nodded silently. What next? he wondered.

The Long Beach fire inspector stepped aboard the *Sea Launch Commander* promptly at 8 A.M. After performing a cursory examination of the charred conduit room, he proceeded to interview the fire response team and other crewmen on duty when the fire started. He then returned to the site of the blaze and methodically examined the burn damage, taking photographs of the blackened room and making notes. After carefully scrutinizing the charred cables and melted fittings for nearly an hour, he satisfied himself that there was no evidence present indicating arson.

It would have taken an excruciatingly attentive analysis to detect the proof. But beneath his soot-covered boots, there were the peculiar minuscule remains of a frozen orange juice container. A chemical analysis of the container would show that a home-made napalm mixture of gasoline and Styrofoam chunks had been mixed and stored in the small container. Planted by one of Kang's men days before and ignited by a small timer, the tiny fire bomb had splattered its flaming goo about the conduit room in a rain of fire, quickly incinerating its contents. With the overhead sprinkler system sabotaged to appear faulty, the damage was assured, as scripted. Enough damage to delay the *Sea Launch Commander* from sailing for several days, but not enough to raise suspicions that the cause was anything but accidental.

Stepping past the charred and indistinguishable juice container, the inspector paused outside the conduit room as he completed his fire assessment. 'Electrical short due to faulty wiring or improper grounding,' he wrote in a small notebook, then stuck his pen in his shirt pocket and made his way off the ship past a gang of oncoming construction workmen.

41

A slow gray drizzle was falling at McChord Air Force Base south of Tacoma when the C-141 lumbered in from its transpacific flight. The big jet's tires screeched on the damp runway before the aircraft rolled to a stop in front of a transit terminal, where its engines were shut down and the large rear cargo door lowered to the tarmac.

Holding true to his word, Dirk had slept nearly the entire flight and exited the ramp feeling refreshed but hungry. Summer followed behind in a groggier state, having slept unevenly in the noisy aircraft. An air transit lieutenant located the pair and escorted them to the base officers' club for a quick hamburger before returning them to the flight line. Spotting a phone booth, Dirk eagerly dialed a local number.

'Dirk, you're all right!' Sarah answered with obvious relief.

'Still kicking,' he chimed.

'Captain Burch told me you were aboard the NUMA ship that sank in the East China Sea. I've been worried sick about you.'

Dirk beamed to himself, then proceeded to tell her an abbreviated version of events since flying to Japan.

'My gosh, the same people that released the cyanide

in the Aleutians intend to launch a larger attack?'

'It appears that way. We hope to find out more when we get back to D.C.'

'Well, keep your friends at the CDC informed. We have a terrorism emergency response team in place to combat sudden chemical or biological outbreaks.'

'You'll be the first one I call. By the way, how's the leg?'

'Fine, though I'm still getting used to these blasted crutches. When are you going to autograph my cast?'

Dirk suddenly noticed Summer waving him toward a small jet parked on the runway.

'When I take you to dinner.'

'I'm off to Los Angeles tomorrow for a weeklong conference on environmental toxins,' she said with disappointment. 'It will have to be the following week.'

'Consider it a date.'

Dirk barely had time to sprint to the Gulfstream V jet that was warming its engines on the tarmac. Climbing aboard, he was chagrined to find Summer sitting at the center of attention, surrounded by a small group of Pentagon colonels and generals on the jet bound for Andrews Air Force Base.

The large executive jet buzzed over the Jefferson Memorial at six the next morning en route to landing at the Air Force base located just southeast of the nation's capital. A NUMA van was waiting for the pair and whisked them through the light early morning traffic to the headquarters building, where Rudi Gunn greeted them in his office.

'Thank God you're safe,' Gunn gushed. 'We were turning Japan upside down looking for you and that cable ship.'

'Nice idea but wrong country,' Summer said with a gibe.

'There's some folks here who'd like to hear about your ordeal firsthand,' Gunn continued, hardly giving Dirk and Summer a chance to relax. 'Let's go to the admiral's office.'

They followed Gunn as he led them around the bay to a large corner office overlooking the Potomac River. Though Admiral Sandecker was no longer the director of NUMA, Gunn subconsciously refused to acknowledge the fact. The door to the office was open and they walked in.

Two men were seated at a side couch discussing coastal port security, while Homeland Security Special Assistant Webster sat in a chair across from them, studiously reviewing a file folder.

'Dirk, Summer, you remember Jim Webster from Homeland Security. This is Special Agent Peterson and Special Agent Burroughs, with the FBI's Counterterrorism Division,' Gunn said, motioning a hand toward the two men on the couch. 'They've met with Bob Morgan already and are very interested to know what happened to you after the *Sea Rover* was sunk.'

Dirk and Summer settled into a pair of wingback chairs and proceeded to describe the entire course of events, from their imprisonment on board the *Baekje* to their escape on the Chinese junk. Summer was surprised to note that three hours rolled by on an antique ship's clock mounted on the wall by the time they finished their saga. The homeland security administrator, she noted, appeared to turn whiter shades of pale as their report progressed.

'I just can't believe it,' he finally muttered. 'Every shred of evidence we had pointed to a Japanese conspiracy. Our whole investigative focus has been centered on Japan,' he said, shaking his head.

'A well-designed deception,' Dirk stated. 'Kang is a powerful man with considerable resources at his disposal. His means and abilities should not be under-estimated.'

'You are certain he aims to target the United States with a biological attack?' asked Peterson.

'That's what he insinuated and I don't believe he was bluffing. The incident in the Aleutians would seem to have been a test application of their technology to disperse a bioweapon into the air. Only now they have boosted the strength of their smallpox virus to a much more virulent form.'

'Not unlike stories I've heard that the Russians may have created a vaccine-resistant strain of small-pox back in the nineties,' Gunn added.

'Only this one's a chimera. A deadly combination of more than one virus that takes on the lethal elements of each,' Summer said.

'If the strain is immune to our vaccines, an outbreak could kill millions,' Peterson muttered, shaking his head. The room fell silent for a moment as the occupants considered the horrifying prospect.

'The attack in the Aleutian Islands proves that they have the means to disperse the virus. The question becomes, where would they target a strike?' Gunn asked.

'If we can stop them before they have the chance to strike, then it doesn't matter. We should be raiding Kang's palace, and his shipyard, and his other sham businesses, and we should be raiding them right now,' Summer said, slapping a hand on her leg for emphasis.

'She's right,' Dirk said. 'For all we know, the weapons are still on board the vessel at the Inchon Shipyard and the story can end there.'

'We'll need to assemble more evidence,' the homeland security man said flatly. 'The Korean authorities will have to be convinced of the risk before we can assemble a joint investigative force.'

Gunn quietly cleared his throat. 'We may be on the verge of providing the necessary evidence,' he said as all eyes shifted his way. 'Dirk and Summer had the foresight to contact Navy Special Forces before leaving Korea and briefed them on Kang's enclosed dock facility at Inchon.'

'We couldn't authorize them to act, but a well-placed call by Rudi got them to at least listen to what we had to say,' Summer grinned toward Gunn.

'It's well beyond that now,' Gunn explained. 'After

you and Dirk departed Osan, we formally requested an underwater special ops reconnaissance mission. Vice President Sandecker went out on a limb to obtain executive approval in hopes we'll be able to locate a smoking gun. Unfortunately, with the ruckus over our military deployment in Korea it's a sensitive time to be nosing around our ally's backyard.'

'All they need to do is snap a picture of the *Baekje* sitting at Kang's dock and we've got proof positive,' Dirk said.

'That would certainly boost our case. When are they going in?' Webster asked.

Gunn looked at his watch, then mentally calculated the fourteen-hour time difference between Washington and Seoul. 'The team will be deployed in about two hours. We should know something early this evening.'

Webster silently gathered his papers, then stood up. 'I'll be back after dinner for a full debriefing,' he grumbled, then made his way toward the door. As he left the room, the others could hear just a single word being muttered repeatedly from his lips as he vanished down the hall: 'Korea.'

42

Commander Bruce McCasland looked up at the Korean night sky and grimaced. A heavy bank of low rain clouds had drifted in over Inchon, obscuring the earlier clear skies. With the low clouds came illumination, the optical boomerang of light waves from thousands of the port city's streetlamps, residences, and billboards. Refracting off the clouds, the lights brightened the midnight hour with a fuzzy radiance. For a man whose livelihood depended on stealth, the dark of night was his best friend, the arrival of clouds a curse. Perhaps it will rain, he thought hopefully, which would improve their cover. But the dark clouds silently rolled by, holding their moisture with taunting stubbornness.

The Navy SEAL from Bend, Oregon, hunched back down in the rickety sampan and glanced at the three men lying low under the gunwale besides him. Like McCasland, they were clad in black underwater wet suits, with matching fins, mask, and backpack. As their mission was one of reconnaissance, they were armed for only minimal close quarters combat, each carrying a compact Heckler & Koch MP5K 9mm submachine gun. Clipped to their vests were an assorted mix of miniature still and video cameras, as well as a pair of night vision goggles.

The weathered boat putted past the commercial docks of Inchon, trailing a pall of blue smoke from its sputtering outboard motor. To the casual eye, the sampan appeared like a thousand others in the region used by merchants and tradesmen up and down the coastal Korean waters as a common mode of transport. Hidden beneath its aged-appearing exterior, however, was a fiberglass-hulled assault craft. With a high-speed inboard motor, the covert boat was specially built to launch and retrieve small teams of underwater special forces.

Meandering through the quiet north corner of the harbor, the sampan approached within two hundred meters of the Kang Marine Services entry channel. Exactly on cue, the twenty-two-foot boat's motor sputtered and coughed several times, then died. Two SEALs, disguised as a pair of derelict fishermen, began swearing loudly at each other in Korean. While one of the men tugged at the outboard motor to restart it, the other made a loud show of grabbing an oar and splashing it in the water in a clumsy attempt to row them toward shore.

McCasland peered over the gunwale with a pair of night vision binoculars trained on the sentry post at the mouth of the channel. Two men looked back from the interior of their guard hut but made no move toward a black speedboat tied up a few feet away. Satisfied the guards were too lazy to investigate further, he called quietly to the three men besides him.

'In the water. Now.'

With the gracefulness of a Persian cat leaping from a settee, the three men slipped quietly over the side and into the water with barely a gurgle. McCasland adjusted his faceplate, gave a thumbs-up to the two 'fishermen,' then followed the frogmen over the side. Having grown hot in the boat wearing the insulated wet suit, he was refreshed by the cool water as it seeped against his skin. Clearing his ears, he submerged to a depth of twenty feet, then leveled off, peering around into the black gloomy murk. The dank polluted harbor water offered only a few feet of visibility, which fell to zero at night without a flashlight. McCasland ignored the blind diving conditions and spoke into a wireless underwater communication system attached to his face mask.

'Audio and nav check,' he barked.

'Bravo here. Nav confirmed. Out,' came one voice.

'Charlie here. Nav confirmed. Out,' followed a second voice, this one with a slight Georgia twang.

'Delta here. Nav confirmed. Out,' the third diver's voice copied.

'Roger, stand by,' McCasland replied.

Above them, the two SEALs in the sampan had beached the boat next to a battered and abandoned pier within sight of Kang's security men. Making a show of repairing the boat, the two men clanged tools together and cursed loudly as they pretended to fumble with the motor while the men in the water carried out their mission.

Below the surface, McCasland activated his Miniature Underwater GPS Receiver (MUGR), or 'Mugger' as it was nicknamed. No larger than a Palm Pilot, the small device contained a navigation system that was calibrated by signals from the GPS satellite system. McCasland briefly kicked up to a depth of ten feet, where the underwater receiver could pick up the GPS signal and establish a fixed base point. A muted green display screen popped on, displaying an animated trail that zigzagged through and around a series of obstacles. Based on aerial survey photographs and the description provided by Dirk and Summer, McCasland had programmed a series of GPS waypoints into the Mugger. The aggregate points created a path to the covered dock entrance they could follow while completely submerged. All four divers held one of the devices, which also showed one another's relative position with a tiny flashing light. Swimming in complete darkness, they could follow the path to the covered dock while staying within just a few feet of one another.

'Okay, let's move,' he spoke into his faceplate after descending again.

With a deep thrust of his fins, McCasland kicked forward into the inky water, his eyes glued to the electronic compass and depth gauge, which he ensured never wavered from the twenty-foot mark. Reaching the entrance to the private ship channel, he turned and swam into the narrow inlet, passing almost directly beneath the security guards' speedboat, which bobbed on the surface well above him. Over McCasland's shoulder, the three other SEALs followed in a triangular pattern a few feet behind.

Day or night, the SEAL divers would have been nearly impossible to detect due to their use of rebreathers. Forgoing the standard dive tank of compressed air, which generates telltale exhaust bubbles visible on the surface, the Navy divers utilized a Carleton Technologies VIPER system for their air supply. Embedded within a sleek-looking backpack, the VIPER rebreather provided pure oxygen to the divers that was recirculated through a chemical scrubber, which removed harmful carbon dioxide while dispelling only a minute amount of exhaust. The streamlined system could enable the divers to remain underwater for up to four hours should the need arise. But with no visible exhaust bubbles rising to the surface, their whereabouts were safely concealed from the naked eye.

Following the Mugger's imaginary trail, the four divers swam through the winding inlet, kicking through the black water until they approached the entrance to the enclosed dock. The quarter-mile submerged swim would have exhausted most sport divers, but years of demanding physical training made it seem like crossing the street to the hardened SEALs. Their heartbeats thumped just above resting as they regrouped in front of the massive door to the enclosed dock. McCasland then swam in a circular pattern until his hands found a pylon that supported one side of the entrance. Following the pylon up, he ascended slowly until finding the lower edge of the sliding door, which hung three feet beneath the water's surface. Confident he was at the proper location, he descended again to the depth of the other divers.

'Proceed with preliminary recon. Regroup this position in three-zero. Out.'

From this point on, each diver had a different trail to follow inside the covered dockyard. Dirk and Summer had drawn a detailed map of the dock layout from memory, which was used to establish a different reconnaissance point for each diver. McCasland had the farthest and most dangerous assignment, to swim to the land's-end side of the dockyard for a frontal view of the facility. Two other divers would reconnoiter the main dock to verify and film the *Baekje*, while the fourth diver would stand by as backup near the entrance door.

The bright overhead lights of the hangar illuminated the upper water shallows, casting a dark shadow from the dock's supporting concrete pilings. McCasland found that at a depth of fifteen feet, he could just make out the dark outline of the pilings in the water ahead of him. He held the Mugger to his chest and kicked harder, using his vision to guide him quickly down the length of the dock. After passing dozens of pilings, a solid wall of concrete suddenly rose up before him and he knew that he had reached the end of the pier. Resting against a pylon, he readied a digital camcorder and prepared to surface, fighting back an uneasy feeling of defeat. He had felt a strange void while swimming beneath the pier, sensing an absence of the mass he thought he should feel nearby even though it was out of sight.

Quietly breaking the water's surface beneath the edge of the dock, his eyes confirmed the empty feeling in his stomach. The giant covered dockyard was bare. There was no four-hundred-foot cable ship tied up in front of him. In fact, the main dock was completely empty. McCasland silently scanned the facility with his camera, finding only one vessel in the entire structure, a beat-up tugboat perched on a dry dock. Nearby, a group of bored dockworkers on the graveyard shift were chasing each other around in a forklift, the only signs of life in the massive structure.

His filming complete, McCasland ducked underwater and kicked back along the dock toward the main entrance door. Reaching the support pylon, he pulled up the Mugger and saw that the other three divers had already returned and were waiting in the surrounding waters a few feet away.

'Mission complete,' he said curtly, then swam off into the inlet.

The four SEALs made their way back to the beached sampan and silently crawled inside. The mock fishermen suddenly found the cure to the ailing motor and restarted the outboard engine. With more vocal cursing, they cruised past Kang's inlet and motored off into the night.

Once out of sight, McCasland sat up and took off his faceplate, taking a breath full of the dank port air while staring at the twinkling waterfront lights. A drop of rain struck him on the face, then another and another. Shaking his head, he sat silently while a healthy deluge opened up from the skies on the frustrated commando.

43

Webster, Peterson, and Burroughs returned to the NUMA headquarters building at exactly six o'clock and found a subdued scene when they arrived at Gunn's office. The results of the SEAL team's reconnaissance mission had just been received, and Gunn, Dirk, and Summer sat morosely discussing the report.

'Disappointing news, I'm afraid,' Gunn said. 'The cable ship wasn't there.'

'How could it come and go without being seen?' Webster wondered. 'We've got Interpol and customs authorities on the lookout for that vessel all throughout Asia Pacific.'

'Perhaps a few of them are on Kang's payroll,' Summer said.

Webster brushed aside the suggestion. 'We're certain the reconnaissance team didn't misidentify anything?'

'There apparently was nothing in the enclosed dock to see. A video feed of the surveillance is being sent by satellite right now. We can take a look for ourselves on the admiral's viewing monitor,' Gunn replied. For the second time that day, he led a procession to the admiral's former office. As he approached the corner suite, he was surprised to hear a familiar laugh emanating from the office as a hazy cloud of smoke drifted out the open door.

Entering the threshold, Gunn was shocked to find Al Giordino sitting on the couch. With a wild wave of his dark curly hair askew, the newly appointed NUMA director of underwater technology sat reclining with his legs up on the coffee table, a stubby cigar dangling from his lips. He was dressed in a worn NUMA jumpsuit and looked like he just stepped off a boat.

'Rudi, my boy, here flogging the crew a little late tonight, aren't we?' Giordino asked before blowing a puff of smoke from the cigar skyward.

'Somebody's got to mind the store while you're out basking on a warm tropical beach.'

Dirk and Summer grinned as they entered the room and spotted Giordino, who was like a favorite uncle to them. They didn't immediately see their father, who stood at the opposite end of the office gazing at the lights across the Potomac. His six-foot-three frame stood tall against the window, having lost little of its younger muscular leanness. A touch of gray at the temples and a few slight wrinkles around the eyes hinted at his age. The weathered, tan face of Dirk Pitt, the legendary special projects director and now head of NUMA, broke into a broad grin at the sight of his children.

'Dirk, Summer,' he said, his sparkling green eyes glowing with warmth as he threw his arms around his two kids.

'Dad, we thought you and Al were still in the Philippines,' Summer said after giving her father a hug and a peck on the cheek.

'Are you kidding?' Giordino piped in. 'The old man practically swam across the Pacific to get back here when he heard you were missing.'

The elder Pitt smiled. 'I was just jealous of you two taking a tour of Northeast Asia without me,' he grinned.

'We made some notes of places to avoid,' Dirk laughed in reply.

Pitt visibly warmed in the presence of his two kids. The veteran marine engineer brimmed with a radiant serenity at the world that had recently changed around him. His personal life had been completely jarred by the sudden appearance of his two grown children just a few years earlier whom he never knew existed. But they quickly became a close part of his life, joining him in his underwater work, as well as sharing personal time with him and his new wife. The sudden dose of responsibility had nudged him to take stock of his life and he had finally married his longtime love, Colorado congresswoman Loren Smith. But the changes continued, as even his professional life saw an upheaval. With Admiral Sandecker unexpectedly taking the vice presidency, Pitt was suddenly thrust into the top spot at NUMA. While special projects director, he experienced several lifetimes' worth of adventure and challenges that took him to the four corners of the globe. The hazards had taken a toll on him, both physically and mentally, and now he was glad to ease back on the more vigorous demands of the job. As NUMA's chief director, his administrative and political duties often exceeded his interests, but he still ensured that he and Al spent plenty of time in the field, testing new equipment, exploring prospective marine sanctuaries, or just pushing the limits of the deep. Deep inside, the flame still burned brightly when it came to exploring the unknown or solving an ancient mystery and his old-fashioned sense of propriety never waned. The kidnapping of his children and the sinking of the *Sea Rover* triggered an anger inside that brought back the old resolve he'd felt time and again to make right in the world.

'Dad, what's the situation with the toxic Japanese cargo ship in the Philippines?' Dirk asked. 'I understand that it was leaky chemical munitions causing the reef kill.'

'That's right, a mixture of mustard and lewisite in this case. More biochemical hazards left over from World War Two. We actually have the leak contained. Nobody was volunteering to conduct a costly excavation and removal of the munitions, so we did the next best thing. Bury them.'

'Lucky for us that underwater sandbank was right there,' Giordino explained. 'We just fired up a water pump and filled the cargo hold with sand, then sealed it back up. As long as nobody goes digging around down there, there should be no more toxic leakage and the damaged reef should rejuvenate itself in a few years.'

An administrative aid poked her head through the door and spoke to Gunn. 'Sir, the video feed from the Pentagon is available for viewing now,' she said, then disappeared out the door like a rabbit down a hole.

Gunn seized the moment to introduce the Homeland Security and FBI men to Pitt and Giordino, then herded everyone toward a large, flat-panel monitor that was hidden behind a sliding panel. Typing in a few quick commands on a keyboard, the screen suddenly illuminated with the image of a large, enclosed dockyard. The camera's eye panned around the facility, showing a series of empty docks. After less than a minute's running time, the video ended and the screen went blank.

'That's Kang's facility, no doubt about it. But there's no sign of the *Baekje*,' Dirk said.

'The Navy report stated that a small tug and a speedboat were the only vessels observed on Kang's property,' Gunn said. 'Like Elvis, the *Baekje* has apparently left the building.'

Webster cleared his throat. 'I have confirmed with Interpol and the Korean National Police that Inchon port traffic has been monitored around the clock since the crew of the *Sea Rover* were rescued and the alert bulletin issued. No vessel matching the *Baekje*'s description has been seen entering or departing the port since.'

'Someone's on the take,' Giordino sneered.

Webster returned the comment with an indignant look. 'A remote possibility but not likely. Despite its heavy traffic, Inchon is not a particularly large port. Somebody should have reported seeing her depart.'

'She may have made a stealthy getaway right after Dirk and Summer left the ship,' Gunn conjectured, 'which was before the Interpol alert was issued.'

'Or there's another possibility,' Pitt suggested. 'The ship may have been camouflaged or reconfigured to resemble another vessel. She may have sailed out of port in broad daylight looking like an ordinary tramp freighter.'

'Or the *Love Boat*,' Giordino added.

'Whatever her disposition, the fact remains that without the ship we have insufficient evidence to make a move against Kang with the Korean authorities,' Webster said.

'What about Dirk and Summer?' Pitt replied with rising anger. 'Do you think they showed up on Korean soil aboard the *Queen Mary*?'

'The proof against Kang has to be ironclad,' Webster replied with a stressed look. 'There's a serious political problem with South Korea right now. Our people in the State Department have their knees shaking, and even the Pentagon is nervous as hell. The prospect of losing our military presence in Korea is very real and nobody wants to jeopardize a precarious situation at this critical juncture in time.'

'So you're afraid to ask South Korea to investigate Kang?' Pitt asked.

'This comes from the top. We're to stay away from Korea until after the National Assembly vote on the expulsion of our military forces.'

'What does the admiral have to say about this?' Pitt asked of Gunn.

Gunn shook his head slowly. 'Admiral, er, Vice President Sandecker has informed me that the president is deferring to the State Department for reaction to the sinking of the *Sea Rover*. Dirk and Summer's indictment of Kang has unfortunately resulted in the edict that Jim just mentioned. Everyone is to lay low until after the National Assembly vote. Apparently, intelligence reports have revealed secret business dealings between Kang and the president of South Korea that go well beyond their known public friendship. The president is afraid of losing his support against the National Assembly measure if a potentially embarrassing investigation is initiated.'

'Doesn't he understand the magnitude of the risk involved with the weapons Kang possesses?' Summer asked incredulously.

Gunn nodded. 'The president has iterated that once the resolution has been voted upon, he will request an immediate and full investigation from the Korean authorities into Kang's involvement with the sinking of the *Sea Rover* and his potential connections to North Korea. In the meantime, he has authorized Homeland Security to issue a heightened domestic security advisory, with emphasis on aircraft and marine vessels arriving from Japan and South Korea.'

The younger Pitt began pacing across the room in frustration. 'It's too little too late,' Dirk finally said in a low tone. 'Promoting the removal of U.S. forces in South Korea is part of Kang's strategy, using the perceived terrorist threat from Japan as a diversion. Don't you see? If he's going to attempt a strike on the U.S., it will happen before the vote comes up in the National Assembly.'

'Which is just ten days from now,' Gunn said.

'Then we have to anticipate Kang's next move,' Pitt injected with a logical calmness. 'We know he operates a large shipping line and therefore has comprehensive knowledge of American port facilities. It would figure that he would try to bring the weapons in via a commercial freighter, most likely on the West Coast.'

'Much easier than smuggling it on an airplane,' Giordino agreed. 'Probably send them over on a Japanese-flagged carrier.'

'Or perhaps the elusive *Baekje*,' Dirk added.

'Yaeger has the rundown on what to look for in the way of biological components and likely storage,' Gunn said. 'I'll see that customs is appropriately educated for their port inspections.'

'That may still be too late,' Pitt replied. 'They could release the agent as they're sailing into port, contaminating the whole region before they dock. Think of San Francisco Bay, for example.'

'Or even before they arrive at port, if there is a prevailing wind. The release in the Aleutians was apparently launched by boat offshore of Yunaska Island, so it's certainly possible they could strike without entering port,' Dirk said.

'The Coast Guard is tasked with port security under Homeland Security jurisdiction and presently boards and inspects all incoming commercial vessels shortly before arrival in port,' noted Webster.

'But do they board and inspect offshore commercial vessels that are not port bound?' Dirk asked.

'I do not believe that the Coast Guard's resources are sufficient for that to be considered part of their security mission. They have beefed up their sea marshal program but still have a limited number of vessels available that they can put to sea. Asking for expanded coverage along the entire West Coast is well beyond their resource ability.'

'What about the Navy?' Summer asked. 'Why can't some ships of the Pacific Fleet be pressed into service? With the national security at risk, it seems to me we should press every available military vessel into blockade duty.'

'A good question with a sticky answer,' Gunn responded. 'It's a gray area of the Navy's mission. They're never big on playing a supporting role to the Coast Guard. They'd likely balk at the request until we got the secretary of defense or the White House to press the issue. I'll bring it up with the vice president, but, realistically, we're talking a week at best before they could be brought online. And that might be too late.'

'There is another option,' Pitt said, reaching into a desk drawer and withdrawing a daily report of NUMA research vessel assignments. 'Let's see, the *Pacific Explorer* just arrived in Vancouver, the *Blue Gill* is conducting a marine survey off Drake's Bay north of San Francisco, and the *Deep Endeavor* is testing a submersible in San Diego. It's not a fleet of battleships but I can reassign three of my research vessels to be in position off the major West Coast metropolitan ports assisting the Coast Guard in two days.'

'That would be a significant boost in offshore resources. And I'm sure the Coast Guard would be grateful for the support,' Webster said.

'Call it a temporary loan,' Pitt said. 'At least until Rudi can find a way to bill back the charges.'

'I'm sure we can work out some sort of compensation for our support during this heightened state of alert,' Gunn said, eyeing Webster with a sharklike grin.

'It's settled, then. The West Coast NUMA fleet will initiate offshore bomb-sniffing exercises at once. One thing, though,' Pitt said to Webster in a rigid tone. 'Kang already sank one of my vessels, I don't want to lose another. I want an armed cutter in the vicinity of my ships at all times.'

'Agreed. The interdiction teams will be alerted as well to the possibility of an armed response.'

'Good. Our team here will coordinate with the

regional Coast Guard surveillance squadrons. Rudi, you'll have to tear yourself out of the headquarters building. I'd like you to fly to San Francisco to set up the *Blue Gill* with the regional Coast Guard squadron and then see that the *Pacific Explorer* is similarly assigned in the Seattle/Vancouver region. Dirk and Summer, I'd like you back on the *Deep Endeavor* in San Diego to assist with surveillance off Southern California,' Pitt directed.

'What about me, boss?' Giordino asked with mock indignation. 'Don't I get a boat inspector's pass?'

'Oh, no,' Pitt replied with a mischievous smile. 'I have something much higher in store for you.'

44

There was little fanfare when a pair of scruffy tug-boats began slowly nudging the Sea Launch platform *Odyssey* away from her home dock. The excitement surrounding a new launch had waned over the years, to the extent that only a handful of family, friends, and corporate managers stood and waved good-bye to the crew. A smaller platform crew also brought out fewer than normal well-wishers. Only forty-two men manned the big platform, roughly twenty fewer than usual, as Launch Director Stamp held back many of the launch engineers to aid the fire repairs being made on the support ship. Captain Christiano watched restlessly from the bridge of the *Sea Launch Commander* as the rocket-laden platform crept away from the pier, offering a farewell to the crew and vessel with a long blast from his ship's horn. Several decks beneath him, an army of electricians and computer technicians worked feverishly around the clock to repair the control room fire damage in hopes that the command ship could follow the platform out to sea in another three or four days.

Christiano's greeting was met by a short horn blast from the *Odyssey* that seemed to come from the clouds. The *Odyssey*'s main platform deck towered nearly a hundred feet above the water. An oceangoing vessel in her own right, the floating platform relied on tugboats to get her cleanly in and out of port. Although she could position herself on a dime, visibility of small boats and harbor obstacles was precarious from the pilothouse positioned high atop the structure so tugs were utilized for safe navigation in congested waters.

The massive structure moved slowly past the port entrance jetty, appearing like a mammoth tarantula creeping across the calm waters. The converted North Sea oil platform rode high atop five thick support columns aligned along each flank. Slicing through the waves barely above the surface, the base of the columns rested upon a huge pair of underwater pontoons, each stretching over four hundred feet in length. Affixed to each aft pontoon hull was a pair of four-bladed propellers, which could push the ungainly craft through the swells at speeds of up to 12 knots. At over thirty thousand tons of displacement, the *Odyssey* was the largest self-propelled catamaran vessel in the world and easily the most impressive to the eye. Gliding past the entrance to Long Beach Harbor, the platform crept another two miles offshore before the tugs ground to a halt.

'Stand by to take up towlines,' barked the *Odyssey*'s commander, a no-nonsense ex-tanker captain named Hennessey.

The tugs released their towlines, which were

quickly reeled in by the *Odyssey*'s crew. The platform's four three-thousand-horsepower direct current motors were engaged, and, as the tugs peeled off to the sides, the *Odyssey* moved forward under her own power. Riding high atop its large pair of pontoons, the crew on the elevated platform swayed slowly back and forth as if in a skyscraper during a windstorm. The powerful Zenit rocket, tightly secured in its horizontal berth, was immune to the gentle motion. The experienced crew went casually about their duties, falling into a relaxed routine during the slow journey toward the launch site as the beige coast of California gradually disappeared from view. Hennessey gently increased power until the platform was chugging along at 9 knots, then laid in a course to the southwest toward the designated launch site fifteen hundred miles south of Hawaii at the equator. No one suspected it was to be a destination they would never see.

Fifteen hundred miles to the west, the *Koguryo* raced across the Pacific like a greyhound chasing a rabbit. Only a diversionary stop in the Ogasawara Islands to retrieve Tongju had slowed her pace since departing Inchon. After skirting a storm front west of Midway, the vessel had encountered calm seas and a strong tailwind, allowing her to churn east at top speed. Stripped of her bulky cable-laying equipment and the miles of heavy cable normally stored belowdecks, the *Koguryo* rode nine feet higher in the water than usual.

Her four diesel engines pushed the lightened ship along at a rapid 21 knots, propelling her across the ocean at nearly six hundred miles a day.

On board, the large team of engineers and technicians readied themselves for the coming Zenit rocket launch. A launch control center, nearly an exact duplicate of the control room on the *Sea Launch Commander*, had been constructed on a lower deck of the *Koguryo* and was the site of continuous activity. The final batch of launch software had been received from the Inchon lab and the software support team loaded up a series of mock launch scenarios for the operations team. Each day, the launch team worked their way through a series of sample test launches until, after a week at sea, the simulations were performed flawlessly. Told only that they would be controlling the launch of a Kang satellite from a floating platform, the team had no idea of the illicit mission they were actually supporting and looked forward to firing off the actual rocket.

Tongju utilized the time at sea to hone his tactics for the assault on the *Odyssey*. He and his commando team pored over blueprints of the launch platform, calculating strike positions and coordinating force movements, until he had a minute-by-minute plan of attack. The commandos memorized their moves, cleaned their weapons, and generally stayed out of sight of the other crewmen as the ship moved closer and closer to its target. After an evening meal with his assault team, Tongju invited his second-in-command

Kim back to his cabin. In the privacy of his room, he explained Kang's order to scuttle the *Koguryo*.

'I have provided Captain Lee with the rendezvous position where we are to meet the waiting freighter. I did not inform him, however, of the plan to sink his ship, only that we would be transferring the launch crew to the other vessel for safety.'

'You do not trust his obedience to Kang?' Kim asked, unaffected by the prospect of murdering two hundred of his fellow shipmates.

'No, it is not wise. No sea captain desires to sink his own ship and abandon his crew. We shall make our escape without him.'

'How is the ship to be destroyed?'

Tongju reached under his cot and pulled out a small satchel, which he handed to Kim.

'Semtex plastic explosives with wireless detonators. I intend to activate the charges while the ship is in motion.'

He walked to a bulkhead and pointed at a small cutaway diagram of the *Koguryo* pinned to the wall.

'By blasting a series of holes in the forward hull and bow sections beneath the waterline, the momentum of the ship will force a rapid flooding of the lower decks. The vessel will plunge to the bottom like a submarine before the crew has a chance to react.'

'There may still be the chance for some to escape on the lifeboats,' Kim countered.

Tongju shook his head with a malignant smile. 'I

have applied a liquid weld compound to all of the lifeboat davits. None of those boats will be leaving this vessel without a considerable effort.'

'And what about us?' Kim asked, a slight uncertainty creeping into his voice.

'You and two others will leave with me on the assault boat. I will convince Lee to let us depart the ship for an advanced surveillance check once the freighter is detected within radar range. When he has brought the *Koguryo* back up to speed, we will detonate the charges.'

Kim let out a quiet sigh and nodded deeply. 'It will not be easy to abandon my assault team,' he said quietly.

'They are all good men but expendable. I will leave it to you to pick the two men to join us. But first we must get the explosives planted. Take your demolitions man, Hyun, and set the charges in the forward bow compartments E, F, and G. Don't let any of the ship's crew observe you.'

Kim grasped the satchel tightly and nodded again. 'It will be done,' he said, then left the cabin.

After he left, Tongju stared at the diagram of the ship for several minutes. The whole operation was a hazardous mission fraught with risks and hidden dangers. But that was exactly the way he liked it.

45

On a collision course with evil, the *Odyssey* plodded along from Long Beach at its meager pace, the ungainly assembly churning up ten miles of foam over the course of an hour. Cutting past the California channel island of San Clemente, the *Odyssey* cruised due west of San Diego shortly before midnight and soon after departed the territorial waters of the United States. Fishing boats and pleasure craft gradually vanished from the horizons as the platform pushed farther into a desolate section of the Pacific Ocean west of Baja California. By the end of the third day at sea, cruising some seven hundred miles from the nearest landfall, the *Odyssey* shared the ocean with only a small dot on the northeast horizon.

Captain Hennessey watched with mild interest as the distant speck slowly grew larger, bearing down on a southerly heading. When it approached within five miles, he aimed his binoculars at the vessel, eyeing a stout blue ship with a yellow funnel. In the fading evening dusk, Hennessey made it out to be a research vessel or special-purpose ship rather than a commercial freighter. He noted with annoyed curiosity that the ship was on a perfect collision course with the *Odyssey*'s current heading. Hennessey stuck close to the helm for the next hour, watching the other vessel as it inched to within a mile of his starboard flank before appearing to slow and nose toward the southwest behind him.

'He's slowing to cross our wake,' Hennessey said to the helmsman, dropping his binoculars from the mysterious blue ship. 'The whole empty Pacific Ocean and he's got to run right down our path,' he muttered, shaking his head.

The thought never occurred to him that it was anything more than a coincidental encounter. Nor would he ever suspect that a trusted crewman, one of a handful of Kang's men working on board as launch technicians, was feeding their exact position to the ship using a simple GPS receiver and portable radio transmitter. After crossing the length of the Pacific, the *Koguryo* had picked up the radio transmission twenty-four hours earlier and vectored in on the *Odyssey*'s path like a homing pigeon to roost.

As the lights of the unknown ship twinkled off the *Odyssey*'s port stern in the evening darkness, Hennessey put the ship out of his mind and focused on the empty blackness before him. They were still nearly ten days to the equator and there was no telling what other obstacles might cross their path.

The experienced assault team came quickly, in the dark of night and with complete surprise. After shadowing the *Odyssey* for most of the evening, the *Koguryo* had suddenly stopped its engines, letting the self-propelled platform churn on toward the horizon. In the pilothouse of the *Odyssey*, the night shift helmsman and watch officer relaxed as the lights of the other ship fell away. With an autopilot steering the platform, their only concerns were monitoring the radar screen and weather forecast. But on an empty sea in the dead of night, there was little cause for concern. Focus on duty waned as the two men paced the bridge, engaging in a tireless debate about World Cup soccer rather than studying the electronic monitors about them. Had either man watched the radarscope more closely, they would have had an inkling of things to come.

Far from changing course or making repairs, the *Koguryo* had stopped to launch its high-speed tender. The open-decked, thirty-foot boat was a spacious and luxurious assault craft for Tongju, Kim, and the dozen other men dressed in black commando outfits who sat brandishing their assault rifles on leather-cushioned seats. Though low on stealth, the boat provided a fast and stable means of crossing open water to strike the platform with an ample attack force.

The tender bounded in darkness across the rolling waves, racing across the open sea under a bright canopy of stars that spread from horizon to horizon. The speedy boat quickly gobbled up ground between itself and the moving platform, which was lit up against the night sky like a Times Square marquee. As the tender's pilot approached the shadow of the massive platform, he steered the boat dead center under the structure, threading the boat between the *Odyssey*'s twin pontoons. Holding its speed, the boat darted under the platform and past the thick support columns, barely skimming under a set of massive triangular supports that horizontally crisscrossed the columns just twelve feet above the water. Slowing to match speeds with the *Odyssey*, he inched toward the forward starboard column, where a salt-encrusted steel stairway led up to the heights above. When he edged to within a few feet, one of the commandos leaped from the bow with a small line and quickly tied it to the stairwell post. One by one, the remaining commandos jumped onto the stairwell and began the long climb to the platform above. Pausing at the top steps to catch their breath, the team paused for a moment to regroup before Tongju nodded his head to proceed. The secure door to the stairwell had been left unlocked by one of Kang's crewmen already aboard and the commandos quickly slipped through and fanned out across the deck.

Though Tongju had studied photos and plans of the *Odyssey*, he was still overwhelmed by the massive scale of the launch deck, which stretched well over a football field in length. At the far end stood the launch tower, separated by a large tract of open deck that led to the launch vehicle hangar. Along the recessed starboard beam sat the massive fuel storage tanks, which would gas up the rocket shortly before launch. On either side of the launch vehicle hangar stood two small buildings that housed the crew's quarters, offering accommodations for sixty-eight men plus a galley and medical station. That would be the first target.

The assault team was primed to strike simultaneously, five men to the hangar, three to the bridge, and the balance to the crew's quarters. Most of the forty-two-man crew aboard the *Odyssey* had little to do until the platform reached the launch site and spent the hours reading, playing cards, or watching movies. By 3 A.M., only a handful of men were still awake, mostly crewmen assigned to sail the platform or monitor the launch vehicle. When the commandos struck the crew's quarters with drill precision, the confused technicians and engineers were too stunned to react. With a blast of light and prodding from the muzzles of AK-74 assault rifles, the sleeping men were quickly roused at gunpoint. Two men playing cards in the galley thought it was some sort of equatorial prank before a swinging rifle butt knocked one to the floor. A startled chef in the kitchen dropped a stack of pans at the sight of the armed men, doing more to wake the disbelieving crew than the gunmen themselves.

In the launch vehicle hangar, it was a similar story. The small commando team rapidly swept through the air-conditioned building that housed the cradled Zenit rocket, rounding up a handful of engineers without a fight. On the bridge situated high atop the launch vehicle hangar, the two men manning the helm couldn't believe their eyes when Tongju walked in and calmly leveled his Glock pistol at the executive officer's ear. In less than ten minutes, the entire platform was secured by Tongju's men. Not a shot fired, the Sea Launch crew never expected to be commandeered in the middle of the Pacific.

The commandos were surprised to find that most of the platform's marine crew were Filipino while the launch team was an assorted mix of American, Russian, and Ukrainian engineers. The subdued multinational crew was herded to the galley where they were held at gunpoint, except for the dozen of Kang's planted crew members and satellite company representatives, who took over operational control of sailing the platform. Even Captain Hennessey, captured and roughly bound by one of Kim's men, was forced to the galley in shock, with the rest of his crew.

On the bridge, Tongju radioed the *Koguryo* that the platform was taken with no resistance. Examining an unfurled navigation chart left on a side table, he barked at one of Kang's crewmen now manning the helm.

'Revise bearing to fifteen degrees north-northeast. We are diverting to a new launch site.'

As the crack of dawn approached, the *Koguryo* maneuvered alongside the northbound *Odyssey* and slowed to match speeds with the platform as it mashed through five-foot swells. Edging to within twenty feet of the *Odyssey*, Captain Lee held the *Koguryo* perfectly in tandem with the moving platform's starboard beam. In the wheelhouse of the *Odyssey*, a nervous helmsman ensured that the autopilot was properly engaged as the ex-cable-laying ship hove to alongside.

On the top deck of the hangar, Tongju supervised the movement of a large crane as it was swung out over the starboard edge of the platform. A heavy block and hook swung wildly from the end of the crane for a moment before being lowered to the rear deck of the *Koguryo*. A ready signal was relayed over the marine radio and the crane began hoisting up a square metal container the size of a sofa, which was swung over and lowered to the platform's main deck. Stored inside were the special canisters containing the freeze-dried chimera cultures ready to be inserted into the payload aerosol dispenser.

While the deadly virus was being hoisted to the platform, the *Koguryo*'s tender ferried over a dozen launch and payload specialists, who immediately swarmed into the rocket hangar and began dissecting the Zenit's payload section. An additional security contingent was also ferried over to help relieve Tongju's assault commandos.

Tongju returned to the pilothouse and peered out the heavy-paned windows at the rolling sea two hundred feet beneath him. The swaying of the platform was slight as the motion rolled up from the distant pontoons beneath the surface. Gazing to his right, he saw the *Koguryo* begin to peel away from the *Odyssey*, its ferrying services complete for the time being.

'Increase speed to maximum,' he said to the helmsman.

The nervous Filipino adjusted the propulsion controls on both pontoons and then watched as the digital speed indicator slowly counted upward.

'Twelve knots, sir. Maximum cruising speed,' the seaman replied, his eyes twitching back and forth.

Tongju nodded in satisfaction, then reached for an overhead radio transmitter and called Captain Lee on the *Koguryo*.

'We are progressing on schedule. Please notify Inchon that we are in control of the launch vessel and intend to initiate launch countdown in approximately thirty hours. Out.'

The apprehensive helmsman stared straight ahead, avoiding the gaze of Tongju. Whatever fearful thoughts tumbled around his head about Tongju's intent were minuscule compared to the commando leader's true objective.

46

It took the launch vehicle engineers just under twenty-four hours to convert the rocket's payload into a weapon of mass horror. Like surgeons conducting a transplant operation, the engineering team carefully removed several sections of the outer payload fairing and delved into the inner workings of the mock satellite. Fake components, built to resemble communication transponders, were removed and replaced with small electric pumps, which would drive the aerosol system. Lines and fittings were attached to the phony solar panels, which would open in flight to spread the rejuvenated virus, disseminating it as a fine mist across the California sky.

Working in protective clean room bunny suits, the technicians performed a final test on the dispensing system, ensuring it was fully functional for the short rocket flight. The final step of the operation was then reached: inserting the chimera virus into the payload vehicle. The canisters from Inchon containing the freeze-dried germs were carefully mounted to the satellite frame and steel braided lines from the hydrogenation tanks were connected to the aerosol system. When activated, a software-controlled program would vacuum-mix the powdered substance with purified water, then transfer the live fluid through the vaporizer and out into the atmosphere.

With the deadly cocktail loaded aboard, the payload fairing was reassembled around the satellite. Propellant explosives were inserted at key points inside the fairing to blast the payload doors away at the appointed moment during flight. When the final section of the nose cone housing was sealed into place, the tired engineering team congratulated one another briefly and then staggered toward the crew's quarters. A few precious hours of sleep was all they could ask for before it would be time to start the final launch countdown.

Without publicly raising the color-coded Threat Advisory System, the Department of Homeland Security quietly issued an elevated marine port and airport security alert. Stepped-up screening and random searches were performed on all aircraft and vessels originating from an Asian locale, with special inspections for biological and chemical agents. At Vice President Sandecker's insistence, the Coast Guard was ordered to stop, board, and search all Japanese- or Korean-flagged inbound ships with a fully armed security contingent. All available Coast Guard cutters were put to sea along the West Coast, concentrated around the commercial hubs of Seattle, San Francisco, and Los Angeles.

In San Francisco, Rudi Gunn coordinated NUMA's interdiction support with the local Coast

Guard commandant. When the research vessel *Blue Gill* arrived from Monterey, Gunn immediately assigned her picket duty ten miles off the Golden Gate Bridge. He then jumped up to Seattle, where he directed local NUMA resources in support of coastal screening, and enlisted the aid of the Canadian Coast Guard in Vancouver to search all British Columbia-bound ships.

Dirk and Summer flew to San Diego, where they were welcomed by the city's trademark seventy-two-degree balmy weather. Taking a short cab ride from San Diego International Airport's Lindbergh Field to Shelter Island, it took them only a few minutes to locate the *Deep Endeavor* tied up at the end of a large municipal dock. As they approached the ship, Dirk noticed that an odd-shaped submersible painted a metallic burnt orange sat on the vessel's stern deck.

'Well, if it isn't the Prisoners of Zenda,' Jack Dahlgren called from the bridge wing upon spotting the twosome boarding the ship. Dirk's close friend hopped down a stairwell and met them at the head of the gangway.

'Heard you two enjoyed a seaside tour of the Korean Peninsula,' Dahlgren laughed as he shook Dirk's hand firmly, then gave Summer a hug.

'Yes, but we somehow missed the *Michelin*-rated attractions,' Summer grinned back.

'Now, wait, that DMZ tour was pretty stimulating,' Dirk said, feigning seriousness. Turning to Dahlgren, he asked, 'You and the crew ready to do a little search-and-seizure work?'

'Yep. A Coast Guard team joined us an hour ago so we're ready to shove off at any time.'

'Good. Let's get after it, then.'

Dahlgren escorted Dirk and Summer up to the bridge, where they were greeted by Leo Delgado and Captain Burch, then introduced to a uniformed Coast Guard sea marshal named Aimes.

'What's our intercept procedure, Lieutenant?' Dirk asked, noting the insignia on Aimes's uniform.

'Call me Bill,' replied Aimes. A studious man with cropped blond hair, Aimes took his duty seriously but hated unnecessary formality. 'We'll be assisting the regional Coast Guard vessels as a backup, when and if commercial traffic gets particularly heavy. Otherwise, we'll be assigned to ad hoc survey and reconnaissance. Under legislative rule, we can intercept and board all inbound commercial vessels up to twelve miles offshore. As NUMA's Coast Guard representative, I will lead all boardings and searches with my team but will be assisted by several of your crewmen who have undergone a brief training session.'

'What are the chances we could actually locate a weapons cache or bomb hidden on a large containership?' Summer wondered.

'Better than you might think,' Aimes replied. 'As you know, we work closely with the Customs Department under the direction of the Homeland Security

Department. Our customs agents are located at foreign ports around the globe and are on site to inspect and seal all cargo containers before the goods are allowed to ship. Upon arriving in U.S. ports, containers are verified by customs agents as having not been opened or tampered with before acceptance into this country. The Coast Guard provides an advance check of the ship and containers before they have a chance to reach port.'

'There's plenty of places on a ship outside of the cargo containers where somebody could hide a bomb,' Dahlgren stated.

'That's a more difficult problem, but it's where the dogs come into play,' Aimes replied, nodding his head toward the far end of the bridge. Dirk noticed for the first time that a pair of yellow Labrador retrievers were tied to a bulkhead stanchion and lay asleep on the deck. Summer had already made her way over to the dogs and begun scratching them contentedly behind the ears.

'The dogs are trained to sniff out a variety of explosive compounds commonly used in bomb manufacture. Best of all, they can run through a ship in quick order. If a biological bomb is being smuggled in on a containership, there's a good chance those boys could sniff out the explosives component of it.'

'That's what we're looking for,' Dirk said. 'So, we'll be working off of San Diego?'

'No,' Aimes replied, shaking his head. 'There's only minimal commercial traffic that moves through

San Diego and the regional Coast Guard vessels are more than adequate to handle the volume. We've been ordered to patrol a quadrant southwest of the Port of Los Angeles in support of the L.A. – Long Beach Coast Guard Marine Safety Group. Once on site, we'll coordinate local positioning and boarding through *Icarus*.'

'*Icarus?*' Dahlgren asked.

'Our all-seeing eye in the sky on the project,' Dirk said with a knowing smile.

As the *Deep Endeavor* chugged toward the Pacific, cruising past Coronado Island and a Navy aircraft carrier inbound from the Indian Ocean, Dirk and Summer went aft and studied the strange submersible that faintly resembled a steroid-augmented earthworm. The bullet-shaped vessel was dotted with a series of bladed propulsion units mounted irregularly about the main body like glued-on heat pumps. Strutted beneath the front of its bullet nose stood a giant coring device that stood ten feet long, protruding upward like a unicorn's horn. Bathed in its garish orange/red metallic hue, the submersible reminded them of a giant insect from a fifties horror film.

'What's the story on this contraption?' Summer asked of Dahlgren.

'Your father didn't tell you about the *Badger*? It's a prototype that he authorized. That's why we were here in San Diego. Some of our engineers have been working on a joint venture with Scripps Institute to develop this hot rod. It's a deep-water corer designed to gather sediment samples from the seabed. The scientific community is anxious to gather sediment and organism samples around volcanic hydrothermal vents, many of which are located ten thousand feet or deeper.'

'What's with all the propulsion units?' Dirk asked.

'To get to the bottom in a hurry. She's a real speed buggy. Rather than waiting for gravity to pull her to the seafloor, she has a hydrogen fuel cell power plant that allows her to submerge at speed to the bottom. She allows you to descend, take a core sample, and then pop back to the surface without twiddling your thumbs all day. Less time spent diving and surfacing means more core samples for the geologists to pick through.'

'And the boys at Scripps were actually willing to trust you behind the wheel?' Summer asked with a laugh.

'They didn't ask how many speeding tickets I have on land so I didn't feel compelled to tell them,' Dahlgren replied with mock innocence.

'Little do they know,' Dirk grinned, 'that they just loaned their new Harley-Davidson to Evel Knievel.'

The *Deep Endeavor* steamed up the California coast for three hours before turning out to sea just before darkness. Dirk stood on the bridge watching the ship's progress on a colored navigation map displayed on an overhead monitor. As the coastline fell away behind them, he observed the island of San Clemente scroll up on the map to the west of their aligned path. He studied the map for a moment, then turned to Aimes, who stood nearby examining a radarscope.

'I thought your interdictions were restricted to no more than twelve miles from the coast? We're headed by San Clemente Island, which is over fifty miles from the mainland.'

'For normal coastal duty, we recognize the twelve-mile limit from the mainland. The Channel Islands are technically a part of California, however, so, legally, we can operate from the islands as an origination point. For this mission, we have been given temporary authorization to expand our normal interdiction zone, with the Channel Islands as a baseline. We'll set up position about ten miles west of Santa Catalina as our base monitoring position.'

Two hours later, they cruised beyond the large island of Catalina and the engines slowed as they neared their station point. At a slow crawl, the *Deep Endeavor* began patrolling a large north-to-south loop west of the island, using the ship's radar as surveillance eyes. A sprinkling of pleasure craft and fishing boats was all the radar detected, along with a Coast Guard cutter on patrol nearby to the north.

'We are positioned well south of the main shipping lane to L.A. and not likely to catch much night traffic in this quadrant,' Aimes said. 'We'll get tossed into the fray in the morning when *Icarus* shows up for work. In the meantime, I suggest we take shifts and get some sleep.'

Dirk took the hint and walked out onto the bridge wing, inhaling a deep breath of sea air. The night was still and damp and the seas almost as flat as a pancake. As he stood in the darkness, his mind tumbled over his meeting with Kang and the less-than-implicit threat that the mogul had delivered to Summer and him. Another week and the South Korean Assembly vote would be history and the legal authorities could pursue Kang with full fury. That's all they needed. A week without incident. As he stared at the sea, a chilled gust of wind suddenly whisked his face, then fell away again just as suddenly, leaving a tranquil and seeming calm.

47

By 9 P.M., the *Odyssey* had backtracked some three hundred miles and was now approaching the designated launch position calibrated in Inchon. Tongju, catching up on some lost sleep in Captain Hennessey's cabin, was startled awake by a rapid pounding at the door. An armed commando entered the room and bowed as Tongju sat up and began pulling on his boots.

'So sorry to intrude,' the commando said apologetically. 'It's Captain Lee. He has requested that you return to the *Koguryo* at once. There is some sort of dispute with the Russian launch engineers.'

Tongju nodded, then shook off the cobwebs and made his way to the pilothouse, where he verified that the platform was still cruising north-northeast at 12 knots. Radioing for the *Koguryo*'s tender, he made his way down the long flight of stairs on the forward piling and hopped into the idling boat that awaited him. A short ride took him to the nearby support ship, where Captain Lee was waiting for him.

'Come with me to the Launch Control Center. It's those damn Ukrainians,' the captain cursed. 'They can't agree on where to position the platform for launch. I think they're going to kill one another.'

The two men made their way down a flight of stairs and along an interior passageway to the expansive Launch Control Center. As Lee opened a side entry door, a loud staccato of foreign swearing burst upon their ears. At the center of the room, a group of launch engineers were huddled loosely around the two Ukrainian launch specialists, who stood toe-to-toe with their arms in the air arguing violently with each other. The crowd of engineers parted as Tongju and Lee approached, but the Ukrainians didn't skip a beat. Looking on in disgust, Tongju turned and grabbed a padded console chair, then lifted it over his head and hurled it at the two jabbering engineers. The gathered spectators gasped as the chair flew into the two men, smashing into their heads and chests before ricocheting to the floor with a crash. The stunned Ukrainians finally fell silent as they shook off the blow from the flying chair and turned toward the two men.

'What is the issue here?' Tongju growled.

One of the Ukrainians, a goateed man with shaggy brown hair, cleared his throat before speaking.

'It is the weather. The high-pressure front over the eastern Pacific, specifically off North America, has stalled due to the push from a low-pressure system in the south.'

'And what does this mean?'

'The normally prevailing high-altitude easterly winds have, in fact, reversed and we are instead facing a strong headwind at the moment. This has thrown off our planned mission flight profile by a considerable margin.' Shuffling through a file of papers, he pulled out a sheaf of algorithmic paper containing numerous calculations and trajectory profiles handwritten in pencil.

'Our base mission plan has been to fuel the Zenit rocket first stage at fifty percent of capacity, which will produce an estimated downrange flight trajectory of 350 kilometers. Approximately fifty kilometers of this distance is over the target region, where the payload system will be activated. Thus, our planned launch position was three hundred kilometers west of Los Angeles, assuming normal local weather patterns. Given the present weather scenario, we have two options: either wait for the low-pressure front to yield to the prevailing winds or reposition the launch platform closer to the target.'

'There's a third option,' the other Ukrainian grumbled irritably. 'We can increase the fuel load in the Zenit to reach the target from the original launch position.' As he spoke, his counterpart stood shaking his head silently.

'What is the risk of that?' Tongju asked the doubter.

'Sergei is correct in that we can adjust the fuel load to reach the target from the original launch position. However, I have grave doubts about the accuracy that we would achieve. We do not know the wind conditions for the entire flight trajectory. Given the current unusual weather pattern, the wind conditions along the entire flight path might vary significantly from what we can measure directly above us. The launch vehicle could easily be diverted north or south of the intended target by a large deviation. We could also overshoot the target by tens of kilometers or, alternatively, undershoot the target by a similar degree. There is just too much potential variability in the flight path from this distance.'

'A minor risk, compounded by speculation,' countered Sergei.

'How long before normal weather patterns return to the area?' asked Tongju.

'The low-pressure front has already showed signs of weakening. We expect it to collapse over the next day and a half, with the dominant high-pressure system prevailing in approximately seventy-two hours.'

Tongju silently contemplated the arguments for a moment, then made his decision without debate.

'We have a timetable to meet. We can ill afford to sit and wait for the weather to change, nor can we risk diluting the target strike. We shall move the platform closer to the target and initiate countdown as soon as possible. How far must we move to mitigate the atmospheric uncertainty?'

'To minimize the impact of the adverse winds, we must shorten the trajectory. Based on our latest wind measurements, we must position ourselves here,' the goateed Ukrainian said, pointing to a map of the North American seaboard. 'One hundred and five kilometers from the coast.'

Tongju studied the position silently for a minute, calculating the added distance to cover. The proposed position was dangerously near the coastline, he observed, noting a pair of offshore islands in close proximity. But they could reach the spot and still launch within Kang's desired time schedule. As all eyes in the room waited for his command, he finally turned and nodded toward Lee. 'Alter course at once. We will position both vessels at the new position before dawn and initiate launch countdown at daybreak.'

48

'You've got to be kidding me. A blimp?'

Giordino scratched his chin, then shook his head at Pitt. 'You dragged me all the way across country to go for a ride in a blimp?'

'I believe the preferred term is *airship*,' Pitt said, throwing his partner a mock look of indignation.

'A *gasbag*, by any other name.'

Giordino had wondered what Pitt had up his sleeve after the two arrived at LAX on an overnight flight from Washington. Rather than heading south from the airport, toward the Port of Los Angeles and adjacent Coast Guard Marine Safety regional command, Pitt had turned their rental car north. Giordino promptly fell asleep in the passenger seat as the head of NUMA drove them out of the Los Angeles metro area. Awakening later to find the specter of strawberry fields rushing past the window, he rubbed his eyes as the car entered the tiny Oxnard Airport and Pitt parked the vehicle near a large blimp moored to a truck-mounted vertical boom.

Peering at the blimp, Giordino cracked, 'I didn't think the Super Bowl was scheduled for another couple of months.'

The 222-foot long Airship Management Services

Sentinel 1000 was, in fact, much larger than the usual advertising blimps seen hovering over football games and golf tournaments. An enlarged version of the company's popular Skyship 600 series of blimps, the Sentinel 1000 was designed to lift a useful load of nearly six thousand pounds by way of an envelope that held ten thousand cubic meters of gas. Unlike the rigidly framed dirigibles of the twenties and thirties that relied on highly flammable hydrogen for lift, the Sentinel 1000 was a true nonrigid blimp that utilized the safer element of helium to rise off the ground.

'Looks like a runt nephew of the *Hindenburg*,' Giordino moaned, eyeing the silver-skinned airship warily.

'You happen to be looking at the latest in surveillance and tracking technology,' Pitt said. 'She's fitted with a LASH optical system. NUMA is testing her out for possible survey use on coral reef and tide studies. The system has already been used successfully to track migrating whales.'

'What is a "LASH system"?'

'Stands for "Littoral Airborne Sensor-Hyperspectral." It's an optical imaging system that uses a breakdown in the color band to detect and track targets that the eye cannot see. Homeland Security is considering using it for border security and the Navy for antisubmarine warfare.'

'If we can give it a test run over Malibu Beach, then I'm all for it.'

A ground crewman wearing a NUMA identification badge climbed out of the gondola as Pitt and Giordino approached the airship.

'Mr. Pitt? We've installed the radio set that the Coast Guard sent up, so you'll be able to conduct secure communications with their vessels. The *Icarus* has been weighed off for a landing equilibrium of plus-one hundred kilograms when your fuel supply runs down to five percent, so just don't run the tanks dry. The airship is also fitted with both a water ballast system and an experimental fuel dump release, should you need emergency lift.'

'How long can we stay aloft?' Giordino asked, eyeing a pair of ducted propellers jutting from either side of the gondola's aft section.

'Eight to ten hours, if you go easy on the throttles. Enjoy your flight, she's a joy to fly,' he said, bowing slightly.

Pitt and Giordino climbed through the gondola door and into a spacious cabin that was comfortably outfitted to seat eight passengers. Squirming through a forward opening into the flight compartment, Pitt took up the pilot's controls while Giordino plopped into the copilot's seat. With a muffled roar, Pitt started the pair of turbocharged Porsche 930 air-cooled engines mounted on the rear flanks of the gondola, which served as propulsion. With the engines idling, Pitt obtained clearance to take off from the airport control tower, then turned to Giordino.

'Ready for takeoff, Wilbur?'

'Ready when you are, Orville.'

Launching the blimp was not a simple action handled solely by the pilots but rather a carefully orchestrated maneuver assisted by a large ground crew. Outside the gondola, the *Icarus*'s support crew, all attired in bright red shirts, took up positions around the airship. A pair of ropes attached to the blimp's nose were pulled taut by three men standing off either side of the bow while four additional men grabbed onto side rails running the length of the gondola. Directly forward of the wide cockpit window that ran nearly to his feet, Pitt stared toward the crew chief, who stood at the base of the mobile mooring mast. At Pitt's command, the crew chief signaled another crewman, standing high atop the mooring mast, to release the nose tether. In unison, the ground crew then tugged at the weightless blimp, walking it away from the mooring mast several dozen yards to a safe launching point clear of obstacles.

Pitt gave a thumbs-up signal to the crew chief, then reached over and pulled down a pair of levers protruding from the center console, increasing the throttle to the twin engines. As the ground crew let free of their clutches and moved clear, he gently pulled back on a center yoke control mounted in front of his seat. The controls manipulated the motor-driven propellers, which were each enclosed in swiveling ducts. As he pulled on the yoke, the ducts tilted upward, providing additional lift from the churning propellers. Immediately, the blimp began to rise, creeping forward as it climbed. Almost without the feeling of movement, the big airship rose off the ground and into the sky with its nose pointed high. Giordino cheerfully waved out an open side window to the ground crew below, who shrank to the size of bugs as the airship rapidly gained altitude.

Despite Giordino's request for a low-flying pass over Malibu, Pitt steered the airship directly offshore from Oxnard after leaving the grounds of the airport and soon leveled the blimp off at a height of twenty-five hundred feet. The Pacific Ocean resonated a deep aqua color under a bright sun, and the men easily counted out the northerly Channel Islands of Santa Cruz, Santa Rosa, and San Miguel under the clear skies. As they floated east, Pitt noticed dew dripping off of the blimp, its fabric sides warming under the rays of the morning sun. He glanced at a helium pressure gauge, noting a slight rise in the needle as the helium expanded from the warming temperatures and higher cruising altitude. An automatic venting system would release any excess gas if the pressure rose too high, but Pitt kept the blimp well below its pressure height so as not to needlessly stave off helium.

The controls of the Sentinel 1000 were heavy in his hands and he noted that the sensation of flying the blimp felt closer to sailing a twenty-meter racing yacht than piloting an airplane. Turning the huge rudders and elevators required some muscling of the yoke, which resulted in an anxious pause before the ship's nose would gradually respond. Correcting course, he absentmindedly watched the lines dangling off the blimp's nose sway back and forth. A boat bobbed into view beneath them, which he recognized as a charter fishing boat. The tiny-looking day fishermen on the boat's stern suddenly waved up at them with friendly abandon. There was something about an airship that always seemed to strike a warm chord with people. They captured the romance of the air, Pitt decided, offering a reminder of times past when flying was still a novelty. With his hands on the controls, he could feel the nostalgia himself. Floating at a leisurely pace over the water, he let his mind churn back to the days of the thirties when mammoth dirigibles like the *Graf Zeppelin* and *Hindenburg* shared the skies with the huge Navy airships *Akron* and *Macon*. Like the opulent cruise ships of the same era, they offered a certain relaxed majesty that simply no longer existed in modern travel.

When they reached a distance of thirty miles offshore, Pitt angled the blimp south and began navigating a large, lazy arc off the Los Angeles metropolis. Giordino powered up the LASH optical system, tied into a laptop computer, which enabled him to spot the images of incoming surface vessels up to thirty-five miles away. The freighters and containerships came chugging in toward the ports of Los Angeles and Long Beach at a sporadic yet endless pace. The big vessels hailed from a variety of exotic-sounding homeports, from Mumbai to Jakarta, though China, Japan, and Taiwan accounted for the largest volume of traffic. More than three thousand vessels a year entered the adjacent ports, creating a constant stream of traffic that crawled across the Pacific toward America's busiest port like ants to a picnic. As Giordino studied the laptop, he reported to Pitt that he could spot two large vessels inbound in the distance that figured to be commercial ships. Squinting out the cockpit window, Pitt could just make out the leading vessel on the horizon.

'Let's go take a look,' Pitt replied, aiming the nose of the airship toward the approaching ship. Flicking a button on the Coast Guard radio set newly installed in the cockpit, he spoke into his headset.

'Coast Guard Cutter *Halibut*, this is airship *Icarus*. We are on station and preparing to survey two inbound vessels approximately forty-five miles due east of Long Beach, over.'

'Roger, *Icarus*,' came a deep-voiced reply. 'Glad to have you and your eyes in the sky with us. We have three vessels deployed and engaged in current interdiction actions. We'll await your surveillance reports on new inbound vessels as they approach. Out.'

'Eyes in the sky,' Giordino grumbled. 'I'd rather be the stomach on the sofa,' he said, suddenly wondering if anyone had packed them a lunch aboard the airship.

*

Throughout the night, the *Odyssey* had churned west, inching her way closer to the California coast that she had departed just days before. Tongju returned to the platform after resolving the launch position dispute and stole a few hours of sleep in the captain's cabin before rising an hour before dawn. Under the first trickles of morning light, he watched from the bridge as the platform followed in the *Koguryo*'s wake, noticing the shadow of a sizable island in the distance off the starboard bow. It was San Nicolas Island, a dry and windblown rock farthest from shore of all the Channel Islands and owned by the Navy for use primarily as an amphibious training site. They continued west for another hour before the radio crackled with the voice of Captain Lee.

'We are approaching the location that the Ukrainian engineers have indicated. Prepare to halt engines, and we will take up position to the southeast of you. We will be standing by to initiate launch countdown at your direction.'

'Affirmative,' Tongju replied. 'We will set position and ballast the platform. Stand by for positioning.'

Tongju turned and nodded to one of Kang's undercover crewmen who was piloting the *Odyssey*. With skilled confidence, the helmsman eased off the platform's forward-propulsion throttles, then activated the self-positioning thrusters. Using a GPS coordinate as a fixed target, the computer-controlled system of forward, side, and rear thrusters was activated, locking the *Odyssey* in a fixed position as if parked on a dime.

'Position control activated,' the helmsman barked in a crisp military voice. 'Initiating ballast flooding,' he continued, pushing a series of buttons on an illuminated console.

Two hundred feet below the pilothouse, a series of gate valves were automatically opened inside the twin pontoons and a half-dozen ballast pumps began rapidly pumping salt water into the hollow steel hulls. The flooding was imperceptible to those standing on the platform deck, as the computer-controlled pumps ensured an even rate of flooding. On the bridge, Tongju studied a computerized three-dimensional image of the *Odyssey* on a monitor, its catamaran hulls and lower columns turning a bright blue as the seawater poured in. Like a lethargic elevator ride, as the men on the bridge watched rather than felt, the platform sank slowly toward the waves. Sixty minutes passed before the platform gently dropped forty-six feet, the bottom of its twin hulls submerged to a stabilizing depth seventy feet below the surface. Tongju noted that the platform had ceased its slow swaying evident earlier. With its submerged pontoons and partially sunken pilings, the *Odyssey* had become a rock-stable platform from which to launch a million-pound rocket.

A buzzer sounded as the designated launch depth was attained, the rising blue water on the monitor graphic having reached a red horizontal line. The helmsman pressed a few more buttons, then stood back from the console.

'Flooding complete. Platform is stabilized for launch,' he said.

'Secure the bridge,' Tongju replied, nodding toward a Filipino crewman who stood near the radar-scope. A guard standing near the door was waved over and quickly escorted the crewman off the bridge without saying a word. Tongju followed out the rear of the bridge, entering a small elevator, which he rode to the floor of the hangar. A dozen or so engineers were hovering around the huge horizontal rocket, examining an array of computer stations that were wired directly into the launch vehicle. Tongju approached a thick-haired man with round glasses named Ling who headed up the launch operations team. Before Tongju could speak, Ling gushed with a nervous testimony.

'We have verified final tests on the payload with positive results. The launch vehicle is secure and all electromechanical systems have tested nominal.'

'Good. The platform is in the designated position and ballasted for launch. Is the rocket ready to be transported to the launch tower?'

Ling nodded enthusiastically. 'We have been await-ing word to proceed. We are prepared to initiate launch vehicle transport and erection.'

'There is no reason to dawdle. Proceed at once. Notify me when you are ready to evacuate the platform.'

'Yes, of course,' Ling replied, then hurried over to a group of nearby engineers and spoke at them rapid-fire. Like a band of scared rabbits, the engineers scattered in a fury to their collective posts. Tongju stood back and watched as the massive hangar doors were opened, revealing a railed path across the deck to the standing launch tower at the opposite end of the platform. A series of electrical motors were then started, which reverberated loudly off the hangar's interior walls. Tongju walked behind a console panel and peered over Ling's shoulder as the launch leader's hands danced over the control board. When a row of lights suddenly glowed green, Ling pointed to another engineer, who activated the mobile cradle.

The two-hundred-foot horizontal rocket rocked sluggishly toward the hangar doors, its support cradle creeping forward on a countless mass of wheels that churned like the legs of a centipede. With its base thrusters leading the way, the rocket crept through the doors and into the daylight, its white paint glistening under the morning sun. Tongju strolled alongside the rolling launch vehicle, admiring the potent power of the huge rocket while amazed at its massive girth in the prone position. Several hundred yards away, the *Koguryo* stood off the platform, a throng of crew and engineers craning from her top deck to catch a glimpse of the big rocket under way.

Crossing the open deck, the mechanical caterpillar ground to a halt as it reached the base of the launch tower. The upper section of the rocket had not completely cleared the hangar and a sliding panel in the hangar roof suddenly crept open to provide clearance. The transporter was locked securely in place to the deck and then the erector mechanicals were engaged, activating hydraulic pumps that pushed gently against the rocket's cradle. With delicate patience, the launch vehicle was slowly tilted upright, its nose sliding through the hangar roof opening, until it stood vertically against the launch tower. A series of support braces clamped the rocket to the platform, while a jumble of fuel, cooling, and venting lines were affixed and checked. Several workmen on the tower plugged in a series of data cables that allowed the engineers on the *Koguryo* to monitor the dozens of electronic sensors embedded under the rocket's skin. Once the Zenit was affixed upright, the erector/transporter support cradle was gently eased away, leaving the rocket braced only by the launch tower. With a hydraulic murmur, the cradle was slowly lowered to its original horizontal position and returned to the hangar, where it would be sheltered out of harm's way during launch.

Ling spoke anxiously by radio to the Launch Control Center on the *Koguryo* before dashing over to Tongju.

'Some minor anomalies, but, overall, the launch vehicle meets all major prelaunch parameters.'

Tongju looked up at the towering rocket with its payload of deadly virus, aimed to rain death on millions of innocent people. The suffering and deaths meant nothing to him, a man purged of emotional empathy decades ago. The power he felt before him was all that mattered, a power greater than he had ever known before, and he relished the moment. Gradually, his eyes played down from the tip of the rocket to its base, then swept slowly across the breadth of the platform, before settling on Ling. The engineer stood waiting anxiously for a reply. Tongju let Ling wallow in discomfort a moment longer before breaking the silence in a deep, firm tone.

'Very well,' he said. 'Begin the countdown.'

49

The crew of the *Deep Endeavor* had quickly found interdiction support duty to be a monotonous assignment. After two days on station, they had only been requested to board and search one ship, a small freighter from the Philippines carrying a shipment of hardwood timber. The commercial shipping traffic that approached Los Angeles from the southwest had been light and ably handled by the nearby Coast Guard cutter *Narwhal*. The NUMA crew preferred to be put to work rather than circle aimlessly waiting for action and quietly hoped traffic would pick up in their quadrant.

In the ship's galley, Dirk sat sipping a cup of coffee with Summer while she studied a report on coral mortality in the Great Barrier Reef when a crewman approached and told them that they were wanted on the bridge.

'We've received a call from the *Narwhal*,' Delgado reported. 'They're halfway through a container vessel search and asked us to confirm identification on a vessel approaching west of Catalina and then stand by for possible interdiction.'

'No advance identification from our eye-in-the-sky?' Dirk asked.

'Your father and Al took off in the *Icarus* this morning. They're working their way down from the north and will probably make a pass through our quadrant within the next couple of hours.'

Summer peered out the bridge window to the north, spotting the *Narwhal* bobbing alongside a large containership that rode low in the water from its heavy cargo. Farther west, she spotted a red speck approaching on the horizon. The *Deep Endeavor*'s pilot was already steering an intercept course toward it.

'Is that her?' Summer asked, pointing a finger toward the object.

'Yes,' Delgado replied. 'The *Narwhal* has already radioed her to halt, so we'll intercept her after she's had a chance to slow. She's reported herself as the *Maru Santo* out of Osaka.'

An hour later, the *Deep Endeavor* hove to alongside the *Maru Santo*, a rusty, multipurpose cargo freighter of small size by inter-Pacific standards. Aimes's Sea Marshal team, along with Summer, Dahlgren, and three other NUMA crewmen, climbed into a small launch and motored over to the freighter, tying up to a rust-stained stairwell that was lowered over the side. Having made fast friends with the bomb-sniffing dogs, Summer quickly volunteered to take the leash of one of the retrievers. As Aimes and Dahlgren met with the freighter's captain to review the manifest, the remaining contingent began a bow-to-stern search of the ship. With the dogs leading the way, the search crew wedged through the ship's holds, checking the container seals and examining several loose crated shipments of running shoes and apparel manufactured in Taiwan. A gritty Malaysian crew looked on with bored amusement as the yellow Labs sniffed their way through the dimly lit crew's quarters.

Dirk stood on the bridge of the *Deep Endeavor*, studying the Japanese cargo ship. A pair of the freighter's crew stood on the deck looking back at the NUMA vessel. Dirk tossed a friendly wave as the two men leaned against a railing in disheveled clothes, smoking cigarettes and cracking jokes in an obviously relaxed manner.

'There is no threat from this ship,' he turned and said with certainty to Captain Burch.

'How can you be so sure?'

'The crew is too lax. The men on Kang's ship were no-nonsense professionals, not the ragtag jovial sort on this tub. There would be a slew of paranoid undercover security types running around as well,' he added, recalling the image of Tongju and his men.

'Be worth noting to Aimes when he gets back. If nothing else, it's still a good practice exercise for the boys. And, heck, I got Dahlgren off the bridge for a few minutes at least,' the captain smiled.

'We've still got to find them first. There's just too many places to hide at sea,' Dirk muttered.

As the search team appeared above decks for a moment, Captain Burch picked up a pair of binoculars and scanned the horizon. He noted a pair of dots far to the southwest, then scanned to the north, taking in the *Narwhal* as she started to pull away from the container-ship. Burch started to drop the binoculars when a sudden glint caught his eye. Raising the glasses and adjusting the focus, he smiled broadly, then spoke to Dirk.

'I guess there will be a few less places to hide on the sea now that our illustrious leaders of the deep are checking things out from the balcony.'

Two thousand feet above the calmly rolling swells of the Pacific, the silver *Icarus* floated gracefully across the sky at thirty-five miles per hour. While the elder Pitt handled the blimp's flight controls, Giordino adjusted a row of dials at the base of a flat-panel color monitor. A WESCAM long-distance camera mounted to the side of the gondola, a supplement to the LASH imaging system, fed into the monitor, providing a zoom image of objects located hundreds of yards away. Pitt glanced from the flight controls to the monitor, which displayed a close-up picture of the stern of a small boat where two bikini-clad women were stretched out sunbathing.

'I hope your girlfriend doesn't catch wind of your voyeuristic tendencies,' Pitt laughed.

'Just testing the resolution,' Giordino replied in a serious tone while prankishly zooming the image in and out on one of the women's behinds.

'Ansel Adams you're not. Let's see what that setup will read with a real target,' Pitt said, turning the airship west toward an outbound vessel a few miles away. Dropping down a few hundred feet, Pitt nosed the *Icarus* to starboard and increased the throttle, gradually gaining ground on the departing ship. While still nearly a half mile away, Giordino zoomed the camera lens onto the stern of the black-hulled freighter, easily reading the name: '*Jasmine Star . . . Madras.*' He raised the camera along the ship's deck, noting a stacked array of containers, before settling on the bridge mast, where the monitor revealed a flag of India snapping crisply in the breeze.

'Works like a champ,' Al said proudly.

Pitt looked at the LASH screen on the laptop, which showed an empty swath of sea in advance of the Indian freighter. 'Nothing coming up on the main shipping channel for the time being. Let's keep going south, where it looks like there's a little more activity,' he said, noting several images on the left edge of the screen.

Maneuvering the blimp south, they soon passed over the *Narwhal* and the containership she just searched, then they cruised over a portion of Catalina Island. Passing back over the water, Giordino pointed out the windshield toward a turquoise ship in the distance.

'There's the *Deep Endeavor*. Looks like she has gotten into the act as well,' he said, noting the red freighter idling nearby.

Pitt guided the blimp toward the NUMA ship, calling it up on the radio as they approached.

'*Icarus* to *Deep Endeavor*. How's the fishing down there?'

'Nary a nibble,' Burch's voice replied. 'How are you gentlemen enjoying your sightseeing flight?'

'Delightful, except for Al's incessant crunching at the caviar table, which is interrupting my enjoyment of the in-flight movie. We'll see if we can't rustle you up some more business.'

'Roger, we'd be much obliged.'

Giordino adjusted the blimp's LASH system, examining it for targets.

'Looks like we've got an inbound vessel in the main shipping channel about twenty-two miles to the northwest and what looks like a couple of stationary targets eighteen miles to the west of us,' he said, pointing to some gray-and-white patches on the monitor that contrasted with the blue ocean background.

Pitt looked at the laptop, then glanced at his watch. 'We ought to be able to catch the northwest ship on the fly. Let's go see what's parked out here first,' he replied, aiming the blimp to the west and toward the two large smudges on the screen that were oddly sitting still.

50

Firing a rocket off the Sea Launch platform is traditionally preceded by a seventy-two-hour launch countdown. During the three-day preparation, dozens of tests are performed to ensure that all support systems are operational and all mechanical and computer systems aboard the rocket are ready to withstand the violent rigors of launch. At T-15 hours before launch, the engineers and all but a handful of crewmen are evacuated from the platform as the final stages of the countdown progresses. The assembly and command ship is then moved to a safe operating area four miles uprange of the platform.

At T-5 hours, the last of the crewmen are evacuated from the platform aboard a helicopter and the remaining countdown procedures are handled remotely from the support ship. With less than three hours to go, the hazardous operation of fueling the launch vehicle is performed automatically, the kerosene and oxygen combustibles remotely pumped into the rocket from the large storage tanks housed on the platform. Once fueled, the decision is then left to the launch engineers aboard the support ship to proceed with the launch and fire the rocket when ready.

Absent the luxury of time, Ling's team of launch engineers consolidated the Sea Launch firing procedures into a bare-minimum schedule. Redundant and nonessential tests were scrapped, built-in launch holds were eliminated, and the fueling time reduced on account of the shortened flight plan. By their accord, they could launch the Zenit in just eight hours from the time the *Odyssey* was ballasted and stabilized.

Tongju stood on the platform near the base of the launch tower and gazed at a large digital clock mounted on the roofline of the hangar. The red illuminated numbers read 03:32:17, with the digits clicking backward a second at a time. Three hours and thirty-two minutes until liftoff. Barring a major technical difficulty, there would be no halting the launch now. In Tongju's eyes, it would soon come down to the simple task of fueling the rocket and lighting it off.

But before the button could be pushed, the *Koguryo* had to obtain total control of the launch process. Ling and his engineers first established a radio link to the automated launch control system, which was tested and verified through the *Koguryo*'s launch control center. Then there was the transfer of the *Odyssey*'s own command system. A wireless marine positioning system allowed the launch platform to be remotely controlled after all personnel were evacuated for launch. Like a radio-controlled toy, the platform could be raised, lowered, or moved by the touch of a keypad aboard the *Koguryo*. Once the controls had been passed to the support ship, Ling approached Tongju on the deck.

'My work here is complete. Full system control now lies on the *Koguryo*. My team and I must return to the support ship to resume launch countdown activities.'

Tongju glanced again at the countdown clock. 'My compliments. You are ahead of schedule. I will call for the *Koguryo*'s tender and you may take your men off the platform at once.'

'You will not be joining us now?' Ling asked.

'I must secure the prisoners first, then my assault team will follow along. It is my desire to be the last man off the platform before launch,' Tongju said. 'That is, except for the men who will not be coming off at all,' he added with a sinister smile.

'There's not supposed to be an oil platform located here.'

Giordino's eyes shifted from the large square object on the water ahead of them to an over-sized navigational chart he'd folded on his lap. 'No man-made hazards are indicated in this region at all. I don't think the Sierra Club is going to take kindly to some stealth drilling this close to the coast.'

'They might be even more perturbed when you tell them the oil platform has a rocket aboard,' Pitt replied.

Giordino squinted out the airship's windshield toward the approaching platform. 'I'll be. Give that man with the eagle eye a cookie.'

Pitt turned the blimp as they approached, making a wide loop around the platform and adjacent support ship, careful to avoid its airspace.

'Sea Launch?' Giordino asked.

'Must be. I didn't think they'd move it around with the rocket standing upright, though.'

'I think they're parked,' Giordino replied, noting there was no wake from the nearby support ship. 'You don't suppose they would be launching from here?'

'No way. They are supposed to fire those things off from the equator. They would at least be up north off the Vandenberg range if they were going to try a live launch around here. Probably some sort of test, but let's find out.'

Pitt punched a switch on a marine band radio and hailed the platform through his headset.

'Airship *Icarus* to Sea Launch platform. Over.'

An empty pause ensued and then Pitt repeated the call. After another lengthy lull, an accented voice finally replied.

'This is Sea Launch platform *Odyssey*. Over.'

'*Odyssey*, what is the nature of your position? Do you require assistance? Over.'

Another long pause. 'Negative.'

'I repeat, what is the nature of your position?'

A pause again. 'Who is requesting inquiry?'

'Friendly sorts, aren't they?' Giordino said to Pitt.

Pitt shook his head slightly and spoke again into the radio. 'This is airship *Icarus*, supporting Coast Guard border security. Please identify current state. Over.'

'This is *Odyssey*. We are conducting system tests. Please stay clear. Over and out.'

'The guy's a regular Gabby Hayes,' Giordino said. 'Do you want to stick around? We need to roll back north if we want to intercept that incoming vessel,' he said, pointing to the radar screen.

'I guess there's not much we can do from up here. Okay, we'll do our job and play tag with the next inbound vessel. But let's have one of the boys downstairs check this out,' Pitt said, turning the airship around to the north.

Giordino took to the radio as Pitt laid in an intercept course toward the inbound commercial ship. 'The *Deep Endeavor* and the *Narwhal* are working this region. *Deep Endeavor* is still searching a Japanese freighter, but the *Narwhal* is freed up at the moment. She says the platform is outside their twelve-mile operating limit, however.'

'We're not asking for an interdiction boarding. Just request a remote visual survey and verification with Sea Launch authorities.'

Giordino spoke into the radio again, then turned to Pitt. '*Narwhal* agrees and is on her way.'

'Good,' Pitt replied, watching the platform fade away in the distance behind them. But he didn't feel good. A nagging sensation told him they had missed something on their flyover. Something important.

Kim stood with Tongju on the bridge of the *Odyssey* watching the blimp circle away to the north.

'They did not loiter for very long. Do you think they suspect anything?' Kim asked.

'I do not know,' Tongju replied, his eyes moving from the blimp to a chronometer mounted on the bulwark. 'The launch will take place in just over two hours. There is no room for interference now. Return to the *Koguryo*, Ki-Ri, and stand by with Captain Lee. If there is any attempted outside hindrance, deal with it decisively. Do you understand?'

Kim looked his commander squarely in the eye and nodded. 'I understand completely.'

Dirk and Captain Burch listened in on the *Deep Endeavor*'s Coast Guard radio as Giordino asked the *Narwhal* to survey the Sea Launch platform and support ship. Minutes later, the *Narwhal* called up the NUMA vessel.

'*Deep Endeavor*, we have completed inspection of the containership *Andaman Star* and are proceeding to the offshore platform for a visual inspection. No incoming traffic in our quadrant is presently in range, so you may accompany us at your convenience if desired. Over.'

'Shall we take a look?' Captain Burch asked of Dirk.

'Why not? Business is slow. We can follow along once we're finished here.'

Burch glanced at the Japanese freighter, noting that Aimes and the search crew were beginning to assemble at the rail, their inspection nearly complete.

'Affirmative, *Narwhal*,' Burch radioed to the Coast Guard vessel. 'We'll shadow you upon completion of our current inspection, in another five or ten minutes. Out.'

'Wonder what piqued the old man's interest,' Dirk asked rhetorically as he and Burch peered across the horizon trying to make out the image of the floating platform.

Three miles away, the *Narwhal* had stoked up its twin diesel motors and was skimming across the waves at its top speed of 25 knots. The eighty-seven-foot cutter was one of the newer Barracuda-class patrol boats employed by the Coast Guard, designed to work out of smaller ports and harbors. With their mission focused primarily on inspection and sea rescue, the boat's crew of ten was only lightly armed with a pair of 12.7mm machine guns mounted on the bow deck.

Lieutenant Bruce Carr Smith braced himself against a bulkhead in the cramped bridge as the white-and-orange-trimmed boat lurched over a swell, her bow slapping the sea with a spray of foam.

'Lieutenant, I've radioed command headquarters. Dispatch is going to contact the Sea Launch port office to determine what's up with their platform,' the *Narwhal*'s red-haired communications officer stated from the corner.

Smith nodded in reply, then spoke to a boyish-looking helmsman manning the wheel. 'Steady as she goes,' he said firmly.

The two dots they chased on the horizon gradually grew larger until the distinct shapes of an oil platform and a utility ship drew into focus. The support ship was no longer aside the platform and Smith could see that it was in fact moving away from the stationary platform. Smith took a quick glance over his shoulder and saw that the *Deep Endeavor* had completed her freighter inspection. The turquoise vessel was moving away from the freighter and appeared to be following his path in the distance.

'Sir, would you like to approach the platform or the ship?' the helmsman asked as they drew nearer.

'Bring us alongside the platform for starters, then we'll go take a look at the ship,' Smith replied.

The small patrol boat slowed as it eased near the platform, which now rode fourteen meters lower in the water under its ballasted state. Smith looked in awe at the huge Zenit rocket standing at its launch tower near the stern edge of the platform. Peering through binoculars, he studied the platform deck but saw no signs of life. Surveying the forward section of the platform, he caught sight of the launch count-down clock, which now read 01:32:00, one hour and thirty-two minutes.

'What the hell?' Smith muttered as he watched the digital numbers tick lower. Grabbing the marine radio transmitter, he called to *Odyssey*.

'Sea Launch platform, this is Coast Guard cutter *Narwhal*. Over.' After a pause, he tried again. But he was met only with silence.

'Sea Launch director of information, how may I help you?' a soft, feminine voice answered over the phone line.

'This is the Eleventh District U.S. Coast Guard, Marine Safety Group, Los Angeles, central dispatch.

We're requesting mission and location status of Sea Launch vessels *Odyssey* and *Sea Launch Commander*, please.'

'One moment,' the information director hesitated, shuffling through some papers on her desk.

'Here we are,' she continued. 'The launch platform *Odyssey* is en route to her designated launch site in the western Pacific, near the equator. Her last reported position, as of eight A.M. this morning, was at approximately 18 degrees North Latitude, 132 degrees West Longitude, or roughly seventeen hundred miles east-southeast of Honolulu, Hawaii. The assembly and command ship *Sea Launch Commander* is presently at port in Long Beach undergoing minor repairs. She is expected to depart port tomorrow morning to rendezvous with the *Odyssey* at the equator, where the Koreasat 2 launch is scheduled in eight days.'

'Neither vessel is currently located at sea off the coast of Southern California?'

'Why no, of course not.'

'Thank you for the information, ma'am.'

'You're welcome,' the director replied before hanging up, wondering why the Coast Guard would think the platform was anywhere near the coast of California.

Smith was too anxious to dally for a response from the Los Angeles Coast Guard Group and brought his vessel closer to the platform. The Coast Guard lieutenant was annoyed at the lack of response from the *Odyssey*, which had ignored his repetitive radio calls. He finally turned his attention toward the support ship, which had now crept a quarter mile away from the platform. Repeated radio calls to the ship went unanswered as well.

'Sir, she's flying a Japanese flag,' the helmsman noted as the *Narwhal* moved toward the vessel.

'No excuse for ignoring a marine radio call. Let's move alongside the vessel and I'll try to talk to them over the PA system,' Smith ordered.

As *Narwhal* moved out of the shadow of the platform, pandemonium struck at once. Coast Guard dispatch broke over the *Narwhal*'s radio with word that the *Odyssey* was reported a thousand miles away from California and that her support ship was sitting docked in Long Beach. Aboard the *Koguryo*, a handful of crewmen pushed aside a lower deck siding, revealing a row of large cylindrical tubes pointing seaward. Though in disbelief, Smith's instincts took over, correctly assessing the situation and barking orders before he even realized the words were flowing from his lips.

'Hard to port! Apply full power! Prepare for evasive maneuvers!'

But it was too late. The helmsman was just able to swing the *Narwhal* broadside to the *Koguryo* when a plume of white smoke suddenly billowed from the larger ship's lower deck. The smoke seemed to build at its source before a bright flash burst forth. Then, out of the smoke, a Chinese CSS-N-4 Sardine surface-to-surface missile erupted from its launch tube, bursting horizontally away from the ship. Watching mesmerized from the bridge, Smith had the distinct sensation of being shot between the eyes with an arrow as he observed the missile charge directly toward him across the water. The nosetip of the missile seemed to smile at him in the fractional second before it smashed into the bridge just a few feet away.

Carrying 365 pounds of high explosives, the Chinese missile had enough demolition power to sink a cruiser. Striking at short range, the cutter had no chance. The nineteen-foot missile ripped into the *Narwhal* and exploded in a massive fireball, blasting the Coast Guard ship and its crew into fiery bits that scattered across the water. A small black mushroom cloud rose like a macabre tombstone above the devastation as the flames died quietly on the water's surface. The incinerated white hull, the only material remains of the ship left intact, clung to the sea's surface in a futile battle to stay afloat. Around her, flaming chunks of debris blazed in the water before slowly sinking to the seabed. The smoldering hull clung to the surface for nearly fifteen minutes before the fight left her and the last remains of the *Narwhal* slipped under the surface with a gasping sizzle and a wisp of steam.

52

'My God, they've fired a missile at the *Narwhal*!' Captain Burch cried out as he watched the Coast Guard ship disappear in a cloud of smoke and fire two miles ahead of the *Deep Endeavor*. Delgado immediately attempted to raise the *Narwhal* on the marine radio as the others peered out the bridge window. Summer grabbed a pair of high-power binoculars but there was little to be seen of the *Narwhal*, its shattered remains obscured by a thick veil of smoke. Looking past the smoke, she scanned the platform and the adjacent support ship, which she studied for a long while.

'There's no response,' Delgado said quietly after repeated attempts to contact the Coast Guard vessel were met with silence.

'There may be survivors in the water,' Aimes stuttered, stunned at the sudden demise of a boat and crew he knew well.

'I can't dare move any closer,' Captain Burch replied with angst. 'We're completely unarmed, and they may well be aiming their next missile at us as we speak.' Burch then turned and ordered his helmsman to stop engines and hold their present position.

Delgado spoke to Aimes. 'The captain is right.

We'll call for help but we can't endanger our crew. We don't even know who or what we are up against.'

'It's Kang's men,' Summer said, handing the binoculars to her brother.

'You're sure?' Aimes asked.

She nodded silently with a shiver as Dirk surveyed the vessels.

'She's right,' he said slowly. 'The support ship. It's the same vessel that sank the *Sea Rover*. She's even flying a Japanese flag. They've painted and reconfigured her, but I'll bet my next paycheck it's the same ship.'

'But why are they standing off here with the platform?' Aimes added, a mask of confusion crossing his face.

'There can only be one reason. They are preparing to launch a strike with the Sea Launch rocket.'

A subdued silence fell across the bridge as the gravity of the situation sunk in. A disbelieving Aimes finally broke the hushed confines.

'But the *Narwhal*. We've got to see if anyone's alive.'

'Aimes, you need to get some help out here, and now,' Dirk replied brusquely. 'I'll go see if there are any survivors.'

Delgado looked at Dirk with a furrowed brow. 'But we don't dare bring the *Deep Endeavor* any closer,' he cautioned.

'I don't intend to,' Dirk replied without explanation as he quickly exited the bridge.

*

Tongju gazed down from the *Odyssey*'s bridge at the smoldering debris of the *Narwhal* and stared quietly. There was no choice but for the *Koguryo* to act against the Coast Guard vessel. It was what he had ordered Kim to do. But they were positioned far enough off shore that they should never have been detected in the first place. He knew now that it was the encounter with the blimp that had raised suspicions. Silently, he cursed the Ukrainian engineers for moving the launch site closer to shore, neglecting to consider that the final decision had been his.

Pacing the *Odyssey*'s bridge anxiously, he noted the launch countdown clock read 01:10:00, one hour and ten minutes to go. A radio call from the *Koguryo* crackled through the air, breaking his thoughts.

'This is Lee. We destroyed the enemy vessel, as you directed. There is another vessel standing off two thousand meters. Do you wish us to destroy her also?'

'Is she another military vessel? Over,' Tongju asked, peering out the bridge toward the distant ship.

'Negative. Believed to be a research vessel.'

'No. Save your armament, we may need it later.'

'As you wish. Ling reports that his launch team is securely aboard the *Koguryo*. Are you ready to evacuate the platform?'

'Yes. Send the tender back to the platform, my remaining team will be ready to evacuate shortly. Out.'

Tongju hung up the radio transmitter, then turned

to a commando standing at the rear of the bridge.

'Transfer the Sea Launch prisoners in small groups to the launch vehicle hangar and lock them in the storage bay located inside. Then assemble the assault team for transport back to the *Koguryo*.'

'You do not fear that the platform crew may survive the launch inside the hangar?' the commando asked.

'The exhaust gases will likely kill them. I do not care whether they live or die just as long as they are unable to interfere with the launch.'

The commando nodded, then slipped out the rear of the bridge. Tongju slowly walked across the pilothouse, carefully examining the array of marine electronics built into the lower forward bulkhead. Finding a panel that contained the manual override switches to the automated controls, he pulled out a combat knife and jammed the blade into a side seam and pried open the cover. Grasping the mass of wires inside, he yanked the serrated edge of his knife across and through the bundle, rendering the switches useless. Continuing his trek through the bridge, he gathered up a half-dozen keyboards attached to various navigational and positioning computers and tossed them through an open window, watching patiently as they splashed into the ocean below. A trio of laptop computers quickly followed the long plunge to a watery demise. For good measure, he pulled out his Glock and fired several rounds into an assortment of computer and navigation monitors positioned about the bridge. As Ling had been ordered to do with the launch control computers in the hangar, Tongju disabled the navigation computers in the pilothouse, destroying any possibility of last-minute intervention. With less than an hour till liftoff, all control of the platform and the rocket was in the hands of the *Koguryo*, and there it would remain.

'Let me go with you,' Summer said. 'You know that I can pilot anything under the sea.'

'It's just a two-seater, and Jack is the only one with experience in this thing. It's better that he and I go,' Dirk replied, nodding toward Dahlgren as he prepared the deep-probe submersible for launching. Grabbing his sister's hand, he looked deeply into her pearl gray eyes.

'Get ahold of Dad and tell him what happened. Tell him we need help right away.'

Giving his sister a quick embrace, he added quietly, 'Make sure Burch keeps the *Endeavor* in a safe position even if something happens to us.'

'Be careful,' she said as he quickly climbed up and into the submersible, sealing the hatch behind him. Squirming into the pilot's seat beside Dahlgren, he saw that the submersible was fully powered up and ready to go.

'Thirty knots?' Dirk asked with skepticism.

'That's what the owner's manual states,' Jack Dahlgren replied, then turned and gave a thumbs-up signal through the view port window. On the stern of the *Deep Endeavor*, a crane operator nodded in reply and lifted the bright red submersible off the ship's deck and over the side, dropping it hurriedly into the ocean. The two men caught a quick glimpse of Summer waving to them on the deck before they were engulfed in the green water. With the NUMA ship's bow pointed toward the platform, the submersible was effectively blocked from view by the *Deep Endeavor*'s superstructure and they were deployed without being seen. A diver in the water released the cable hook, then gave a rap on the side to signal they were free.

'Let's see what she'll deliver,' Dirk said, activating the six thrusters and pushing the throttles to their stops.

The cigar-shaped submarine surged rather than leaped forward, amid a whine of electric motors and rushing water. Dirk adjusted a pair of diving planes slightly until they were at a submerged depth of twenty feet, then followed a compass-directed path toward the wreck of the *Narwhal*.

Through his hands, the ride felt like driving a vacuum cleaner. The submersible bobbed and weaved through the current and maneuvered like they were in a bowl of molasses. But with the buzzing of the thrusters in his ears, there was no denying she was a speed demon. Even without a relative speed gauge inside the submersible, Dirk could tell from the water rushing past the view port that they were moving at a rapid clip.

'I told you she was a thoroughbred,' Dahlgren grinned as he monitored an elapsed time clock on the console. Turning serious, he added, 'We should be approaching *Narwhal*'s position in about sixty seconds.'

Dirk gradually eased off the throttles a minute later, throwing the motors into idle as the *Badger*'s forward momentum waned. Floating to the surface, Dahlgren adjusted the ballast tanks to keep them low in the water in order to remain as covert as possible. With his expert touch, the submersible just barely broke the surface, showing less than a foot of its topside surfaces above the water.

A few yards in front of them, they could see the demolished hull of the smoldering *Narwhal*, her stern raised high in the air at an awkward angle. Dirk and Dahlgren barely had a chance to gaze at the hulk before her stern tipped upward even higher, then the entire remnant slipped quietly under the waves. Scattered about was a handful of floating debris, some smoldering but none larger than a doormat. Dirk guided the *Badger* in a small circle around the wreckage, but there was no sign of life in the water. Dahlgren solemnly radioed Aimes on the *Deep Endeavor* and reported that all appeared lost in the explosion.

'Captain Burch asks that we return to the *Deep Endeavor* at once,' Dahlgren added.

Dirk acted as if he didn't hear the comment and guided the submersible closer to the platform. From their vantage point low in the water, there was little on the platform deck they could see beyond the top half of the Zenit and the upper portion of the hangar. But suddenly he halted the *Badger* and pointed a finger past the rocket.

'Look, up there.'

Dahlgren peered past the rocket but just saw the roof of the hangar and an empty helipad. Squinting harder, he gazed down slightly. Then it struck him. The large digital launch clock that read 00:52:00, fifty-two minutes.

'That thing is going to fire off in less than an hour!' he exclaimed, watching the seconds tick down lower.

'We've got to stop it,' Dirk said, a tinge of anger in his voice.

'We'll have to get aboard and quick. Though I don't know about you, pardner, but I don't know a thing about missiles or platform launches.'

'Can't be anything more than a little rocket science,' Dirk replied with a grimace, then jammed the submersible's throttles forward, surging the *Badger* toward the platform.

53

The metallic red submersible surfaced again near the stern of the platform almost directly beneath the launch tower and Zenit rocket. Dirk and Dahlgren peered up at a large set of panels that protruded from the underside of the platform just below the base of the rocket. The flame deflector was designed to divert and dampen the rocket's fiery thrust, directing the launch tempest through the platform to the ocean below. Thousands of gallons of fresh water were released seconds before launch into the trench to help cool the exposed portions of the platform during the blazing inferno during the rocket's slow rise off the pad.

'Remind me not to park here when that torch goes off,' Dahlgren said, trying to visualize the conflagration that would surround them if the rocket was ignited.

'You don't have to ask twice,' Dirk replied.

Their attention turned to the platform's thick support columns, searching for a way up to the main deck. Dahlgren was the first to spot the *Koguryo*'s tender, tied up at the opposite side of the platform.

'I think I see a stairwell on that forward column where the boat's tied up,' he said.

Dirk took a quick bearing, then submerged the *Badger* and quickly ran her between the *Odyssey*'s sunken pontoons to the bow end of the platform. Bobbing to the surface, they rose just astern of the white tender, where they floated cautiously eyeing the other craft.

'I don't think anyone is home,' Dirk said, satisfied the boat was empty. 'Care to tie us off?'

Before he could get an answer, Dahlgren had already opened the submersible's top hatch and climbed out. Dirk purged the *Badger*'s tanks of all seawater to attain maximum buoyancy, then nudged the submersible forward till he tapped the stern of the tender. Dahlgren immediately hopped from the sub to the boat, then from the boat to the platform, tightly clutching a mooring line while he moved. Dirk quickly shut down the submersible's power systems and climbed onto the platform as Dahlgren tied off the mooring line.

'This way to the penthouse,' Dahlgren said in a gentlemanly tone as he motioned an arm toward the adjacent stairwell. Climbing onto the metal stairs, the two men moved rapidly, racing up the steps in a measured pace, while careful to minimize the clamor of their movements. Reaching the top flight of steps, they stopped for a moment and caught their breath, then stepped onto the exterior deck of the platform.

Standing on the forward corner of the platform, they came eye to eye with two enormous cigar-shaped fuel tanks that were encompassed by a maze of pipes and tubing. The massive white tanks stored the Zenit's flammable diet of kerosene and liquid oxygen. Beyond the tanks, at the rear of the platform, they saw the Zenit itself standing like a lonely monolith surrounded by open deck. They stood for a moment, mesmerized by the size and sheer power of the rocket without even considering the lethality of its payload. Dirk then looked up at the hangar towering beside them, capped by a helipad at its forward edge.

'I'm pretty sure the bridge sits above the hangar. That's where we need to get to.'

Dahlgren studied the structure methodically. 'Looks like we'll have to go through the hangar to get there.'

Without another word, the two men took off at a fast jog, wary of being observed as they dashed to the end of the five-story-high hangar. Reaching the deck side with its open barn doors, Dirk carefully peered around the edge to look inside. The long narrow hangar looked like a huge empty cavern without the Zenit lying prone inside. With Dahlgren on his heels, Dirk slipped around the door and into the hangar, moving quietly behind a large generator mounted next to the wall. Voices suddenly echoed across the empty chamber and the men froze in their tracks.

Midway down the length of the hangar, a door flew open on the opposite side and the voices fell quiet. Three gaunt-looking men in Sea Launch jumpsuits staggered through the door and into the hangar followed by two armed commandos. Dirk recognized the black commando outfits and the AK-74 assault rifles as those he'd seen on the men who attacked the *Deep Endeavor*. He and Dahlgren watched as the three men were marched to a fabricated storage room situated near the far end of the hangar. Two additional commandos stood guard over the storage bay and helped to herd the Sea Launch workers inside before closing and locking the door behind them.

'If we can get to the Sea Launch crew, they'll know how to stop the launch,' Dirk said in a low voice.

'Right. We ought to be able to take care of Mutt and Jeff, once their friends leave,' Dahlgren replied, motioning toward the two storage bay guards.

Creeping to a vantage spot near the transporter/ erector, they waited and watched as the first two commandos chatted with the guards for a moment, then left through the side door. Ducking and weaving through an array of electronic test racks and tool bins that lined the sides of the hangar, Dirk and Dahlgren quietly crept closer to the guarded storage bay. Along the way, they passed a rack of tools marked HYDRAULIC ENGINEER. Hesitating for a second, Dirk grabbed a long-handled wooden block mallet while Dahlgren grabbed an oversized box wrench for insurance. Scrambling past the end of the transporter/erector, they silently darted behind a work platform that sat a hundred feet from the storage room.

'What now, maestro?' Dahlgren whispered, seeing that there was nothing but open deck between them and the storage bay.

Dirk crouched against a wheel of the work platform and looked across toward the guards. The two armed commandos were engaged in an animated conversation with each other, paying little attention to the rest of the hangar. He then took a studious look at the platform they had ducked behind. It was a motorized work platform that rose up and down to allow access to the topsides of the thirteen-foot-diameter rocket. Dirk patted his hand on the wheel beside him and threw a crooked grin toward Dahlgren.

'Jack,' he whispered, 'I believe you shall drive in the front door while I waltz in the back door.'

Seconds later, Dirk quietly made his way down the side of the hangar, careful to move only when the guards showed their backs in his direction. After several short running bursts, he reached the rear of the hangar, where he made his way across the width section undetected. As long as the guards stayed positioned near the front of the storage bay, he could approach from behind without being seen.

Dahlgren, meanwhile, was left with the more daring part of the offensive. Climbing onto the motorized work platform, Dahlgren grabbed hold of the cabled control box, then lay flat on the platform. A canvas tarp was partially rolled up on one side, which he used to cover himself with. Peering through a crack at the guards, he gently tapped at the RAISE button on the controls when the guards were turned the other way. With barely a whir, the platform rose a half foot. Out of audio range, the two guards were oblivious. Dahlgren waited again until the guards were looking away, then hit the control button again, this time holding it down firmly. The work platform rose quietly like an elevator, its electric motor barely humming. Dahlgren held his breath and waited until the scaffold reached a height of fifteen feet before releasing the button to stop. Peeking down at the guards, Dahlgren could see that the movement had gone undetected.

'Now for the fun part,' he muttered to himself.

Hitting the drive controls, the entire work platform lurched forward on its four wheels, rolling ahead at a slow crawl. Dahlgren adjusted the drive mechanism to aim the platform directly toward the storage building and two guards, then hunkered down under the canvas tarp and lay still.

The towering platform crept halfway across the hangar like a robot before one of the guards detected its movement. From under the tarp, Dahlgren heard an excited rush of gibberish in an Asian tongue, but, thankfully, no sound of gunfire followed. A loud cry of 'Saw!' screeched through the air, and was repeated a few seconds later as the confused guards called for the contraption to halt. Dahlgren ignored the cry and kept rolling across the floor. Peeking through a crack in the canvas, he saw the roofline of the storage shed approaching and knew he was close to the guards. He waited until the platform rolled to within five feet of the storage building, then pressed the STOP button. The confused guards fell silent as the raised platform quietly rolled to a standstill.

The tension in the air was palpable and Dahlgren milked it for full effect. Beneath him, the two guards stared nervously at the mysterious platform, their fingers sweaty on the triggers of their guns. From their vantage, the bewildering platform had rolled across the floor empty but for a tarp and a loose spool of rope. Perhaps it was just a simple mechanical failure that caused it to roll forward. Cautiously, they stepped closer to inspect the platform. Concealed in the tarp, Dahlgren held his breath and then hit the control button.

Like a mechanical ghost, the platform suddenly began lowering itself. The two guards jumped back as the accordion-support structure slowly collapsed and the wooden scaffold dropped toward the ground. Then, at a height of six feet, the platform abruptly stopped. The platform stood a good six inches taller than either man and they both stood back several feet, trying to eye who or what was driving the thing. Finally, one of the guards approached on his tiptoes and began thrusting the muzzle of his assault rifle into the roll of canvas while his partner stood back peering around the hangar suspiciously.

Dahlgren knew that he would have only one chance to disable the guard and discreetly extended his right arm above his head to prepare for the blow. Through the ruffled canvas, he could feel the prodding of the guard move closer until the thrusting muzzle finally struck home against his thigh. The startled guard hesitated for a second before pulling the gun back to fire. But it was all the time that Dahlgren needed to swing the heavy box wrench out from under the canvas and down hard in a pendulum motion toward the man's head. The hard metal face of the wrench struck the guard square on the jaw with a muffled thump, by some miracle not crushing the bone. But the blow was powerful enough to send the man straight to sleep and the unconscious guard crumpled raggedly to the floor without firing a shot.

Dahlgren's strike had yanked back the screening cover of the canvas as the second guard swung around to find his partner lying senseless on the floor. Dahlgren stared back helplessly at the guard, holding the bloody wrench clasped in his hand. Without hesitation, the guard raised his AK-74 at Dahlgren and squeezed the trigger. But a simultaneous blur from behind flew through the air and collided with the back of the man's head, sending him tumbling to the ground as the burst of fire sprayed from his gun. The jolt was just enough to alter his aim and the bullets struck harmlessly beneath Dahlgren's raised perch. As the guard fell to the ground, Dahlgren could see the tall figure of Dirk standing twenty feet behind, a determined expression on his face. In a desperate move to save his friend's life, Dirk had tossed the mallet like a long-handled ax, the hammer spinning through the air until the business end struck the guard's head like a croquet ball.

The guard was only stunned by the blow, however, and dazedly rose to his knees, trying to retrain his gun. Dahlgren quickly jumped from the scaffold and reeled back to swing the wrench again when a burst of gunfire split the air. Dahlgren froze as a neat row of bullet holes popped through the platform support just inches from his head. The sound of spent shell casings rattled across the floor as the echo of the gunfire through the hangar gradually subsided.

'I would advise you not to move either, Mr. Pitt,' spat the menacing voice of Tongju, who stood in the side doorway cradling a machine gun.

54

Dirk and Dahlgren were held at gunpoint as Tongju and his team of commandos herded the remaining Sea Launch crew members into the storage shed. When Captain Christiano was lastly escorted in, one of the guards turned to Tongju.

'These two as well?' he asked, nodding toward the NUMA captives.

Tongju shook his head no with a faint look of pleasure. The guard then sealed the heavy metal door to the storage bay shut, securing the handle with a chain and padlock. Locked inside, thirty Sea Launch crewmen were crammed into a black, windowless box with no means of escape.

Once the door was secured, Tongju walked over to the hangar wall, where Dirk and Dahlgren stood staring at a pair of gun muzzles aimed at their ribs. Tongju gazed at Dirk with a mixed look of respect and disdain.

'You have an annoying proclivity for survival, Mr. Pitt, which is exceeded only by your irritating penchant for intrusion.'

'I'm just a bad penny,' Dirk replied.

'Since you have taken such a keen interest in our operation, perhaps you would enjoy a front-row viewing of the launch?' Tongju said, nodding toward three of the guards.

Before Dirk could reply, the guards were prodding rifles into their backs, steering them in the direction of the open hangar doors. One of the guards reached up onto Dahlgren's work platform and snatched the coil of rope that lay next to the canvas roll. Tongju hung back a moment, ordering his remaining assault team to the tender, before following behind. As they walked, the two prisoners glanced at each other in mental search of an escape plan, but their options were slim. Dirk knew that Tongju would not hesitate to kill them instantly, and relish the opportunity.

Tongju caught up with them as they marched out of the hangar and into the bright sunshine that washed down on the open deck.

'You know, of course, that military units are on their way to the platform at this very moment,' Dirk said to the assassin, silently hoping his words were true. 'The launch will be stopped and you and your men will be captured, or perhaps killed.'

Tongju looked up at the launch clock, then turned to Dirk and smiled, his yellow-stained teeth glistening in the sunlight.

'They will not arrive in time. And if they do, there will be no consequence. The soft American military will not attack the platform for fear of killing the innocent workers aboard. There is no way to stop the countdown now. The launch will proceed, Mr.

Pitt, and bring an end to the meddlesome activities of both you and your countrymen.'

'You'll never escape alive.'

'Nor you, I'm afraid.'

Dirk and Dahlgren fell silent as they trudged across the open platform, feeling like two men marching to the gallows. As they approached the launch tower, all of the men could not help but look up at the shimmering white rocket that towered over them. The captives were led to the very base of the standing rocket, which clung to the tower several feet above them. Dirk and Dahlgren were shoved against a tower bracing and ordered to stand still as the guard with the rope began cutting it into several lengths with a serrated knife.

Tongju stood and casually unholstered his Glock, aiming it at Dirk's throat, as a guard hog-tied his wrists and elbows behind his back and around a tower support beam. The guard then tied his ankles together and wrapped them to the beam before moving over to Dahlgren and roping him to the tower in the same fashion.

'Enjoy the launch, gentlemen,' Tongju hissed, then turned and walked away.

'We shall, knowing that vermin like you won't have long to breathe,' Dirk cursed.

He and Dahlgren watched silently as Tongju and his men jogged across the platform toward the forward support column and disappeared down the stairwell. A few minutes later, they observed the tender speeding away toward the *Koguryo*, which was now positioned nearly two miles from the *Odyssey*. From their captive position, they had a clear view of the launch clock as it ticked down to 00:26:00, twenty-six minutes. Dirk looked up and morbidly studied the Zenit's huge thrusters that hung several feet above their heads. At the first seconds of launch, 1.6 million pounds of thrust would be expelled onto them like a firestorm, incinerating their bodies to ashes. At least it would be a quick death, he thought.

'I guess that's the last time I let you talk me into crashing a party uninvited,' Dahlgren said, breaking the tension.

'Sorry, I guess we were a little underdressed,' Dirk replied without humor. He tugged and twisted at the binding ropes, searching for an avenue of escape, but there was little room to even wiggle his hands.

'Any chance you can slip your ropes?' he asked hopefully of Dahlgren.

'Afraid not. This guy definitely earned his merit badge in knot tying,' Dahlgren said, pulling at his restraints.

A loud clanging across the platform seized their attention, which was followed by a deep rumbling beneath their feet. The rushing sound of flowing liquid bellowed up behind them, roaring up and overhead through a series of pipes built into the launch tower. The pipes creaked and groaned around them as they protested the flow of the supercooled liquid oxygen and kerosene being pumped into the Zenit.

'They're fueling the rocket,' Dirk observed. 'Too dangerous to do with the crew aboard so they wait until just prior to launch, after the platform has been evacuated.'

'That makes me feel so much better. I just hope the guy manning the pump doesn't get sloppy and overfill the tank.'

They both looked up at the rocket in apprehension, knowing that a spill of liquid oxygen would burn right through their skin. The rocket shuddered and wailed as it drank in the liquid fuel, seeming to come alive with the infusion. Pumps and motors whirred above their heads as priming fuel was released into the rocket engine's initial combustion chamber. Both men stared up in numbed silence at the mouth of the rocket thrusters, contemplating the impending conflagration that would rain upon them. Dirk thought of Sarah and felt a sudden pang in his chest, realizing he would never see her again. Worse still, he remembered that she was visiting Los Angeles. She, too, might well succumb to the effects of the missile launch, a launch that he had failed to prevent. Then his sister and father sprang to mind and he felt remorse in that they would never know what befell his disappearance. There certainly wouldn't be any remains left to bury, he thought morbidly. His attention was drawn to a low hiss, caused by puffs of white steam venting out of several safety valves along the Zenit's exterior. As the chilled oxygen warmed in the daytime air, the expanding vapor was purged from the rocket, accumulating in wispy clouds above their heads. To the cruel irony of the two captives awaiting death in their last minutes, the sky seemed to darken over them as the vapor shadows obscured the rays of the sun. But Dirk's heart suddenly skipped a beat when he realized that the shadow cast over them above the rocket was slowly creeping across the platform deck.

Even from high in the sky, the Sea Launch platform and Zenit rocket looked impressive. But for the men in the *Icarus*, the focus was not one of sightseeing. There was no puttering around the airspace this time as the blimp came floating directly over the stationary platform.

'There's the *Badger*. She's tied up alongside the forward support column,' Giordino said, pointing toward a corner of the platform where the red submersible could be seen bobbing in the water.

'Dirk and Jack clearly made it aboard,' Pitt replied with a touch of concern.

Upon receiving a radio call from Summer on the *Deep Endeavor* that the *Narwhal* had been attacked, Pitt immediately yanked the blimp around to the south and came charging back at full speed. The twin Porsche engines affixed to the gondola whined as the rpms climbed and the airship was pushed to its top speed of 50 knots. On the horizon, Pitt and Giordino could see the black smoke from the *Narwhal*'s smoldering hull rising like a beacon before the ship slipped underwater. Pitt willed the blimp toward the debris as fast as the ungainly airship would go while Giordino focused the long-distance camera at the site ahead. As they grew nearer, they observed the *Koguryo* distancing herself from the platform, while discovering little remains of the Coast Guard vessel through the magnified camera lens.

'You might not want to cruise too close to that support ship,' Giordino cautioned after several tight passes over the *Narwhal* site failed to reveal any survivors.

'You think she's carrying SAMs?' Pitt asked.

'She stung the *Narwhal* with a surface-to-surface, so it's a betting chance.'

'I'll keep the platform positioned in between us. That should dissuade them from firing on us and, hopefully, alleviate your *Hindenburg* fears.'

Pitt brought the airship down to an altitude of five hundred feet and eased back on the high-revving motors as they approached the platform. Giordino focused the WESCOM camera onto the *Koguryo* standing off in the distance, eyeing it warily for signs of a potential strike on the blimp. The shuttle boat suddenly lurched into view on the monitor as it pulled up alongside the ship. Pitt and Giordino watched as Tongju and the last of his assault team climbed onto the larger vessel. Pitt noted that Jack and his son were not among the group.

'The last of the rats leaving the platform?' Giordino asked.

'Could be. Doesn't look like they are sending the tender back. Let's see if we can find anyone left minding the store.'

The blimp drifted over the stern of the platform and Pitt guided the airship along the length of the portside deck toward the bow. Not a soul could be seen wandering the deck below. Giordino pointed out the backward-ticking clock on the hangar, which read 00:27:00, twenty-seven minutes. As they floated past the forward edge, Pitt turned and ran across the *Odyssey*'s bow and alongside the roof-mounted pilothouse. Giordino swung the camera until it pointed into the windows of the platform's command station. On the monitor, they could see clearly into the bridge. Scanning back and forth, there was not a solitary sign of life.

'Looks like the ghostship *Mary Celeste* around here,' Giordino said.

'No doubt about it. They're getting ready to light the fuse.'

Pitt turned the blimp's controls again and brought the airship down the length of the starboard side, then circled tightly around the Zenit rocket. Plumes of white smoke spewed from the release valves on the rocket, venting the warming fuel. Giordino panned up and down the rocket with the camera system.

'She looks gassed and ready to roll at any minute.'

'Twenty-six minutes, to be precise,' Pitt said, eyeing the countdown clock.

Giordino let out a whistle as he glanced at the clock. A slight movement on the monitor brought his eyes back to the rocket display, but he still almost missed it. He curiously tweaked the focus down the length of the rocket until the monitor suddenly filled with the image of two men standing at the base of the tower.

'It's Dirk and Jack! They're tied to the tower.'

Pitt stared at the screen for a moment and nodded, his eyes squinting in recognition. Without saying a word, he quickly scanned the platform for a spot to bring the blimp down. Though the rear deck of the platform offered a large open space between the hangar and the launch tower, a tall crane was angled up and inward, impeding the airspace. The airship's fabric sides might gash open if contact were made with the structure.

'Nice of them to leave the can opener out for us,' Giordino said as he peered at the imposing crane.

'No troubles. We'll just have to make like a helicopter.'

Skimming over the hangar and descending rapidly, Pitt eased the blimp down toward the large round helipad mounted above the pilothouse. With a finesse touch, he eased the blimp down until the gondola lightly kissed the pad.

'Can I trust you not to go off sightseeing without me?' Pitt asked as he hastily climbed out of the pilot's seat.

'Cross my heart.'

'Give me ten minutes. If we're not back, then just get this thing the hell away from the platform before she lights up.'

'I'll keep the meter running,' Giordino replied, giving Pitt a nod of good luck.

In a flash, Pitt was out the gondola door and sprinting across the pad. As he disappeared down a stairwell, Giordino looked at his watch and anxiously started counting the seconds.

55

Tongju climbed aboard the *Koguryo* and immediately raced to the bridge, where Captain Lee and Kim stood surveying the *Odyssey*.

'You cut your departure a little thin,' Lee said soberly. 'They have already commenced fueling the rocket.'

'A minor delay, due to an unexpected interruption,' Tongju replied. Scanning the horizon, he noted the airship drifting slowly back toward the platform. 'Have you detected any more approaching vessels?'

The captain shook his head. 'No, none yet. Besides the airship, there has just been the lone research ship that was following behind the Coast Guard vessel,' he said, pointing to a radar blip on the opposite side of the platform. 'She's remained in her present position, two miles to the northeast of the platform.'

'And no doubt has radioed for assistance. Those damn Ukrainians,' he spat. 'They have brought us too close to shore and placed the mission in peril. Captain, we must get under way immediately after liftoff. Adjust course due south at full power to Mexican waters before laying in for our rendezvous point.'

'What about the airship?' Kim asked. 'It must be destroyed as well, for it can track our escape.'

Tongju studied the silver blimp, which sat hovering on the *Odyssey*'s helicopter pad.

'We cannot fire upon them while they are positioned near the platform. They can do no harm at this late time. Perhaps they will stupidly burn in the launch themselves. Come, let us enjoy the liftoff. We will dispense with them later.'

With Kim in tow, Tongju left the bridge and quickly made his way aft to the launch control center. The brightly lit bay was packed with white-coated engineers sitting at workstations arranged in a horseshoe shape around the room. On the front center wall was a large flat-panel video screen that showed a full image of the Zenit rocket at the launch tower, wisps of vapor emanating from its sides. Tongju spotted Ling hunched over a monitor conversing with a technician and approached the launch operations engineer.

'Ling, what is the launch status?' Tongju asked.

The round-faced engineer squinted at Tongju through his glasses.

'The fueling will be complete in another two minutes. One of the backup flight control computers is not responding, there's a low-pressure reading in one of the cooling lines, and the number two auxiliary turbopump indicator shows a fluid leakage.'

'What does that mean for the launch?' Tongju asked, a sudden flush rising over his normally placid face.

'None of the items, either individually or collectively, are mission critical. All other systems are showing nominal. The launch will proceed as scheduled,' he said, eyeing a digital launch clock beneath the video panel, 'in exactly twenty-three minutes and forty-seven seconds.'

At twenty-three minutes and forty-six seconds, Jack Dahlgren looked up from the *Odyssey*'s ticking launch clock to the *Icarus*, which seemed to be fixed hovering above the pilothouse. He knew there was no chance that they could have been spotted by the high-flying gondola, but he still wondered if Pitt or Giordino might somehow find a way to stop the launch. He strained to turn toward Dirk beside him, expecting his friend to be looking at the blimp with hopeful optimism. Instead, Dirk was oblivious to the airship, his full attention focused on defiantly trying to break the bounds of his ropes. Jack started to offer some words of encouragement but his lips froze when he saw a movement inside the hangar. He blinked and took another hard look. Sure enough, he could see it was a man sprinting through the hangar directly toward them.

'Dirk, there's somebody coming our way. Is that who I think it is?'

Dirk glanced toward the hangar while continuing to strain at his bound hands and feet. He squinted at the lone figure bursting out of the hangar and tearing across the platform carrying what looked like a long stick in his hand. The figure was tall and lean with dark hair and Dirk suddenly stopped struggling at the ropes when he recognized the gait.

'I don't ever recall seeing my father move that fast before,' he said to Dahlgren, a broad grin spreading across his face.

As the head of NUMA drew closer, they could see that it was a fire ax, not a stick, that he toted in his right hand as he ran. Sprinting up to the tower, the elder Pitt smiled in relief at seeing that the two men were uninjured.

'I thought I told you boys never to accept a ride with strangers,' he gasped, patting his son on the shoulder as he examined the rope restraints.

'Sorry, Dad, but they offered us the moon and the stars,' Dirk grinned, then added, 'Thanks for dropping by to get us.'

'I've got a taxi waiting. Let's just get out of here before they ignite this thing.'

Eyeing the center of the rope, he took a full swing and laid the blade through the rope that secured Dirk's elbows. With another swing, he cut the wrist binds, the blade of the ax tinging loudly as it cut through to the tower beam. As Dirk worked to untie his ankles, Pitt repeated his Paul Bunyan routine on Dahlgren's ropes. The two men quickly scrambled to their feet as Pitt tossed the ax aside.

'Dad, the Sea Launch platform team is locked up inside the hangar. We need to get them out.'

Pitt nodded. 'I thought I heard some banging around in there. Lead on.'

Almost as one, the three men dashed back across the open platform at full speed, knowing that every second counted. As they ran, Dirk looked at the launch clock above his head. Just twenty-one minutes and thirty-six seconds remained before the platform would be engulfed in a blasting inferno. As if that wasn't enough motivation to move faster, a sudden whirring noise erupted from inside the hangar. An electronic command had been issued from the *Koguryo*'s launch control software and the hangar's large barn doors began sliding closed in preparation for the blastoff.

'The doors are closing,' Dahlgren huffed. 'We've got to hurry.'

Like a trio of Olympic sprinters heading to the tape, the men bolted side by side toward the shrinking gap of the closing doors. Though he still had plenty of fire in his step, Pitt eased back as they approached the opening and let Dirk and Dahlgren jump through first. Following single file, he turned and slid sideways through the gap just before the doors sealed shut.

Midway down the hangar, they could hear the sound of muffled voices and a metallic banging as the men inside the metal shed fought to extricate themselves. Dirk, Dahlgren, and Pitt scurried to the shed and examined the chained and padlocked door as they caught their breath.

'That chain isn't going to give, but maybe we can pry the door off its hinges . . . if we can find a crowbar around here,' Dahlgren said, scanning the area for a potential tool.

Pitt glanced at the motorized work platform Jack had ridden across the hangar and reached up and grabbed the control box, which dangled from the railing.

'I think we've got our crowbar right here,' he said, lowering the platform a few feet, then rolling the device up to the front of the shed. As Dirk and Dahlgren looked on, Pitt grabbed a loose end of the padlock chain and wrapped it tightly around the platform's railing, then yelled at the men inside the shed: 'Stand back from the door.'

Waiting a second, he then hit the RAISE button and watched as the platform rose slowly, drawing the chain tight. The lifting mechanism groaned and strained for a moment as the wheels of the platform rocked across the floor. Then, with a loud crack, the shed's door ripped off its hinges and popped into the air, slamming against the platform with a shudder before dropping and dangling from the chain midair. Pitt quickly backed the platform out of the way as the Sea Launch crew surged out of the claustrophobic shed.

The crewmen had been given little to eat since the *Odyssey* was commandeered and they appeared weak and haggard from the stress of their captivity. Yet an underlying anger purveyed over the men, a group of seasoned professionals who didn't take kindly to having given up their rocket and platform.

'Is the captain and launch manager here?' Pitt shouted over the cries of thanks from the released crew.

A battered Captain Christiano elbowed his way through the throng, followed by a thin, distinguished-looking man with a goatee.

'I'm Christiano, captain of the *Odyssey*. This is Larry Ohlrogge, platform launch manager,' he added, nodding to the man beside him. 'Has the platform been secured from those scum?' he spat with contempt.

Pitt shook his head. 'They've evacuated the platform in preparation for launching the rocket. We don't have much time.'

Ohlrogge noted the erector/transporter had been returned to the hangar and that the hangar doors had been closed.

'We're talking minutes,' he said with alarm in his voice.

'About eighteen, to be precise. Captain, get your crew to the helipad now,' Pitt directed. 'There's an airship waiting that can evacuate everyone from the platform if we move quick.'

Turning to Ohlrogge, Pitt added, 'Is there any way we can stop the launch?'

'The launch sequence is completely automated and controlled by the assembly and command ship. Presumably, these terrorists have duplicated that functionality on their own vessel.'

'We can mechanically halt the fueling of the rocket,' Christiano noted.

'It is too late,' Ohlrogge said, shaking his head. 'There is an override control in the bridge that would be our only hope at this late time,' he added grimly.

'The elevator at the rear of the hangar leads to the bridge deck. The helipad is just above,' Christiano said.

'Then let's get moving,' Pitt replied.

Quickly, the group shuffled en masse to the rear of the hangar and crowded around a medium-sized elevator.

'There's not enough room for all,' Christiano stated, regaining his captain's form. 'We'll need three trips. You eight men first, then this group, then you ten men over there,' he ordered, dividing the crowd into three groups.

'Jack, you go with the first group and help them onto the *Icarus*. Let Al know there's more on the way,' Pitt said. 'Dirk, you bring up the last group, make sure everyone makes it out of here. Captain, we need to visit the bridge now,' he said, turning to Christiano.

Christiano, Ohlrogge, Dahlgren, and Pitt crowded into the elevator with eight other men and waited impatiently as the elevator zipped up to the bridge level above the hangar. Dahlgren quickly located a stairwell off to one side that led to the helipad and herded the crewmen up to the exposed deck.

As promised, the silver airship hung hovering several feet above the pad, Giordino at the controls smoking a fat cigar. He quickly rotated the swiveling propulsion ducts and brought the gondola down to the deck as Jack ran up.

'Hi, sailor. Give a few girls a ride?' Dahlgren asked, poking his head into the gondola doorway.

'Coitainly,' Giordino replied. 'How many do you have?'

'About thirty, give or take,' Dahlgren replied, looking suspiciously at the gondola's passenger compartment.

'Shove 'em in, we'll make them fit. But we better toss any unnecessary weight if we want to get off the ground. Just make it quick, as I have an aversion to getting baked alive.'

'You and me both, pardner,' Dahlgren replied, herding the first of the crewmen aboard.

In addition to the two-seat cockpit, the gondola's passenger compartment was configured to seat eight passengers in oversized leather airplane-type seats. Dahlgren studied the arrangement and grimaced at the prospect of squeezing all the men in and possibly grounding the blimp. As the crew climbed aboard, he checked the mountings of the seats and found that they had a quick-release mechanism for temporary removal. He quickly unlatched five of the seats and, with the help of a Russian engineer, tossed them out the door of the gondola.

'Everybody to the back of the bus,' he barked. 'It's going to be standing room only.'

As the last man in his group wedged into the passenger compartment, Dahlgren turned to Al.

'How much time do we have?'

'About fifteen minutes, by my count.'

The next group of crewmen began spilling off the stairs and sprinting across the deck of the helipad. Dahlgren let out a slight sigh. There would be time, if not room, to get every man to the blimp before blastoff. But would it be enough time to stop the launch, he wondered, catching sight of the Zenit rocket standing fueled and ready across the platform.

56

Inside the *Odyssey*'s bridge, Captain Christiano turned pale and shook his head silently as he surveyed the bullet-ridden computer stations and shattered glass that littered the floor. Walking to the navigation station, he curiously noticed a lonely computer mouse dangling by its cord, its companion keyboard nowhere to be seen. Ohlrogge observed that the computer drive itself was undamaged.

'I've got scores of laptop computers downstairs. We can plug one in and activate the platform controls,' he offered.

'They have no doubt secured the automated controls,' Christiano said with disgust, thrusting a thumb over his shoulder toward the window. Pitt followed his motion, observing the *Koguryo* sitting defiantly in the distance. Returning his gaze to the captain, Pitt caught sight of the *Badger*, still tied up in the water off the starboard support column far below.

'There is no time. It might take hours to work around,' Christiano continued, moving to the bridge's center console with a look of despair on his face.

'You said there was a manual override on the bridge?' Pitt asked.

Christiano anticipated the results before his eyes

reached the console. They had simply known too much. How to navigate and ballast the platform, how to fuel the Zenit, how to control and launch the rocket from their own support ship. There was simply too much inside knowledge for the terrorists not to have sabotaged the manual override. With disappointing confidence in his beliefs, he looked down at a jumbled mass of cut wires and smashed controls that offered the last hope of halting the launch.

'Here's your manual override control,' he swore, flinging a segregated clump of wires and switches across the bridge. The three men stood in silence as the mass of electronics bounced across the deck before coming to a halt against the bulkhead. Then the bridge door opened and Dirk thrust his head into the bay. From the looks on the other men's faces, he knew that their attempt to prevent the launch had failed.

'The crew is all aboard the airship. I respectfully suggest we abandon the platform, and now.'

As the last four men aboard the platform began to scramble up the helipad stairwell to the waiting airship, Pitt stopped and grabbed his son by the shoulder.

'Get the captain aboard the blimp and tell Al to take off without me. Make sure he gets the airship uprange of the platform before the rocket fires.'

'But they said there was no getting around the

automated launch controls,' the younger Pitt protested.

'I may not be able to stop the rocket from launching, but I just might be able to change its destination.'

'Dad, you can't stay aboard the platform, it's too dangerous.'

'Don't worry about me, I don't intend to stick around,' Pitt replied, giving his son a gentle shove. 'Now get going.'

Dirk looked his father in the eye. He had heard numerous tales of his father placing the safety of others above himself and now he was seeing it firsthand. But there was something else in his eyes. It was a calm look of assurance. Dirk took a step toward the stairwell, then turned back to wish his father luck but he had already vanished down the elevator.

Sprinting up the stairwell two steps at a time, the younger Pitt leaped onto the deck of the helipad and looked on in amazement at the waiting blimp. The gondola looked like a windowed can of sardines, with the fish replaced by humans. The entire Sea Launch crew had managed to squeeze aboard the passenger compartment, cramming into every available square inch. The weakest of the crew were given the three passenger seats that Dahlgren did not remove while the rest of the men stood shoulder to shoulder in the remaining space. Scores of men hung their heads out the side windows while one or two were even jammed into the small bathroom at the rear of the gondola.

The sight made a New York City subway at rush hour look spacious by comparison.

Dirk ran over and wedged himself through the door, hearing Dahlgren's voice somewhere in the mass telling him that the copilot's seat was vacant. Half-crawling, he squirmed his way into the cockpit, taking the empty seat alongside Giordino, who had moved to the left-hand pilot's seat.

'Where's your dad? We need to get off this barbecue grill, pronto.'

'He's staying put. Has one last trick up his sleeve, I guess. He said to get the blimp uprange of the platform, and that he'll meet you for a tequila on the rocks after the show.'

'I hope he's buying,' Giordino replied, then tilted the propeller ducts to a forty-degree angle and boosted the throttles. The gondola chugged forward, pulling the helium-filled envelope with it. But instead of rising gracefully into the air as before, the gondola clung to the deck, dragging across the helipad with a dull scraping sound.

'We've got too much weight,' Dirk stated.

'Get up, baby, get up,' Giordino urged the mammoth airship.

The gondola continued to skid across the pad, heading to the forward edge, which dropped straight down two hundred feet to the sea. As they approached the lip of the helipad, Giordino adjusted the propellers to a higher degree of inclination and jammed the throttles to their stops but the gondola continued to scrape along the deck. An eerie silence filled the cabin, as every man held his breath while the gondola slipped over the edge of the helipad.

A falling surge suddenly hit the pit of everyone's stomach as the gondola lurched down ten feet, then halted. The occupants were roughly thrown forward as the blimp's fabric-covered tail bounced off the helipad, pushing the nose of the blimp at a steep decline as the airship's balance of weight cleared the edge. Continuing to jar forward, the tail finally scraped past the platform edge and the entire blimp rushed nose first toward the sea.

Giordino had a split-second decision to make in order to save the airship. He could either pull the thrusters all the way back to a ninety-degree vector and hope the engine propulsion would overcome the excess weight and hold the blimp at altitude. Or he could do the complete reverse: by pushing down the thrusters, he could try to increase the blimp's forward velocity, which would generate lift if he gained sufficient speed. Staring at the looming ocean, he let the momentum of the blimp guide his decision and calmly pushed the yoke forward, accelerating their downward dive.

Cries of alarm wafted from the rear passengers as it appeared Giordino was deliberately trying to crash into the sea. Ignoring the pleas, he turned to Dirk in the copilot's seat.

'Above your head there is a water ballast release control. At my command, hit the release.'

While Dirk located the button on the overhead console, Giordino focused his eyes on the altimeter. The dial was rolling backward quickly from two hundred feet as their descent speed increased. Giordino hesitated until the dial read sixty feet, then barked: 'Now!'

In unison, Giordino yanked back on the yoke while Dirk activated the water ballast system, which instantly dumped a thousand pounds of water stored in a compartment beneath the gondola. Despite the sudden actions, there was no immediate response from the blimp. The massive airship moved at its own deliberate pace, and, for an instant, Giordino thought he had acted too late. As the approaching ocean filled the view out the cockpit windshield in a rush of speed, the nose gently began to pull up in a sweeping arc. Giordino eased off the yoke to level the airship as the gondola surged closer toward the sea, its nose rising with agonizing slowness. With a sudden jolt, the base of the gondola slapped the water's surface as the airship flattened from of its dive but bounded quickly up and off the surface. As every man aboard held his breath, the blimp staggered forward a short distance before slowly climbing a few feet above the water and holding steady. As the seconds ticked by and the airship held in the air, it became apparent that Giordino had pulled it off. Though risking a high-speed impact, the accelerated dive and last-second ballast release had been just enough to keep them airborne.

The relieved men in the passenger compartment let out a cheer as Giordino gingerly coaxed the blimp up to an altitude of one hundred feet, the big airship slowly stabilizing under his steady hand.

'I guess you showed us who's master of the airship,' Dirk lauded.

'Yeah, and almost commander of a submarine,' Giordino replied as he eased the nose of the blimp to the east and away from the platform.

'Uprange and away from shore isn't exactly the direction I'd like to be going at this altitude,' he added, eyeing the *Koguryo* warily out the window to port. 'I radioed *Deep Endeavor* to get out of the way of the rocket's flight path, so they should be cutting a wide swath around to the north. We ought to keep them in sight in case we have to ditch.'

Dirk scanned the horizon, keeping one eye locked on the launch platform. Far to the southwest, he spotted the distant mass of San Nicolas Island. Peering to the northeast, he saw a tiny blue dot, which he knew to be the *Deep Endeavor*. Then, just to the north of the NUMA ship, he noticed a small brown mass rising from the sea.

'That landmass up ahead. I recall from the navigation charts that it's a small channel island called "Santa Barbara." Why don't we head that way? We can drop the crew there and have *Deep Endeavor* pick them up before we get into any more trouble.'

'And get back to find your dad,' Giordino said,

finishing Dirk's thought. Dirk looked back at the platform with hesitation.

'Can't be much time left,' he muttered.

'About ten minutes,' Giordino replied, wondering like Dirk what Pitt could possibly pull off in such little time.

57

Physically surviving a launch on board the *Odyssey* was not impossible. When a rocket was fired, the main thrust was directed beneath the platform at ignition. The *Odyssey* had been constructed as a re-usable launch platform, and, in fact, had already withstood more than a dozen launches. The deck, hangar, crew compartment, and pilothouse were all built to withstand the fiery heat and exhaust gener-ated from a powerful rocket launch. What a human inhabitant was not likely to survive, however, was the noxious fumes that engulfed the platform at blastoff. A massive billow of exhaust from the spent kerosene and liquid oxygen fuel all but buried the *Odyssey* in a thick cloud of smoke for several minutes after liftoff, smothering the breathable air in the vicinity of the platform.

But that was of little concern to Pitt as he jumped off the elevator and raced out a back door of the hangar. He had no interest in hanging around the platform when the Zenit was lit off. Instead, he was hell-bent on making it to the bright red submersible he saw bobbing in the water from the pilothouse window. Like a contestant running a timed obstacle course, Pitt ran, jumped, and hurdled his way across the platform to the corner column support and sprinted down the steps to the water's edge. In their haste to evacuate the platform, Tongju and his men had not thought it necessary to let adrift the NUMA sub. Pitt was thankful to find her still tied to the column steps as he exhaustedly reached the water's edge.

Untying the line, he jumped aboard and scrambled down the *Badger*'s top hatch, sealing it closed behind him. In seconds, he had activated the submersible's power systems and opened the ballast tank for submersion. Engaging the throttles, he quickly maneuvered away from the *Odyssey*'s forward column and proceeded down the interior length of the platform before positioning the submersible for the task at hand. Holding the submersible steady, Pitt activated the controls to the bow-mounted coring device and, with just minutes to spare, prayed that his cockamamie plan would work.

The Korean launch team aboard the *Koguryo* watched the video screen with curiosity as the silver blimp touched down on the *Odyssey*'s helipad and the crew of the platform jammed into the gondola. Kim grimaced with anger but noted that Tongju remained calm.

'We should have killed the crew and destroyed that airship when we had the opportunity,' Kim hissed as they watched the *Icarus* lurch off the platform. An alternate camera was turned toward the blimp, showing the airship fight for altitude before turning out to sea. Tongju nodded toward the video image with assurance.

'She is overloaded and unable to make speed. We shall easily catch and destroy her after the launch,' he said quietly to Kim.

His eyes returned to the launch countdown and the noisy jabber of the engineers within the control center. The room was a flurry of activity and pressure as the final minutes drew to a close. Ling stood nearby, reviewing the output from a series of launch vehicle assessments. Beads of sweat rolled from his forehead in tense anticipation despite the cool temperature of the air-conditioned bay.

For Ling, there was every reason to be nervous. In the world of space vehicle delivery, there was an astounding rate of mortality. He knew all too well that roughly one in ten satellite launches ended in failure, and that the fault could come from a thousand and one sources. Failure of the rocket at launch was still not an uncommon occurrence, though most satellite losses were due to deploying the payload in an incorrect orbit. The short, suborbital flight of the mission at hand eliminated a great deal of the problematic issues associated with most rocket flights, but the risk of a catastrophic launch failure never went away.

Ling breathed easier as he digested the latest status updates. All critical systems appeared operational. There was nothing to indicate that the trustworthy

Zenit rocket would not fire off in its usual dependable manner. With less than five minutes to go, he turned to Tongju and spoke with a glimmer of confidence.

'There will be no launch holds. The countdown will proceed unimpeded.'

Their attention turned to the image of the rocket on the video screen in its last minutes before takeoff. Despite the multitude of studious eyes converged on the image of the rocket and platform, no one in the room noticed the tiny movement at the periphery of the picture. Only the camera saw as a dark-haired man ran to the edge of the platform and scrambled out of sight down the corner column stairwell.

Pitt had wasted no time in engaging the full set of thrusters that powered the *Badger*. Though he knew it was the worst possible place to be, he quickly guided the submersible down the underbelly length of the platform and maneuvered the vehicle to a stop alongside the rear starboard support column. Directly above him was the recessed launchpad flame deflector, which would route the titanic blast of the Zenit's thrust toward the sea at liftoff.

Pitt turned the nose of the submersible until it was aimed at the column, then backed away from the rotund support leg as he submerged the vessel to a depth of fifteen feet. Using a set of manipulator controls, he lowered the huge coring probe until it stretched perfectly horizontal in front of the submarine's prow, protruding like a medieval jousting lance. Pitt braced his feet against the metal deck plate and muttered, 'Okay, *Badger*, let's see your bite,' as he jammed the throttles to FULL FORWARD.

The shiny red submersible clawed its way through the water, quickly gaining speed over the short distance to the column. Pushed by the full weight and force of the submersible, the coring probe slammed into the side of the massive steel column with a bang. Pitt held his breath as he was jolted forward and continued to slide ahead until the nose of the submersible slapped against the column. Rammed to a halt, he quickly threw the thrusters in reverse and peered through the surging bubbles as the submersible backed away from the column. A metallic grating sound echoed back at him as the probe was drawn roughly off the column. Through the murky and turbulent water, he caught a glimpse of the coring probe jutting intact off the bow and he exhaled in relief. As Pitt had hoped, the momentum of the speedy submersible had driven the tip of the coring probe cleanly through the side of the support column, opening an eight-inch-diameter hole.

Pitt felt a little like Ezra Lee on the *Turtle*. The Revolutionary War volunteer had attempted to sink a British warship in David Bushnell's small wooden submarine by drilling a hole in the side and attaching a mine. Though the attempt failed, the *Turtle* would be remembered in history as the first submarine ever used in combat. With the benefit of propulsion, Pitt backed the *Badger* away twenty feet and adjusted his depth slightly, then reversed the thrusters and charged into the column again. Once more, the probe tore through the outer wall of the column, leaving a neat round hole for the seawater to pour into.

Though abjectly crude, Pitt's mad ploy had an element of simple genius to it. He calculated that if there was no way to stop the rocket from lifting off, then, perhaps, there was a way to change its intended destination. By creating an imbalance in the platform, he might at least angle the rocket off its intended flight path. On such a short flight, the rocket's guidance system would not have sufficient time to fully correct the deviation and could miss its intended target by miles. And there was no doubt that the Achilles' heel of the platform at launch were the rear support columns. With the rocket standing vertically at the extreme rear edge of the platform, the *Odyssey* had to maintain a careful balance to handle the uneven weight distribution across the entire platform. An active trim-and-heel system utilized ballast tanks in the columns and pontoons to maintain stability, managed by six large ballast pumps. By flooding the rear support columns, there was a chance of destabilizing the launch deck. For Pitt, it would be a desperate race against the ballast pumps to create a material imbalance.

Like a passenger on a carnival ride gone amok, Pitt was violently thrown about the submersible as he rammed into the column time and time again. Electronic equipment was jarred from its mounts, crashing and flying about his feet with each impact. The nose section of the submersible soon became battered after repeated collisions with the column wall and small rivulets of salt water began streaming into the interior through the damaged seams. But none of this mattered to Pitt. The risk to himself and the submersible was the last concern on his mind as the seconds to launch ticked down. One more time, he flung the force of the submersible against the support column, poking a hole in its surface like a rampant mosquito, the jab not drawing blood but letting in a flood of water.

After more than a dozen strikes at the starboard column, Pitt spun the leaking *Badger* around and raced toward the rear port support. Glancing at his Doxa watch, he calculated there was less than two minutes before liftoff. With a towering crash, he slammed into the other support column, driving the probe to its base and further crumbling the nose of the submersible. More water began leaking into the interior but Pitt ignored it. With salt water sloshing around his feet, he calmly reversed thrust and backed away for another stab at the column. As he lined up for another assault, he wondered if his actions were the futile gesture of an underwater Don Quixote charging at an errant windmill.

Unknown to Pitt, his very first blow on the starboard support column had activated one of the ballast pumps. As the number of holes and the amount of inrushing water increased, additional pumps were activated, until all six pumps were engaged. The pumps operated at the base of the columns, which were already submerged some forty feet under the water. While the automated ballast system easily kept each pontoon level with one another side by side, there was only limited means of maintaining balance fore and aft. With the water level rising rapidly in the stern support columns, it didn't take long before Pitt's drilling overwhelmed the rear ballast pumps. The sinking stern of the platform created a programming dilemma for the automated stabilization system. Under normal conditions, the trim-and-heel system would compensate the aft list by flooding the forward compartments and lowering the overall platform depth. But the platform was in launch position and had already been flooded to launching depth. Ballasting the platform lower, the computer knew, risked damaging the low-hanging thrust deflectors. In a handful of nanoseconds, the computer program reviewed its software logic for priority actions. The results came back unambiguous. During a designated launch countdown, the stabilization system was to maintain launch depth as its first priority. The sinking aft columns would be ignored.

58

Aboard the *Koguryo*, a red warning light began blinking in the launch control room with less than two minutes to go. A bespectacled engineer studied the platform stabilization warning for a moment, then jotted down some notations and briskly stepped over to Ling.

'Mr. Ling, we have a platform stabilization warning,' he reported.

'What is the deviation?' Ling asked hurriedly.

'An aft list of three degrees.'

'That is inconsequential,' he replied, brushing off the engineer. Turning to Tongju, who stood at his side, he said, 'A list of five degrees or less is no cause for concern.'

Tongju could almost taste the results of the launch now. There could be no turning back now.

'Do not halt the launch for any reason,' he hissed at Ling in a low voice. The chief engineer gritted his teeth and nodded, then stared nervously at the waiting rocket that stood shimmering on the video screen.

The interior of the *Badger* was a jumbled mess of tools, computer parts, and interior pieces that sloshed back and forth across the floor with each jerk of the sub. Pitt remained oblivious to the carnage as he rammed the submersible against the platform column for the umpteenth time. Seawater slapped at his calves as he braced himself for yet another collision, listening for the warning bam of the core probe as it punched into the column side. Thrown harshly forward at impact, he detected the smell of burned wiring as yet another electrical component shorted out from saltwater immersion. Pitt's hammering had turned the submersible into a shattered hulk of its former self. The rounded exterior bow had been pounded nearly flat, its coating of glittery red paint roughly scraped away from the repeated blows. The coring probe was bent and twisted like a piece of licorice and barely clung to the *Badger* by a pair of mangled brace supports. Inside, the lights flickered, the water level rose, and the propulsion motors began dying one by one. Pitt could feel the life ebbing from the submersible as he listened to the groans and gurgles of the flailing machine. As he tried to reverse the thrusters and back away from the column, a new sound struck his ears. It was a deep rushing noise emanating far above his head.

To the casual observer, the first sign of an imminent rocket blast off the Sea Launch platform is the roaring rush of fresh water as it is pumped into the deluge system. At T-5 seconds, a veritable flood of dampening water is released into the flame trench positioned beneath the launchpad. The effect of the massive water dousing is to lessen the thrust exhaust effects to the platform, and, more important, minimize potential acoustic damage to the payload from the maelstrom at launch.

At T-3 seconds, the Zenit rocket begins groaning and stirring as its internal mechanisms are activated and the massive rocket comes to life. Inside its metal skin, a high-speed turbine pump begins force-feeding the volatile liquid propellant through an injector into the rocket engine's four combustion chambers. Inside each chamber, an igniter is activated, detonating the propellant in what amounts to a controlled explosion. The exhaust from the fiery detonation, seeking the path of least resistance, comes blasting out of each chamber through a constricted nozzle at the base of the rocket. The power of thrust is generated by the purged exhaust, enabling the Zenit rocket to defy the force of gravity and lift itself off the launchpad.

But the final three seconds of countdown are all critical. In those brief few seconds, onboard computer systems quickly monitor the engine start-up, checking propellant mixture, flow rates, ignition temperature, and a host of other mechanical readings affecting engine burn. If a significant deviation is discovered in any of the engine parameters, the automated control system takes over, shutting down the engine and scrubbing the launch. A reinitialization of the entire launch process is then required, which may take upward of five days before another launch can be attempted.

Ling ignored the video screen of the Zenit at the launch tower and instead stared at a computer display of critical measurements as the final seconds of the launch countdown ticked toward zero. At T-1 second, a row of green lights burst onto the screen and Ling allowed himself a slight breath of relief.

'We have main engine thrust up!' he shouted aloud as the display told him the computers were ramping up the rocket's RD-171 engine to maximum launch thrust. Every eye in the room turned to the video screen as the propellant floodgates were opened and the fuel burst through the rocket's engine in a torrent. For a long second, the rocket sat still on the pad as the fiery exhaust burst from its nozzles, the flames licking the water deluge and spraying a thick cloud of white smoke beneath the platform. Then, with a burgeoning burst of power, the Zenit surged up off the pad. The launch tower clamps fell away as the white rocket, erupting with 1.8 million pounds of thrust, climbed up past the tower and into the sky with a blinding glare and deafening roar.

A cheer rang through the launch control center as the engineers watched the Zenit rise successfully off the platform. Ling broke into a broad smile as the rocket climbed higher, grinning good-naturedly at Tongju. Kang's henchman simply nodded back in satisfaction.

At the far side of the bay, the bespectacled engineer who monitored the platform continued to stare mesmerized at the video image of the rocket as it climbed into the crisp blue sky. Oblivious to him was the computation on his computer monitor, which showed that the platform stabilization deviation had continued to rise, creeping past fifteen degrees in the last seconds prior to launch.

Fifteen feet beneath the water's surface, Pitt's ears were bleeding from the acoustical barrage. What started with the sound of a distant freight train had rumbled into the bombardment of a thousand erupting volcanoes as the Zenit's engine reached full thrust. The deafening sound, Pitt knew, was only a warning of the real savagery to come. The building force of the rocket's exhaust was deflected into the flame trench, where thousands of gallons of water dampened the inferno. The blasting force of the exhaust was little repressed, however, gathering into a steaming cloud of fury that proceeded past the deflectors to the open sea below the platform, where it pounded the water like a sledgehammer.

Positioned almost directly beneath the launchpad, the *Badger* was pummeled like a small toy, surging twenty feet down in a blast of bubbles and vapor. Pitt felt as if he were trapped in a washing machine as the submersible was tossed violently about. The seams of the vessel twisted and groaned from the force of the surge and the interior lights flickered from the shaking. A loose battery pack bounced off Pitt's head, gashing his temple as the submersible nearly turned turtle in the bellowing turbulence. Shaking off the blow, he discovered a new worry when he braced a hand against the bulkhead during a side roll. To his surprise, the bulkhead was searing hot. He quickly pulled his hand away, cursing as he shook it in the air to cool. A sickening thought drew over him as he felt a heavy mist of sweat dripping down his forehead and realized the water sloshing at his feet was rapidly warming. The rocket's exhaust was creating a boiling tempest around him, which might poach him alive before the rocket cleared the platform.

A second, more powerful surge stuck the submersible as the rocket's full thrust came to bear. The force of the current pushed the *Badger* charging through the water in a contorted angle, nearly on its side. Pitt clung to the controls for balance, unable to see ahead through the turbulent water, which offered no visibility. Had he an inkling where the submersible was headed, he might have braced himself for the impact. But the collision came without warning.

Ripping with the surge like a raft down the Colorado River, the submersible tore head-on into the side of the *Odyssey*'s flooded port pontoon. A metallic clap thundered through the water as the submersible smacked against the immovable hull. Pitt was jerked from the pilot's seat and flung against the forward bulkhead amid a rain of loosened electronic debris as the interior lights fell black and a series of hissing sounds erupted throughout the compartment. A grinding noise told Pitt that the *Badger* was sliding along the pontoon until another clang erupted and the submersible tilted over to one side and jerked to a sudden stop. As Pitt collected his senses, he realized that the submersible was wedged against the platform hull from the force of the rushing water, perhaps entangled in one of the pontoon's drive propellers. Turned on its side against the huge pontoon, there was no way that Pitt could open the entry hatch, dare he try to flood the interior and escape to the surface. With a sickening awe, he realized that if he wasn't soon baked alive he would face a swift death by drowning trapped inside the leaking submersible.

59

Tongju watched intently as the Zenit climbed up past the launch tower with a thundering reverberation that could be felt even inside the bowels of the *Koguryo*'s control center. A lingering applause still rang through the control center as the jubilant launch crew cheered the rocket's ascent. Ling afforded himself a wide smile as the computer display told him that the Zenit's engine was operating at full thrust. He peered at Tongju, who returned the glance by nodding tight-lipped in approval.

'The mission is still far from over,' Ling said, visibly relieved that the rocket was finally under way. But the riskiest phase of the mission was behind them now, he knew. Once the rocket was ignited, he had little control, if any, over the outcome of the mission. With a quiet uneasiness, he settled in as a spectator to monitor the balance of the flight.

Six thousand miles away, Kang smiled weakly as he watched a satellite feed of the rocket bursting off the deck of the *Odyssey*.

'We have opened the genie's bottle,' he said quietly

to Kwan, sitting across his desk. 'Let us hope he follows his master's wishes.'

From the cockpit of the *Icarus*, Al, Dirk, and Jack watched with dread as the blast of the rocket shook across the open sea. Just seconds before, Giordino had eased the struggling airship down onto a flat clearing atop Santa Barbara Island, where the relieved Sea Launch crew quickly jumped out of the over-crowded gondola. Captain Christiano hesitated at the cockpit doorway, stopping to shake hands.

'Thank you for saving my crew,' Christiano said through a grim face pained with disgrace for losing command of the *Odyssey*.

'Now that we can get airborne again, we'll make sure they don't get away,' Dirk replied with shared anger. He then pointed out the cockpit windshield toward an approaching blue dot on the horizon.

'The *Deep Endeavor*'s on her way. Get your men down to the shoreline and prepare to transfer aboard.'

Christiano nodded then stepped off the gondola, leaving it empty save for Jack.

'All ashore,' he uttered into the cockpit.

'Then let's get this gasbag back into the sky,' Giordino grunted, turning the propeller ducts upward and advancing the throttles. With roughly eight thousand pounds of human cargo suddenly off-loaded, the blimp rose easily into the air. As Giordino aimed the airship back toward the *Odyssey*, their eyes collectively caught the first billows of smoke that indicated the launch was initiated.

The fuming exhaust of the burning liquid oxygen and kerosene propellant bursting against the platform's water dampener system created a massive white cloud of vapor that quickly enveloped the entire platform and surrounding sea. For what seemed like minutes, the Zenit stood still at the launch tower. To the men in the airship, there was a hopeful moment where it appeared that the rocket was not going to leave the pad, but finally the tall white rocket began to rise, its blinding exhaust glaring like a fireball. Even a half-dozen miles across the water, they could hear the sharp crackling sound of the combusting fuel as the hot explosive thrust met the cool surrounding air, creating the echo of an ax ripping through a pine log.

Though it was a powerful, almost beautiful sight, Dirk felt a sickening knot in his stomach as he watched the rocket ascend. The glistening white missile would host the most savage terrorist attack the world had ever seen, resulting in a horrifying death for millions. And he had failed to stop it. As if that was not punishment enough, he knew that Sarah was somewhere in the target area of Los Angeles and might very well be one of the strike's first victims. And then there was the fate of his father. Glancing forlornly at Giordino, he saw a grimace on the old Italian's face the likes of which he had never seen before. It was not a look of anger with the terrorists but an expression of concern for the loss of a lifelong friend. As much as Dirk did not want to face it, he knew that amid the noxious inferno of the rocket's blastoff his father was somewhere on the platform fighting for his survival, or worse.

Aboard the *Deep Endeavor*, Summer felt the same pangs of dread swell through her body. Dirk had radioed the ship with news that the Sea Launch crew had been rescued, but also that their father was somewhere aboard the platform. When Delgado was the first to observe the rocket igniting, she thought her legs had turned to rubber. Grasping the captain's chair for support, she stared stoically toward the platform as tears welled in her eyes. All fell silent on the bridge around her as they watched in disbelief at the rocket as it surged off the launchpad. As one, their thoughts were on the fate of the NUMA leader, lost somewhere in the rocket's white plume of smoke.

'It can't be,' Burch muttered in shock. 'It just can't be.'

60

Inside the *Badger*, the temperature was unbearable. The superheated metal skin created a sauna effect with the water that was rising inside. Pitt could feel himself on the verge of passing out from the heat as he clawed his way back to the tilted pilot's seat. A handful of lights still blinked on the control panel, indicating that the emergency life-support system still had power, but the propulsion systems were long expired. Though his body was numb from the heat, his mind quickly calculated that he had one chance to break free from the grip of the pontoon. Through sweat-laden eyes, he reached forward and mashed a control button market BALLAST PUMP. Then, grasping the control yoke, he flung himself backward into the rising water, using his full weight and remaining strength to yank the sub's rudder against the burgeoning current. The rudder blade protested at first, then swung slowly against the rushing water, fighting against Pitt's every movement. With muscles aching and spots appearing before his eyes, Pitt clung desperately to the yoke, fighting not to pass out. For a second, nothing happened. All Pitt could hear was the churning torrent of the water rushing against the sub, while the temperature inside continued to rise. Then, almost imperceptibly, a grinding noise struck his ears. Gradually, the noise grew louder, matching the sound he had heard before. A faint smile crossed Pitt's lips as he fought to maintain consciousness. Hang on, he told himself, gripping the yoke tightly. Just hang on.

An eagle-eyed flight engineer, standing on a rocky hilltop of Santa Barbara Island amid his stunned Sea Launch colleagues, was the first to detect it. A subtle, almost invisible waggle at the base of the rocket as it cleared the launch tower.

'She's oscillating,' he said aloud.

His surrounding crewmates, exhausted and stunned by the entire ordeal, ignored his words and watched in angry disbelief as somebody else launched their rocket from their platform. But as the rocket climbed higher and higher into the sky, more of the experienced launch veterans detected something amiss with the flight trajectory. At first, just a murmur rippled through the assembled crew; then, an excited buzz jolted the men like an electric shock. One man started to yell, cursing at the rocket to burst, and then another followed suit. Before long, the entire crew was jumping up and down while shouting at the soaring rocket, cajoling the mechanical beast like some last-dollar bettors urging a long-shot nag to the wire at Pimlico.

*

On board the *Koguryo*, the excitement of the launch had yet to wane when a seated flight engineer turned to Ling and said, 'Sir, the Stage One engine indicates an active gimbaling beyond nominal flight plan parameters.'

The Zenit-3SL, like most modern rockets, was steered in flight by adjusting, or gimbaling, the launch vehicle's engine, redirecting its thrust to govern the rocket's heading. As Ling was aware, the initial launch sequence called for no gimbaling until the rocket was in a stabilized climb, then the navigation system would initiate slight steering adjustments to guide the rocket toward the target. Only an undetected imbalance would create an immediate steering correction from launch.

Ling walked over to the engineer's station and peered at the man's computer monitor. His mouth fell open as he saw that the rocket's engine was gimbaled to its maximum degree. He watched in silence as, a second later, the engine adjusted back to its neutral position, then gimbaled to the full extent in the opposite direction. Almost immediately, the whole cycle started over again. Ling immediately surmised the cause.

'Choi, what was the launchpad horizontal deviation at T-0?' he shouted to the platform engineer.

The engineer looked back sheepishly at Ling and uttered in a barely audible voice, 'Sixteen degrees.'

'No!' Ling gasped in a raspy voice as his eyes scrunched closed in a panic of disbelief. The color rushed from Ling's face and he felt himself grasping the computer monitor to steady his suddenly weakening knees. With dire foresight, he slowly opened his eyes and stared at the video screen of the charging rocket, waiting for the inevitable.

Pitt had no way of knowing the impact from his frenetic hole drilling. But the dozens of gouges poked into the side of the support columns had opened up a flood of incoming seawater that quickly overpowered the *Odyssey*'s ballast pumps. With the automated controls set to maintain the prescribed launch depth, the incoming water collected in the rear support columns and tugged the platform down by its aft side. Firing off the platform, the Zenit rocket was over fifteen degrees off vertical center as it left the launchpad and immediately tried to correct the deviation from its prescribed flight plan by shifting the engine thrust. But at the low speed of takeoff, the initial command was diluted so the engine position was tweaked again to its maximum adjustment. As the launch vehicle gained speed, the adjustment quickly became an overcorrection and the rocket's computers gimbaled the engine in the opposite direction to counterbalance the movement. Under normal conditions, the rocket might have been able to stabilize itself with a few minor adjustments. But on this flight, the Zenit's fuel tanks were only half full. The partially empty fuel tanks allowed the liquid propellant to slosh back and forth during the thrust inclinations, creating a whole new set of balancing dynamics. The overtaxed stabilization control system tried vainly to smooth the flight but, ultimately, exacerbated the situation and the rocket began to waffle.

On video screens and satellite feeds, out an airship cockpit window, and from a barren rocky island in the Pacific Ocean, a thousand eyes stared transfixed at the streaming white rocket as it began a slow and morbid gyration across the sky. What started as a slight wobble at liftoff grew into a continuous waggle during ascent until the entire rocket was shaking uncontrollably toward the clouds like an anorexic belly dancer. Had Sea Launch been managing the flight, an automated safety control would have detonated the rocket as it veered out of parameter. But the abort command had been deleted from the flight software by Kang's crew and the Zenit was left to struggle upward in a tortuous dance of death.

To the unbelieving sight of those who watched, the huge rocket swung wildly in the sky before tearing itself apart from the inside out and literally snapping in two. The lower Stage 1 immediately disintegrated in a massive fireball as the fuel tanks were simultaneously ignited, swallowing everything in its radius with a cauldron of flame. Chunks and pieces of rocket machinery not dissolved by the explosion rained down over a swath of empty sea, while the high-altitude mushroom cloud from the explosion hung in the blue sky as if painted there.

The nose cone and upper stage of the Zenit oddly

sailed free of the carnage and continued speeding across the sky like a streaking bullet, fueled only by momentum. In a graceful parabolic arc, the smoke-trailed payload gradually lost energy and nosed down toward the Pacific, smacking the surface with a watery geyser of debris miles downrange from the initial explosion. As the sudden sound of silence drifted over the water, the stunned observers stared miraculously at the white rainbow of smoke that trailed the death flight and arched quietly from horizon to horizon.

61

On a rocky beach of Santa Barbara Island, an elephant seal awoke from a leisurely nap and cocked an ear toward the inland. The odd sound of cheering wafted down the hillside from thirty or so men congregated on a small bluff. The seal looked quizzically up at the disheveled group of men, then stretched back out and resumed his nap.

For the first time in their lives, the Sea Launch platform crew of technicians and engineers were happy to witness a launch failure. Men cheered and whistled while others poked their fists in the air in celebratory victory. As the launch vehicle blew up above their heads, even Christiano grinned a sigh of relief as Platform Launch Manager Ohlrogge slapped him on the back.

'Somebody was smiling down on us for once,' Ohlrogge said.

'Thank God. Whatever those bastards were trying to launch could not have been good.'

'One of my flight engineers noted a roll oscillation right from launch. Must have been a nozzle adjustment malfunction, or a stabilization issue with the platform.'

Christiano thought of Pitt and his comment before

departing the *Odyssey*. 'Maybe that fellow from NUMA worked some magic.'

'If so, we owe him big.'

'Yes, and somebody owes me, too,' Christiano replied.

Ohlrogge looked at the captain quizzically.

'That was a ninety-million-dollar launch vehicle that just went up in flames. There will be hell to pay when we pass that bill to the insurer,' the captain said, finally letting loose a laugh.

Kang flinched as he watched the satellite feed of the Zenit disintegrate before his eyes. As the camera caught pieces of falling debris, he silently reached for the remote control and turned off the monitor.

'Though the strike has failed, the specter of the attack will still represent a serious provocation to the American public,' Kwan assured his boss. 'Anger will be high and the fallout against Japan significant.'

'Yes, our staged media security leaks should ensure that,' Kang said, suppressing his anger at the failure. 'But the disappearance of the *Koguryo* and launch team remains at hand. Their capture would corrupt much of our hard work to date.'

'Tongju will fulfill his duties. He always has,' Kwan replied.

Kang stared at the darkened television monitor for a moment, then slowly nodded.

*

The mood in the *Koguryo*'s launch control center quickly turned from joy to shock to sullen disappointment. In an instant, the mission requirements of the launch team fell away and the assembled technicians and engineers sat silently at their computer stations, staring at the displays that no longer provided any launch data. No one seemed to know what to do next and whispered quietly with one another.

Tongju threw a long, frigid glare toward Ling, then left the control center without saying a word. As he made his way toward the bridge, he called Kim on a portable radio and spoke briefly in a low voice. On the bridge, he found Captain Lee staring out the starboard bridge window at the smoke-trailed rain of debris that scarred the blue sky with white strips of vapor.

'She shook herself apart,' he said with wonder, then looked into the blank eyes of Tongju.

'A problem with the platform,' Tongju replied. 'We must evacuate the area immediately. Can we get moving at once?'

'We are standing by for departure. We just need to hoist in the tender, then we can be under way.'

'There is no time,' he hissed suddenly. 'The American Coast Guard and Navy may already be looking for us. Proceed under full power at once, and I will personally cut the tender loose.'

Lee looked at Tongju warily, then nodded.

'As you wish. Our course is already laid in. We shall make for Mexican waters, then divert under cover of darkness for the rendezvous position.'

Tongju took a step to exit the bridge, then stopped suddenly. Out of the forward window, he gazed at the smoke-enshrouded Sea Launch platform. Approaching the platform from the northwest was the silver blimp, now cruising several hundred feet above the water. Tongju waved an arm in the direction of the *Icarus*.

'Alert your surface-to-air missile team. Take out that airship immediately,' he spat, then vanished out the door.

As the *Koguryo*'s twin four-bladed propellers began churning the water beneath the ship's hull, Tongju hustled his way back to the portable stairwell that ran down the vessel's port flank. At the base of the stairwell bobbed the white tender, a mooring line tied across to the railing. He noted bubbles of smoke rising from the boat's stern, alerting him that the engine was running at idle. Quickly untying the line, he coiled it in his hand and waited until the next passing wave pushed the tender up against the side of the ship. With barely a step, he hopped aboard the bow of the boat and shuffled toward the cabin, tossing the coiled line into an empty bucket on deck. Inside the cabin, he found Kim and two of his commandos standing beside the wheel.

'Everything aboard?' Tongju asked.

Kim nodded. 'During the excitement of the launch, we moved our arms and provisions on board, and even hoisted extra fuel aboard, without any inter-ference.' Kim tilted his head toward the rear open deck where four fifty-five-gallon drums of gasoline were tied off against the gunwale.

'Let us drift off the stern for a moment, then we shall make our run to Ensenada. When will the charges detonate?'

Kim glanced at his watch. 'In twenty-five minutes.'

'Plenty of time for the missile crew to destroy the airship.'

The *Koguryo* quickly churned away from the small boat as the tender continued to idle in the low swells. When the former cable ship had cleared a quarter mile of open water, Kim moved the throttles to SLOW and crept forward with the bow pointed southeast. In no time, he figured, they would look like another ordinary fishing charter heading home to San Diego.

Long after the Zenit had climbed into the sky and detonated, a thick cloud of white smoke still hung over the *Odyssey* like a fogbank. Ever so gently, the light sea breeze began poking holes through the exhaust, revealing sporadic patches of the launch platform through the haze.

'Looks like a bowl of clam chowder down there,' Giordino said as he banked the *Icarus* over the plat-form. While Giordino and Dahlgren visually surveyed the platform for any signs of Pitt, Dirk activated the LASH system and scanned for optical anomalies that might signify a human being.

'Don't quote me but I think that baby is sinking,' Dahlgren said as they glided around the aft end of the platform and could make out an exposed section down to the water. The men in the gondola could clearly see that the aft support columns appeared shorter than the bow columns.

'She's definitely taking on water in the stern,' Dirk replied.

'Wonder if that's the handiwork of your old man? He may have just cost somebody a new rocket,' Giordino said.

'And maybe a new launchpad,' Dahlgren added.

'But where is he?' Dirk asked aloud. They could all detect that there was no apparent sign of life on the platform.

'The smoke is starting to clear. Once the helipad opens up, I'll take us in for a closer look,' Giordino replied.

As they drifted back toward the bow of the platform, Dahlgren looked down and grimaced.

'Damn. The *Badger*'s gone, too. Must have sank during the launch.'

The threesome fell quiet, reflecting that the disappearance of the submersible was the least of their losses.

Three miles to the south, a gunnery crewman on the *Koguryo* was transferring the radar-derived coordinates of the blimp into a Chinese CSA-4 surface-to-air missile guidance system. The slow-moving airship was as easy an objective as the gunnery crew could ever hope to target. With such a large object at close range, the odds of failing to strike the blimp were nearly zero.

In an enclosed room adjacent to the dual missile canister, a weapons control expert stood at a console transferring the firing guidance through a missile command link. A row of green lights flashed at him as the engagement radar embedded in the missile acknowledged a target lock. The man immediately picked up a telephone receiver that ran directly to the bridge.

'Target acquired and missile armed,' he said in monotone to Captain Lee. 'Awaiting orders to fire.'

Lee looked out a bridge side window toward the blimp hovering over the platform in the distance. The high-powered missile exploding into the airship would make for a spectacular display, he thought childishly. Perhaps they should also destroy the distant turquoise vessel that lingered on the edge of their radar screen and then make a clean escape. But, first things first. He moved the receiver to his mouth to issue the command to fire when suddenly his lips froze. His eyes had detected a small pair of dark objects emerging from behind the airship. He stood frozen and watched as the objects quickly materialized into a pair of low-flying aircraft.

The F-16D Falcon fighter jets had been scrambled from an Air National Guard base in Fresno minutes after a NORAD satellite had detected the launch of the Zenit rocket. While flying toward the launch site, the pilots were directed to the *Koguryo* with the help of the Coast Guard distress call that had originated from the *Deep Endeavor*. The sleek gray jets flew low above the water and burst over the *Koguryo* just a few hundred feet above her forebridge. The crackling roar of the jets' engines struck a second after their shadows had whisked by overhead, rattling the windows of the bridge where Lee stood with a sickened look on his face.

'Stand down! Stand down and secure the battery!' he barked over the phone. As the SAM was stowed away, Lee watched as the two fighter jets gained altitude and began crisply circling the fast-moving ship.

'You!' he cursed at a crewman standing nearby. 'Find Tongju and bring him to the bridge ... at once.'

The men in the blimp beamed in relief at the sight of the Air National Guard jets circling above the *Koguryo*, having no idea how close they were to being blasted out of the sky by the ship's SAM battery. They knew that a horde of Navy ships was on the way and that there was little chance the ship would escape apprehension now. They again turned their attention to the smoke-covered platform below.

'The haze is lifting off the helipad,' Giordino observed. 'I'll set her down if you boys want to jump off and take a look around.'

'Absolutely,' Dirk replied. 'Jack, we can start with the bridge, then move down to the hangar if the air is breathable.'

'I'd start with the ship's lounge,' Giordino said, trying to cut the somber mood. 'If he's okay, my money says he's mixing a martini and eating up the ship's store of pretzels.'

Giordino swung the blimp wide of the platform, bringing the airship around with its nose into the wind. As he lined up on the helipad and began dropping altitude, Dahlgren stuck his head back into the cockpit and pointed out the side window.

'Take a look over there,' he said.

Several hundred feet off the side of the platform, a sudden surge of bubbles erupted from beneath the surface. A few seconds later, a mottled gray metallic object broke the surface.

'Launch debris?' Dahlgren asked.

'No, it's the *Badger*!' Giordino exclaimed.

Guiding the airship toward the object, the three men could see that it was in fact the NUMA submersible bobbing low in the water. The underwater vehicle's bright metallic paintwork had been cooked off in the launch blast, leaving its skin a dappled mix of primer and bare metal. The bow section was bent and mangled, as if it had been involved in a head-on traffic accident. How the thing still managed to float was anybody's guess, but there was no denying it was the experimental submersible Dirk and Dahlgren had sailed to the platform.

As Giordino brought the blimp down for a closer look, the three men were stunned to see the top hatch suddenly twist and pop open. A cloud of steaming vapor streamed from the open hatch as they looked on incredulously. For several agonizing seconds, their eyes hung glued to the hatch, hoping against hope. Finally, they saw the odd apparition of a pair of stockinged feet rise up and out of the hatch. A patch of dark hair then appeared and they realized that the feet they observed were actually hands covered in a pair of socks. The stocking-wrapped hands, protected from the hot metal, quickly hoisted up the lean, racked body of their owner from the enclosed oven.

'It's Dad! He's okay!' Dirk exclaimed with glaring relief.

Pitt climbed to his feet and swayed on the rocking sub, sucking in lungfuls of the cool ocean air. He was a haggard mass of blood and sweat, and his clothes stuck to him as if they were glued to his skin. But his eyes shined as he looked skyward and threw a jaunty wave to the men in the gondola.

'Going down,' Giordino announced as he proceeded to guide the blimp down toward the sea until the gondola was skimming just inches above the waves. With a deft touch, Giordino gently eased the blimp alongside the submersible. Pitt leaned down and secured the *Badger*'s top hatch, then took a few steps and staggered into the open door of the gondola, where Dirk and Dahlgren grabbed his arms and yanked him safely aboard.

'I believe,' he said to Giordino in a dry parched voice, 'I'll take that drink now.'

Pitt slipped into the blimp's copilot seat and gulped down a bottled water as Al, Dirk, and Jack described the fiery disintegration of the Zenit rocket minutes before. While studying the vapor trails in the sky and eyeing the *Koguryo* fleeing in the distance, Pitt countered with a description of his drilling attack on the *Odyssey*'s support columns and the tumultuous assault from the wake of the blastoff.

'And here I had good money down that you were lolling about in the *Odyssey*'s lounge nursing a martini,' Giordino grumbled.

'I was the one shaken and stirred,' Pitt laughed. 'Would have been baked alive when the *Badger* got jammed against the side pontoon, but I was able to manually force the rudder against the surge and broke free into cooler water. Even with the ballast tanks purged, it took me a while to surface until I got the bilge pump working. There's still a lot of water sloshing around inside, but she should stay afloat a while longer.'

'I'll radio *Deep Endeavor* and have her fish the *Badger* out once they've picked up the platform crew on Santa Barbara Island,' Giordino replied.

'I will have a furious sister on my hands if you first don't let her know you are safe,' Dirk chided.

Summer nearly fell over when her father's voice crackled through the *Deep Endeavor*'s radio, jokingly ordering a beer and a peanut butter sandwich.

'We feared the worst,' she gushed. 'What on earth happened to you?'

'It's a long story. Suffice it to say that the Scripps Institute isn't going to be too happy with my submarine-driving skills,' he said, leaving all on the bridge of the *Deep Endeavor* scratching their heads.

As Giordino lifted the airship up off the water, Pitt noticed the F-16s circling the fleeing *Koguryo*.

'Cavalry finally arrive?' he asked.

'Just moments ago. The Navy has an armada headed this way as well. She's not going to get away.'

'Her tender is sure making haste,' Pitt said, nodding toward a white speck to the south.

Lost in the spectacle and confusion was the *Koguryo*'s tender, which had slipped quietly away from her mother ship and was now motoring south toward the horizon at high speed.

'How do you know that's her tender?' Giordino asked, squinting downrange.

'Over here,' Pitt replied, tapping the WESCAM monitor. Pitt had been fooling around with the zoom lens while talking and happened to catch the speeding boat flash by. The focused image clearly showed it was the *Koguryo*'s tender, which they had observed earlier.

'The jets definitely aren't tracking her,' Dirk said from the rear, noting the F-16s circling tightly around the *Koguryo* as she sailed farther to the west.

'Let's stay on her,' Pitt stated.

'She has nary a chance against our fleet wings aflutter,' Giordino snarled, pushing the throttles to FULL and watching as the airspeed indicator crept slowly toward 50 knots.

62

'Why haven't they fired on the aircraft, or that infernal airship?' Tongju swore as he stared at the *Koguryo* through a pair of binoculars. The bouncing movement of the tender as it ran at full speed through the waves made it impossible for him to steady his gaze and he finally threw the glasses down harshly onto a cowling.

'The aircraft have intimidated Lee,' Kim said over his shoulder as he clutched the steering wheel tightly. 'He will pay with his life in about two more minutes.'

The *Koguryo* was growing smaller on the horizon as the tender accelerated south. But when the planted explosives detonated, they could clearly see puffs of water spray into the air along the ship's hull line.

Standing on the bridge, Captain Lee at first thought that the F-16s had fired on him. But the warbirds still circled lazily above, and there was no sign that they had fired any missiles. As the damage assessments came in reporting that the lower hull was compromised in several locations, Lee suddenly realized the culprit. Minutes before, a crewman had reported observing Kim and Tongju board the tender and the small boat was now seen running south at high speed. With a sick sensation of betrayal, Lee knew that he and his ship had been deemed expendable.

But a miscalculation would save them. Kim's demolition team had planted ample explosives to rip the bowels out of a normal ship *Koguryo*'s size. But a critical piece of information about the cable ship had not been considered: she had a double hull. The detonated charges easily ruptured the vessel's inner hull but only buckled the plates of the outer hull. Seawater gushed into the lower holds, but not with the massive force that would submerge the running ship as Tongju had envisioned. Lee immediately stopped the ship, deployed portable pumps to the damaged holds, and then sealed off the high-risk areas behind watertight doors. The ship would list and be unable to run at speed but she would not founder.

Once the flooding was halted, the captain peered through a set of field glasses at the speeding tender escaping in the distance. Lee knew that he had little to live for now. As the captain of the vessel that launched the aborted missile attack against the United States, he would be the prime scapegoat if captured. If he somehow escaped, or was released, there would be no telling what sort of reception he'd receive from Kang. Satisfied that the ship was stabilized, Lee excused himself from the bridge and retired to his cabin. Retrieving a Chinese-made Makarov 9mm pistol from beneath a dresser drawer filled with pressed shirts, Lee lay down neatly on his bed, held the barrel to his ear, and pulled the trigger.

While pursuing the speeding tender, the men in the *Icarus* caught sight of the series of explosions that ripped along the hull of the *Koguryo*.

'Are those lunatics trying to scuttle her with all hands?' Dahlgren wondered.

For several minutes, they watched the ship as she slowed but held steady. Pitt noticed that there was no apparent rush for the lifeboats, and he could see several members of the crew standing idly at the rail watching the jets overhead. He studied the water-line for a significant change but could only detect a slight list.

'She's not going to disappear on us anytime soon,' he said. 'Let's keep after the tender.'

Giordino glanced at the LASH system output on the laptop computer, spotting several gray shapes to the southeast approximately thirty miles away.

'Our Navy pals are on the way,' he said, tapping the screen. 'They won't be alone for long.'

With a nearly 20-knot advantage in speed, the airship began easily gaining ground on the fleeing white boat. The *Icarus* had only ascended to a five-hundred-foot altitude when Giordino gave chase and he didn't waste power on any further climb-ing. The blimp glided smoothly toward the boat's wake, driving fast and low over the water. As the airship moved closer, Pitt focused the surveillance camera on the boat's open rear deck and cabin. Through the covered portico, he could only make out indiscriminate shapes at the helm.

'I count four men abovedecks,' he said.

'Apparently, they're not ones for a crowded escape,' Giordino replied.

Pitt scanned the camera about the deck, relieved to find no heavy armament but noting the extra drums of fuel near the stern.

'Plenty of gas for a run to Mexico,' he said.

'I think our Coast Guard friends in San Diego might have something to say about that,' Giordino replied, tightening his bearing on the boat.

Tongju and his men had been focused on the *Koguryo*, but one of the commandos finally noticed the approaching blimp. While Kim manned the helm, the other three men instinctively stepped to the rear open deck to better observe the airship. Pitt focused the zoom lens of the camera on the men until their faces could clearly be distinguished.

'Recognize any of these characters?' Pitt asked over his shoulder to Dirk and Dahlgren.

The younger Pitt studied the screen for just a moment before gritting his teeth hard. The flash of anger subsided quickly, though, as a contented smile returned to his face.

'The Fu Manchu character standing in the center. His name is Tongju. He's Kang's master of ceremonies for torture and assassination. Appeared to be calling the shots aboard the *Odyssey* earlier.'

'For such a nice guy, it would be kind of a shame to ruin his Mexican vacation,' Giordino replied.

As he spoke, he dipped the prow of the blimp down and held steady as the airship slowly dove toward the water. When it looked like he was going to drive the nose into the sea, Giordino gently pulled up on the controls, leveling the gondola just fifty feet above the water. The *Icarus* had closed the gap between the two vessels during the dive, and Giordino guided the airship along the port side of the tender until the gondola was suspended side by side.

'You want to step off and have a beer with these guys?' Pitt asked as he eyed the men on the boat just a few dozen feet away.

'No, just want to let them know that they ain't going to outrun Mad Al and his Magic Bag of Gas,' he grinned.

Giordino eased back on the throttles until he matched speeds with the bouncing tender, the large envelope of the blimp casting a shadow over the topsides of the boat. Above the din of the tender's twin inboard engines and the airship's Porsche motor-driven propellers, the men in the *Icarus* suddenly detected an unwelcome staccato. Glancing back at the tender, Pitt saw that Tongju and the two commandos had retrieved automatic weapons and were standing on the stern deck blasting away at the blimp.

'I hate to be the one to tell you but they're shooting holes in your gasbag, Mad Al,' Pitt said.

'The jealous lowlifes,' Giordino replied, goosing the throttles.

Before departing Oxnard, they had been told that the airship could withstand a profusion of holes and gashes to the air bags and still retain its lift. Tongju and his men would have to exhaust a crate of ammunition to threaten the airworthiness of the helium-filled blimp. But the safety of the gondola was less assured. After a momentary pause in the firing, the floor of the main cabin suddenly erupted in a spray of splinters as the gunmen redirected their weapons at the gondola.

'Everybody down!' Pitt yelled as a burst of fire smashed the side cockpit window, the bullets grazing just over his head. The sound of shattering glass resonated through the cabin as a rain of bullets poured into the gondola. Dirk and Dahlgren lay flat on the floor as several bursts stitched past them and into the ceiling above. Giordino jammed the throttles all the way forward, and, while waiting anxiously for the blimp to speed ahead, turned the yoke full to port to turn away from the tender.

'No,' Pitt yelled at him, 'turn and fly over him.'

Giordino knew not to question Pitt's judgment and, without hesitation, threw the rudder over in the opposite direction, pushing the *Icarus* back toward the tender. Glancing at Pitt, he could see him studying the tender below with an arched brow. The blistering fire continued to tear into the gondola for a second, then abruptly stopped as Giordino steered the gondola above and slightly ahead of the tender's cabin roof, temporarily obscuring the field of fire.

'Everyone all right?' Pitt asked.

'We're okay back here,' Dirk replied, 'but one of the engines isn't faring too well.'

As the sound of gunfire fell away, the men could hear sputtering and coughing emanating from the starboard gondola motor. Giordino glanced at the console gauges and shook his head.

'Oil pressure falling, temperature rising. Going to be tough to run away from these guys on one leg.'

Pitt peered down at the deck of the tender, spotting Tongju and the two gunmen moving toward the stern of the boat reloading their weapons.

'Al, hold your position,' he said. 'And lend me your cigar.'

'It's one of Sandecker's finest,' he replied, hesitating before handing Pitt the saliva-soaked green stub.

'I'll buy you a box of 'em. Hold steady for ten seconds, then turn hard to port and get us the hell away from the boat.'

'You're not going to do what I think you are?' Giordino asked.

Pitt just flashed a sly look, then reached up for an overhead ripcord with one hand while he turned a dial marked FUEL BALLAST to the open position. Pulling on the cord, he silently counted to eight, then released the line and closed the lever. At the stern of the gondola, an emergency dump valve opened on the fuel tank, releasing a flood of gasoline that surged out the bottom of the tank.

Pitt's quick discharge released more than seventy-five gallons of gasoline out of the gondola tank, which sprayed down directly onto the stern deck of the tender. Pitt looked down and could see that the rear deck was awash in fuel that sloshed along the rear gunwale as the boat charged through the waves. Tongju and the two gunmen covered their faces and sprinted under the portico as the rain of liquid splattered down on them but quickly returned after the deluge ended and raised their weapons again to finish off the blimp. Pitt watched curiously as the pool of gasoline washed around their feet and splashed over some deck chairs, a bench, and the four fifty-five-gallon drums tied to the side. He stoked a few puffs on the cigar to brighten its ember, then stuck his head out the shattered side cockpit window. Just a few yards away, Pitt eyed Tongju and smiled as the assassin looked up and swung his assault rifle toward him. Through his legs, Dirk could feel the blimp begin pulling to one side as Giordino threw the controls over. With a calm nonchalance, he took a last puff on the cigar and casually tossed it toward the stern of the tender.

A wave jostled the tender, and Tongju braced himself against a side railing as he jerked the stock of the AK-74 assault rifle to his shoulder. He barely noticed the small green object that fluttered down and struck the deck beside him as he took aim at Pitt's head poking out the cockpit window. His finger was just tightening on the trigger when a loud poof erupted at his feet.

The cigar's glowing ember ignited the gasoline vapors rising off the deck before the stogie even struck the surface. The airship's rain of gasoline had sprayed everywhere and in seconds the whole stern of the boat was a wall of flame. A commando standing besides Tongju had been drenched in fuel and the flames shot up his legs and torso in a rush. The panicked man dropped his weapon and danced frantically about the deck, his arms flailing wildly to douse his burning clothes. Screaming in pain, he finally ran to the railing and flung himself over the side, the ocean waters quickly extinguishing the human torch in a whiff of smoke. Kim watched from the helm as the man leaped off the boat but made no move to turn the boat around and rescue the scorched commando.

Tongju, too, was temporarily engulfed in flames, angrily lowering his rifle without firing and leaping under the portico, where he was able to stamp out the flames burning his shoes and pants. Kim gazed from the blazing stern to Tongju with a look of alarm in his eyes.

'Keep going,' Tongju shouted, 'the flames will burn themselves out.'

The wind and sea spray from the charging boat had, in fact, extinguished some of the peripheral flames, but pools of burning gasoline still sloshed across the deck and deep black plumes of smoke revealed that more than just the fuel was on fire.

'But the fuel barrels!' Kim cried, watching as the flames licked at the drums of gasoline.

Tongju had forgotten about the full barrels of gasoline tied to the rear deck amid the blazing fire. The flames were initially concentrated to the rear of the barrels, but the sloshing gas on the deck brought the fire up to the base of the drums. Scanning the helm console, Tongju spotted a small fire extinguisher mounted to the bulkhead. With a quick lunge, he scooped up the extinguisher, pulled its lockpin, and sprinted onto the rear deck to protect the fuel drums. But he was too late.

A seal cap on one of the drums had not been tightened all the way, allowing a thin wisp of vapor to escape. The constant jarring from the pounding boat had generated more vapor pressure inside the drum, which expanded further by the heat of the nearby fire. When the flames finally drew near enough to ignite the vapor, the fuel drum exploded like a powder keg. In quick succession, the other three fuel drums ignited with devastating effect.

As the blimp peeled away from the boat, Pitt and the others watched in awe as the first fuel drum exploded right into Tongju. A chunk of flying shrapnel from the drum burst through his body, tearing an oblong hole the size of a softball through his chest. A stunned look crossed the assassin's face as he sunk to his knees. In the last seconds of life, he peered skyward toward the blimp and scowled defiantly before he was swallowed up in an inferno of flames.

The subsequent explosions leveled the entire superstructure of the boat in a maelstrom of flying timbers and debris. A huge fireball rolled into the sky as the stern of the boat rose into the air briefly, its still-driving propellers churning at the sky. The explosion blasted a gaping hole through the hull, which quickly sucked the boat under the waves in a boil of froth and smoke, taking the bodies of Tongju, Kim, and the third commando to the seafloor.

Giordino had sharply turned the *Icarus* away from the exploding boat, but flying debris still splattered against the airship, shearing an additional array of holes into the fabric skin. More than a hundred rips, tears, and bullet holes peppered the surface, creating avenues for helium to escape. The bruised and damaged airship refused to go down, however, and clung to the sky like a battered fighter.

The men in the gondola surveyed the surreal scene around them. In the sky above, a heavy white plume of smoke still hung in the air, marking the Zenit rocket's explosive demise. Across the water, a Navy frigate and destroyer could be seen bearing down on the *Koguryo* as a swarm of fighter jets circled overhead. And beneath them, a scattering of burning timbers smoldered in the water, denoting the grave of Tongju and the sunken tender.

'Guess we showed your pal a hot time,' Giordino said to Dirk as he stuck his head into the cockpit.

'I have a feeling he'll be burning in hell for quite some time to come.'

'We gave him a nice head start,' Pitt said. 'You and Jack okay back there?'

'Just a few scratches. We both managed to dance around the flying lead.'

'But look what they did to my airship,' Giordino muttered with feigned hurt, waving a hand about the shot-up gondola.

'At least all of our vital signs are good. Despite the gunshots to the envelope, our helium pressure is holding up, and we've got fifty gallons of fuel to get us back to shore,' Pitt replied, eyeing the console gauges before shutting down the damaged engine. 'Take us home, Mad Al.'

'As you wish,' Giordino replied, easing the nose of the *Icarus* toward the east. Slowly steering the battered airship back to the mainland on its one good engine, he turned to Pitt and said, 'Now, about those cigars . . .'

63

It took only the mere sight of the U.S. Navy frigate and destroyer for the captainless crew of the *Koguryo* to throw in the towel. As more and more fighter planes appeared in the sky overhead, it became obvious to all aboard that trying to flee would result in their destruction. And with the damaged hull, they were not about to outrun anybody. As the Navy ships approached, the *Koguryo*'s executive officer wisely radioed their surrender. In minutes, a small boarding party arrived from the destroyer USS *Benfold* and took custody of the ship. A repair team was then sent aboard to assist in stabilizing the damaged hull, and then the Japanese-flagged ship was sailed to San Diego at a slow crawl.

Arriving at San Diego early the next morning, a media frenzy erupted. As word broke of the attempted rocket attack on Los Angeles, scores of small boats packed with reporters and cameramen buzzed around the harbor trying to get a close-up glimpse of the terrorist ship and crew. For their part, the crew and technicians aboard the *Koguryo* looked down at the swarming media with befuddled amusement. Their greeting at the San Diego Naval Station was less inviting as teams of government security and intelligence officers whisked the crew into heavily guarded buses, where they were hurriedly driven away to a secure facility for detailed interrogation.

Back at the dock, investigators combed every inch of the ship, removing the launch control data and securing the surface-to-surface and surface-to-air missile systems. Marine engineers studied the hull damage, proving with certainty that it had been created by internally detonated explosive charges. It would take several days before intelligence analysts would discover that all the software data related to the mission flight profile and rocket payload had been systematically destroyed prior to the ship's capture.

Interrogation of the ship's crew proved equally frustrating. The majority of the crew and launch team had believed they were actually launching a commercial satellite and had no clue how close they were to the continental United States. Those who knew otherwise refused to talk. Investigators were quickly able to finger Ling and the two Ukrainian engineers as kingpins for the mission, despite their vehement denials.

Publicly, the launch created a furor, which magnified as word leaked that the payload carried smallpox virus. The Japanese Red Army was behind the attack, newspapers and television reports screamed, fueled in part by the staged media leaks perpetrated by Kang operators. The government silently made no denials while piecing together their own evidence, further inciting the public rage against Japan. The attempted attack, though unsuccessful, seemed to have achieved Kang's desired outcome. The single-minded media applied their full reporting resources to the incident. Constant news coverage focused strictly on the investigation and speculation about possible retaliation measures to take against the shadowy Japanese terrorist group. Lost in the news was the issue of Korea and the pending vote in the National Assembly over the removal of U.S. troops from the South Korean Peninsula.

As the media ran dry of new facts about the failed rocket launch, they turned their attention toward hero-making. The Sea Launch platform crew was nearly mugged by reporters when they stepped off the *Deep Endeavor* in Long Beach. Many of the tired crewmen were given just a few hours' rest, then helicoptered back to the *Odyssey* to patch up the holes Pitt had carved in the support structure and sail the listing platform back to port. Those escaping work duty were badgered for in-depth interviews about their capture and imprisonment aboard the platform, as well as their later rescue by Pitt and Giordino in the blimp. The men from NUMA were lionized as heroes and every news media organization was on the hunt for them. But they were nowhere to be found.

After setting the perforated blimp down on an unused runway at LAX, the men beat it down to Long Beach, where they met the docking *Deep Endeavor*. Slipping quietly aboard after the Sea Launch crew departed, they were warmly greeted by a relieved Summer and the ship's crew. Dahlgren was happy to see the mangled *Badger* sitting upright on the fantail deck.

'Kermit, we've got another search ahead of us,' Pitt said to Burch. 'How soon can we be under way?'

'Just as soon as Dirk and Summer step ashore. Sorry, son,' he said, turning to the younger Pitt, 'but I'm afraid Rudi called. He's been trying to track all four of you guys down for the last two hours. Says the top brass wants to talk to you and Summer. They need your insight on the bad guys, and right away.'

'Some guys get all the luck,' Giordino said, grinning at Dirk's misfortune.

'Seems like we never get much time with you,' Summer frowned at her father.

'We'll get the next dive in together,' Pitt said, throwing an arm around each of his kids' shoulders. 'I promise.'

'I'll be counting on it,' Summer replied, giving her father a kiss on the cheek.

'Me too,' Dirk said. 'And thanks for the blimp ride, Mad Al. Next time, I'm going Greyhound.'

'The highbrow type, eh?' Giordino replied, shaking his head.

Dirk and Summer said a quick good-bye to Dahlgren and the other men on the bridge, then hopped off the *Deep Endeavor* as the vessel backed away from the dock. A feeling of satisfaction should have beat through them, but, with Dirk, an underlying anger still brewed. The deadly virus strike had been prevented, the *Koguryo* was captured, and even Tongju was dead. More selfishly, Sarah was safe as well. But on the other side of the world, Kang still breathed. As they moved down the pier, Dirk felt Summer hesitating beside him and he turned and stopped so she could wave a friendly farewell to the ship. He stared and waved as well, but his mind was churning elsewhere. Together, they stood and watched a long while as the turquoise NUMA ship chugged out the harbor and eased slowly toward the western horizon.

Well before the Homeland Security investigation team thought to round up all available search and salvage vessels and comb for the sunken rocket debris, the *Deep Endeavor* had already slipped her towed sonar array fish over the side and was scanning the depths for the remains of the payload. Captain Burch had anticipated a salvage operation and knew precisely where to start searching. While standing on the deck of the *Deep Endeavor* watching the Zenit disintegrate across the sky, he had carefully tracked the trajectory of the debris and marked on a nautical chart an impact zone where he thought the nose cone struck the water.

'If the payload remained intact, it should be somewhere within that box,' he told Pitt as they chugged back to sea, pointing to a nine-square-mile grid penciled on the chart. 'Though we're probably dealing with a scattered debris field.'

'Whatever is left has only been sitting on the bottom a few hours, so we'll have a fresh profile at least,' Pitt replied, studying the chart.

Burch guided the *Deep Endeavor* to a corner of the grid, where they began running north/south survey lanes. Just two hours into the search, Pitt identified the first scattering of debris visible against the rolling bottom. Pointing to the sonar monitor, he fingered a cluster of sharp-edged objects protruding in succession.

'We've got a string of man-made objects running in a rough line to the east,' he said.

'Either a local garbage scow spilled her goods or we've got a pile of rusting rocket parts,' Giordino agreed, eyeing the data.

'Kermit, why don't we break off the lane and run a tack to the east. Let's see if we can follow the debris trail and see where it leads.'

Burch ordered the ship about and they followed the trail of wreckage for several minutes as it intensified in quantity before slowly petering out. None of the debris appeared larger than a few feet long, however.

'That's one heckuva jigsaw puzzle someone's gonna have to piece together,' Burch said as the last of the wreckage fell away from the screen. 'Shall we resume the survey lane?' he asked Pitt.

Pitt thought for a moment. 'No. Let's hold our course. There's got to be more substantial remains.'

Pitt's years of underwater exploration had refined

his senses to almost psychic ability. Like an under-water bloodhound, he could nearly sniff out the lost and hidden. There was a lot more of the Zenit still out there and he could feel it.

As the sonar monitor reeled off nothing but flat bottom, the men on the bridge began to have their doubts. But a quarter mile later, a few small pieces of ragged-edged debris crept onto the screen. Suddenly, the silhouette of a large rectangular object filled the monitor lying perpendicular to the other debris. As it rolled off the screen, a new image crawled into view. It was the shadow of a large, high cylinder.

'Boss, I think you've just found the whole enchilada,' Giordino grinned.

Studying the image with a nod, Pitt replied, 'Let's go have a taste.'

Minutes later, the *Deep Endeavor* fixed its position by engaging its side thrusters and lowered a small remote-operated vehicle over the stern railing. A large winch unrolled the ROV's power cable as the machine sunk to the seafloor nine hundred feet beneath the surface. In a dimly lit electronics bay beneath the wheelhouse, Pitt sat in an oversized captain's chair where he controlled the unmanned submersible's thrusters with a pair of joysticks. A rack of video monitors lined the wall in front of him, displaying multiple images of the sandy bottom fed from a half-dozen digital cameras mounted on the ROV.

Adjusting the thrusters so that the ROV hovered

a few feet above the bottom, Pitt gently guided the submersible toward a pair of dark objects nearby. Protruding from the sandy bottom, the cameras revealed, were two jagged pieces of white metal several feet long, which were clearly chunks of skin from the Zenit rocket. Pitt kept the ROV moving past the debris until the initial sonar targets materialized in the inky water, two unmistakable sections of the launch vehicle rising high off the bottom. As the ROV moved closer, Pitt and Giordino could see the first section was nearly fifteen feet long, and almost as high, but flattened on one side. The rocket section had tumbled before impact, smacking the water lengthwise in a jarring blow that had given it the rectangle shape identified by the sonar. Guiding the ROV to one end, the cameras showed a large thruster nozzle protruding from a mass of pipes and chambers that constituted a rocket engine.

'An upper stage engine?' Giordino asked, eyeing the image.

'Probably the Zenit's third stage motor, the uppermost propulsion unit designed to drive the payload section into final orbit.'

The unfueled section appeared to have broken cleanly from the lower Stage 2 component during the explosion. But the payload section that rode above it had separated also and was no longer attached. A few yards away, a large white object stretched into the murky range of the camera lens.

'Enough with the preliminaries. Let's go take a

look at that big boy,' Giordino said, pointing to the edge of one of the video monitors.

Pitt guided the ROV toward the object, which quickly filled the video screens with white. It was clearly another section of the Zenit rocket, even more intact than the Stage 3 section. Pitt estimated it was about twenty feet long, and noticed that it appeared to have a slightly larger diameter. The nearest end was a mangled mass of carnage. Twisted and jagged edges of the white metal skin jutted inward as if mashed by a giant sledgehammer. Pitt maneuvered the ROV to peer inside but there was little to be seen besides mashed metal.

'This has to be the payload. It must have struck the water on its end,' Pitt remarked.

'Maybe there's something exposed on the other side,' Giordino said.

Pitt quickly guided the ROV along the length of the horizontal rocket section until reaching the opposite end, then glided the submersible around in a wide U-turn. Shining the ROV's illuminating lights into the exposed end, Pitt and Giordino craned at the monitor to get a closer look. The first thing that Pitt noticed was an inward-flared ring around the interior edge. It was apparent that the smaller-diameter Stage 3 rocket section had been mated to the section at this end. Inching the ROV closer, they could see that a vertical piece of fairing had been stripped off the rocket along the exposed top side. Raising the ROV until it hovered just above the prone rocket, Pitt guided the submersible along its upper side, following the open seam with the cameras pointed inside. After viewing a maze of tubes and wiring, Pitt stopped the ROV as the video image suddenly displayed a flat board that glistened under the submersible's high-power lights. A wide grin quickly spread across Pitt's face.

'I do believe that there's a solar panel shining back at us,' he said.

'Well done, Dr. von Braun,' Giordino replied, nodding.

As the ROV inched forward, they could clearly see the folded wings of the solar panels and the cylindrical body of the mock satellite through the open seam. Though the nose cone had been mashed at impact, the satellite payload inside had survived intact, and, with it, the deadly cargo of virus.

After carefully studying the integrity of the entire payload section with the remote video, Pitt returned the ROV to the *Deep Endeavor* and directed the vessel into salvage mode. Though *Deep Endeavor* was primarily an exploration vessel, she was equipped to handle light salvage with the help of her onboard submersibles. Despite the loss of the *Badger*, Pitt and Giordino employed a backup submersible to affix a sling support around the payload and slowly bring the rocket section to the surface with the aid of large lift bags. Under cover of darkness and away from the prying eyes of the occasional media boat, the payload was hoisted out of the water and onto the deck of the

Deep Endeavor. Pitt and Giordino looked on as the rocket piece was secured and covered under a shroud of canvas.

'That'll give the intelligence boys something to chew on for a while,' Giordino said.

'It will certainly prove that the attack was not attempted by an amateur group of terrorists. Once the lethality of the payload is revealed to the public, the ignoble Mr. Kang will wish he was never born.'

Giordino waved an arm toward a fuzzy glow of light on the eastern horizon. 'All things considered, I'd say the good people of Los Angeles owe us a beer for protecting their fair city . . . and maybe the keys to the Playboy Mansion.'

'They have Dirk and Summer to thank.'

'Too bad they weren't here to see this baby come up.'

'I still haven't heard from the kids since we dropped them at the dock.'

'They're probably doing the same thing their old man would have done,' Giordino grinned. 'Slipped the intelligence interview and headed down to Manhattan Beach for some surfing.'

Pitt laughed briefly then looked out at the dark sea as his thoughts wandered. No, he knew, now wasn't the time for that.

64

Forty-two thousand feet above the Pacific, Dirk sat in the cramped seat of a government jet trying to get some sleep. But the adrenaline still surged through his body, keeping him awake as the plane nosed closer to South Korea. It was just hours before that he and Summer had been summoned off the *Deep Endeavor* to brief FBI and Defense Department intelligence officials on their meeting with Kang and to provide details about the industrialist's fortified residence.

They learned that Sandecker had finally persuaded the president, and the White House had issued orders to get Kang, swiftly and silently and without informing the South Korean government. An assault plan had been formulated, targeting several of Kang's facilities, including the shipyard at Inchon. The mysterious leader had not been seen in public for days so his private residence was moved to the top of the list of incursion targets. Because few Westerners had ever been invited to the residence, Dirk and Summer's insights were critical.

'We'll be happy to provide you with a full lay-out of the site, identify entry points and passage-ways, even give you the security force positions and monitoring technology,' Dirk offered to the delight of the intelligence agents. 'But I expect one thing in return,' he added, 'and that's a ticket to the show.'

Dirk smiled to himself as he watched the color drain from their faces. After some grumbling counterarguments and a few calls to Washington, he won out. There would be value, they knew, in having him on the ground with the assault force. For her part, Summer thought he was crazy.

'You actually want to go back to that chamber of horrors?' she asked incredulously when the agents had left the room.

'You bet,' he replied. 'I want a front-row seat when they slip the noose around Kang's neck.'

'Once was enough for me. Please be careful, Dirk. Leave the assault work to the professionals. I nearly lost both you and Dad today,' she said with sisterly concern.

'Not to worry. I'll keep quietly to the rear with my head down,' he promised.

Two hours of intense briefings later, he was whisked to LAX and bound again for Korea. Shortly after the jet's wheels touched down at Osan Air Base after the long flight across the Pacific, he was at it again, this time briefing the Special Operations Forces that would be carrying out the assault. Dirk was particularly thorough, providing every detail and scrap of information about Kang's residence that he could remember. He then sat back and listened intently as the tactical assault plans were presented in precise detail. Two Army Special Ops teams were tasked with infiltrating Kang's marine dock and nearby telecommunications center in Inchon while a Navy SEAL team would broach his residence. The operations would be conducted simultaneously, with backup teams standing by to strike additional Kang properties, should the enigmatic leader not be found at the initial targets. After the briefing, a no-nonsense Navy captain responsible for coordinating the SEAL assault approached Dirk.

'You've got five hours to relax before we assemble. You'll go in as part of Commander Gutierrez's team. I'll see that Paul has you outfitted ahead of time. Sorry, but we can't issue you a firearm. Orders.'

'I understand. I'm just grateful to join the ride.'

Grabbing a quick meal and nap at a temporary officers' quarters, Dirk assembled with the SEAL team, where he was issued a set of black camouflage fatigues, an armored vest, and a pair of night vision goggles. After a final briefing, the men boarded a pair of enclosed trucks and were driven to a small dock south of Inchon. Under cover of darkness, the twenty-four-man SEAL team boarded a nondescript support boat and quickly shoved off, proceeding north into the Yellow Sea toward Kyodongdo Island. The team of highly trained commandos anxiously rechecked their weapons under the enclosed main cabin's dim lights as the boat sped across the open sea. Commander Paul Gutierrez, a short but husky man who wore a thin mustache, approached Dirk when they neared the mouth of the Han River.

'You'll be going in with my squad in boat number two,' he said. 'Just stick close by when we hit the ground and follow my lead. With any luck, we'll be in and out without firing a shot. But, just in case,' he paused and handed Dirk a small satchel.

Dirk unzipped the bag and pulled out a SIG Sauer P226 9mm automatic pistol with spare ammunition clips.

'Much obliged. I was hoping I wouldn't have to walk into a potential firefight unarmed,' Dirk replied.

'The Kevlar vest will keep you safe, but this will add some insurance. Just don't tell anyone where you found it,' he nodded with a wink, then turned and ambled off to the wheelhouse to check their progress.

A half hour later, the support boat sped past the cove entrance that led to Kang's residence and continued upriver another two miles before suddenly cutting the engines. As the boat slowed to a stop against the current and began drifting back downriver, three Zodiac black rubber boats were quickly lowered over the side. With quiet efficiency, eight SEALs quietly climbed into each boat and paddled away from the support craft, Dirk joining the men in the second rubber boat. Nearly invisible against the darkened night, the three boats moved easily downriver with the current before silently turning into the inlet to Kang's property.

A cloudy sky softly reflected the lights of Kang's

compound as the three rubber boats turned the last corner of the winding inlet and entered the expansive cove beneath the residence. Dirk gripped a paddle tightly and rowed in silent unison with the heavily armed SEAL team members beside him in the boat. The lingering effects of jet lag and exhaustion from the aborted Sea Launch strike were quickly shaken off at the sight of Kang's stone fortress.

Halfway across the cove, the boats split up, two heading left to land on the sandy beach near the boat dock while the third moved toward the right. The third boat's wet suit-clad occupants would swim ashore first, creeping in along the rocky landing on the opposite side of the dock. Dirk rowed in one of the boats that headed to the beach, wondering if the advance SEAL team had missed neutralizing any of the surveillance video cameras Kang had mounted around the inlet.

As they paddled closer to shore, Dirk noticed the same configuration of boats tied up at the dock as when he escaped with Summer. Kang's big Benetti yacht and the blue high-speed catamaran were tied up in a row, while the small speedboat was centered in between. The yacht and catamaran quickly became the focus of all the men in Dirk's rubber boat. Their mission was to secure Kang's docked vessels while the other SEAL teams rushed the compound. Surveying the dock and surrounding area, Dirk smiled to himself at the sight of the missing skiff.

The two rubber boats hung offshore for several

minutes as the submerged SEALs crept ashore on the far side. From his vantage point in the cove, Dirk watched as a handful of black shapes moved silently out of the water and along the rocky shoreline. A pair of dark shapes crept up to the security booth and quickly subdued the on-duty guard, whose nose was buried in a newspaper.

At the bow of Dirk's boat, Commander Paul Gutierrez quietly raised his hand and the ops team dipped their paddles in the water, rapidly driving the rubber boat ashore after a few dozen hard strokes. The boat's hull barely scraped the sand when its occupants burst out and sprinted down the shoreline toward the dock. All remained quiet about the compound as the following boat's team simultaneously raced up to the cliff entrance under cover of the advance squad.

Dirk followed his team of eight men as they hustled onto the dock ramp, then split in two. Four men peeled off and leaped aboard the catamaran while Commander Gutierrez and three men continued down the dock toward the Benetti. Dirk kept running past the catamaran, opting to join the men headed for the larger yacht. But twenty yards from the yacht, he suddenly froze in his tracks as a yellow flash of light burst from the stern deck. The clatter from an AK-74 shattered the night air a microsecond later, followed by a sickening series of dull thumps as the bullets slammed into the bodies of the two men in front of him. Ducking behind a barrel, Dirk yanked the SIG Sauer 9mm pistol from a side holster and quickly squeezed ten shots toward the source of the gunfire. A few yards ahead of him, Gutierrez had also returned fire, sweeping the yacht's rear deck with a Heckler & Koch MP5K submachine gun. Their combined bursts silenced the unseen gunman amid a spray of flying splinters and shattered glass.

The sudden bursts of gunfire seemed to awaken the whole island as small arms fire erupted throughout the compound. A pair of pistol-wielding gunmen popped out of a cabin door on the catamaran with guns blazing but were quickly mowed down by the SEAL team already positioned aboard. A guard in the main security house noticed the murdered beach guard over a video camera and quickly alerted the residence security forces. The approaching SEALs found themselves walking into the fire from a half-dozen armed guards.

Back on the dock, Dirk leaned over the two men sprawled on the ground in front of him. To his shock, he found the first man was dead, a series of bullet punctures noticeable across his neck and clavicle. The second man was wriggling about, gasping in pain. He had been saved by his Kevlar combat vest, the burst having caught him across the stomach, his unprotected hips and thighs catching the worst of the fire.

'I'm okay,' the tough SEAL grunted as Dirk tried to assess his wounds. 'Finish the mission.'

As he spoke, the powerful motors of the Benetti yacht gurgled to life. Dirk looked up to see more gunfire erupt from the boat's dock-side gunwale as a pair of crewmen worked down the length of the vessel, one cutting the mooring lines while the other sprayed covering fire across the deck.

'We'll get them,' Dirk said to the prone man, patting his shoulder. Reluctantly leaving the injured soldier, he stood up and sprinted toward the yacht. The yacht's motors began to rumble loudly as the throttles were shoved to FULL. A foaming torrent boiled off the transom as the boat's propellers cut into the water.

A few feet ahead of Pitt, Gutierrez let off a quick burst of fire aimed at the starboard passageway, then stood and barked, 'Let's get aboard!'

Dirk bolted past Gutierrez and the other SEAL at a dead run as the two commandos scrambled to chase after the departing yacht. The crack of an automatic pistol belched somewhere above Dirk three times and he could hear the whine as the bullets flew just over his head. A loud thud resonated from the dock behind him and a voice shouted out 'I'm hit' just as Dirk leaped off the dock.

The fleeing yacht was only a few feet removed from the dock when Dirk jumped and he easily grasped the side railing midair and pulled himself aboard in a single fluid move, dropping to the deck and lying still on the darkened stern. A second later, a thump banged against the side as another body jumped onto the side of the moving boat. Dirk saw the outline of a black-camouflaged man quickly slide over the railing and onto the deck a few feet behind him.

'It's Pitt here,' he whispered back to the shadow, not wishing to get shot by mistake. 'Who's there?'

'Gutierrez,' came the gravelly voice of the SEAL commander. 'We need to get to the wheelhouse and stop this craft.'

Gutierrez started to get up and creep forward when Dirk stuck out his hand in a halting motion. Both men froze as Dirk trained his eyes and ears on the port side of the deck. On the far side, he could see that a stairwell led down from an open observation deck above their heads. As the yacht headed into the cove, the lights from the dock flared over the boat's stern and Dirk detected a slight movement in the shadows of the stairwell. Slowly unholstering his 9mm, he took a bead on the shadowy spot and waited. When the shadow suddenly appeared to descend a step, Dirk squeezed the SIG Sauer's trigger twice.

A metallic clunk rang across the deck from a fallen handgun and the long shadow slumped down the stairwell into the visible mass of a crumpled man dressed in black fatigues.

'Nice shooting,' Gutierrez grumbled. 'Now, let's move.'

As the commando crept forward, Dirk followed close behind, nearly losing his footing and slipping to the deck at one point. Glancing down, he noticed the deck was covered in a pool of blood from the gunman Gutierrez had shot from the dock. The dead man's body lay facedown next to a teak bar, a bent cigarette still clenched between his lips.

Roaring away from the brightly lit dock, the yacht was now enshrouded in total darkness as it sped across the cove at top speed. Nearly all of the boat's lights had been extinguished, save for a few dim interior floorlights. The two men felt their way along to the main rear cabin that housed the dining salon and skirted around to the starboard-deck passageway. Gutierrez suddenly raised a hand and stopped, taking a step back toward the salon.

'There's next to no cover along the side passageways. It would be better if we split up. Take the port passage and try to move forward. I'll work up the starboard side here,' Gutierrez directed, knowing another gunman was likely waiting around the corner. 'We better work fast, before we end up sailing to the wrong side of the DMZ.'

Dirk nodded. 'See you on the bridge,' he whispered, then darted across the stern deck. With his senses tuned high, he edged around the portside corner and stepped onto the teak passageway leading forward. Distant gunfire from the shore rattled over the yacht's pulsating engines, but Dirk was focused on the sounds aboard the boat. Padding silently, he crept forward until the passageway ended at a stairwell. The bridge was almost in reach now, just up a level and another thirty feet. As he peered up the stairs, the loud bark of automatic gunfire suddenly cracked through the air. His heart skipped a beat, but then he realized it was on the other side of the yacht.

Gutierrez had been waiting for the burst. Slinking forward on the starboard side, he kept low to the ground in anticipation of an unseen gunman. Reaching the opposite stairwell, he climbed it like a cat, poised on the balls of his feet for a sudden barrage. He didn't have to go far to find it. The SEAL had barely set foot on the landing when a spray of gunfire whistled over his head. Hiding off the bridge wing, a black-clad gunman fired with an AK-74.

Gutierrez barely escaped the initial fusillade. The gunman's burst was thrown high when the yacht suddenly slowed and swerved into the narrow cove inlet. Diving back for the stairwell, Gutierrez slid down the first few steps before twisting around and aiming his MP5K. The SEAL waited calmly for several seconds until the gunman's muzzle flashed again. The incoming burst chewed up the deck just inches from his head, peppering his face with teakwood splinters. Calmly adjusting his aim, Gutierrez let off a solid burst from the Heckler & Koch into the darkness. A brief muffled cry rang out, then another flash of fire spewed from the concealed shooter's gun. Only this time, the spray of yellow fire arced skyward, then ceased altogether as the mortally wounded gunman fell dead to the deck.

On the other side of the yacht, Dirk heard the gunfire fall silent and wondered whether Gutierrez had survived the firefight. Moving up the port stairwell, he climbed two steps then froze at the sound of a faint click behind him. Tilting his head back, he detected that the sound came from a side cabin door at the base of the stairs. Descending silently, Dirk crept back down the stairs until he stood in front of the doorway. Gripping the SIG Sauer firmly in his right hand, he reached for the brass door handle with his left hand and gently turned it to its stops. Holding the latch open for a second, he took a deep breath, then shoved the door open and lunged in.

He had expected the door to fly fully open, but, instead, it abruptly stopped from the mass of a human being. Slightly thrown off balance by the sudden jar, Dirk found himself bouncing off a muscular guard standing with a surprised look inside the doorway. Facing just inches away, Dirk noted a deep L-shaped scar on the man's chin and a bent angular nose that had once been broken. In his hands he held an AK-74 rifle, which he was attempting to reload. The rifle's barrel was pointed at the floor as the man fumbled with the clip, but he immediately swung the stock up toward Dirk's right side. Lurching back a step in order to bring the SIG Sauer to bear, Dirk was struck by the rifle before he could aim and his shot fired harmlessly into the wall. But rather than stiffly absorbing the blow, Dirk rolled to his right as the rifle struck, at the same time swinging his left arm around. As he pivoted with the force, he balled his left fist and threw a sharp uppercut, which landed firmly on the jaw of the man's face. The blow sent the gunman staggering backward, where he tripped and fell over a basket of laundered clothes.

For the first time, Dirk noticed that the cabin was a small laundry room. A tiny washing machine and dryer sat against the far wall while an open ironing board stood next to the doorway. Regaining his balance, he quickly leveled the SIG Sauer at the guard's chest and squeezed the trigger.

There was no loud bark from the muzzle nor a kick to his wrist. Instead, just a metallic click as the gun's firing pin beat down on an empty chamber. Dirk grimaced as he realized that he had emptied the pistol's thirteen-round magazine. Smiling in the face of the empty handgun, Kang's guard rolled to his knees. In his right hand, he still held the full ammo clip, which he expertly jammed into the stock of the assault rifle. Dirk knew there was no way he could reload the SIG Sauer in time, but his body was already reacting with an alternate plan. Barely seen out of the corner of his eye, the shiny object that his hand was already reaching for was a last-gamble defense.

The chrome iron sitting atop the ironing board was not hot, nor even plugged in. But it made for a sharp and nasty projectile. With a toss that would have made John Elway proud, Dirk grabbed the iron and fired it at the gunman like a bullet. The gunman, intent on training his loaded rifle at Dirk, didn't even bother to duck. The flat side of the iron struck his head like an anvil, smacking his skull with an audible crack. The assault rifle fell to the floor first, followed by the gunman, his eyes rolled far back in his head.

Beneath his feet, Dirk felt the boat's motors suddenly rumble louder again. The yacht had cleared the inlet and was accelerating into the Han River. It would easily outrun the special forces support vessel stationed off the inlet. If it was to be stopped, he and Gutierrez would have to act quick. But how many more gunmen were aboard? And, more important, where was Gutierrez?

65

Gutierrez kneeled at the top of the starboard stairwell peering down the passage, searching for shadows. The black silhouette of the gunman he had dropped lay motionless on the deck beside the bridge. He could detect no movement around the area, and no one was firing at him, at least for the moment. No sense in waiting for reinforcements to appear, he decided. Vaulting from the stairwell, he dashed across the open passageway to the bridge wing and leaped over the dead gunman, then burst through the open bridge door.

He half-expected a horde of armed guards waiting to greet him with a cluster of hot muzzles pointing his way, but it was not the case. Just three men stood on the expansive bridge, their eyes turned to him with contempt. A burly, salt-faced man who was obviously the captain stood at the helm, guiding the yacht toward the center of the Han River. Near the port wing door stood a surly guard fingering an assault rifle, who glared at the SEAL with anticipation. And at the rear of the bridge, sitting in a raised leather captain's chair with a look of disdain on his face, was none other than Kang himself. The mogul, whom Gutierrez recognized from a briefing photo, was dressed in a burgundy silk robe, having slept on his yacht in preparation for a last-minute getaway.

As the four sets of eyes locked on one another, Gutierrez's reflexes were already in motion. The trained SEAL quickly aimed his weapon at the guard and squeezed the trigger, a full second before the other man reacted. In a quick burst, three rounds spat from his gun, striking the guard in a clean cluster across his chest. A stunned look spread over the guard's face as he was thrown back against the bulkhead, but his finger instinctively tightened in the trigger guard. A wild spray of fire burst from his assualt rifle, ripping across the deck and toward Gutierrez. The SEAL stood helpless as a seam of lead flew in his direction before the gunman sagged to the floor dead.

It took a split second for Gutierrez to take stock. He had been hit by one round, which nipped him in the thigh. He felt a warm rivulet of blood from the wound run down his leg and collect in his boot. Another round nearly struck him in the abdomen but was deflected by his own machine gun. The bullet had smashed into the MP5K's breech, he realized, and rendered the firearm useless.

The other men on the bridge noticed it as well. The burly captain, standing just a few feet from Gutierrez, let go of the ship's wheel and plunged at the wounded SEAL. Unsteady from the wound to his left leg, Gutierrez stood inert as the captain barreled into him. The captain used his bulk to throw a bear hug around the SEAL and then slam him into the helm. Gutierrez could feel the breath forced from his lungs and felt as if his ribs were going to snap as the captain tried to squeeze the life out of him. But in Gutierrez's right hand, he still held the compact MP5 machine gun, which he swung upward and smashed against the back of the captain's skull. To his astonishment, nothing happened. The captain seemed to squeeze even tighter, and Gutierrez could see a kaleidoscope of stars starting to shimmer before his eyes as the oxygen in his blood ebbed. Sharp pains flared from the wound in his leg while hammering pangs throbbed against his temples. Again, he thrust the gun's stock against the man's head and, again, the grip seemed only to tighten. Desperation started to seep into the SEAL's mind as he approached the verge of passing out and he wildly thrust the gun at the man's head again and again. Gutierrez sensed his body falling and presumed he was blacking out. But he was suddenly jarred conscious by a collision to his body.

The repeated blows had finally knocked the stubborn captain cold and the two of them fell hard to the deck, Gutierrez still embraced in the captain's bear hug. The SEAL gasped for breath as the man's iron grip fell slack and he crawled to his knees inhaling deeply.

'An impressive display. But, regrettably, it shall be your last.' The voice of Kang spat with the flavor of venom. While grappling with the yacht's captain,

Kang had approached and leveled a Glock automatic pistol at Gutierrez's head. The SEAL searched for a defense but there was none. The guard's K-74 was wedged in the dead man's hands across the bridge and his own weapon lay empty and useless in his right hand. On his knees, weakened from gunshots and the struggle with the captain, there was nothing he could do. With a resolute look of defiance, he stared up at Kang and the Glock pistol aimed inches from his face.

The single gunshot burst through the bridge like a crack of thunder. Gutierrez felt nothing and was surprised by the sudden stunned look in Kang's eyes. Then he realized that the Korean's hand, the one holding the pistol, had disappeared along with the gun amid a shower of crimson blood. Two more cracks filled the air and a splattering of blood flew out of Kang's left knee and right thigh. With a garbled cry of agony, Kang fell to the deck, grasping the remains of his bleeding hand and writhing in misery. As he fell, Gutierrez looked across the bridge to where the gunshots had originated.

Standing across the deck in the port doorway, Dirk held an AK-74 at eye level, the smoking barrel still leveled at the prone figure of Kang. A relieved look spread across his face as he made eye contact with Gutierrez and realized the SEAL was still alive.

Dirk walked across the bridge, noting the pilotless yacht was still barreling across the width of the Han River at nearly 40 knots. Off the starboard beam but falling rapidly behind was the SEAL support ship, fighting to keep up with the faster yacht. Across the river, but now directly ahead, was the brightly illuminated river dredge he had seen before, slowly scooping a channel lane near the opposite bank. Dirk stared at the dredge a moment, thinking of the dead SEAL on the dock and the Coast Guardsmen killed in Alaska. Then he turned back to the wriggling figure of Kang and stepped close to the mogul, who was bleeding heavily onto the deck.

'Your ride is over, Kang. Enjoy your stay in hell.'

Kang peered up at Dirk with an angry look and grunted an obscenity but Dirk turned and walked away before he could finish. Stepping to the helm, he reached down and yanked Gutierrez to his feet.

'Nice going, partner, but what took you so long?' Gutierrez rasped.

'Just had to get a few things ironed out,' Dirk replied as he half-dragged the SEAL to the side railing.

'We better stop this cruise ship now,' Gutierrez grunted. 'I didn't expect to find the big cheese aboard. Intel will be anxious to get him under the hot spotlight.'

'I'm afraid Kang has an appointment with the grim reaper,' Dirk said, grabbing a life preserver off the bulkhead and throwing it over Gutierrez's head and shoulders.

'My orders are to take him alive,' Gutierrez protested. But before he could argue further, Dirk grabbed him firmly by the lapels and rolled the both of them over the side railing and into the water below. Dirk ensured he was positioned beneath Gutierrez and took the brunt of the blow as they struck and bounced across the water, nearly knocking the wind out of him from the high-speed impact. After a quick submersion, they bobbed to the surface as the yacht roared past them, Dirk holding the SEAL commander afloat.

The crew of the following support ship saw them go over the side and quickly broke off the chase to pull them out of the water. But Dirk's and Gutierrez's eyes were on the yacht as they floated in the water, watching Kang's vessel race across the river. The Benetti's course held firm as it crossed midriver and streaked toward the dredge and the opposite bank. As it drew closer to the opposite shore, it became apparent to everyone who watched that the vessel was headed directly for the dredge. The dredge's pilot, seeing the speeding yacht heading toward him, let loose with a long blast from his whistle but the rapidly approaching boat held steady.

With a thunderous shriek, the gleaming white yacht burst into the dredge ship like a charging bull, her bow plowing into the rusty steel vessel amidships. Striking at top speed, the yacht disintegrated into a cloud of white smoke, followed by a small fireball that floated into the air as the fuel tanks were crushed and ignited. Splinters of wood and debris rained across the dredge and around the river as the mashed remains of the vessel slid off the dredge and sank to the bottom. When the smoke and flames cleared, there was little evidence to indicate a 165-foot yacht had existed moments before.

Dirk and Gutierrez drifted in the river, watching the carnage with grim captivation as a rescue dinghy from the support ship puttered toward them.

'Might be hell to pay for not bringing him in alive,' Gutierrez said after the flames and smoke had dissipated.

Dirk shook his head bitterly. 'So he could spend the rest of his days in a country club prison? No thanks.'

'You get no argument from me. I think we just bestowed a colossal favor upon humanity. But his death might bring repercussions. My superiors are not going to be happy if we create an international incident with Korea.'

'When the facts come out, there will be no tears shed for Kang and his enterprise of murderers. Besides, he was still alive when we left the yacht. It looked like a boating accident to me.'

Gutierrez thought for a moment. '"A boating accident,"' he repeated, trying to convince himself. 'Sure, that might just fly.'

Dirk watched as the remaining smoke from the collision slowly dissipated over the river, then smiled a tired grin at Gutierrez as the rescue boat approached and fished them out of the river.

Referendum

66

As Kang was obliterated, so fell his empire. The SEAL forces that swept through his residence captured his assistant Kwan alive, along with a cache of incriminating documents that he was desperately trying to destroy in his employer's private office. To the south at Inchon, additional Special Forces teams sped through Kang's shipyard and neighboring telecommunications facility. Heavy security resistance at the facility raised suspicions and a large intelligence team quickly descended on the building. The secret biological research lab in the basement was soon discovered, as were the staff's ties to North Korea. Faced with mounting evidence and the death of his master, Kwan quickly folded under the duress and fully confessed Kang's sins in a self-serving ploy to save his own neck.

Back in the United States, news of the 'accidental death of Kang as he was fleeing authorities' brought a similar reaction from Ling and his top engineers. Threatened by officials with attempted mass murder charges, they cooperated as well, offering the ill excuse that they were just following orders. Only the Ukrainian engineers refused to cooperate, which eventually ensured their lengthy stay in a federal penitentiary.

The government authorities, meanwhile, held their cards to the vest publicly until the final piece of damning evidence had been uncovered. The remains of the rocket payload that Pitt and Giordino had retrieved were transferred under secrecy to Vandenberg Air Force Base north of Los Angeles. In a tightly guarded hangar, a team of space engineers carefully disassembled the payload, uncovering the mock satellite that disguised the virus canisters and vapor-dispensing system. Army and CDC epidemiologists removed the canisters of the freeze-dried virus, finding, to their shock, that they contained the lethal chimera of smallpox and HIV organisms. Samples from the Inchon lab were quietly matched up and the horror confirmed. Despite an interest by the Army in maintaining samples, the recovered viruses were ordered destroyed in their entirety by the president. Fears lingered that additional samples escaped capture and destruction, but the chimera engineered by Kang's scientists was in fact fully eradicated.

With the *Koguryo* and her crew traced to Kang Enterprises and the ties from Kang to North Korea firmly established, officials from the Homeland Security Department finally went public. A firestorm of media attention broke worldwide as details of the deadliest attempted terrorist attack on U.S. soil were fully released. The global press transferred its focus from Japan to North Korea as the diplomatic assassinations were additionally linked to Kang. The failed rocket attack brought worldwide outrage against the North Korean totalitarian regime despite the Korean Workers' Party blanket denial of involvement. The few trading partners North Korea had cultivated before the incident retaliated by placing even tighter restrictions on imports and exports. Even China joined in the sanctions by halting its trade with the outlaw regime. Once again, the starving peasantry in the North began to quietly question the dictatorial rule of their nepotistic leader.

In South Korea, the overwhelming evidence against Kang and the actions of his accomplices hit Seoul like a nuclear strike. Any displeasure the South Korean government initially manifested at the American unilateral military intervention was quickly put aside by the ensuing global uproar. South Korean sentiment turned from shock and disbelief to anger and outrage at their country's duping by Kang and his servitude to North Korea. The fallout was rapid. Political cronies and deal makers who had supported Kang were publicly vilified. A wave of resignations swept through the National Assembly, leading right up to the office of the presidency. Revelations of close personal ties with Kang forced even the South Korean leader to resign from office.

The national embarrassment and anger led the government to quickly nationalize the holdings of Kang Enterprises. The yachts and helicopters were dispensed with first and his fortress residence turned into a think tank devoted to the study of South Korean sovereignty. His name was removed from any association with his former assets, which were later broken up and sold to competing businesses over time. Soon there was nothing left to remind any of his very existence. Almost by silent decree, the name of Kang was entirely purged from the South Korean lexicon.

The exposé of Kang's ties to the north impacted every level of society. Youthful demonstrations for reunification fell away as a wariness of the neighbor to the north reemerged in the national psyche. The massive North Korean military force poised across the border was no longer conveniently overlooked. Reunification remained a national goal, but it would have to come on South Korea's terms. When reunification finally did arrive on the Korean Peninsula some eighteen years later, it was driven by a growing hunger for capitalism in the Korean Workers' Party. Acceding to the personal freedoms that came with it, the party at last purged itself of dictatorial family rule and unilaterally converted the bulk of its military troops into a civilian economic workforce.

But before all that could occur, the South Korean National Assembly had to vote on Bill 188256, the legislative measure calling for the expulsion of U.S. military forces from within the national borders. In a rare show of bipartisan accord, the measure lost by a unanimous vote.

*

At Kunsan City, Korea, Air Force Master Sergeant Keith Catana was quietly walked out of a dingy municipal jail cell just before dawn and released into the waiting custody of an Air Force colonel attached to the American embassy. Far beyond his comprehension of events, Catana was told nothing about the reason for his release. Catana would never know that he had been set up for the murder of an underage prostitute as part of a concerted plot to influence public sentiment against the U.S. military presence in Korea. Nor would he know that Kang's own assistant, Kwan, had revealed the details of the staged murder. Ensuring full blame fell to the dead assassin Tongju, Kwan readily confessed to the plot, along with the political assassinations that occurred in Japan. None of this mattered to the stunned serviceman as he was whisked onto a U.S.-bound military jet. He knew only one thing. He would happily oblige the order given by the Air Force colonel never to set foot on Korean soil again for as long as he lived.

In Washington, D.C., NUMA was briefly exalted for the role played in diverting the launch and preventing the release of the deadly virus over Los Angeles. But with the death of Kang and the public release of his culpability for the attack, Pitt's and Giordino's exploits quickly fell to yesterday's news. Congressional hearings and investigations into the attack were the order of the day, and a drumbeat for war with

North Korea beat loudly for a spell. But emotions eventually cooled as the diplomats were held at bay and the focus gradually shifted to Homeland Security's border resources and ensuring that such an act could never occur again.

Shrewdly seizing the moment, the new head of NUMA appealed to Congress for a special appropriations supplement for his organization, to fund a replacement helicopter, research ship, and two submersibles for those damaged or destroyed by Kang's men. In a wave of patriotic gratitude, Congress heartily approved the measure, the bill sweeping through both houses in just a matter of days.

Much to Giordino's chagrin, Pitt had sneaked an additional funding item into the approved bill, requesting a mobile atmospheric marine surveillance platform for the agency to use in coastal research. It was otherwise known as 'a blimp.'

67

It was a clear, crisp afternoon in Seattle, the type of day that was just a few degrees shy of invigorating. The declining sun was casting long shadows from the tall pines dotting Fircrest Campus when Sarah hobbled out the front door of the Washington State Public Health Lab. A heavy plaster cast coated her right leg, which she was heartened to know would finally be removed in just a few more days.

She winced slightly as she set her weight on a pair of aluminum crutches, her wrists and forearms sore from carrying the load of her broken leg for the past few weeks. Hobbling a few paces out the doorway, she dropped her eyes to the pavement and navigated herself down a short flight of steps. Carefully picking the next spot along the ground to jab her crutches, she did not notice the car parked illegally at the sidewalk entrance and nearly bumped into it. Looking up, she dropped her jaw in amazement.

Parked in front of her was Dirk's 1958 Chrysler 300-D convertible. The car looked to be in a semi-state of restoration. The pockmarked leather seats had been temporarily taped over while the bullet holes in the body had been sealed with bondo. Assorted spots of gray primer paint across the turquoise body gave the car the look of a giant camouflaged manta ray.

'I promise not to break the other leg.'

Sarah turned to the deep voice behind her to find Dirk standing there with a bouquet of white lilies and a mischievous grin on his face. Lost in emotion, she dropped her crutches and threw her arms around him in a warm hug.

'I was beginning to worry. I hadn't heard from you since the rocket attack.'

'I was away on an all-expense-paid trip to Korea for a farewell cruise on Dae-jong Kang's yacht.'

'The virus they concocted . . . it's just mad,' she said, shaking her head.

'There is no need to worry anymore. Confidence is high that all the samples were retrieved and destroyed. Hopefully, that bug will never appear on earth again.'

'There's always some crazy working on the next biological Pandora's box for money or notoriety.'

'Speaking of crazies, how's Irv doing?'

Sarah laughed at the simile. 'He's going to be the only modern-day survivor of smallpox in the world. He's fast on his way to a full recovery.'

'Glad to hear it. He's a good man.'

'Looks like your car is on the road to recovery as well,' she said, nodding toward the Chrysler.

'She's a tough old beast. I had the mechanicals refurbished while I was away but haven't got to the body and interior yet.'

Dirk turned and looked at Sarah tenderly. 'I still owe you that crab dinner.'

Sarah looked deep into Dirk's green eyes and nodded. With a quick scoop, Dirk bent over and picked Sarah up and placed her gently on the front seat of the car with the lilies, then kissed her lightly on the cheek. Tossing the crutches into the backseat, he jumped in behind the wheel and fired up the car. The rebuilt motor kicked over easily and idled with a deep purr.

'No ferries?' Sarah asked, snuggling close to Dirk.

'No ferries,' Dirk laughed, slipping an arm around Sarah. Tapping on the accelerator, the old convertible rumbling deeply, he steered across the lush grounds and into the pink-tinted dusk.

DIRK PITT® ADVENTURES

ARCTIC DRIFT
CLIVE CUSSLER AND DIRK CUSSLER

A foundered Victorian ship looking for the fabled Northwest Passage holds a secret in its icy grave . . .

When Dirk Pitt of NUMA is almost blown to pieces in a lab explosion, he suspects sabotage. The lab in question belongs to a scientist hoping to use a rare mineral to combat greenhouse gases – but who would want to destroy our one chance to save the planet?

But there are those who will do anything to control such a valuable prize. Pitt's investigations take him to the Arctic in search of a clue to the origins of this precious mineral. There he and NUMA colleague Al Giordino must battle for survival against the hostile elements and an evil megalomaniac who is about to plunge the North American continent into war . . .

Arctic Drift is a white-knuckle ride of a novel that once picked up you won't want to put down.

DIRK PITT® ADVENTURES

TREASURE OF KHAN
CLIVE CUSSLER AND DIRK CUSSLER

From the frigid lakes of Siberia to the hot wastes of the Gobi desert, Dirk Pitt is on the trail of fabled treasure …

Rescuing an oil survey team from a freak wave on Russia's Lake Baikal is all in a day's work for adventurers Dirk Pitt and partner Al Giordino. Yet when their ship is sabotaged and the survey team vanishes, Pitt is forced to get to the bottom of a mystery with far-reaching consequences.

Soon he's on his way to Mongolia. There, a powerful and ruthless business tycoon holding an astonishing secret about Genghis Khan is hoping to emulate the legend's greatest conquests – but on a global scale!

With the legacy of Khan and the lost treasures of Xanadu as the prize and the future security of the world at stake, Dirk Pitt for one isn't going to stand idly by …

He just wanted a decent book to read ...

Not too much to ask, is it? It was in 1935 when Allen Lane, Managing Director of Bodley Head Publishers, stood on a platform at Exeter railway station looking for something good to read on his journey back to London. His choice was limited to popular magazines and poor-quality paperbacks – the same choice faced every day by the vast majority of readers, few of whom could afford hardbacks. Lane's disappointment and subsequent anger at the range of books generally available led him to found a company – and change the world.

'We believed in the existence in this country of a vast reading public for intelligent books at a low price, and staked everything on it'
Sir Allen Lane, 1902–1970, founder of Penguin Books

The quality paperback had arrived – and not just in bookshops. Lane was adamant that his Penguins should appear in chain stores and tobacconists, and should cost no more than a packet of cigarettes.

Reading habits (and cigarette prices) have changed since 1935, but Penguin still believes in publishing the best books for everybody to enjoy. We still believe that good design costs no more than bad design, and we still believe that quality books published passionately and responsibly make the world a better place.

So wherever you see the little bird – whether it's on a piece of prize-winning literary fiction or a celebrity autobiography, political tour de force or historical masterpiece, a serial-killer thriller, reference book, world classic or a piece of pure escapism – you can bet that it represents the very best that the genre has to offer.

Whatever you like to read – trust Penguin.